LAROUSSE

El conde de Montecristo

Alexandre Dumas

Adaptación al portugués: Telma Guimarães Castro Andrade
Ilustraciones: Cecília Iwashita
Traducción al español: Beatriz Mira Andreu y Mariano Sánchez-Ventura

LAROUSSE

© 2001, Editora Scipione Ltda., São Paulo, Brasil
Título de la edición original: O conde de Monte Cristo
"D. R." © MMIII, por E. L., S. A. de C. V.
  Dinamarca núm. 81, México 06600, D. F.
ISBN 85-262-3859-0 (Editora Scipione, Ltda.)
ISBN 970-22-0730-4 (E. L., S. A. de C. V.)
ISBN 970-22-0726-6 (Colección completa)
PRIMERA EDICIÓN — 1ª reimpresión — I / 05

"Leer es de buenos mexicanos"

CANIEM

CONSEJO DE LA
COMUNICACIÓN, AC
VOZ DE LAS EMPRESAS

Índice

La llegada

En el puerto de Marsella, los navíos siempre eran recibidos por una multitud curiosa. Aquella tarde, el señor Morrel notó algo extraño en cuanto avistó a su navío *Faraón*.

—La bandera del *Faraón* está a media asta... ¡Eso significa que alguien murió!, exclamó a uno de sus hijos.

—No te preocupes... El capitán Leclère se habrá hecho cargo de todo, tranquilizó el joven al padre.

En el puerto, la linda Mercedes esperaba con impaciencia a su novio Edmundo Dantés, segundo oficial de la nave. Se iban a casar cuando regresara de ese viaje.

Fernando Montego, primo de Mercedes, también estaba enamorado de la joven. Al ver la bandera a media asta, deseó que fuera Dantés el que hubiera muerto. Sin embargo, para desilusión de Fernando y alegría de Mercedes y del señor Morrel, Edmundo Dantés les hacía señas desde la nave mientras ésta atracaba. Se apresuró a recibir a bordo al señor Morrel. Alto, esbelto, de ojos y cabellos negros, Edmundo vestía pantalones blancos con botas altas, y una elegante casaca de color azul marino con relucientes botones dorados.

—¡Te esperábamos con ansiedad!, exclamó el señor Morrel al joven Dantés. ¿Dónde está el capitán?, preguntó mirando a su alrededor.

—Por desgracia, señor, el valiente capitán Leclère murió a causa de una fiebre. A partir de entonces, yo asumí el mando del *Faraón*. Respecto a la carga que transportamos, señor, no se preocupe. Está segura.

El señor Morrel se afligió con la noticia de la muerte del capitán. Afortunadamente, a pesar de su juventud, Edmundo era muy hábil.

Mientras éste se encargaba de otras tareas, el intendente Danglars se acercó al señor Morrel.

—La muerte de nuestro capitán fue una gran pérdida, ¿verdad, señor Morrel? Lo peor es que tuvimos que someternos a la voluntad de Edmundo, agregó con una mirada de odio.

—¿A qué te refieres, Danglars?

—Edmundo asumió el mando sin consultar a nadie. Por su culpa tuvimos que desviar el curso para ir a la isla de Elba. Al parecer, Leclère le había pedido que entregara una carta a alguien.

Danglars, gordo y bajo de estatura, tenía una mirada inquieta. La tripulación del barco lo aborrecía, pero esperaba asumir el puesto de capitán. Con desdén, siguió criticando a Edmundo, que apenas tenía diecinueve años, mientras Danglars tenía veintiséis; también habló del exceso de confianza del joven haciendo insinuaciones:

—¡Actúa como si fuera capitán!, concluyó impaciente.

—¡Eso es, en efecto!, replicó el señor Morrel, confirmando así que Edmundo asumiría el mando del *Faraón*.

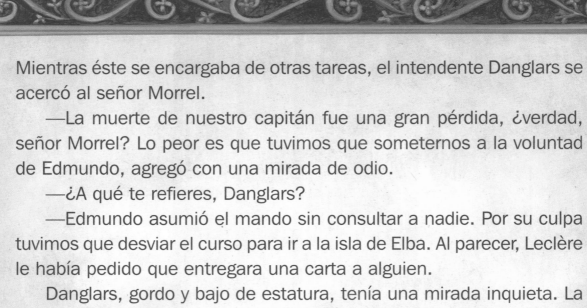

Continuó diciendo que el joven poseía la suficiente experiencia para ello.

—Respecto a su visita a la isla de Elba, ¡tendrá que darme explicaciones!

En cuanto terminó sus tareas, el joven capitán le explicó al señor Morrel:

—El capitán Leclère me rogó, en su lecho de muerte, que le entregara una carta al mariscal Bertrand en la isla de Elba.

—¿Quieres decir que estuviste con Napoleón Bonaparte?, susurró el señor Morrel temiendo que alguien escuchara, pues en aquel entonces Napoleón había sido desterrado de Francia.

—Sí, pero apenas hablamos, señor.

—¿Le entregaste la carta al mariscal?, continuó Morrel.

—Así es, se la di personalmente, y de él recibí una carta para ser entregada a una persona en París.

Satisfecho con las respuestas del joven, Morrel quiso saber su opinión sobre el intendente Danglars. Edmundo respondió que aunque el intendente no era amable con él, llevaba a cabo sus obligaciones adecuadamente.

—Como capitán, ¿lo mantendrías en la tripulación?

—¿Capitán? El señor me da a entender que yo…, tartamudeó Edmundo sorprendido con la pregunta de Morrel.

—Acabo de nombrarte, Edmundo. ¡Espero que aceptes!

—¡Estoy muy agradecido, señor! En cuanto a Danglars, sí lo mantendría en la tripulación. Pero, señor, antes de que partamos de nuevo, quisiera pedirle un par de semanas para ausentarme de mi puesto. Además de hacer los preparativos para mi boda, debo entregar esa carta en París.

—¡Desde luego que sí, muchacho!, accedió Morrel.

Tras agradecerle infinitamente al señor Morrel, Edmundo bajó a tierra. Tenía que contarle la gran noticia a Mercedes. Su bella novia, que lo esperaba en lo alto del muelle, corrió a abrazarlo. El joven capitán fue a su encuentro. Desde el barco, Fernando observaba a la pareja. Con el corazón lleno de envidia, se dirigió a la taberna de don Charny.

El señor Dantés

Mientras iban hacia la casa del padre de Edmundo, los novios acordaron celebrar su boda al día siguiente.

—Hablaré con papá. Quiero que nuestra boda sea una hermosa ceremonia, dijo Mercedes besando a su amado.

—Todo saldrá bien, querida. ¡Nacimos el uno para el otro!

Cuando llegaron a la casa del señor Dantés, los novios se separaron. El joven estaba ansioso por contarle sus aventuras a su padre. Abrió la puerta con cuidado y lo vio regando las flores de la ventana.

—¡Hijo mío! ¡Has regresado!

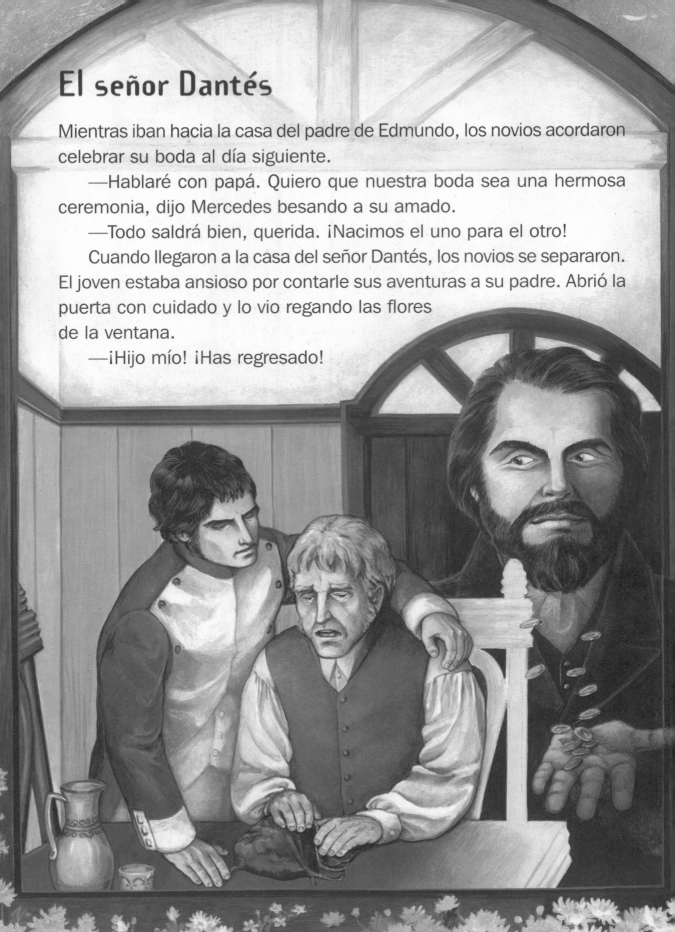

—¡Padre! ¿Has estado enfermo? ¡Te ves muy pálido! ¿Qué te preocupa?, preguntó Edmundo abrazando al padre con cariño.

—Estoy enfermo, sí, ¡de tanto extrañarte, hijo mío!

Edmundo le pidió a su padre que se sentara para oír las nuevas noticias: la muerte del capitán Leclère, su viaje a la isla de Elba y su ascenso al grado de capitán del *Faraón*.

—¡Capitán! ¡Eso es maravilloso!

—¡Mira, padre!, exclamó Edmundo sacando de la casaca una bolsa con monedas. He recibido una buena cantidad de dinero. Voy a comprar una casa con jardín para ti. Así podrás cuidar de todas las plantas que quieras. Y otra cosa más: ¡mañana me casaré con Mercedes!

El viejo Dantés no quería inquietar a su hijo, pero acabó por contarle las dificultades que había tenido durante su ausencia. Su vecino Caderousse, con quien tenía una deuda, amenazó con ir a cobrársela al señor Morrel si no la pagaba. Temiendo perjudicar a su hijo, el pobre hombre saldó la deuda con el dinero que Edmundo le había dejado.

Edmundo se quedó asombrado. ¿Cómo pudo sobrevivir su padre sin dinero durante su ausencia? En ese momento, alguien tocó la puerta, y el señor Dantés acudió a abrir.

—Pasa, Caderousse.

El vecino, de barba oscura y tupida, venía a felicitar al nuevo capitán del *Faraón*.

—Todo mundo sabe la noticia, Edmundo. Vine para felicitarte. Con sus ojos de águila, Caderousse de inmediato vio el saco de monedas sobre la mesa. Al parecer, las cosas mejoran por aquí, ¿verdad?

—Y van a mejorar más todavía después de mi boda con Mercedes y de la nueva casa que pretendo comprarle a mi padre, respondió con frialdad el joven.

—Bien, Edmundo, solamente vine para felicitarte. No me guardes rencor. Yo les presté dinero a ustedes, y ustedes me lo devolvieron. Estamos a mano, ¿no es así?

—Nunca estaremos a mano con aquellos que nos amenazan, respondió Edmundo.

Al salir, Caderousse se encontró con Danglars, quien tenía curiosidad por la familia Dantés:

—Vamos a la taberna de don Charny, así podrás contarme qué has sabido de los Dantés. ¡Yo invito!

Caderousse aceptó encantado la invitación. Le agradaba la idea de una buena conversación acompañada con buen vino.

Tras un ligero refrigerio, Edmundo tomó sus binoculares y llamó a su padre para mostrarle una casa que estaba en venta. Parecía ser ideal para él, pues tenía un bello jardín. Cuando miraba a través de los binoculares, el joven alcanzó a ver a Fernando, a Danglars y a Caderousse tras la ventana de la taberna, y se extrañó de que estuvieran reunidos. Entonces su padre quiso dar un vistazo a la casa y él se olvidó de los hombres. Ignoraba lo que estaban tramando los tres.

La conspiración

Fernando Montego ya se encontraba en la taberna cuando Caderousse y Danglars llegaron. Caderousse conocía a Fernando y se lo presentó a Danglars. Decidieron sentarse en la misma mesa. Mientras les contaba a los otros dos lo que había sucedido en casa de los Dantés, Caderousse se embriagaba rápidamente. Danglars y Fernando, entre copa y copa de vino, descubrieron que tenían algo en común: el odio por Edmundo.

—¡Siempre he amado a Mercedes! ¡Tengo que encontrar la manera de apartarla de Edmundo!, exclamó Fernando Montego, golpeando la mesa, cuando supo que se casarían al día siguiente.

—Edmundo tiene una carta con órdenes secretas. Podemos aprovecharnos de eso, ¿estás de acuerdo? La cárcel puede separar a una pareja para siempre…, dijo Danglars con una mirada extraña.

El pescador Fernando Montego asintió con una sonrisa y llamó al tabernero. Necesitaban papel, pluma y tinta. Mientras tanto, Caderousse despertó de su sopor y pudo escuchar parte de la conversación; quiso decirle a ambos que Edmundo no había hecho nada para merecer la prisión, pero por su embriaguez no alcanzaba a articular siquiera una frase.

—Vamos a denunciarlo al procurador del rey. Diremos que es un agente secreto de Napoleón. El hecho de haber ido a la isla de Elba es una prueba convincente, concluyó Danglars.

Entonces tomó la pluma y comenzó a escribir una carta con la mano izquierda para que nadie pudiera reconocer su letra:

Al Procurador del Rey:
Excelentísimo Señor Villefort,
Edmundo Dantés, segundo a bordo del navío Faraón, trajo de la isla de Elba una carta dirigida a los seguidores de Napoleón Bonaparte en la ciudad de París. La carta debe estar en su poder, ya sea en casa de su padre o en su camarote.

—¿Qué tal?, preguntó Danglars a su nuevo amigo y compañero.
—El mensaje es perfecto… ¡Y no hay testigo alguno!
Caderousse dormía a pierna suelta.

Mientras esto pasaba, Edmundo y Mercedes visitaban a algunos parientes y amigos para invitarlos a su boda, entre ellos al señor Morrel y a su familia.

Al día siguiente, la iglesia resultaba pequeña para tantos invitados. Edmundo y Mercedes ya se encontraban ante el altar cuando unos soldados interrumpieron la ceremonia.

—Edmundo Dantés, venimos a apresarlo. ¡Venga con nosotros en nombre de la ley!, ordenó el comandante dando un paso al frente.

Edmundo palideció:

—¿Qué significa esto? ¿Qué crimen he cometido?

El señor Morrel corrió a su lado e intentó calmarlo.

—Debe ser una equivocación, Edmundo.

—¡No es posible, debe haber un error! ¡Edmundo no ha hecho nada malo…!, exclamó Mercedes buscando el apoyo de sus padres.

Edmundo Dantés no tuvo más remedio que acompañar a los soldados. Éstas fueron sus últimas palabras antes de partir:

—¡Regresaré, Mercedes! ¡Te lo juro! ¡Espérame! ¡Padre, no te preocupes! ¡Todo saldrá bien!

El juez Villefort

El juez Villefort era un hombre alto, rubio, de impenetrables ojos azules. Cuando la cuadrilla de soldados entró en su despacho, se sorprendió por el aspecto elegante del prisionero.

A una señal del juez, los soldados le quitaron las esposas a Dantés, depositaron sus pertenencias sobre la mesa y salieron de la habitación.

—Dígame su nombre y su profesión.

—Mi nombre es Edmundo Dantés. Soy el capitán del navío *Faraón* y estaba a punto de casarme, señor.

El juez se levantó y caminó alrededor de Edmundo.

—He sabido que recientemente se encontró con Napoleón Bonaparte. ¡También corre el rumor de que usted es un hombre muy peligroso!, afirmó el juez mostrando la carta que había recibido.

—¡Ignoro quién pudo ser el autor de esa infamia! Señor, tengo apenas diecinueve años y acaban de nombrarme capitán de un navío. Eso habrá despertado la envidia de alguien que inventó la calumnia para vengarse…, concluyó Edmundo.

Villefort le preguntó sobre el episodio en la isla de Elba. Edmundo confirmó que sí había estado ahí. Explicó que el capitán Leclère le había rogado que entregara una carta al mariscal Bertrand. Éste, a su vez, le pidió que llevara una carta a una persona en la ciudad de París.

—¿Dónde está esa carta?, preguntó el juez.

—Probablemente junto con mis pertenencias, señor.

—¿Sabes quién es el destinatario?

—Sí, lo sé… se llama François Noirtier, y vive en…

—¡Un momento! ¿Usted conoce a ese hombre? ¿Ya estuvo con él o ha hablado acerca de él con alguien?, preguntó Villefort revolviendo los papeles sobre la mesa hasta encontrar la carta.

—Ni lo conozco ni he hablado con nadie sobre este asunto.

Villefort rompió el sello de lacre del sobre y leyó la carta rápidamente. Enseguida la quemó y suspiró con alivio.

—Lo hice por su propia seguridad, caballero. Nada malo le sucederá si no habla con nadie de nuestra conversación. Esa carta era la mayor prueba contra usted. Ahora ya no existe la evidencia.

—¿Quiere decir que soy libre?

—Todavía no, pero mañana será liberado. Le doy mi palabra.

—¿Por qué no ahora mismo?, preguntó Edmundo decepcionado.

—Es necesario cumplir con las formalidades de la justicia. Al decir esto, el juez ordenó a los guardias que acompañaran al prisionero.

—¡No sé cómo agradecérselo, señor!

El juez Villefort enjugó el sudor de su frente. Su padre era François Noirtier y había estado a punto de arruinarle su carrera. Aquella carta que había enviado el mariscal hubiera sido la prueba de que aquél conspiraba para el regreso de Napoleón. Si el rey se hubiera enterado, el juez estaría perdido.

El castillo de If

Al día siguiente Edmundo fue conducido hasta una embarcación por cuatro soldados, que lo hicieron subir a bordo. Esto le pareció muy extraño. ¿A dónde lo llevaría la nave? El juez le había prometido que sería liberado al día siguiente. ¿Por qué lo escoltaban cuatro soldados?

—¿Adónde me llevan?, preguntó.

—A la prisión para los traidores, el castillo de If.

"¡El juez me engañó! ¡Él me prometió que hoy quedaría libre!", se decía Edmundo indignado. "¡En el castillo de If los prisioneros ni siquiera tienen derecho a un juicio!".

Aterrorizado, observó la isla donde se levantaba el castillo de piedra. Intentó saltar al mar, pero los soldados lo inmovilizaron rápidamente, y sólo lo soltaron para desembarcar. Lo escoltaron hasta el castillo. Un carcelero abrió la enorme puerta de hierro de la prisión y los condujo al interior.

—¡Deténganse! ¡Se equivocan! El señor Villefort dijo que yo sería liberado hoy mismo!, imploraba inútilmente el muchacho.

Al llevarlo a su celda, a lo largo de pasillos húmedos y escaleras estrechas, podía oír los gritos de los prisioneros. El carcelero abrió un calabozo y los soldados empujaron a Edmundo dentro.

—¡Auxilio! ¡Por favor, avisen al señor Villefort! ¡Se molestará mucho si no me dejan libre!, gritó el desdichado.

Uno de los soldados regresó y le respondió burlándose:

—¿Y quién es ese tal Villefort? ¡Jamás hemos oído hablar de él!

Entonces Edmundo se dio cuenta de que había caído en una trampa. Caminó alrededor de la celda apenas iluminada por los últimos rayos del sol que entraban por los barrotes de la pequeña ventana. Desde allí se podían ver las olas que chocaban contra el peñasco sobre el cual se elevaba el castillo.

A la mañana siguiente, el carcelero llegó con el café del desayuno y lo introdujo por un hueco de la puerta.

—No quiero nada. Quiero hablar con el director.

—Ni el prisionero que le ofreció un tesoro consiguió verlo, respondió el hombre entreabriendo la puerta.

—¿Quién es ese hombre? ¿Dónde está ahora?

—En una celda debajo de la tuya, le respondió.

—Si no le avisas a mi novia Mercedes dónde estoy y qué me sucede, ¡te voy a estrangular!

Edmundo no logró contener su rabia y empujó al carcelero dentro de la celda. De no haber acudido otros guardias en su auxilio, lo habría herido.

Al día siguiente, el joven fue llevado a una celda más fría y oscura en los sótanos del castillo, reservada para los prisioneros peligrosos. La comida era tan infame que muchas veces tuvo que dormirse sin haber probado bocado durante todo el día.

Sucio, con los cabellos y la barba crecidos y la ropa hecha harapos, parecía estar al borde de la locura. Su única distracción era conversar con los insectos y las alimañas. Gritaba sin cesar:

—¡Díganme qué hice! ¡Necesito hablar con el director de la prisión!

Edmundo Dantés jamás pudo hablar con el director. En el libro de registros del castillo aparecía la siguiente nota:

Edmundo Dantés, prisionero número 34, es un revolucionario peligroso, seguidor de Napoleón Bonaparte. Debe ser encerrado en la celda de seguridad máxima.

15

El sacerdote Faria

Había pasado tanto tiempo desde que Edmundo cayó en prisión, que ya no creía volver a conversar con otra persona y mucho menos recuperar su libertad. Un día oyó un golpeteo suave y recorrió la celda para saber de dónde procedía; descubrió que era del suelo. Parecían golpes de martillo. Él mismo dio unos golpes pero no obtuvo respuesta. Al poco rato, escuchó los golpes de nuevo, esta vez más cerca de su cama. Empujó la cama y puso su oreja sobre el suelo. Buscó algún objeto afilado, pero en su celda solamente había una cama, una silla, una mesa y una jarra de agua. Desesperado, rompió la jarra. Con uno de los pedazos empezó a raspar entre las baldosas de las cuales surgía el ruido, hasta que finalmente una de ellas se aflojó. Retiró la primera piedra, luego la segunda. Se asustó mucho al ver aparecer a un hombre viejo, pequeño, cubierto de polvo, con barba y cabellos blancos, y con un crucifijo colgado del cuello.

—¿Quién…? ¿Quién es usted?

—Un prisionero, el número 27, ¿y tú?

El viejo empujó con gran esfuerzo y dificultad dos piedras laterales. Edmundo lo ayudó a salir del hoyo.

—Me llamo Edmundo Dantés. Dicen que soy un seguidor de Napoleón Bonaparte.

Desde hacía mucho tiempo, la única persona con quien ambos podían comunicarse era el carcelero. La emoción los hacía hablar atropelladamente. Cuando se calmaron, Edmundo relató su historia y el viejo lo escuchó con atención. Después, éste contó que llevaba cuatro años cavando aquel túnel.

—¡He trabajado inútilmente!, suspiró desanimado.

—¿Por qué lleva usted ese crucifijo?, preguntó el joven.

—Soy sacerdote. Me llamo Faria y llevo quince años en esta prisión, llegué en 1810. Hace algunos años planee una fuga. Pasé un año haciendo cálculos, otro construyendo los instrumentos necesarios, y cuatro más cavando. Pensaba que esta pared daba al mar…

Edmundo tuvo lástima del religioso. El túnel que había cavado llegaba sólo hasta su celda, ubicada en el sótano de la prisión.

Faria invitó a Edmundo a visitar su celda. Los dos bajaron al túnel cuidando de colocar la cama y las piedras en su lugar para que el carcelero no se diera cuenta de nada. El clérigo iba al frente y alumbraba el camino con una antorcha.

—¡Hemos llegado! Ésta es mi celda, afirmó apartando unas piedras cubiertas con paja.

Edmundo observó admirado varios objetos que había sobre la mesa. El religioso le explicó qué eran.

—Con esta piedra hice un reloj solar que también funciona como calendario y mapa astronómico. Le mostró que la aguja que indicaba la hora era una espina de pescado.

Edmundo estaba impresionado con las habilidades del cura, quien acostumbraba trabajar durante la noche para que el carcelero no sospechara nada. El viejo le explicó que usaba la grasa, que sacaba de la carne del almuerzo, como combustible para su lámpara. Para encenderla, fabricaba fósforos con el azufre que el carcelero le había dado para curar una supuesta enfermedad de la piel. Incluso había elaborado una navaja y una daga con parte del armazón de la cama.

—Tanto sacrificio para nada… pasé años cavando un túnel que tan sólo me llevó hasta tu celda, dijo el anciano desalentado.

—El túnel que usted cavó sigue la misma dirección que la galería externa. Desde mi ventana puedo ver el mar. La mitad del túnel va en la dirección correcta. Si cavamos juntos unos cien metros a partir del punto central, alcanzaremos el mar, observó Edmundo.

—¿Cuánto tiempo crees que nos tomará?, preguntó Faria animándose.

—¡Tal vez unos cuatro años!

Ambos se abrazaron imaginándose que pasado ese tiempo serían libres para siempre.

Faria parecía frágil, pero también se veía como alguien inteligente. Edmundo lo percibió en cuanto observó los objetos que había creado.

—Mientras preparamos la fuga, ¿podrá usted enseñarme todo lo que sabe?, preguntó el joven.

—Claro que sí, hijo mío. El clérigo sonrió complacido, pues lo que más deseaba en la vida era poder enseñar todo lo que sabía sobre filosofía, teología, matemáticas, historia y los idiomas que dominaba.

El tiempo fue pasando. Ambos conversaban, hablaban de sus recuerdos, de sus familiares y amigos, intercambiaban confidencias y cavaban desviando el túnel en dirección al mar. La tierra que iban sacando la tiraban cuidadosamente por la ventana. Las olas que golpeaban los peñascos se encargaban de eliminar las evidencias.

Edmundo escuchaba las enseñanzas del viejo. Además, ejercitaba su cuerpo en la celda para desarrollarlo y fortalecerlo aún más.

Mientras trabajaban, el religioso le preguntó a Edmundo sobre las causas de su encarcelamiento:

—¿No crees que el hecho de ser capitán de un navío y novio de una bella joven fueron motivo suficiente para despertar la envidia de alguien? Piénsalo bien: ¿a quién podía beneficiar tu encarcelamiento?

—¡A Danglars! Me acuerdo que en esa ocasión, cuando fui a entregar la carta a la isla de Elba…, y Edmundo le narró el episodio de la carta.

Así, el sabio religioso, con la ayuda del joven, acabó por resolver el rompecabezas: la pasión de Fernando por su novia Mercedes, la reunión de Caderousse, Danglars y Fernando en la taberna, y finalmente, la peor de las revelaciones…

—Dices que le mostraste a Villefort la carta dirigida a un señor Noirtier. ¡Pues sucede que François Noirtier es el padre de Villefort!

—¡Ahora todo está claro! Puse en riesgo al juez Villefort. Si alguien hubiera sabido que su padre estaba involucrado con Napoleón Bonaparte, ¡el rey lo habría destituido de su cargo!

Edmundo se sentía muy indignado. El sacerdote intentó calmarlo, pero el joven no cesaba de recordar a cada momento cuatro nombres: Danglars, Caderousse, Fernando y Villefort.

Una mañana, mientras cavaban, el viejo cura exclamó un grito de dolor. Edmundo se apresuró a atenderlo.

—Faria, ¿qué le pasa?

—Me siento… muy… muy mal. Apenas podía respirar. No alcanzaré a llegar… al final de esta jornada… hijo mío…

Fatigado, con voz débil, el sacerdote pidió a su joven amigo que lo condujera de regreso a su celda. Necesitaba compartir con él un secreto que cambiaría su vida.

Cuando llegaron, el anciano se acostó en su camastro y abrió el crucifijo que siempre tenía colgado del cuello. Desdobló con cuidado una tira de papel muy viejo.

—¿Qué es eso?, preguntó Edmundo intrigado.

El cura, haciendo un gran esfuerzo, le explicó el significado de ese papel.

Un secreto

—Es un mapa. Es el mapa del tesoro de César Spada, quien murió en 1498. Es uno de las mayores fortunas del mundo.

El sacerdote respiró profundamente antes de continuar:

—La fortuna fue enterrada en la isla de Montecristo hace más de trescientos años.

—Junto al mapa hay un mensaje.

—Sí, léelo, dijo con voz débil el cura.

Edmundo tomó el papel y leyó:

"Yo, César Spada, he sido invitado hoy, 25 de mayo de 1498, a una comida con César Borgia. Temo que quiera asesinarme para apropiarse de mis riquezas. Por tal motivo, deseo heredar mis bienes a Guido Spada después de mi muerte. Escondí mi fortuna en oro y joyas en un lugar que él conoce bien: la isla de Montecristo. En el sudeste de la isla se encuentra una barrera de piedras. En la parte baja, a ras de la arena, hay una gran piedra en forma de T. Partiendo de ésta, contando de izquierda a derecha, se debe quitar la vigésima segunda piedra, allí hay un hueco. Hay que bajar los escalones y entrar en la segunda sala a la derecha. En el muro de enfrente se ve una piedra redonda. Hay que empujarla con fuerza. Ahí se encuentra el tesoro.

César Spada, 25 de mayo de 1498"

El clérigo explicó que él había sido gran amigo de un príncipe que fue descendiente de César Spada. El príncipe pasó muchos años investigando la vida de sus antepasados para descubrir el lugar donde César Spada había escondido el tesoro. Tras la muerte del príncipe, el sacerdote heredó todos sus libros. Una noche, mientras hojeaba uno de los tomos bajo la luz de una pequeña lámpara, descubrió que debido al calor de ésta habían aparecido unas letras amarillentas en el separador de páginas. Como parecían contener un mensaje, tomó una pluma y delineó cuidadosamente las letras hasta descubrir el texto.

—¡Era el mensaje de César Spada! Por desgracia, cuando me preparaba para salir en busca del tesoro, me encarcelaron.

Faria dijo que hubiera querido rescatar el tesoro junto con Edmundo, pero sabía que ahora ya no sería posible.

—Voy a morir, hijo mío... En cuanto al tesoro, es todo tuyo. Solamente te pido que lo uses para ayudar a la gente. Prométeme que harás buen uso de tanta riqueza.

—¡Faria, sus enseñanzas son mi verdadero tesoro!, respondió Edmundo aferrando las manos de su amigo.

Faria sonrió. Entonces sus ojos se cerraron y sus manos soltaron las de Edmundo.

—Señor cura... señor Faria...

Edmundo lloró al ver que el religioso había muerto. Decidió que era mejor regresar a su celda, pues se acercaba la hora de la cena y pronto aparecería el carcelero.

El joven era siempre el último en recibir los alimentos. Cuando el carcelero llegó con la cena, le comentó:

—Un prisionero más partió a mejor vida... ¡o a peor vida! Murió ese cura loco que quería ofrecerle su tesoro al director. Creí que estaba dormido y hasta sacudí su hombro. Ya lo pusimos dentro de un saco, lo arrojaremos al mar esta noche.

Edmundo intentó disimular la tristeza por la muerte de su amigo. Se levantó de la cama y fue a mirar el mar por la ventana para esconder sus lágrimas. En cuanto salió el carcelero se puso a pensar: "Después de la cena iré a la celda de Faria. Sacaré su cuerpo del saco y lo traeré hasta mi cama para taparlo con mis trapos. Luego regresaré a su celda y me introduciré dentro del saco para tomar su lugar".

Así lo hizo. Llevó el cuerpo de su amigo a su celda y lo colocó sobre la cama. Antes de cubrirlo, le besó la frente. Regresó a la celda del cura, tomó su daga y se introdujo en el saco.

"¡Si los guardias sospechan algo, estaré perdido! Pero no me rendiré tan fácilmente... ¡Si es necesario, me defenderé con la daga!". Edmundo estaba decidido a morir si su plan no funcionaba.

Pronto oyó voces y pasos. Había llegado la hora. Sólo le quedaba rezar para que el saco no golpeara contra alguna peña cuando lo tiraran al mar. Si eso pasara, ¡seguramente moriría! Los hombres entraron en la celda, ataron el saco y lo llevaron hasta el borde del gran peñasco sobre el que se alzaba el castillo de If. Sujetaron piedras a una de las extremidades para que el cuerpo se hundiera enseguida. Edmundo contuvo la respiración. Tenía que actuar rápidamente en cuanto cayera al mar.

—Tengan cuidado de que no caiga sobre las peñas. ¡El director nos obligará a bajar para rescatar al muerto!, previno uno de los hombres.

—¡Listos!, y arrojaron el saco.

—¡Vayamos a tomar un trago en memoria del viejo!

Edmundo contuvo la respiración mientras cortaba el saco. Poco después pudo sentir la brisa de la libertad en su rostro.

¡Piratas!

Edmundo miró hacia lo alto del peñasco. Los hombres ya se habían ido, así que podía comenzar a nadar.

Los rayos iluminaban el cielo y truenos aterradores rasgaban el silencio de la noche. Comenzó a caer una fuerte tempestad. El joven nadó varias horas bajo la lluvia. Si no hubiera ejercitado su cuerpo en la prisión, no habría tenido la fortaleza física para hacer frente a aquellas olas enormes.

Mientras nadaba, pensó en el carcelero, quien pronto entraría en su celda y descubriría el cadáver de Faria. Por primera vez sintió miedo, pues su libertad peligraba. Le dolían todos los músculos, tenía hambre y sed, y el agua estaba helada. Por fortuna, encontró un tronco flotante al que pudo aferrarse. Cerró los ojos tratando de no quedarse dormido: Necesitaba descansar.

Perdió la noción del tiempo que estuvo flotando con el tronco. Cuando el sol comenzaba a mostrar sus primeros rayos, Edmundo se frotó los ojos. ¿Sería un espejismo lo que veía o era de verdad un barco? Gritó lo más fuerte que pudo y levantó los brazos haciendo señas desesperadas. Alguien le respondió desde la cubierta del barco. Entonces Edmundo comenzó a nadar; se alegró mucho al ver a dos hombres que se aproximaban en un bote de remos. Lo sacaron del agua totalmente agotado y lo llevaron al barco. Cuando despertó, estaba rodeado de algunos marineros curiosos. Le habían quitado la ropa mojada y lo habían cubierto con una manta. Su aspecto no era muy bueno. Se irguió mirando a su alrededor y sintió gran alivio al ver que la embarcación navegaba en dirección opuesta al castillo de If.

"¡Estoy a salvo!", pensó entusiasmado.

El capitán de la nave se acercó y le preguntó:

—¿Qué te sucedió?

—Mi barco naufragó en la tempestad, señor. No sé cómo agradecer lo que sus hombres hicieron por mí…

—¿Qué edad tienes?, indagó el capitán.

—Treinta… y cuatro… señor. Edmundo casi se atragantó. ¡Había estado quince años en prisión!

—Si quieres puedes quedarte con nosotros, pero tendrás que trabajar. ¡Y mucho!, le invitó el capitán.

Edmundo aceptó de inmediato. El capitán ordenó a los marineros que le dieran algo de comer, un poco de agua dulce para lavarse y ropa limpia. Después de esto, Edmundo se sintió un hombre nuevo.

Al poco tiempo se dio cuenta de que se encontraba en un barco de piratas. Entregaban mercancías de madrugada en los puertos para evitar el pago de impuestos. Edmundo no estaba de acuerdo con ese tipo de actividades, pero dada su situación no tenía otra opción.

Jacobo, uno de los marineros, le cortó el pelo y la barba. Lleno de curiosidad, Edmundo se miró en un espejo. ¡Se veía tan diferente! Ni siquiera su propio padre lo reconocería. Su cabello negro estaba lleno de hilos plateados; su rostro, más delgado, parecía de piedra; su piel estaba mucho más blanca; y sus ojos, fríos como el acero. Hasta su manera de hablar había cambiado: era más pausada, más segura.

Al principio, la tripulación y el propio capitán le tenían desconfianza. Con el paso de los días, sin embargo, todos se acostumbraron a su presencia. El capitán quedó satisfecho, pues el nuevo marinero era muy experimentado.

Edmundo adoraba la sensación de libertad que el mar abierto le otorgaba. La había soñado todo el tiempo que estuvo en la prisión.

Tras muchos días de trabajar a bordo, Edmundo avistó las altas peñas de la isla de Montecristo, que parecían tocar el cielo.

24

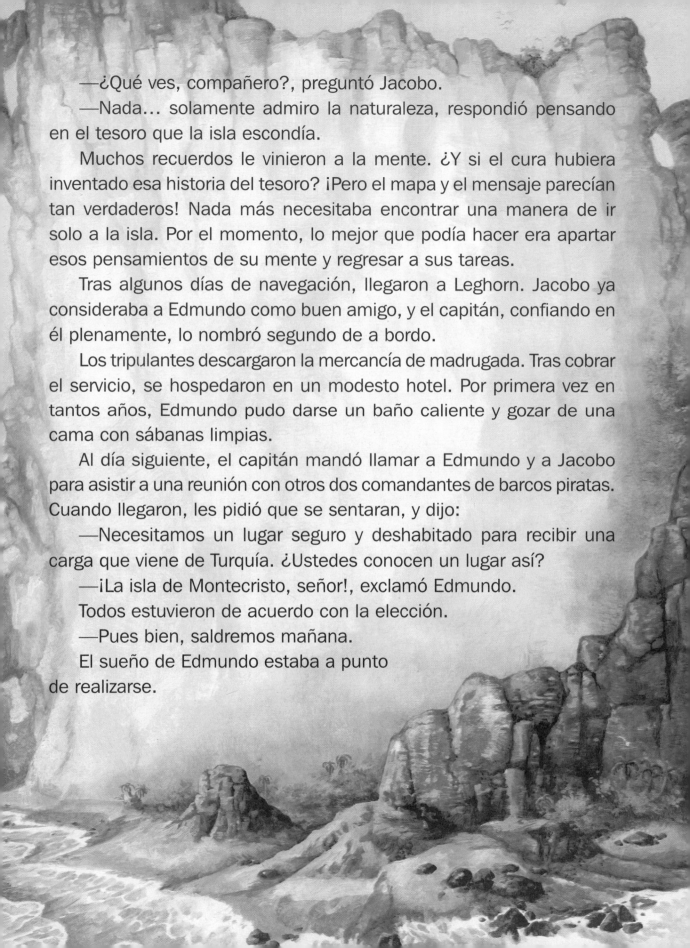

—¿Qué ves, compañero?, preguntó Jacobo.

—Nada... solamente admiro la naturaleza, respondió pensando en el tesoro que la isla escondía.

Muchos recuerdos le vinieron a la mente. ¿Y si el cura hubiera inventado esa historia del tesoro? ¡Pero el mapa y el mensaje parecían tan verdaderos! Nada más necesitaba encontrar una manera de ir solo a la isla. Por el momento, lo mejor que podía hacer era apartar esos pensamientos de su mente y regresar a sus tareas.

Tras algunos días de navegación, llegaron a Leghorn. Jacobo ya consideraba a Edmundo como buen amigo, y el capitán, confiando en él plenamente, lo nombró segundo de a bordo.

Los tripulantes descargaron la mercancía de madrugada. Tras cobrar el servicio, se hospedaron en un modesto hotel. Por primera vez en tantos años, Edmundo pudo darse un baño caliente y gozar de una cama con sábanas limpias.

Al día siguiente, el capitán mandó llamar a Edmundo y a Jacobo para asistir a una reunión con otros dos comandantes de barcos piratas. Cuando llegaron, les pidió que se sentaran, y dijo:

—Necesitamos un lugar seguro y deshabitado para recibir una carga que viene de Turquía. ¿Ustedes conocen un lugar así?

—¡La isla de Montecristo, señor!, exclamó Edmundo.

Todos estuvieron de acuerdo con la elección.

—Pues bien, saldremos mañana.

El sueño de Edmundo estaba a punto de realizarse.

El tesoro de la isla de Montecristo

Cuando los piratas desembarcaron en la isla de Montecristo, Edmundo pidió permiso para cazar cabras salvajes. De prisa se dispuso a buscar la entrada del escondite del tesoro. Siguió paso a paso las instrucciones del mensaje, y finalmente descubrió la cueva secreta. Al entrar, encontró tres compartimientos: En el primero había montones de monedas de oro; en el segundo, cientos de barras de oro; en el tercero, diamantes, perlas y rubíes. Edmundo guardó varias piedras preciosas en sus bolsillos. Al salir, ocultó cuidadosamente la entrada

de la caverna. Después cazó a dos cabras salvajes y las llevó al barco. Dentro de una semana estarían en Marsella y él podría regresar después a la isla con más tiempo.

Unos días más tarde, cuando llegaron al puerto de Marsella, Edmundo le pidió a Jacobo que fuera a la casa de su padre, y luego a la de Mercedes, para enterarse de lo que había sucedido durante su ausencia. Cuando desembarcaron, Edmundo fue a vender algunas piedras preciosas, pues quería comprar un yate para regresar solo a la isla de Montecristo.

Edmundo y Jacobo se reunieron en la fecha convenida. Jacobo le contó que el señor Dantés había muerto de hambre y que Mercedes había desaparecido sin dejar pistas.

—Murió… ¿de hambre? Y de Mercedes, ¿no hay ninguna pista?, Edmundo sintió que su corazón se hundía.

—Fue lo que me contaron…, respondió Jacobo compadeciendo a su amigo.

—Murió de hambre… Nadie ayudó a mi padre…

Jacobo intentó consolar a su amigo diciéndole que Mercedes y un tal señor Morrel quisieron llevarse a su padre a otro sitio, pero que él no quiso abandonar el hogar, pues tenía la esperanza de que su hijo regresaría algún día.

Cuando vio que Edmundo se repuso, le preguntó de quién era el yate que piloteaba. Edmundo acabó por contarle a su amigo lo que le había pasado. Jacobo quedó impresionado con la sorprendente historia que acababa de oír, y preguntó:

—¿Qué pretendes hacer de ahora en adelante?

—Buscar a los responsables de mi encarcelamiento, comenzando por Caderousse.

—¿Revelarás tu verdadera identidad?

—No, querido amigo. Ellos no sabrán quién soy, respondió Edmundo con un extraño brillo en los ojos.

El primero: Caderousse

Edmundo llegó a casa de Caderousse presentándose como un cura italiano que traía noticias de un marinero llamado Edmundo Dantés. Al saber esto, Caderousse preguntó:

—¿Está vivo? Lo quiero mucho, fui amigo suyo.

—No, murió en prisión acusado de crímenes que no cometió. En la prisión, el pobre inocente cuidó de un hombre, quien le dio muchas piedras preciosas como recompensa. El último deseo de Dantés fue pedirme que las distribuyera entre los señores Caderousse, Danglars y Montego, así como el juez Villefort, su novia Mercedes y el señor Morrel.

—Los criminales no deben ser recompensados, señor cura. Un día antes de la boda de Edmundo y Mercedes, Montego y Danglars me emborracharon y escribieron una carta denunciándolo.

—Si usted sabía que Edmundo Dantés era inocente, ¿por qué no testificó en su favor cuando los soldados se lo llevaron preso?

—Fui amenazado de muerte por Danglars y Montego, mintió descaradamente Caderousse.

Caderousse le contó que el señor Morrel estaba arruinado y que debía dinero al banco. Danglars era ahora un rico banquero. El juez Villefort también se había hecho muy rico y ya no vivía en Marsella. En cuanto a Fernando Montego, ingresó al ejército y sirvió en Grecia, donde se hizo rico de manera misteriosa; al regresar se casó con Mercedes.

Edmundo Dantés palideció. ¡Jamás imaginó que Mercedes sería capaz de semejante traición!

—Mercedes lloró durante seis meses, señor cura. Finalmente acabó por aceptar la petición de su primo. Tienen un hijo llamado Alberto, pero parece que ella es muy infeliz, concluyó diciendo Caderousse.

—Tome esta piedra, Caderousse. Adiós, dijo Dantés despidiéndose y viendo cómo Caderousse miraba la piedra codiciosamente.

—¡Gracias, señor cura!

"El dinero que obtenga de su venta le hará feliz... ¡o acaso muy desgraciado!", pensó proféticamente Edmundo.

Ayudando al señor Morrel

Edmundo se apresuró a vender más piedras preciosas para ayudar al señor Morrel. En el banco, el gerente le informó que la deuda de la familia Morrel iba a aumentar, pues el navío *Faraón* había naufragado. De repente, el señor Morrel y su hija Julia irrumpieron desesperados sin notar la presencia de Edmundo.

—Señor gerente, necesito hablar con usted. Acabo de perder otro navío de mi flota. Vine hasta aquí a rogarle que prolongue el plazo para el pago de mi deuda, suplicó el señor Morrel.

—Lo siento mucho, no puedo hacer nada, respondió el gerente.

Morrel y su hija palidecieron. Salieron del banco pensando que sólo un milagro podía salvarlos de la ruina.

Edmundo escribió de prisa unas palabras en una hoja, se despidió del gerente y salió detrás de Morrel y su hija. Cuando los seguía, Morrel se detuvo a conversar con dos marineros, mientras Julia los observaba a cierta distancia. Pasó a su lado y dejó caer la hoja doblada a sus pies. La joven la recogió con la intención de devolvérsela, pero Edmundo ya había desaparecido. Decidió leer la hoja para ver de qué se trataba, y encontró el siguiente mensaje:

Señorita, si quiere salvar a su padre de la ruina, acuda al número 5 de la calle Meilhan. Abra la puerta, entre, y vaya a la habitación principal. En el cajón del tocador hay una bolsa de seda roja. Tómela y llévesela a su padre antes de las once de la noche de hoy. No le cuente nada a él, solamente obedezca estas órdenes.

Simbad, el marino

Julia dio un suspiro de alivio. Tenía que mostrarle el mensaje a su novio y pedirle que la acompañara.

Mientras tanto, Edmundo Dantés llegaba a la casa que había comprado, la casa número 5 de la calle Meilhan. Puso dinero dentro de una bolsa de seda roja y salió inmediatamente.

Julia y su novio Emanuel recogieron la bolsa de seda y corrieron después al despacho del señor Morrel.

—¡Mira cuánto dinero hay aquí, papá! ¡Estás a salvo de la ruina!

Julia le entregó el dinero y le mostró el mensaje que el desconocido había dejado caer a sus pies.

—¿Quién será Simbad el marino? ¡Dios bendiga a ese noble caballero!, exclamó emocionado y besando el papel una y otra vez.

No muy lejos de allí, Edmundo Dantés se hacía a la mar en su yate. Había llegado la hora de partir para hacer justicia.

El joven Alberto

Después de mandar construir un castillo en la isla de Montecristo y comprar algunas casas más en París, Edmundo viajó alrededor del mundo durante muchos años y se dio a conocer como el conde de Montecristo.

Cierta ocasión, en Roma, conoció a dos jóvenes, Franz y Alberto, que se hospedaban en el mismo hotel que él. Era una noche de carnaval en las calles de la ciudad. Alberto buscaba un carruaje. El conde, muy atento, le prestó el suyo. Sin embargo, durante el trayecto, Alberto fue asaltado y tomado como rehén por unos bandidos, quienes pedían un cuantioso rescate por su libertad.

El conde de Montecristo fue informado del incidente y se dirigió de inmediato al escondite de los secuestradores. Cuando llegó, los rufianes lo reconocieron y se disculparon por lo ocurrido. Lo respetaban mucho porque sabían que tenía amigos tanto, en la alta sociedad como en el bajo mundo.

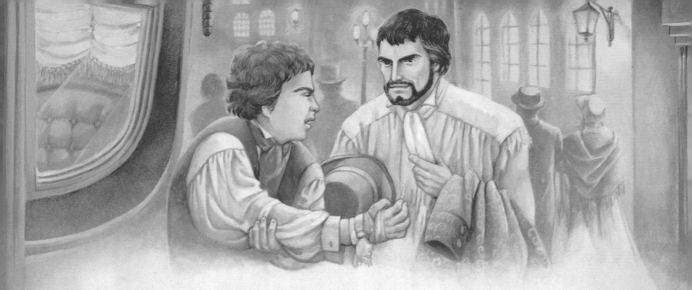

Alberto estaba herido. El conde rasgó en tiras su camisa de seda para improvisar una venda. Luego de curarlo, lo llevó de regreso al hotel.

La mañana siguiente, ya recuperado de sus heridas, el joven se dirigió a los aposentos del conde de Montecristo.

—No sé cómo agradecérselo. ¡Pude haber muerto! Tengo una deuda eterna con usted, dijo apretando la mano del conde.

—No exageres. Conozco a esos bandidos, y era mi deber evitar que perjudicaran a un amigo.

—Me encantaría invitarlo a una cena en mi casa, en París, la semana entrante.

—Acepto complacido, respondió Edmundo, ansioso por volver a ver a Fernando Montego y a Mercedes.

El reencuentro

La mejor sociedad parisiense supo del retorno del conde de Montecristo a París. Se sabía que tenía una protegida griega de rara belleza llamada Haydée, y un esclavo mudo que respondía al nombre de Alí, y que siempre estaban a su disposición dos marineros, Jacobo y Bertuccio. Las jóvenes sólo hablaban de él, del aura de misterio que lo rodeaba, de su fortuna, de su castillo en la isla de Montecristo, de sus hazañas y andanzas alrededor del mundo, y de sus extraños amigos.

Los jóvenes exaltaban su valentía. Su hazaña más comentada era la liberación de Alberto Montego, que había sido secuestrado en Roma por una banda de rufianes.

En casa del joven Alberto todo estaba listo para la cena, a la que acudirían algunas personas importantes, como el barón Danglars, su esposa, y su hija Eugenia, así como el juez Villefort, su esposa, y su hija Valentina.

Los invitados se encontraban en la sala cuando el conde fue anunciado. Su figura imponente, su elegancia impecable y su penetrante mirada dejaron paralizados de admiración a los asistentes.

Alberto Montego recibió al conde y lo presentó a sus padres.

—Éste es mi padre, Fernando Montego, conde de Morcerf.

—Me honra conocerlo, conde de Montecristo, dijo Fernando Montego haciendo una reverencia.

"El conde de Morcerf... está lleno de canas y más gordo... seguramente no me reconoció", pensó Dantés más tranquilo.

El joven continuó:

—Mi madre, Mercedes Montego.

—No tengo... no tengo palabras para agradecerle lo que hizo por mi hijo. Una extraña sensación invadió el corazón de Mercedes.

"Esos ojos… ¡no puede ser! El conde me recuerda a Edmundo…"
Sin embargo, de inmediato intentó convencerse de que estaba soñando.
"Edmundo murió en la cárcel, no puede tratarse de la misma persona."

Otros invitados fueron presentados al conde. Danglars, bastante envejecido, tampoco lo reconoció. La cena transcurrió tranquilamente para todos, menos para Dantés. En su corazón pesaban el odio y el rencor hacia los responsables de su encarcelamiento, además de una gran melancolía por haber visto de nuevo a su amada Mercedes, tan bella como siempre.

Los sirvientes de Morcerf le servían al conde los más finos manjares y los vinos más exquisitos, pero éste no parecía impresionarse. Los asistentes estaban intrigados con su inteligencia: el conde hablaba tanto de política como de economía, religión o costumbres. ¡Además, conocía los clásicos de la literatura y dominaba cinco idiomas!

Más tarde, en su residencia, Edmundo se sentó frente al fuego de la chimenea y se sumió en sus pensamientos, interrumpidos después por la entrada de la princesa Haydée en el salón.

—¿Alguien te reconoció, Edmundo?

—¡Nadie!

—¿Ni siquiera Mercedes?

Edmundo creyó notar un indicio de celos en la pregunta de la joven.

—Creo que dudó un poco, pero después se tranquilizó, comentó mientras destapaba una licorera.

—Tú… ¿tú aún la amas?

—No.

—¡Sólo ella podrá hacerte desistir de tus planes de hacerte justicia!

—¡Ningún ángel, ningún demonio me hará renunciar a mis planes!, respondió Edmundo con determinación.

Los ojos de Haydée se inundaron de lágrimas. En la intimidad de su corazón, abrigaba la esperanza de que un día Edmundo olvidara sus rencores y la amara como a Mercedes.

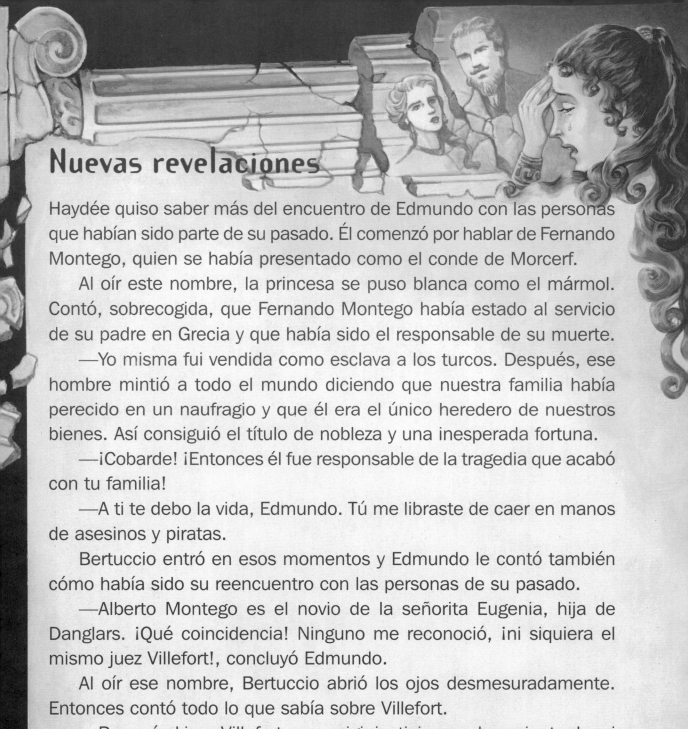

Nuevas revelaciones

Haydée quiso saber más del encuentro de Edmundo con las personas que habían sido parte de su pasado. Él comenzó por hablar de Fernando Montego, quien se había presentado como el conde de Morcerf.

Al oír este nombre, la princesa se puso blanca como el mármol. Contó, sobrecogida, que Fernando Montego había estado al servicio de su padre en Grecia y que había sido el responsable de su muerte.

—Yo misma fui vendida como esclava a los turcos. Después, ese hombre mintió a todo el mundo diciendo que nuestra familia había perecido en un naufragio y que él era el único heredero de nuestros bienes. Así consiguió el título de nobleza y una inesperada fortuna.

—¡Cobarde! ¡Entonces él fue responsable de la tragedia que acabó con tu familia!

—A ti te debo la vida, Edmundo. Tú me libraste de caer en manos de asesinos y piratas.

Bertuccio entró en esos momentos y Edmundo le contó también cómo había sido su reencuentro con las personas de su pasado.

—Alberto Montego es el novio de la señorita Eugenia, hija de Danglars. ¡Qué coincidencia! Ninguno me reconoció, ¡ni siquiera el mismo juez Villefort!, concluyó Edmundo.

Al oír ese nombre, Bertuccio abrió los ojos desmesuradamente. Entonces contó todo lo que sabía sobre Villefort.

—Busqué al juez Villefort para exigir justicia por el asesinato de mi hermano. Por su modo de actuar y sus palabras, me di cuenta de que él había sido el autor intelectual del crimen. Lo seguí durante algunos días y descubrí que una desgraciada mujer acababa de tener un hijo suyo. Lo vi colocar al recién nacido en una caja y buscar un sitio dónde enterrarlo vivo. Cuando se distrajo, logré colocar una piedra en lugar del bebé. Dejé a la criatura con mi madre y partí a correr mundo, como sabes, en la aventura de la piratería. Ese niño, Benedetto, sólo me trajo disgustos y preocupaciones. Mientras yo viajaba, él se involucró en trifulcas, asaltos y crímenes, y acabó en la cárcel. Un día, buscando posada en un puerto durante mis viajes, me recomendaron a Caderousse. Me enteré de que éste había recibido una piedra preciosa de un cura y que hospedaba a un joyero que se la compraría por una enorme suma. Esa noche, Caderousse apuñaló al pobre hombre para quedarse con el dinero y con la piedra. Oí sus gritos y corrí para auxiliar al joyero, pero lo encontré muerto. Caderousse huyó. Cuando llegaron los policías y me vieron manchado de sangre, me detuvieron; pero Caderousse fue apresado más tarde. En la prisión conoció a Benedetto y se hicieron amigos. No obstante, Benedetto logró fugarse tras robar a Caderousse, quien juró vengarse algún día. ¡Ésa es mi historia, señor!

Edmundo Dantés se quedó pasmado con el increíble relato. Inmediatamente pensó: "¡Villefort tiene un hijo ilegítimo! ¡Él me ayudará a desenmascararlo!"

El segundo: Danglars

Para lograr acercarse a Danglars, Edmundo invirtió grandes sumas en acciones españolas en el banco que éste presidía. Luego corrió el rumor en el mercado financiero de que el precio de las acciones españolas estaba subiendo mucho. Sabía que, al enterarse, el banquero entraría en contacto con él.

En efecto, intrigado por la enorme inversión del conde de Montecristo, Danglars fue a visitarlo a su casa.

—¡Buenas tardes!, saludó el conde.

—Disculpe que venga a molestarlo, dijo Danglars haciendo una pequeña reverencia. Lo que aquí me trae, caballero, es mi inquietud respecto de sus inversiones. Sé que usted es dueño de una de las mayores fortunas del mundo, ¿pero tiene la certeza de que invertir en acciones españolas es seguro?

—Desde luego, de otra manera no hubiera invertido tanto dinero en ellas.

Luego de una breve conversación, Danglars se despidió del conde y regresó al banco para invertir en tales acciones. Lo que no sabía es que el conde vendería sus acciones a tiempo, mientras que él perdería todo.

Ese mismo día, Bertuccio apareció en la casa del conde: había encontrado a Benedetto, como se lo pidió su patrón, quien ahora le explicaba su plan.

—Entrégale una suficiente cantidad de dinero al hijo bastardo de Villefort. De ahora en adelante, deberá ser conocido como Andrea Cavalcanti, un noble italiano. Deberá conquistar a la hija de Danglars, para que ella dé por terminado el noviazgo con Alberto Montego.

Además, Edmundo tenía la intención de comprar un periódico importante. Lo necesitaría para poner otros planes en práctica.

Caderousse y Benedetto

Benedetto empezó a frecuentar las mismas reuniones que el conde, y se presentaba como Andrea Cavalcanti.

El plan de Dantés estaba dando resultado: Danglars supuso que el impostor era bastante más rico que Alberto Montego, e hizo lo imposible para que su hija se interesara en él. Eugenia, que en realidad no quería a Alberto, deshizo el noviazgo.

Al perder Danglars todo el dinero invertido en las acciones y quedar al borde de la miseria, imploró a su hija que se casara con Andrea. Ella acabó por aceptar, pues deseaba salvar a su padre de la ruina.

Poco tiempo después, el conde de Montecristo conversaba en su casa con Benedetto respecto de la futura boda cuando una visita inesperada irrumpió en el salón.

—¡Benedetto, por fin te encontré!

Era Caderousse, que arremetió contra el ladrón.

—¡Usted debe de estar loco!, exclamó Benedetto, levantándose de un salto del sofá.

—Pero, ¿qué pretende usted?, preguntó sorprendido Edmundo Dantés quien no contaba con que apareciera Caderousse para vengarse de Benedetto.

Caderousse no percibió que el conde y el cura que le había dado la piedra preciosa eran la misma persona. Solamente quería ponerle las manos encima al traidor que le había robado su dinero en la cárcel.

Benedetto quiso darse a la fuga y corrió hacia la escalera. En su prisa por perseguir al ladrón, Caderousse tropezó en uno de los escalones y cayó recibiendo un tremendo golpe en la cabeza. Edmundo intentó ayudarlo, pero constató que el hombre había muerto.

—¡Fue un accidente! ¡Él quiso atacarme, usted fue testigo, señor conde!, gritaba desesperado Benedetto.

Mientras Alí colocaba el cuerpo sobre un banco y Jacobo iba a buscar a la policía, Edmundo tuvo una idea:

—No te preocupes, Benedetto. El hechizo siempre se vuelve en contra del hechicero: El procurador que te habrá de acusar de haber matado a Caderousse seguramente será Villefort, en cuya alma pesan más crímenes que los que tú jamás hubieras podido pensar en cometer.

—¿Cómo me defenderé? Pueden culparme por otros crímenes, ¡pero en este caso soy inocente!, exclamó Benedetto preocupado.

Dantés se sentó en su escritorio, escribió una carta y la puso junto con otros documentos en un sobre que entregó a Benedetto. Le recomendó que leyera todo y lo guardara cuidadosamente. Poco después llegó la Policía, y se llevó a Benedetto.

El escándalo

Días más tarde, el conde de Montecristo mandó publicar en su periódico una noticia que conmovió a la familia Morcerf.

El artículo afirmaba que Fernando Montego, llevando a cabo una horrenda traición, había asesinado al padre de la princesa griega Haydée, protegida del conde de Montecristo, a quien vendió como esclava a los turcos, para después robar el dinero de su familia.

La noticia causó enorme malestar en la corte de París, pues se sabía que el conde de Morcerf se había hecho rico en Grecia.

Los rumores comenzaron a circular. Alberto le preguntó a su padre si era verdad lo que decían; el falso conde negó haber cometido tales crímenes. Mercedes no creía que fuera capaz de tal monstruosidad.

Durante la semana, la Cámara de Diputados llamó tanto a Fernando como a la princesa Haydée para hacer averiguaciones sobre el caso.

En el día fijado, la princesa mostró en la Cámara todas las pruebas que incriminaban a Montego: documentos, firmas y certificados. Él intentó argumentar que la princesa mentía, pero no pudo probarlo y lo condenaron.

Alberto Montego salió enojado de la audiencia y se dirigió al periódico. Allí le informaron que el autor del artículo era el conde de Montecristo. Furioso, gritaba:

—¡Díganle al conde que lo desafío a un duelo! Dentro de una semana, en el bosque de Vincennes, a las ocho de la mañana.

El conde de Montecristo fue informado enseguida, y pensó en el dolor que Mercedes debía estar sintiendo. No se había imaginado que Alberto fuera tan insensato. ¡Podría matarlo con los ojos cerrados!

En cuanto a Fernando Montego, era justo que fuera condenado. Ahora Haydée podía tener un poco de paz, pues el asesino de su padre finalmente recibiría el castigo justo por su crimen.

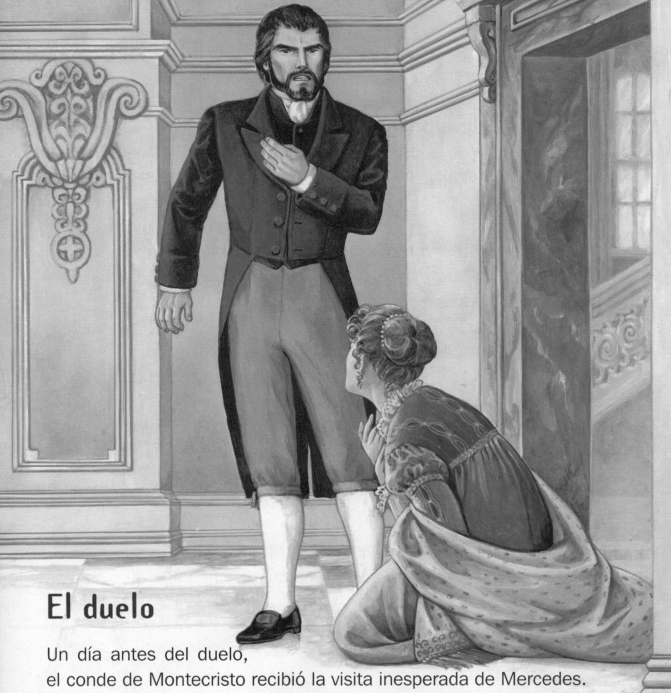

El duelo

Un día antes del duelo,
el conde de Montecristo recibió la visita inesperada de Mercedes.

—Señor conde, vengo a implorarle que no mate a mi hijo…

—Nada puedo hacer, señora. El desafío de duelo vino de él, ¡no de mí!, respondió el conde.

—Edmundo… Edmundo, no mates a mi hijo. ¡Él es todo lo que me queda en el mundo!

—La señora se equivoca. Ése no es mi nombre…

—Te reconocí en cuanto te vi, Edmundo. ¡Por favor, no derrames la sangre de Alberto para hacerte justicia! ¡Yo soy la verdadera culpable, pues no pude soportar el dolor de quedarme sola y acepté casarme con Fernando Montego!

—Siéntate, Mercedes. Tengo una larga historia que contarte. ¡Por causa de esos canallas perdí muchos años de mi vida en prisión!

Y relató con amargura todo lo que había acontecido.

—¿No eres capaz de perdonarme, Edmundo? Que tu castigo se vuelva contra mí o contra Fernando, ¡pero no contra aquel que pudiera ser nuestro hijo!, terminó diciendo Mercedes, quien salió corriendo al carruaje que la esperaba.

Edmundo Dantés decidió no batirse en duelo con el muchacho. Éste no debía ser castigado por los crímenes de su padre.

La mañana siguiente, cuando llegó al sitio elegido para el duelo, Edmundo se encontró a Alberto desarmado y pálido.

—Mi madre me confirmó que sus acusaciones contra mi padre son verdaderas. No me batiré en duelo con usted. Pronto mi madre y yo viajaremos a África para empezar una nueva vida.

—Quise que se hiciera justicia, Alberto, pero bien sabía que eso no me haría feliz.

—Se hizo justicia. ¡Adiós, conde de Montecristo!

En el camino de regreso a casa, Edmundo sintió que tal vez había perdido su alma para siempre.

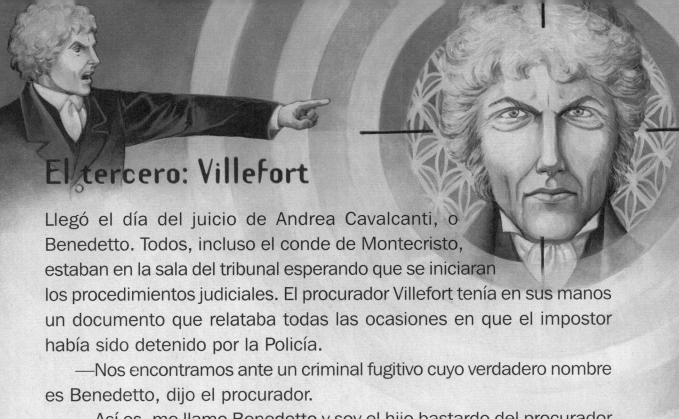

El tercero: Villefort

Llegó el día del juicio de Andrea Cavalcanti, o Benedetto. Todos, incluso el conde de Montecristo, estaban en la sala del tribunal esperando que se iniciaran los procedimientos judiciales. El procurador Villefort tenía en sus manos un documento que relataba todas las ocasiones en que el impostor había sido detenido por la Policía.

—Nos encontramos ante un criminal fugitivo cuyo verdadero nombre es Benedetto, dijo el procurador.

—Así es, me llamo Benedetto y soy el hijo bastardo del procurador del rey, afirmó el reo luego de ponerse de pie.

—¿Qué dices…?, Villefort palideció.

—En 1817, mi padre rentó una casa en un barrio apartado de París con el propósito de esconder a una joven de la sociedad parisiense. Ella estaba embarazada y murió al dar a luz. Mi padre me puso en una caja porque pretendía enterrarme vivo. Para mi fortuna, un hombre que había visto todo colocó una piedra en mi lugar, y salvó mi vida. La hermana de este buen hombre cuidó de mí durante algunos años; luego fui llevado a un orfanatorio. Allí estuve hasta los trece años, cuando escapé, y comencé una carrera de delitos que me ha traído hasta aquí.

—¡Eso es mentira! ¡No tienes pruebas!, gritó Villefort, quien debió ser sujetado por dos soldados para impedir que golpeara a Benedetto.

—Sí que las tengo, padre, replicó con una sonrisa mientras abría un sobre. Aquí tengo el contrato de la casa rentada, el certificado de la muerte de mi madre y la declaración del médico que asistió el parto, atestiguando que usted es mi padre.

El juez verificó que los documentos eran auténticos. Nadie pudo dudar de las palabras de Benedetto ante ese tribunal.

La fuga

Desesperado con tantas deudas, Danglars sacó una buena cantidad de dinero del banco sin que nadie lo supiera. Escribió una carta de despedida a su familia y huyó a Roma.

Edmundo Dantés recibió informes de esta fuga y pidió de favor a dos bandidos que secuestraran a Danglars en Roma. Éstos actuaron de inmediato. Cuando el carruaje de Danglars circulaba por una oscura callejuela, sometieron al cochero. El banquero dormía, pero despertó aterrorizado, pues pensó que la Policía lo había descubierto. Sin embargo, en el camino a las catacumbas se dio cuenta de que era conducido por bandidos. Al llegar a su destino, éstos encerraron a Danglars en un helada celda y salieron riendo a carcajadas.

Danglars se aferró a los barrotes de hierro de la reja y gritó:

—¡Esperen, no se vayan! ¡Tengo dinero! ¿Es eso lo que quieren? Tengo hambre, necesito comer algo…, lloriqueó.

No le hicieron caso. Danglars se acurrucó en un rincón de la celda. Como temía a las ratas y a las cucarachas, no consiguió conciliar el sueño.

Al amanecer se oían pasos, corrió a la reja para pedir algo de comer. Los secuestradores le dijeron que si quería comer, le costaría muy caro. Al término de una semana, el dinero se le había acabado.

—¡Quiero hablar con su jefe! ¿No tienen un jefe? ¿Saben cómo sufre alguien con hambre? ¿Han pasado hambre algún día?, gritaba.

—Yo sí…, respondió alguien con el rostro oculto por una capucha. Deduciendo que aquél era el jefe de la banda, el preso insistió:

—Entonces usted sí sabe lo que estoy sufriendo.

—Lo que estás sintiendo es muy poco comparado con lo que yo padecí cuando tú nadabas en oro. La voz del encapuchado era fría como el hielo.

—Perdóneme…, suplicó Danglars.

—Entonces, ¿te arrepientes del mal que has causado?

—Sí, me arrepiento…, respondió Danglars con el único afán de que ese hombre le diera algo de comer.

—Estás perdonado…, dijo el hombre descubriéndose el rostro.

—¡Conde…! ¡Conde de Montecristo!, exclamó Danglars con los ojos desorbitados.

—Edmundo Dantés, si así lo prefieres. Aquél que traicionaste y que llevaste a prisión injustamente. Te perdono, Danglars, porque yo también necesito que me perdonen. En mi sed de justicia no había lugar para la muerte. Desgraciadamente, Caderousse murió en una pelea con Benedetto, Fernando se mató después de que Mercedes y Alberto lo abandonaran, y Villefort ha enloquecido. Estás en libertad… ¡En la miseria, pero en libertad!

Dantés le abrió la celda a Danglars, quien parecía estar viendo un fantasma. Lo miró temblando de pies a cabeza y después salió corriendo por los oscuros pasillos de las catacumbas.

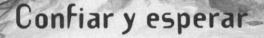

Confiar y esperar

De regreso en París, Edmundo Dantés se preparaba para partir a su isla. Se acordó entonces de Maximiliano Morrel y Valentina Villefort, quienes se habían enamorado en secreto. Llamó a Jacobo y le pidió que les llevara una carta.

Jacobo salió a entregar la carta. Haydée bajó las escaleras que daban al salón. Su mirada era triste.

—¿No te has ido todavía, querida princesa?

—Sé que estoy libre, Edmundo, pero mi corazón no lo está, dijo suspirando. ¿No te has dado cuenta todavía de que te pertenece, que yo te pertenezco?

Edmundo Dantés besó su mano. Sintió que ya no había amargura en su corazón. ¡Estaba enamorado de Haydée!

—Cásate conmigo, Haydée. Solamente tu amor liberará mi corazón para siempre. Y besó sus labios.

Maximiliano y Valentina se sorprendieron con la carta de Dantés. En ella les contaba la historia de su vida y mencionaba la ayuda que le había brindado al señor Morrel, cuando lo salvó de la bancarrota. Se sentía culpable de que Villefort, el padre de Valentina, se hubiera vuelto loco. La carta terminaba así:

Les dejo a ambos, como regalo de bodas, mi casa en París y las joyas que hay en el cofre. Reza por mí, Valentina. Quizá así mi alma podrá quedar libre del remordimiento que aún siento. He aprendido que la sabiduría humana puede resumirse en dos palabras: confiar y esperar.

Edmundo Dantés, conde de Montecristo

—¿Dónde estará el conde? ¿Cuándo podremos verlo para agradecerle su ayuda?, se preguntaban Maximiliano y Valentina.

—Se fue con Haydée a buscar la paz, dijo Jacobo señalando el mar. Un día volverá. Aprendamos también a confiar y esperar.

¿Quién fue Alexandre Dumas?

Alexandre Davy de la Pailletterie nació el 24 de julio de 1802 en Villers-Cotterêts, cerca de París. Quedó huérfano a los dieciocho años. Dos años después decidió ir a París.

El conde de Montecristo es una novela histórica llena de aventuras, tal como fue la vida del autor, quien adoptó el seudónimo de Alexandre Dumas. En la narración aparecen varios personajes y acontecimientos reales: el exilio de Napoleón en la isla de Elba; César Borgia, quien en verdad usaba todos los medios posibles para enriquecerse; y el castillo de If, que se utilizó como prisión de los enemigos del rey.

Alexandre Dumas murió en París completamente arruinado el 5 de diciembre de 1870, a los 68 años de edad. Dejó un hijo natural, Alexandre Dumas hijo, autor de *La dama de las camelias.*

Sus obras más conocidas son: *El conde de Montecristo, Los tres mosqueteros, Veinte años después* (continuación de *Los tres mosqueteros), La reina Margot* y *La máscara de hierro.*

LAROUSSE

El conde de Montecristo

Clásica
A partir de 9 años
lectura

Adaptación al portugués: Telma Guimarães Castro Andrade
Ilustraciones: Cecília Iwashita
Traducción al español: Beatriz Mira Andreu y Mariano Sánchez-Ventura

El joven capitán Edmundo Dantés estaba a punto de casarse con su novia Mercedes cuando su destino cambió totalmente: Una serie de intrigas ocasionó su injusta prisión durante quince años. Aun después de fugarse de la cárcel tuvo que luchar mucho para alcanzar su propósito: encontrar el tesoro de César Spada y buscar a todos los responsables de su infortunio para hacerse justicia.

ENCUENTRO CON LA LECTURA

Conoce los lugares y los personajes de la historia

1 La historia que acabas de leer, ocurrió en algunas ciudades e islas que se localizan en un solo continente. Sus nombres aparecen en el siguiente mapa. Consulta un atlas y observa el mapa de nuevo.

Marsella   Isla de Montecristo   París   Roma   Isla de Elba

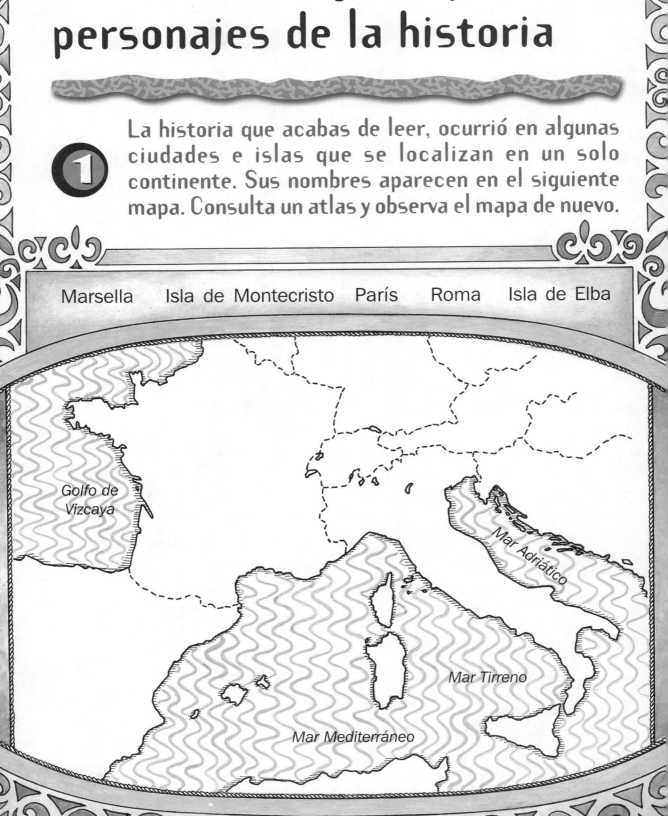

a) Localiza en el mapa, las ciudades y las islas que se citan en la historia; después escribe su nombre en los puntos correctos. Marca con un círculo relleno el lugar donde se ubica cada ciudad.

b) Ahora, responde:

- ¿En qué país está la ciudad de París?

  _____

- ¿Y la ciudad de Roma?

  _____

- Esos dos países, así como las islas que forman parte de la trama de la historia, ¿en qué continente se encuentran?

  _____

c) Colorea de amarillo los países y las islas donde de desarrolla la trama de la historia.

2 ¿Quién es el personaje principal de la historia que acabas de leer?

_____

_____

El personaje principal de una historia también se le llama **protagonista**, y los personajes que se oponen a éste se les nombra **antagonistas**. ¿Puedes identificar a los personajes antagonistas en esta historia? ¿Quiénes son? Escribe su nombre junto a la ilustración de cada uno de ellos. Luego describe las actitudes que los caracterizan como antagonistas. Analiza el siguiente ejemplo:

Villefort: Su padre conspiraba para el retorno de Napoleón Bonaparte. Edmundo, sin saberlo, tenía la prueba de ello: una carta de Napoleón para el padre de Villefort. Si el rey se hubiera enterado, éste habría perdido su cargo como procurador.

Villefort

4 Para lograr que se hiciera justicia y castigar a los responsables de su encarcelamiento, el protagonista contó con la ayuda de algunos amigos. ¿Quiénes fueron éstos? Identifícalos en las ilustraciones siguientes, coloréalos y escribe sus nombres.

5 Busca en la sopa de letras los nombres o apellidos de algunos personajes que aparecen en la historia que acabas de leer. Después, completa las frases con las palabras que encontraste.

```
TMATEMERCEDESUOPCZEISTFQOP
MORRELBNRWGIATCJOLURFÉPCAH
DEVQNYCIWPOALBERTOSYODRKDE
QIUGCBERTUCCIOYPEHEFLANALÍ
QTEUIKAEERIDSOURRLEMCNTIOV
PHMNITBAJEREUGENIAYVETPUQY
TPIBENEDETTOWTUGEDENTÉDYIP
QTEUIKAEERIDSOURRLEMCSTIOV
```

a) _____ era la novia de Edmundo Dantés, pero después de que él fue hecho prisionero no pudo soportar la soledad y se casó con su primo.

b) Cuando salió de prisión, Edmundo se enteró de que el señor _____ estaba arruinado y debía dinero al banco.

c) Cuando conoció al conde de Montecristo, _____ no sospechaba que éste había sido el gran amor de su madre y el rival en amores de su padre.

d) _____, marinero que Dantés conoció en el barco pirata donde trabajó después de su fuga, se convirtió en uno de sus fieles servidores cuando Edmundo regresó a París.

e) El conde de Montecristo tenía un esclavo mudo que respondía al nombre de _____.

f) Aunque era novia del hijo de Mercedes y Fernando Montego, _____ no lo quería y deshizo el noviazgo a petición de su padre.

g) Siendo un bebé, _____ fue rescatado de la muerte por un pirata y estuvo al cuidado de la hermana de éste como si fuera su hijo, pero eso no impidió que tomara el camino del crimen.

h) El señor _____ murió de hambre mientras esperaba el retorno de su hijo.

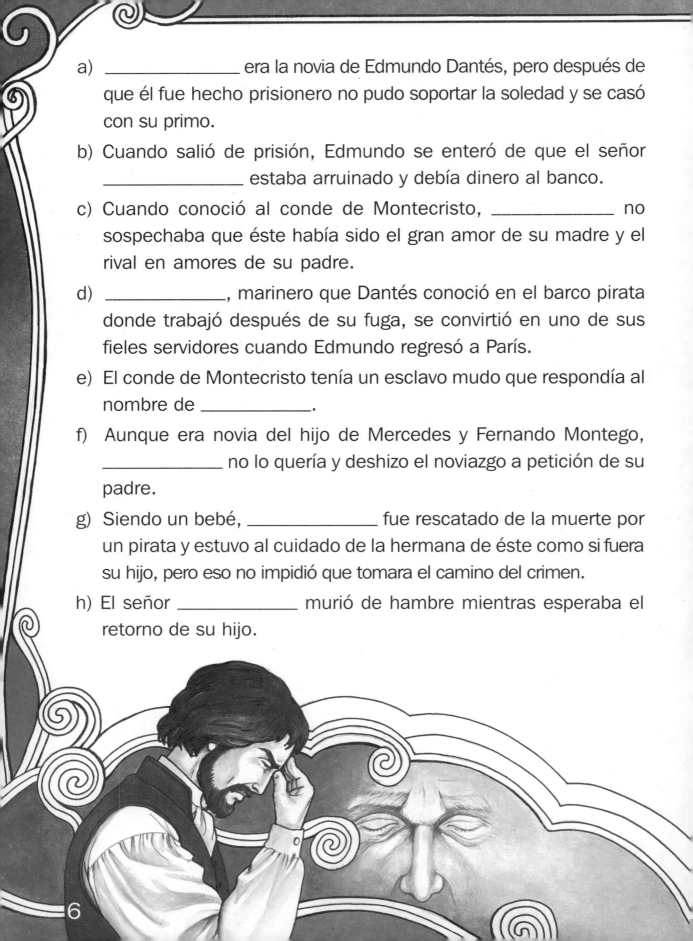

Organiza los hechos y soluciona problemas

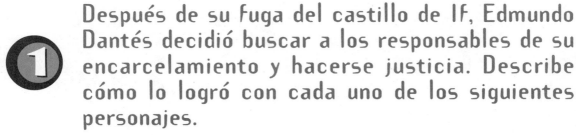

1 Después de su fuga del castillo de If, Edmundo Dantés decidió buscar a los responsables de su encarcelamiento y hacerse justicia. Describe cómo lo logró con cada uno de los siguientes personajes.

Caderousse: _____

_____

_____

_____

Danglars: _____

_____

_____

_____

Fernando Montego: _____

_____

_____

_____

Villefort: _____

_____

_____

_____

2 Las acciones del conde de Montecristo tuvieron consecuencias para sus adversarios. ¿Cuáles fueron esas consecuencias en cada caso?

Caderousse: _____

_____

_____

Fernando Montego: _____

_____

_____

Villefort: _____

_____

_____

Danglars: _____

_____

_____

3 ¿Qué piensas de la actitud del conde ante los responsables de su injusta prisión? ¿Qué harías si estuvieras en su lugar? Justifica tu respuesta.

_____

_____

_____

_____

_____

_____

Representa la historia

1 ¿Qué parte de la historia te gustó más? Dibújala en el siguiente espacio.

Seguramente, durante la lectura de la historia, te imaginaste cómo sería el castillo de If y la isla de Montecristo. Dibújalos en los espacios de abajo.

Castillo de If

Isla de Montecristo

Comprende las expresiones

1 Vuelve a leer las siguientes frases. Fíjate en las expresiones o palabras realzadas para responder cada pregunta.

- "¡Furia, sus **enseñanzas** son mi verdadero **tesoro**!, respondió Edmundo aferrando las manos de su amigo."

  En tu opinión, ¿por qué las enseñanzas del cura Faria eran el verdadero tesoro de Edmundo Dantés?

  _____

  _____

  _____

- "Ni siquiera su propio padre lo reconocería. Su cabello negro estaba lleno de hilos plateados; **su rostro**, más delgado, **parecía de piedra**; su piel estaba mucho más blanca, y **sus ojos, fríos como el acero**."

  ¿Qué interpretas de las expresiones realzadas en esta cita?

  _____

  _____

  _____

- "En el camino de regreso a casa, Edmundo pensó **que tal vez había perdido su alma para siempre**."

  ¿Qué significa "perder el alma para siempre"?

  _____

  _____

  _____

2 Vuelve a leer la frase escrita por Edmundo Dantés en su carta de despedida:

"Aprendí que la sabiduría humana puede resumirse en dos palabras: confiar y esperar."

a) ¿Cómo interpretas la frase "confiar y esperar"?

_____
_____
_____
_____

b) ¿Estás de acuerdo con él? ¿Por qué la sabiduría humana puede resumirse en esas dos palabras?

_____
_____
_____
_____

Identifica y expresa sentimientos

 Edmundo tuvo muchos estados de ánimo, ¿no es así? Identifica los momentos en que él expresó los sentimientos que se indican a continuación.

Rabia: _____
_____
_____
_____

Tristeza: _____
_____
_____
_____

Nostalgia: _____
_____
_____
_____

Alegría: _____
_____
_____
_____

2 La lectura de una historia hace posible imaginar situaciones y vivir las emociones de los personajes. ¿Cuál fue el sentimiento más intenso que experimentaste durante la lectura? Explica por qué.

_____
_____
_____
_____
_____

3 Escoge uno de los sentimientos anotados en el ejercicio 1 y represéntalo mediante un dibujo. Intenta imaginar las sensaciones que te causa ese sentimiento.

Sentimiento: _____

Diviértete

1 Reconstruye la historia de Edmundo Dantés siguiendo el laberinto en el orden correcto.

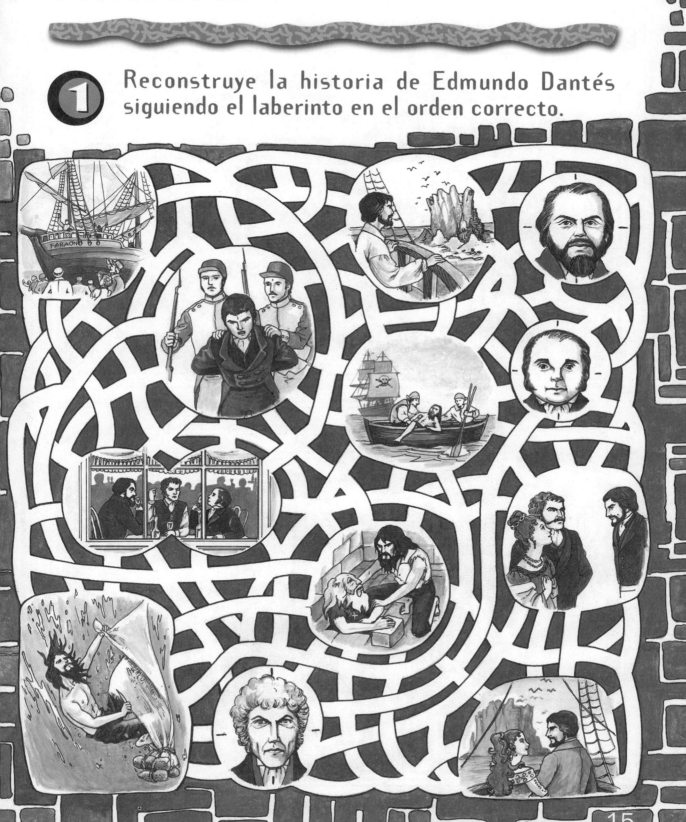

15

BILL RUSSELL'S
AMERICAN MUSIC

BILL RUSSELL'S AMERICAN MUSIC

Compiled and edited by Mike Hazeldine

Jazzology press

To Bill

Jazzology Press
1206 Decatur Street, New Orleans, LA 70116, U.S.A.
© 1993 by GHB Jazz Foundation, New Orleans

First printing October 1993
Printed in the United States of America by Wendel Printing, New Orleans, Louisiana

Library of Congress Cataloging-in-Publication Data

Bill Russell's American Music / Mike Hazeldine.

Biography: p.
Discography: p

Hazeldine, Mike. 1940 -

Library of Congress No 93-73571

ISBN 0-9638890-0-1

Contents

FOREWORD

I am grateful to Mike Hazeldine for producing this book on the American Music recordings, based on notes and interviews of my brother, Bill Russell. I first met Mike in Ascona in 1987 and was impressed with his dedication to learn the history of the AM recordings. Then later in New Orleans I had the opportunity to watch him spend hours pouring over Bill's diaries and conversations, seeking every bit of information he could. I know of no other person who would or could meticulously obtain the material and faithfully present it for the benefit and enjoyment of New Orleans jazz enthusiasts, both present and future. I regret that my brother did not live to see the book, but I am sure he would have endorsed it as a valuable contribution to the history of New Orleans music – although many of his friends may doubt he would ever endorse any book.

William Wagner,
Lexington, KY. 1993

I have worked on projects involving New Orleans jazz with Mike Hazeldine since 1962. During those years he has never wavered in his quest for knowledge of that subject, and even more important is his interest in sharing that knowledge with students of the music. He takes a job and gets it done. It's that simple.

In any field of research, one can talk about doing the work, or do the work. Mike is strictly a worker . . . he loves his work and loves to do his work. Therefore it is with absolute gratitude that, on behalf of Jazzology Press, I welcome this book, *Bill Russell's American Music*, as the first of our literary publications.

This book represents years of hard labor, piecing together Bill's diary notes and verbal and taped commentaries with him and, most of all, the relationship Mike had with Bill that enabled him to draw Bill's interest in the project in the first place. Bill was not a man to endorse writings that praised his efforts in any field, yet, as I watched the two of them working together, I had the feeling that Bill knew that this story was the story of New Orleans music in a certain time and place that was worth telling.

It is told honestly and the editor has sought to preserve Bill's personal observations of the personalities and the events during these years. For many of Mike's generation reading this book, this may seem an exercise in nostalgia. It relates the untold story of how recordings that we all cherished in our youthful days came about. The nostalgia will vanish with the coming generation, but the music never will. It is art with a capital "A" and is part of the American Culture that will defy time and place. It is the story of one man's quest to document that art. Bill Russell succeeded, and so did Mike Hazeldine in telling his story.

Barry Martyn,
New Orleans, LA, 1993

INTRODUCTION AND ACKNOWLEDGMENTS

For many years I had been interested in compiling a discography/biography of the American Music label, but without Bill Russell's co-operation the project would not be worth considering. When I first suggested the idea, he dismissed it, saying the label was hardly Victor or Columbia and I should not "waste (my) time trying to write about it." This was in 1983. At that time he had not released any new American Music records for over twenty years, the Storyville and Dan reissues had long been deleted and he had not accepted George Buck's offer to buy American Music. Resigned to his lack of interest, I partially abandoned the idea, although I started assembling the discography for my own interest.

In 1986 we were both engaged as contributors on early jazz for *The New Grove Dictionary of Jazz*. As he shared with me research information from his files and notebooks, I sensed that he was warming to my American Music interest. However, being impatient to finish his *Jelly Roll Scrapbook*, he doubted if he would ever have enough time to devote to another project.

When I met him again in Ascona, Switzerland, in 1987, I was surprised to find that he had changed his mind and was now ready to help me. During the next ten days, he spent most of his afternoons talking into my tape machine about his recollections of the musicians and sessions. His memory of the events of more than forty years earlier was remarkable, yet he would often get annoyed with himself when he could not recall exact details. Several times during the week he complained, "This is a dumb idea . . . we'll have to do this from my notes if we're going to get it right." This, of course, was what I had wanted to do all along, and so, until his passing in 1992, I spent most of my annual visits to New Orleans at his apartment – talking, reading, taking notes and learning. The first thing I discovered was that the discography I had assembled from previous published sources was, at best, only about 75% correct.

Anyone who has had the privilege of visiting Bill Russell's apartment will recognize the excitement I felt every day as I approached his door on Orleans Street. It was not only his home, but an archive for thousands of photographs, letters, instruments, records, magazines, newspaper cuttings, books and New Orleans ephemera collected over a period of fifty years. His sheet-music collection was wonderful and he surely had the best ragtime collection in private hands. Everything was carefully wrapped in plastic bags and labelled, and he could quickly refer to the price, date and place of every item purchased.

The main source of information was his diaries, and it is these writings that form the basis of this book. The diaries covered his visits to New Orleans, San Francisco, Los Angeles, Chicago, Boston and New York between 1942 and 1949. Almost 2,000 (9½"x 6") pages record events, meetings, conversations, plans, and expenses worked out to the last cent. The detail of the documentation was unbelievable. Some days' events, like his visit to Bunk for the last time in New Iberia, took over thirty pages. In addition, there were several notebooks of random information about musicians he had either met, interviewed or, if dead, researched. All of this built up a clear picture of a man with an insatiable appetite for knowledge, a burning love of New Orleans music and the patience of Job in encouraging musicians to give of their best. It is often difficult to understand how a person of his education, intellect and deep knowledge of music, from Mozart to Schoenberg, could feel such humility when in the company of "folk" musicians like Wooden Joe Nicholas or George Lewis. He found in them a quality that was absent in musicians elsewhere and his admiration of Bunk Johnson (". . .the greatest musician I ever heard") never waivered. His American Music recordings have often come in for considerable criticism, yet, considering the problems he experienced, no other person could have achieved the results he obtained.

The rhythm of his 1940s writing and his 1980s speech were identical, so, in editing his narrative, I have made no distinction between quoting from his diaries and his more reflective comments to me. When we discussed passages in the diaries, he was often able to give a fuller account and a better perspective of events; therefore many stories have been rewritten and his contemporary thoughts edited in. There are gaps of course: no diary entries were found covering Dink Johnson in 1946, George Hornsby in 1947, the Mobile Strugglers and Charlie Thompson in 1949, and the Baby Dodds sessions in the 1950s. I wish, now, I had asked him more about these events. He never tired of answering my questions and I will always be grateful for the patience and kindness that he extended to me.

I would like to thank Bill's brother, William Wagner, for his support and encouragement in the completion of this book, Barry Martyn for his unselfish help, advice and support during its writing, and George Buck for his initial enthusiasm leading to its subsequent publication. Alden Ashforth and John Steiner have been generous with their time in providing information on the sessions in which they were involved, and Caroline Richmond proofread the final draft and made numerous suggestions. Håkan Håkansson and Lennart Fält checked the discography for the many reissues (bootleg or otherwise) that have appeared throughout the world, and my partner and publisher of *New Orleans Music*, Peter Horsfield, compiled the index.

All the illustrations and the majority of photographs used in this book were Bill Russell's, but I am also grateful to Skippy Adelman, Alden Ashforth and William Wagner for the use of photographs from their own collections.

But most of all I am indebted to Bill Russell himself. Without him, this work would never have been started, and without his help and co-operation it would never have been finished. My only regret is that he never lived to see its publication. Although I would never have been able to complete it to his ultimate satisfaction, I hope he might have admitted that the book was worth "wasting my time" on after all.

I can never repay Bill for his hospitality, the hundreds of hours of his time, and the free access to his files, notes and huge collection of memorabilia. But I was not alone, as his generous nature and vast knowledge made him much sought after by researchers, writers and enthusiasts from all over the world. Nobody who sought knowledge was ever turned away.

Thank you Bill. Bunk changed your life and you changed ours.

Mike Hazeldine,
Manchester, England, 1993

DISCOGRAPHY NOTES

The master numbers and titles listed are taken directly from Bill Russell's recording logs made during the sessions. Therefore, where a title was issued under a different name, this has also been listed in italics. In addition, Bill often wrote remarks adjacent to the titles, and when of interest these have been reproduced as ("...........") in italic type.

To avoid confusion, I have listed musicians by their generally accepted names. Therefore Alcide Pavageau appears as Alcide "Slow Drag" Pavageau, although Willie Johnson, Louis Madison, Thomas Valentine, Joseph Pierce, Nathan Robinson and Warren Dodds, etc, appear as Bunk Johnson, "Kid Shots" Madison, "Kid Thomas" Valentine, DeDe Pierce, Jim Robinson and Baby Dodds.

The records and reissues are listed in the order that they appeared, although various issues from any one label have been grouped together. To save space abbreviations have sometimes been used for the record company's name, thus:

AM = American Music	Stv = Storyville
Col = Columbia	(Storyville's export pressings had a 670 or
F'ws = Folkways	671 prefix, thus SLP 204 became 670.204)
Jz Con = Jazz Connoisseur cassettes	Su = Supraphon
P'ny = Penny	Var = Variety
S.S's = Seven Seas	Wf = Wolf

BILL RUSSELL

Born: Canton, Missouri, 26 February 1905; *died:* New Orleans, 9 August 1992

It is impossible to over-estimate Bill Russell's importance to New Orleans music. As a researcher and historian he was without question *the* authority. He not only started searching out pioneer jazz musicians before anyone else, but knew them all better. Over the years he interviewed and collected material on more old-time New Orleans musicians than all the other researchers and writers put together.

Without his insight and single-minded dedication, Bunk would have remained and been forgotten in New Iberia and the recordings that are the very foundation of our understanding of this music would not have been made. Without his leadership and inspiration, two generations of jazz research and the rediscovery of hundreds of New Orleans musicians would never have happened. Tulane Jazz Archives would not exist, nor would Preservation Hall and scores of jazz record labels that have continued his pioneering work.

Bill's grandfather (William Wagner) had emigrated from Germany. He was a carpenter and fought in the Civil War on the Union side. Bill's father (also called William) was also a carpenter and his mother was also of German stock. Bill was the second of four brothers and was christened Russell William Wagner. But when he began to have his compositions published in the early 1930s, he felt that there was only room for one composer called Wagner (although not pronounced in America as "Vägner"), so he reversed his two first names and called himself William Russell.

Russell William Wagner (left) with his older brother, Homer (circa 1912)

All four of the Wagner brothers were taught to play music and Bill began to study the violin at the age of ten. In his teens he studied the violin at the Quincy Conservatory and then attended the local Culver-Stockton College (1923–6), where he gained a teacher's certificate. He then taught music at Ewing High School, Missouri, and Yankton College, South Dakota. In 1927 he continued his violin studies in New York under Max Pilzer, the Concert Master of the New York Philharmonic, and attended Columbia University Teachers College and School of Music Education (1927–9), where he gained a degree in Music Education. He began composing percussion music and was soon amongst the leading "innovators who believed that music should capture the sounds and spirit of the modern world and that traditional European forms, timbres and harmonic systems were not ideally suited to the task. They were attracted, instead to percussion ensembles and to instruments from Asian and Latin American cultures" (*New York Times* reviewing a 1990 concert devoted to his compositions). He taught music in New York (1930–32) and continued to compose a wide variety of percussion music including a ballet *Ogou Badagri*. His teaching and compositions deeply influenced other percussion composers, such as John Cage (who died three days after Bill), Henry Cowell, Lou Harrison and Edgard Varese.

Russell William Wagner in the late 1920s

In 1939 he received his B.S. degree in Physical Science via the University of Chicago and a Music and Education degree from the University of California.

Bill started collecting jazz records in 1929 and compiled the first Louis Armstrong discography. In 1931 he began to study oriental and African music and furthered his studies in Haiti in 1932. In 1934 he joined the Red Gate Shadow Players (a touring Chinese shadow theater), where he accompanied the performances on several oriental instruments. In 1935, with the painter Steve Smith, he formed the Hot Record Exchange as an outlet for many of the records he collected whilst on tour. He first visited New Orleans on February 26, 1937, "the best birthday treat I ever had!" and during that year he wrote several articles for Hugues Panassié's *Hot Jazz* magazine and composed a Trumpet Concerto based on a descending three-note motif from Louis Armstrong's 1929 Okeh recording of *That Rhythm Man*. He began searching out pioneer musicians. He never found Joe Oliver, but met hundreds of others, including Johnny Dodds in Chicago, Zue Robertson in Los Angeles and Jelly Roll Morton in Washington.

It was Zutty Singleton who first mentioned the name "Bunk" to Bill Russell. Clarence Williams thought it was Bunk Campbell and later Louis Armstrong confirmed to Bill that it was Johnson. Bill's letter addressed to the postmaster in New Iberia in February 1938, requesting that he "deliver the enclosed letter to a Negro cornetist known to all musicians in New Orleans, whence he came, as 'Bunk'," changed not only Bunk's life, but, also Bill's and created a new understanding of jazz around the world.

It was only natural that the editors of *Jazzmen* asked Bill to join them when the contract for the book was signed late in 1938. His three chapters (unlike much of the writing in that book) have not dated and still hold the same authority and freshness after more than fifty years. With Bill Russell as one of the editors, the same team later wrote *The Jazz Record Book* (1942).

In 1939–40 Bill studied with Arnold Schoenberg at the University of California and composed his *Chicago Sketches*, a three-movement work based on the playing of Jimmy Yancy, Cripple Clarence Lofton and various washboard bands that he had heard in Chicago between 1938 and 1939. When the work was performed in San Francisco in 1940, Bill played the suitcase. The music reviewer of the *San Francisco Chronicle* wrote: "There was something epical . . . in seeing William Russell pound on a suitcase in his *Chicago Sketches* for the delicious thud that only a suitcase can provide." With a wry smile Bill claimed the suitcase was a Strad or possibly a Guarneri!

With the outbreak of war, he moved to Pittsburgh as a chemist to work in the research department of Electro-Dryer. Living on $3 a week, he saved every cent he could and used his vacations from this company to record Bunk and others in 1942, 1943, 1944 and 1945. In late 1944 he formed his American Music label, and he continued recording until 1953 and distributing the label until the early 1960s.

Bill returned to Canton in the mid-1940s, and moved to Chicago in 1950, and finally settled in New Orleans in 1956. From his shop on Chartres Street he sold records and repaired violins, and it became a mecca for musicians and fans to meet. This activity continued when he moved it to St Peter Street (opposite Larry Borenstein's Associated Artists Studio) in 1960. The shop closed in 1963 when he returned to Canton to look after his parents.

From 1958 until 1965, he was the Curator of the Tulane Jazz Archives and, with Dick Allen, he recorded hundreds of interviews with veteran musicians.

Returning to New Orleans in 1965, he became associated with Preservation Hall. For over twenty five years the nightly appearance of an elderly man perched on a stool in the carriageway became as much a fixture as the Hall itself. It was in the carriageway that one could meet this mild, modest, friendly man, but few of the thousands of tourists that passed through the Hall every night realized he was a legend. Although Bill was stubbornly independent, Alan Jaffe idolized him and did all that he could to make Bill as comfortable as possible in his later years.

In 1967, Bill surprised everyone by agreeing to join the New Orleans Ragtime Orchestra playing violin. With them he recorded numerous albums and together they visited Europe in 1978 and 1987.

In the late 1960s he started writing on a book about Jelly Roll Morton which he completed in January 1992. He then began work on his long awaited book of interviews with musicians defining the New Orleans style. After his death his brother William Wagner, asked Barry Martyn and myself to finish this volume and agreed to allow us to complete other books for which Bill had gathered material.

Bill was due to be presented with an award at the 1992 IAJRC convention being held in New Orleans. Having been persuaded to attend the evening presentation (August 8, 1992), during the afternoon he fell in his apartment and was rushed to hospital. Later that evening, the presentation plaque was brought to his bedside. He died, without pain, the following morning just before 9 am.

Bill Russell at Doc Paulin's recording session – May 23, 1960

AMERICAN MUSIC

The discovery of Bunk Johnson was the inspiration for the American Music label. Although Bill recorded Bunk talking in 1942, the idea of creating a record label to feature his work did not germinate in his mind until late 1944. Even when Bill recorded extensively in New Orleans in 1944, had Alfred Lion (who was present throughout the week) offered to release the records (as he had with the 1943 George Lewis recordings) then Bill probably would have sold them outright. When Lion showed no interest, Bill decided to release them himself, through mail order. However, due to the wartime shortage of shellac, he was forced into having them pressed on the more expensive vinyl, and the first 12" Bunk Johnson American Music releases appeared in March 1945. Selling at $1.75 including postage, the average net profit on each record was no more than a few cents.

Bill Colburn had been one of the enthusiasts instrumental in the discovery of Bunk Johnson, and when the trumpet player stayed at his house in San Francisco, Colburn would write weekly reports to Bill cataloging Bunk's activities. In his letters he always referred to Bunk playing, not jazz, but "The music of America" or "American music." This latter description was duly adopted for the label's title.

Illustration 1

Left (illustration 1) is Bill's original design drawn onto the blank test-pressing label of the first 78; the background has also been colored with a yellow pencil. Some months before, he had read a scientific paper stating that black type on a yellow background was easier for the eye than any other combination of colors, and, in fact, these colors were to be adopted later on all traffic information signs on the highways. Thus the black and yellow labels were used for virtually all of the 78s issues. In the late 1940s, he reissued some Paramount 78s with black type on a green background, and black type on a blue background was used for the Mobile Strugglers' 78 and his 10" LP series in the early 1950s.

The first 12" American Music 78 bears the catalog number 251 (see above and illustration 2 overleaf) and the first 10" 78 is 511 (illustration 3), while the first 10" LP (illustration 4) starts at 638. These were the three house numbers where Bunk Johnson resided in New Iberia during the late 1930s and 1940s. When Bill first made contact with Bunk in February 1938 he was living at 251 School Alley. By 1940, Bunk had moved to 511 Providence Street for a couple of years, then settled in 638 Franklin Street, where he remained until his death. Like most black itinerant workers in the South, Bunk never owned his own house, and paid $8 a month rent for his three-room dwelling on Franklin Street.

Bunk's first orchestral recording was made in a piano store-room using amateur equipment. As no black musicians were allowed in recording studios in New Orleans, the choice was simple: either persuade a local radio station to grant the use of their facilities (Kid Rena' Delta, Bunk's Jazz Information and OWI recordings) or record wherever one could, using portable equipment. In 1943, Bill purchased his own disc recording machine to record Bunk in San Francisco and George Lewis in New Orleans.

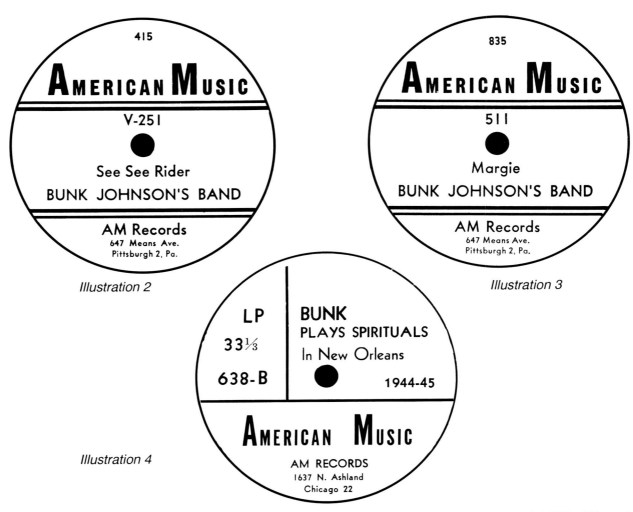

Illustration 2

Illustration 3

Illustration 4

Better equipment was obtained for the recordings in New Orleans in 1944 and 1945. Although considered "portable," the weight and bulk of these machines needed two people to transport them comfortably. In addition, the weight of several wooden boxes of blank masters could be heavier than the recording machine itself. With a more relaxed racial attitude outside New Orleans, it is understandable that Bill hired studios to record pianists Dink Johnson, Charlie Thompson and George Hornsby, as well as Bunk Johnson in 1946. On his final recording trip to New Orleans in 1949, he borrowed John Steiner's tape machine and recorded in the musicians' homes.

When Bunk Johnson died in 1949 the label had largely completed its task, and the 1953 Natty Dominique–Baby Dodds session was Bill's last recording for American Music. With the exception of *Burgundy Street Blues*, none of the records enjoyed huge sales, some taking almost twenty years to exhaust the original pressing quantities. Many record dealers refused to stock his 12" 78s, and a fourth Baby Dodds LP and two projected Natty Dominique LPs were abandoned in 1955 after disappointing sales of the other Baby Dodds recordings.

It was doubtful, in the mid-1950s, that Bill Russell could have foreseen the worldwide interest in American Music. In Europe the LPs proved hard to find, and a new generation of New Orleans jazz enthusiasts discovered Bunk Johnson, Wooden Joe and Kid Shots Madison on bootleg acetates and pressings. These bootleg issues probably exceeded the sales of the original LPs several times over and influenced a generation of Bunk Johnson–George Lewis–Jim Robinson imitators from London to Tokyo. When Bill Russell leased the label to Storyville in Denmark and then to Dan Records in Japan, many previously unissued numbers were released, and this added to the interest in American Music.

Today the sales are better than ever. The first American Music CD (*Bunk Johnson – King of the Blues*) outsold all the original American Music Bunk Johnson recordings put together and the CD series has been an outstanding success in every way.

Bill took an active interest in these new American Music CDs. Barry Martyn worked in tandem with Bill, co-supervising the project. Originally, Bill had laid plans for the first 6 ½ releases. As these were predominantly Bunk Johnson issues, Barry suggested inserting the Wooden Joe Nicholas (AMCD-5) and the Big Eye Louis Nelson (AMCD-7) recordings as earlier catalog numbers. Bill changed the order of his handwritten tech-sheets to accommodate this, and, in addition, he approved the concept of adding live material from Herbert Otto's recordings to both the Big Eye Louis Nelson and Herb Morand CDs (AMCD-7 and 9).

Initially somewhat reticent, he later agreed to the combining of his duet recordings of Bunk and Bertha Gonsoulin with the Geary Theater material, claiming that these rehearsal recordings did not really represent Bunk's best playing. Later he modified this thinking in order to present a more com-prehensive documentation of Bunk's activities in San Francisco (AMCD-16).

They worked together preparing notes and photographs for inclusion in the accompanying booklets, until failing health forced Bill to delegate most of the subsequent planning to Barry. He endorsed the agenda from his sick bed until the time of his death.

Over the last two years I have worked closely with Barry concerning future releases. The yellow label series will now run to 19 CDs (including the one accompanying this book), and this, the most compre-hensive American Music series, is final testimony to the energy, insight and dedication of Bill Russell.

AMERICAN MUSIC
by
BUNK JOHNSON'S BAND

—•—

V-251 Tiger Rag   V-252 St. Louis Blues
       See See Rider   When The Saints Go Marching In

—•—

On 12 inch Vinylite • Records

Price (including packing, shipping, and taxes) $1.75 each

—•—

**Available only by mail from A M Records
647 Means Ave., Pittsburgh 2, Pa.**

_____

* The Flexible plastic with minium surface noise used for radio transcriptions

Left: The first American Music advertisement that appeared in the Record Changer in March 1945

NEW ORLEANS, 1942

BUNK JOHNSON
2nd Floor, Grunewalds Music Store, 327 Baronne Street, New Orleans.
Saturday afternoon, June 13, 1942

Bunk Johnson (talking & whistling)
(12" steel acetate – unnumbered master)

Buddy Bolden's Style   AM LP 643, Purist LP (No number), Dan: VC-4020, VC-7022

Bill Russell: After we made the band numbers with Bunk on the third floor at Grunewalds, a few days later we got Bunk to return with us to make some talking records. Gene Williams wanted to record Bunk talking about his life, so we set up their machine (Federal disc cutter) in a small booth on the second floor. Gene did three sides which came out on Dave Stuart's Jazz Man label.

I still had a 12" blank which I had brought down and didn't want to waste it. I thought I would ask Bunk about Bolden's style and try out the whistling idea. Before we started recording, I asked Bunk if he could whistle the Bolden tune that he had talked to me about the day before. He acted like he was hazy about it, which he wouldn't have been as he had the most remarkable memory of anybody I ever knew. I even tried to hum the tune for him. He didn't even answer and just sat there in silence for two or three minutes, staring into the distance. Finally he said, "Alright, I'm ready," He'd worked it all out in his mind and knew exactly what he was going to do.[1] When the red light went on I said, "Bunk, you're about the only one around who remembers how Bolden played." Without any hesitation he said, "I can explain you thoroughly." He made a remark or two and then whistled chorus after chorus of the Bolden tune. Then I asked him to show how he introduced his "diminished chords," and he whistled all the breaks, with meaningful glances and motions, and the broken chords which he'd played to fill up the gaps between phrases. We played back the 75 cent record straight away and Bunk got quite excited, bouncing up and down and rocking along with that Bolden tune. Listening to himself he pointed out that during the first solo, the descending runs (breaks) at the end of the lines were Cornish's. A few seconds later he said, "That's Bolden to a tee." He also pointed out modulations. I asked him what the piece was or if it had a title. He said, "No, just a make-up chorus of Buddy's. He'd stomp his foot and start off on something. Then Buddy would yell, 'Look out!,' which meant a change of key was coming up. At other times he'd yell A-flat. He might really have been in E-flat or some other key." Dave thought that this side was the best of the afternoon.

Bill Colburn was getting restless and said, "There's no time for a second side." Dave Stuart and Hal McIntyre were all packed up so they could all drive back to California. They were also taking Bunk back to New Iberia. I was sorry I only had time to record the one side. I said goodbye to Bunk and the others and walked around town for a few hours and caught the 8.30 train for Pittsburgh.

Left: Bunk Johnson – New Orleans, 1942

SAN FRANCISCO, 1943

Bill Russell: In early 1943, I got got hold of some recording equipment. I had a Knight amplifier, which cost me about $20, and a turntable with a cold cutting head, also for about $20. Some of it didn't work properly so I got my brother to fix it up for me and added a $5 microphone and a speaker. I don't think the whole thing cost more than $50. My brother was good with electronics and he fitted up the whole thing, which folded into a box measuring about 10"x12"x16", with the speaker in the lid. I was working in the test department of a transformer plant[2] with my brother, who was head of research. The plant was due to close for a few weeks in May, so I planned to go down to New Orleans to record some more sides with Bunk. A few weeks before I was due to leave, I wrote to Bunk to tell him I was coming down and that I would like to record him. About the same time I got a letter from Bill Colburn telling me that Bunk had arrived in San Francisco and was staying with him and his wife at their house. So I wrote to George Lewis and asked him if he could get another trumpet player. I might have suggested a few names myself, like Kid Shots, Louis Dumaine or Herb Morand, but George wanted to use Kid Howard.

I decided to go first to San Francisco to see Bunk before going on to New Orleans. The night before I left, my brother and I made some test recordings with the equipment. I played violin and he played piano. They didn't sound too bad, but we had some thread trouble from the cutting head.

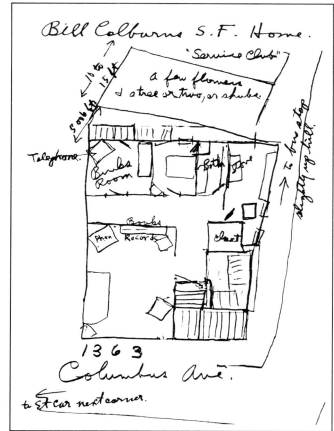

On the way to San Francisco I couldn't get a seat on the train so I stayed in the men's room. It wasn't just a toilet; the room was about seven feet by ten feet with a toilet in the corner. The train was so crowded that two or three other people were also sleeping in there. I put the recording equipment box in a corner and put my feet on it and stayed there for the three day journey. I did manage to get a seat most of the way from San Francisco to New Orleans but, with the war being on, you could never get a Red Cap to help with luggage. As the equipment and blanks were so heavy, when I got off the train I had to leave half of it and carry the rest about fifty feet and then come back for the remainder. With the train being about ten or twelve cars long, it took about half an hour before I got inside the station.

I arrived in San Francisco on Tuesday May 4th, and went directly to Bill Colburn's, arriving around 11.30 am. Bill lived right at the end of Columbus Avenue near the Fisherman's Wharf district. He lived on the ground floor and his landlady lived upstairs. In the kitchen he'd pinned up a big poster of the Geary Theater concert that Bunk was appearing in that Sunday.

The next day Bertha Gonsoulin[3] had told Bunk to come over at 10 am to practice at her home. They were both practicing for the Geary Theater concert. Rudi Blesh had made up a list of about twenty tunes that he wanted Bunk to pick from. Some of them, like *Emancipation March*, Bunk didn't know. In fact, I don't think anybody – particularly Rudi – knew how they went. When we were researching *Jazzmen*, somebody gave us a list of old tunes that nobody knew the music to and I think Rudi's list came from that.

To get to Bertha's from Bill Colburn's we had to take two street cars, and we finally got to Bertha's about 10.30 am. Bertha still wasn't ready, so I fixed Bunk some coffee. About 11 o'clock she wanted me to listen to her program that she had planned for Sunday's concert. She played *Kansas City Stomp*, *The Pearls* and *Froggie Moore Rag*. Then Bunk suggested that they should try *Sidewalk Blues*, playing along with the record, but the result wasn't too hot. At my request they tried *Maple Leaf Rag* and *Careless Love*, which sounded better. I asked about recording her and Bunk and the possibility of getting a drummer for the session.

Bunk talked about how Brock Mumford and Frank Lewis had told him how Bolden had learned *Careless Love* from hearing a prostitute sing it in Carrollton, a suburb up the river from New Orleans, about where Tulane is now.

Bunk then talked about W. C. Handy. At the Museum he had said, "Now, Handy, he played some Memphis blues. Down in New Orleans we had (and played) the real blues." He later stated that Handy didn't really write *St Louis Blues*. Bunk said he was worried about the list of tunes that Bill Colburn had mentioned for the Sunday concert.

We left about 3 o'clock and Bunk wanted to stop at his favorite Chinese restaurant, The Main Inn, on Jackson, above Grant, in Chinatown, but it was closed on Wednesdays.

In the evening we played some records and Bunk wanted to hear again Jelly Roll's *Sidewalk Blues*. He explained how Bertha didn't get it right and wanted to record himself to show her how Jelly meant it to be played.

BUNK JOHNSON
Bill Colburn's home, 1363 Columbus Avenue, San Francisco.
Wednesday, May 5, 1943

Bunk Johnson playing "second cornet part" over Jelly Roll Morton's Red Hot Peppers recording of *Sidewalk Blues* – Victor 20252

2   Sidewalk Blues   Unissued

Bill Russell: The next day (Thursday, May 6) Bunk wanted to buy a ring he had seen for $10, so I gave him the money to get it. Bunk looked at the $10: "You don't have to pay me to make records for you." After he died, Maude gave me the ring, but I haven't seen it for the last twenty years. Bertha had told us to come over at 11 o'clock. We got there a little after that, but, as usual, she wasn't ready. I took over a box of 12" blanks and some 10", which had just arrived (they had been shipped out by mail). Bertha had forgotten all about the drummer she was going to organize. She started off by playing some solos from her program.

Finally they got out Bunk's list and tried *Pallet on the Floor*. Bunk started to play in B-flat and after about three minutes he went into E-flat with that Bolden tune that he'd whistled in

New Orleans. He said, "Bolden used to do that and make that change." Bunk whistled a great deal around the house. They also rehearsed *Darktown Strutters' Ball* and Bunk taught Bertha the Tony Jackson number *Baby I'd Love to Steal You*, on the piano. Then he played *Sister Kate* and had problems trying to get her to play the straight lead so he could play some variations around it. He also had some trouble getting her to stop playing when he played the breaks. He kept saying, "It's a break tune!"

Several people came by from the Bill Robinson show that was in San Francisco. They all wanted Bertha to go and see the show. Bunk wouldn't go. He said his cold was too bad and told me later that he was sick of seeing shows, having travelled with shows most of his life. He went on to explain that he was from a religious family and didn't care to run around or go to shows. He said he never played pool, and gave his regular "no whiskey head" speech, with much stomach thumping. "All the whiskey heads are dead and I'm alive, ain't I?" His only problem was the damp San Francisco weather, as he was always getting colds. "I have my colds and I take a couple of laxatives and compounds." Bunk had always been a strong believer in medicines and his mother always had him take them.

Rudi came by with Douglas MacKay (the Curator of the Museum) to see Bunk and Bertha. Rudi talked to him about finances and jobs in San Francisco. Douglas said to me that Bunk should like it here because there was less race prejudice in California. At that time they were locking up every Oriental in the state – whole families; most had lived there for generations. I reminded him of that.

Bertha wanted Bunk to stay for some red beans and rice, but he had Chinese food on the brain again, and we left about 4 pm for the Main Inn. Bertha asked us to come back in the morning at 11 am, or at 3 pm if Bunk slept late. On the way home Bunk had his shrimp and fried rice. When we arrived back, Bill Colburn was waiting to go out and eat. I went downtown with him and ate a little at Compton's. I bought an evening paper and stopped at two record stores hoping to pick up another "new" Dodds *Weary Blues*. I was always looking out for old records. Sometimes I would find them in "new" condition.

Then I went on to Pat Patton's [banjo player with the Yerba Buena Band]. He'd had an electric recorder since 1927 and still spent most of his time with it. He played part of a series of recordings with Bob Helm and a good San Francisco pianist that lived down in South Frisco [Burt Bales?]. He had dubs of $33\frac{1}{3}$ cuts of Bunk at the Big Bear on April 12 – Bunk and Ellis and the gang. He played me *Maple Leaf Rag, Ballin' the Jack, Down by the Riverside* and the best blues playing I ever heard, with Bunk doing *St Louis Blues* – long off-key notes throughout and choruses which were terrifically blue. No performance of *St Louis Blues* I ever heard approached this. It was a very bad recording except for Bunk, who came through clearly. The clarinet was hardly heard and the rest was all muddy, muddled and noisy.

The next day (Friday, May 7) I got up early, and while Bunk was still asleep the OWI [Office of War Information] called up and wanted to do an interview with him. I referred them as quickly as possible to the Museum, who were running the concert. They wanted to record Bunk reading his letter to the editors of *Jazzmen*, which seemed a dumb idea and it didn't appeal to me.

When Bunk awoke he was slow to get going. He was still complaining about his cold and kept sniffing on Vicks inhalers. He didn't like the cold at Fisherman's Wharf – "Too cold for fish even." He said he wasn't used to sleeping and getting up in the cold. He hinted that Bill should have put some heat in his room and told me about an oil burner he had at home, saying for 25c he could get enough oil to last a long time: "The damp night air is bad for you." He seemed dissatisfied with the food prospects. He had told Bertha that Maude would never come to San

Francisco and told me, "You don't know these country people down there, they'll never leave their home." Bertha had told him he needed his family, and more than once he said he wished he was going back with me. He was also worried because he'd been there a full month without a job. He'd missed one pay day from the School Board who, it seems, had asked him to go back. He didn't want a job in the shipyards and was afraid that "taking care of a country place" would mean he could only get a job heavy farming or truck driving. That broke him down once. He said an elevator operator's job would be okay, but he thought a man would have to be there a long time to get such a job.

He really wanted a job playing music. Bunk agreed that he didn't run the streets in New Iberia and had no reason to now, meaning, I guess, that there wasn't much opportunity for playing music jobs there. He thought that, since they had brought him up for the concert, people would pay good money to hear him and expect to hear something.

BUNK JOHNSON

Bill Colburn's home, 1363 Columbus Avenue, San Francisco.
Friday, May 7, 1943 (morning)

Bunk Johnson (talking)

1	Tony Jackson at the Big 25	AM LP 643, Purist LP, Dan: VC-4020, VC-7022
3	Pete Lala's & Dago Tony's	AM LP 643, Purist LP, Dan: VC-4020, VC-7022
4	Funeral Parades	AM LP 643, Purist LP, Stv: SLP 202, Dan: VC-4009, VC-7011

Bill Russell: After Chloe [Bill Colburn's wife] had left for work, I got Bunk in from the kitchen and set up the recording machine, as I had got him interested in making some talking records. He said he didn't want to sit on the long soft chair in the front room, so I got him a kitchen chair to sit on. Then he helped supervise the microphone placement. He said he wanted to talk about Tony Jackson at the Big 25 and told me to ask him this question: "Can you tell me about when you and Tony Jackson played in the wine room . . . .," and he made me practice the question several times. He knew exactly how he wanted it done. On the next side he talked about Pete Lala's place. I asked him, "Bunk, I'd like for you to explain to us just what kind of place did Pete Lala run and when did you play there?" Bunk knew I had forgotten to ask where it was and he replied in a flash, "And also where it was located I suppose you would like to know?" I gratefully said, "Yes." Then on the third side he talked about the funeral music and

parades. These days, TV/Madison Avenue people refer to them as marching bands. Bunk wouldn't have known what that term meant. He only knew them as brass bands. He wanted to hear everything played back immediately and he seemed pleased with the recordings. In fact, they did sound very good to me.

BUNK JOHNSON & BERTHA GONSOULIN

Bertha Gonsoulin's home, 1782 Sutter Street, San Francisco.
Friday, May 7, 1943 (3.00–6.10 pm)

Bunk Johnson (pno solo)

5a	Baby I'd Love to Steal You	AM LP 643, Dan: VC-4020, VC-7022

Bunk Johnson (tpt); Bertha Gonsoulin (pno)

5b	Temptation Rag	AMCD-16
(both 5a and 5b were cut onto the same master)		
6	Plenty to Do	Unissued
7	Plenty to Do	Dan: VC-4020, VC-7022

Bunk Johnson (pno solo)

8	Maple Leaf Rag (1 minute)	AM LP 643, Wolf: WJS 1001, WJS 1001 CD

Bunk Johnson (tpt), Bertha Gonsoulin (pno)

9 (1)	Sister Kate	AMCD-16
10 (2)	Sister Kate	Unissued
11 (3)	Pallet on the Floor (1)	AM LP 643, Dan: VC-4020, VC-7022
12 (3a)	Pallet on the Floor (2)	Dan: VC-4020, VC-7022
13 (3b)	Pallet on the Floor (3)	Dan: VC-4020, VC-7022
14 (3c)	Pallet on the Floor (4)	AM LP 643, Dan: VC-4020, VC-7022, AMCD-16
15 (4)	Blues in C (*Franklin St. Blues*)	AMCD-16
16 (5)	Blues in C (*Franklin St. Blues*)	

Note: The numbers in brackets against masters 9 to 16 inclusive are the original master numbers assigned during the recording. These masters were reassigned the 9 to 16 numbers the following day. Masters 15 and 16 (*Blues in C*) have been edited together on AMCD-16.

Bill Russell: That afternoon we went over to Bertha's house about 2.15. Bertha had been to the Bill Robinson show and celebrated afterwards with friends by sharing a 27-pound turkey. She had not arrived home till around 7 am. She wanted Bunk to eat something and I set up the equipment while they ate and talked. Bertha was peeved at her landlord, who had told her to get rid of the roomers [tenants]. Bunk told her how once his landlord wanted half the pecans on his tree at 251 School Alley. Bunk never let him have one, but gave plenty of them away to Louis's orchestra.[4] Bunk was complaining that his landlord was about as bad as Bertha's.

At about 3 o'clock we made a short test of Bunk playing Tony's piece on piano (*Baby I'd Love to Steal You*). He'd only just started when Bertha yelled, "Play it, Bunk." That's still on the record, I couldn't cut it out. Then she started playing *Temptation Rag* and Bunk got his horn out and started warming up, so I cut a little of that without them knowing. Then Bertha wanted to teach Bunk her piece (*Plenty to Do*) that she had composed with Lionel Hampton, so she could send a copy to Louis [Armstrong]. She was going to arrange a contract [copyright] for it. She said she would cut Bunk in on it if he would make that record with her. The first try was 'punk' (that's an American word meaning bad), so we did it again. The second take was worse than the first. She wanted another try, but Bunk's lip still wasn't warmed up, so I suggested we should leave it till after other numbers when Bunk's lip would be better. Often

6

Bunk used a mute while he was practicing, but he played open horn here. He hardly ever used a mute when playing a job.

It was almost 4 o'clock when we tried *Sister Kate*, and Bunk couldn't remember the verse, so Bertha went into the back room to look for the music. While she was gone, Bunk had finally worked it out by the time she came back. She couldn't find the music for *Sister Kate*, but brought back a copy of *Basin Street Blues* instead. Bunk didn't know *Basin Street Blues* and said he'd never played it! On the concert the following Sunday, the band played it on the air without a rehearsal and Bunk played a solo. He later played it a lot with the Yerba Buena band and with Louis on a broadcast in 1945, when they renamed Saratoga Street back to Basin Street. That was the broadcast that Leonard Feather (who had no time for Bunk) reviewed the concert from the radio and identified Bunk's solo (after Louis's vocal) as being by Louis. He couldn't tell the difference! We cut a version of *Sister Kate* and played it back. It sounded pretty bad: Bunk's tone still didn't sound natural and had a bad rattle. So I asked him to try it again, but some of the signals got mixed up and the second take was probably as bad. Normally, when I got the machine going, I would signal and they would take a few seconds and then start, but this time when I signalled they came in too quick.

The *Pallet on the Floor* blues was much better. Every time Bunk played it he had a different variation, so I got him to do it four times. Each one was different. It started out as *Pallet* and went into the Bolden number that he had whistled the year before. He did have a remarkable memory. He surprised me two or three times during the week by recalling, even quoting, something he'd said, or shown me, in New Orleans the year before. When I reminded him that the piece he tacked on the end of *Pallet on the Floor* was the same piece he'd whistled, he seemed annoyed that I wouldn't think he'd also remembered it.

It certainly wasn't an ideal day for recording. Throughout the afternoon doorbells rang and friends and roomers came in to pay Bertha their rent. The telephone kept ringing and three kids came in for lessons. One of them, a girl, continuously sniffed and held back sneezes. Another little kid kept saying, "I want to go home," while the other boy kept walking around and tripping on the wires. Bunk was more disgusted than I was and said, "No one should be allowed in the room." Time was growing short and they'd always insist rehearsing everything first, and then, after recording, hearing everything played back. I thought my opportunity was slipping away without getting one good side. Sometimes the thread got tangled up with the cutting head and I had to ask them to do a number over again. When we tried the blues (*Blues in C*), Bunk was peeved that Bertha didn't take a slower tempo and tried to play too fancy. He suggested that she should just play the chords, keep to the tempo and leave out the breaks. The second take of the blues was also messed up, and it was almost 6.15 pm. Bertha suggested that Bunk should come back on Monday morning to try again. Bunk was also more than agreeable to do that.

That night Chloe played for Bunk Louis's record of *Basin Street Blues*. He thought Lil [Armstrong] had made a record of that; in fact, it was Earl Hines. We also played for Bunk *Muskrat Ramble*, *Savoy Blues* and *Ory's Creole Trombone* by Louis's Hot Five. He wanted to hear them over and over again. We played each record about three times and he played very softly along with them. When he heard *Ory's Creole Trombone*, he talked about *Flossy Trombone*. He said it was a similar type of tune to *Lassus Trombone*, *Moses Trombone* and *Sally Trombone*. He said Ory stole it from *Flossy Trombone* and *Carbarlick Acid Rag* – he pronounced it "Car-barr-lick." I had majored in chemistry and I corrected him: I thought he meant to say "Carbolic Acid Rag." It was some years later when I discovered the sheet music that I found out Bunk was right all along – it really was *Carbarlick Acid Rag*.

On the Saturday (May 8) the Ory band arrived on the 9.30 am train from Los Angeles for the concert. Rudi took Ory and part of the band to Bertha's, where they would be staying. Bill drove Mutt [Carey], Tudi [Ed Garland] and Buster [Wilson] back to Columbus Avenue to stay at his house. When Bunk was travelling up to San Francisco, he met Mutt, who was a Pullman porter on the train. Mutt told me how great Bunk had been in New Orleans, and how he had never got the breaks.

The Ory band had expected to play a job that night at the Dawn Club. Mutt had taken all the cards to the Union, but they wouldn't allow the dance to go ahead. So we arranged for an afternoon rehearsal at the Museum for Bunk and Ory's band to go over some numbers. Bunk thought he should be leader and said, "I'll leave the room so you can elect one." Ory got out of it by saying, "Mutt's always our leader." There was probably a lot of truth in this, as Mutt used to get most of the jobs when the band started.[5]

There were a number of local musicians at the rehearsal, like Turk Murphy, Ellis Horne, Paul Lingle and Pat Patton, as well as Hal McIntyre (a disc jockey) and Bill Colburn's sister-in-law, who was working on a story for *Time* magazine. The band played *Muskrat Ramble*, *High Society*, *That's a Plenty*, *Savoy Blues* and *Panama*. After the rehearsal Bill Colburn took Mutt to Fisherman's Wharf for a meal and I took Bunk, Tudi and Buster to the Main Inn. When we got back, we showed Mutt the list of tunes that Rudi had supplied. He put on his glasses and studied the list for a few minutes. He looked a little concerned and a decision was quickly made to stick to the more familiar numbers.

BUNK JOHNSON with KID ORY'S BAND
Blue Network broadcast, Geary Theater, Geary Street, San Francisco.
Saturday, May 9, 1943
Bunk Johnson (tpt); Mutt Carey (tpt); Wade Whaley (clt); Kid Ory (tbn); Buster Wilson (pno); Frank Pasley (gtr); Ed Garland (sbs); Everett Walsh (dms)

Way Down Yonder in New Orleans	AMCD-16
Basin Street Blues	AMCD-16
Muskrat Ramble	AMCD-16
High Society	AMCD-16

Bertha Gonsoulin (pno); Wade Whaley (clt); Frank Pasley (gtr); Ed Garland (sbs); Everett Walsh (dms)

The Wolverines	AMCD-16

Bertha Gonsoulin (pno); Frank Pasley (gtr); Ed Garland (sbs); Everett Walsh (dms)

The Pearls	AMCD-16

Bunk Johnson (tpt); Mutt Carey (tpt); Wade Whaley (clt); Kid Ory (tbn); Buster Wilson (pno); Frank Pasley (gtr); Ed Garland (sbs); Everett Walsh (dms)

Dippermouth Blues	AMCD-16

Note: Although the above session was not recorded by Bill Russell, it has been included here as it is relevant to Bunk Johnson's activity during this period and has since been issued on a yellow label American Music CD.

BUNK JOHNSON & BERTHA GONSOULIN
Bertha Gonsoulin's home, 1782 Sutter Street, San Francisco.
Monday, May 10, 1943 (3.00–5.30pm)

Bunk Johnson (tpt); Bertha Gonsoulin (pno)

| 16½a | Basin Street Blues | Dan: VC-4020, VC-7022 |

Bertha Gonsoulin (pno solo)

| 16½b | The Pearls | Unissued |

Bunk Johnson (tpt); Bertha Gonsoulin (pno)

17	Sweet Georgia Brown	AMCD-16
18	Darktown Strutters' Ball	AMCD-16
19	Maple Leaf Rag (1)	Unissued
20	Maple Leaf Rag (2)	Unissued
21	St. Louis Blues	Dan: VC-4020, VC-7022
22	Bunk's Blues in F	Unissued
23	Bunk's Blues in C (Franklin St.)	Unissued
24	Careless Love	AM Book CD

Bertha Gonsoulin (pno solo)

| 25 | The Pearls #2 | Unissued |

Note : All the above were recorded onto 12" masters with the exception of those masters made on May 5 and 7; and masters 16½a *Basin Street Blues* and 16½b *The Pearls,* which were 10" masters.

Bill Russell: After Bunk had played *Basin Street* at the concert, I suggested we should cut it. Bertha then wanted to do her solo. Bunk seemed pleased with *Sweet Georgia Brown* and *Darktown Strutters' Ball*, so I didn't ask for another take. *Maple Leaf Rag* didn't sound so good. I asked for something like *Bunk's Blues* that he'd played at the concert. They tried it through and it seemed to be great. Bunk liked it a lot and Bertha thought that he'd played it beautifully. He mentioned that at a slower tempo they could really put in the "execution." When they cut it, the piano seemed a little too loud to me, although Bunk had intentionally played quite softly throughout. So I used this as an excuse to ask for another take on it and changed the angle of the mike a little lower, so as to point more directly at Bunk. They played it again, but changed the key from F to C. This take also turned out fine. Bertha played a longer solo than on the first take. I had one more disc left and I asked for one last blues number. Bertha said another ad lib would tend to repeat ideas and suggested *Stormy Weather*. Just as Bunk was about to agree to that, I quickly switched them to *Careless Love* – although it hadn't sounded too good when they rehearsed it last week. But I had hopes, as Bill had told me how Bunk had stomped it on two different nights with Ellis's band. Bunk waited for the groove to get started and then gave two slow beats from the waist. It ran long and his last note just fitted on. We played it back, and while Bunk ran over the street to get a half gallon of bargain beer to take home, Bertha wanted to play one more version of *The Pearls*. I packed away the recording equipment and they helped me load up the car with the records, etc, and Bunk and I drove downtown. The next day I left for New Orleans.

Despite a bad cold, I thought Bunk had played quite well at Bertha's. During the two days of recording, he frequently changed mouthpieces in the middle of a number, with a lot of fumbling around in his case and clicking of locks. He would also have to clear his throat.

BUNK JOHNSON
San Francisco, circa November 1943

Bunk Johnson playing trumpet over the George Lewis New Orleans Stompers recording of *Two Jim Blues* – Climax 102

26   Pacific Street Blues   Dan: VC-4020, VC-7022, Transark 1000, AMCD-16

Bill Russell: I don't know who recorded this. It is doubtful if I knew forty-five years ago. I believe it was made at some San Francisco radio studio, possibly by Hal McIntyre, but that is only a guess. My copy was probably sent to me by Bill Colburn or some musician. I believe the Climax issue of *Two Jim Blues* came out in October 1943, so this might have been recorded around November. Since I was not there it was not given a master number (or title) until it was issued by Dan records in Japan in 1973.

Bill Colburn lived on Columbus Avenue, about four or five blocks west from the intersection with Pacific Street. In 1938, Jelly told me that the nightclub that he and his "wife" [Anita] once ran in San Francisco was on the corner of Columbus and Pacific. Pacific Street was the main street of the old red-light district in San Francisco, with all the honky-tonks and whorehouses along both sides.

BUNK JOHNSON'S HOT SEVEN
Recorded at the CIO Hall, 150 Golden Gate Avenue, San Francisco.
Spring 1944

Bunk Johnson (tpt); Ellis Horne (clt); Turk Murphy (tbn); Burt Bales (pno); Pat Patton (bjo); Squire Girsback (sbs); Clancy Hayes (dms)

Ain't Gonna Give Nobody None of my Jelly Roll #1   AMCD-16
Ain't Gonna Give Nobody None of my Jelly Roll #2   AMCD-16

Note: Although the above two sessions were not recorded by Bill Russell, they have been included here as they are relevant to Bunk Johnson's activity during this period and have since been issued on a yellow label American Music CD.

Bill Russell: Bunk had been in San Francisco about fifteen months. He'd been playing at the CIO Hall. There had been trouble with the Union as he had been working with some of Lu Watters's musicians. There was also the problem that no colored band could work north of Filmore Street. He also didn't like the climate out there; it was too damp and he was always getting a cold. Part of the time he worked on the docks as a longshoreman but found it difficult to lift the 55-gallon tanks of oil at his age. He also worked for the pharmaceutical company MacKesson, but he never forgave them when he lost his job there. Later, when he had one of his colds, he went into one of their drug stores for some medication. While he was waiting a couple of white people got served ahead of him. When he finally did get served, he started telling the assistants a long story of how he had worked for the company as a stock clerk. This caused all the white people in the line behind him to wait for about half an hour.

He finally decided to go back home in the July of 1944. As he had to go down to Los Angeles in order to connect with the Southern Pacific train, Gene Williams got him a record date in Los Angeles making the World Transcription records. World Transcription was a subsidiary of Decca, whom Gene was working for.[6] All the numbers were cut onto a large 16" disc and sold to radio stations. Gene couldn't leave New York to supervise the session, so Bill Colburn went down to Los Angeles to organize things. Dave Stuart had contacted Ory and he agreed that his band should work with Bunk on the date, but about two days before the session Ory said he wanted leader's fee. Bunk felt that it was his record date, so Ory withdrew and wouldn't let his band play the job. Gene had a wonderful letter from Bill Colburn giving all the details about how Ory had pulled out. It was single-spaced typewritten letter and ran to four or five pages. At that time, Gene, Bill and I would pass letters that we received from musicians, etc., on to each other. When Gene sent it to me to read I gave it to a typist at the factory where I worked to do a copy for me. But then she left and the letter must have got thrown out. I wish I had it now, as it was one of the best letters Bill ever wrote and told the whole story of what happened. I can't remember all the details now, but I do remember Bill said Bud Scott wanted to play, though he didn't want to break ranks.[7] What Bud didn't know was that Ory was thinking of firing him and hiring Frank Pasley. Ory kept saying to Bud; ". . . you're a free agent." Bud didn't realize what he was trying to tell him. Bunk was pretty disgusted with Ory's attitude and told how Ory had always wanted to play the "big boss." He recalled how, in the old days, Ory had once signed up many of the dance halls, like the Economy Hall and Hopes Hall, so no one else could play there.

After Bunk had returned home to New Iberia, he came over to New Orleans the following week and we started our recordings at the San Jacinto.

I arrived in New Orleans with my brother [William Wagner] on Thursday morning of the last week in July [July 27]. I put the recording equipment into a taxi and went over to George's house. George showed me the scars he had got from his two accidents. Two months earlier he had been hospitalized with a neck injury when a fifty-pound sling fell on him in a ship's hold and knocked him out for two hours. The second one, just over a month later, also had put him in hospital. This was caused by the handle of a banana truck which had broken loose and caught him in the middle of the right side of his chest. He said he felt short of breath, but he would be able to play. George never weighed more than 110 pounds and, according to the doctors, he only had 30% lung capacity during the last twenty years of his life.

I showed him the brass flutes [fifes] I had with me. I had used them in a school where I taught in Staten Island for a brass-band project. I had bought three or four for a couple of dollars each. I took some of them down as I had this idea of maybe getting some of the kids to play along with a brass band on a number. I gave one to George and, later, one to Bunk.[8] George preferred the brass horizontal model with the transverse mouthpiece.

We set up the recording machine in George's bedroom and we cut a number with George playing the flute and then some numbers on the clarinet. They sounded okay, even though only accompanied by his own foot patting. George had arranged for Slow Drag and Lawrence Marrero to drop by and at about 5.30 we started rehearsing the trio. *Burgundy Street Blues* hadn't got a title then. When I played the record later for Gene in New York, he wrote down about ten New Orleans street names and suggested Burgundy Street because he thought the name had a nice sound to it. George hadn't given the tune a title so I used Gene's idea when I issued it the following year.

Seating plan for the recording

GEORGE LEWIS

George Lewis's bedroom, 827 St. Philip Street, New Orleans. Thursday morning, July 27, 1944

George Lewis (clt, & flute on master 91)

91	"Flute solo"	Dan: VC-4014, VC-7021
91a	My Life Will Be Sweeter Someday	(incomplete — 53 seconds) Unissued
92a	My Life Will Be Sweeter Someday	Dan: VC-4014, VC-7021
92b	My Life Will Be Sweeter Someday	Dan: VC-4014, VC-7021
	(recorded at 33⅓ rpm)	

GEORGE LEWIS TRIO

George Lewis's backyard, 827 St. Philip Street, New Orleans. Same day (5.30 pm start)

Add Lawrence Marrero (bjo); Alcide "Slow Drag" Pavageau (sbs)

92c	My Life Will Be Sweeter Someday	Dan: VC-4014, VC-7021, AMCD-4
93	Ice Cream	Dan: VC-4014, VC-7021
94	Ice Cream	Stv:SLP 203, Dan: VC-7012, VB-1005, VC-4005, AMCD-4
95	"George's Blues"	
	(issued as *Burgundy Street Blues*)	AM V254, AM 531, AM LP639, Stv: SLP 201, DALP2/1944, Dan: VC-4004, VB-1005, VC-7007, Jz Con: JCC 102, Tulane Alumni Fund: LH15555/6, AMCD-2
96	A Closer Walk with Thee	AM 531, N.O. Rarities 4, Dan: VC-4014, VC-7021
97	I Can't Escape from You (issued as *San Jacinto Stomp*)	Dan: VC-4014, VC-7021, AM Book CD
98	I Can't Escape from You (issued as *San Jacinto Stomp*)	Dan: VC-4014, VC-7021

Note: Tom Bethell (*George Lewis* biography) lists *My Life Will Be Sweeter Someday* as master 90. While the logic is understandable, no such master number is listed in Bill Russell's notes.

The "Flute solo" (master 91) listed in Bill Russell's notes is *Sometimes my Burden*.

The second take of *My Life Will Be Sweeter Someday* (master 92b) was recorded at 33 ¹/₃ rpm, whilst takes 1 and 3 (92a and 92c) were recorded at 78 rpm. All three takes are contained on one side of a 13" acetate disc.

Both takes of *Ice Cream* (masters 93 and 94) were also recorded at 33¹/₃ rpm. All other titles were recorded at 78 rpm.

A Closer Walk with Thee (master 96) was not recorded at this session. It was part of the George Lewis New Orleans Stompers session of May 16, 1943, and was not sold to Alfred Lion for issue on Climax records.

San Jacinto Stomp: master 97 is incomplete and master 98 is cut on the Dan issues.

Bill Russell: That evening we went around to see Jim Robinson. It was dark when we arrived and he and Pearl were sitting on the steps. He seemed anxious to make the records and said he would finish early for the Saturday rehearsal, even though he normally worked till 5 pm. He told us on Sunday he had a funeral parade over in Algiers and to be sure that we would be there. He went on to say how impressive the funeral marches were, with soft music and the way they marched slowly, pausing at every other step. George also had a parade that Sunday, but Jim couldn't remember where it was.

Alfred Lion of Blue Note Records (on leave from his army base in Texas) had arrived and wanted George to take him to hear some music. We visited a few places, but the music wasn't up to much. Al spent most of the time arguing about the tunes that Bunk should record and thought they should try a lot of composed pieces like *Sidewalk Blues, Wolverine Blues* and *Sugar Foot Stomp.*

The next day (Friday 28) I took the 8 am train out to New Iberia to see Bunk. He showed me the cornet he'd had since Wednesday. He really preferred the cornet to the trumpet and never did like his Selmer trumpet. He said he would need a month before he could get used to the mouthpiece. He never did play the cornet for me, either in New Iberia or New Orleans. Later, when I gave him the Rudy Muck mouthpiece from Benny Strickler, he thought it was much better than the Conn he had been using. He wrapped a little piece of paper around the mouthpiece and stuck it in the trumpet and blew a few notes. He said he'd break in the mouthpiece and then switch over to the cornet with it later. After dinner that night Bunk got out his trumpet and practiced for about forty minutes on tunes. Then he suddenly cut loose on some technical exercises that really astonished me. All sorts of fast arpeggios, up and down, with diminished chords. After about two minutes he suddenly stopped and said, "I used to love to practice all that stuff. I used to get up in the morning and play exercises for an hour or two." I asked him if he ever practiced much in San Francisco. "Aw, no. Playing once a week . . . ? Now if I played every night my lip would really be hard." Then he told how he used to play in New Orleans all day and every day. The next morning we got up early and caught the 6.20 am train to New Orleans.

Alfred Lion and George had arranged to book San Jacinto Hall for the rehearsal. Some of the men had a job on Saturday night so we agreed to finish early. I arranged to hire the hall for the week, at $10 a night. It was owned by Beansy Fauria and the caretaker was a guy named Roger Mitchell.

George helped to get the band together, as I didn't know who was in town. I thought maybe we would use Jim Little [Sidney Brown] or Austin Young or Chester Zardis on bass, but

George had already lined up Slow Drag. He had a good beat, but he had "a hard ear" as George once put it – he was a little deaf. George only knew him as Slow Drag and didn't know his last name. When he introduced me to him on the Thursday, he thought his name was Novello.

Bunk was talking about hiring a pianist and said, "You know, a piano would set off the band real nice." Remembering how Walter Decou had been afraid to play with George the previous year, I said that I didn't know where we could get a good pianist. Bunk said he'd heard a boy that played with Sidney. I thought he meant Bechet in the old days, but he meant Desvigne. I changed the subject and he never brought it up again.

The drummer was a problem. I didn't want a repeat of the Edgar Mosley business of the year before. George had used him just because he had got George a $2 or $3 job the week before. I'd once talked to Bunk about his ideal "all-star" band and he'd mentioned Baby Dodds as his favorite. Although it wouldn't have been Bunk's idea to bring Baby Dodds down from Chicago, I got John Steiner to talk to Baby to see if he would be interested. He said he was, even though he wasn't feeling too well then. He had high blood pressure. Baby arranged to stay with his nephew, a Pullman porter named Dent.

Baby arrived at George's house after lunch on the Saturday. He was dressed very sharp in a new light sports suit and two-color white and brown shoes. George was interested in the rubber bands that held his sticks together and asked Baby to save them for him. Baby gave him the rubber bands straight away. He was really excited about his trip down to New Orleans on the Panama Limited. "It was the most wonderful trip I have ever had in my life. I won't be able to thank John Steiner enough for fixing it up." I had arranged for John Steiner to get him a roomette on the train. On the way down he was sitting across from a white family from Vicksburg, Mississippi – a mother and father, a baby and a small boy. Baby felt very uncomfortable and sat there with his heart in his mouth. He thought to himself: "Well, I'm just gonna sit here and keep my big mouth shut tight." He even tried to sit over on his side to keep out of their way. Pretty soon the boy must have got his shoes on Baby's pants. The father reacted very sternly and told his son off. A few minutes later he said to his son, "Maybe the gentleman would like some chewing gum?" Baby wasn't sure how to react at first, then answered "I wouldn't mind if I did." The boy offered him two sticks and said he would save him some more for later. The whole family was very polite and treated him well, and Baby couldn't stop talking about this. Mississippi had a bad reputation and I think he thought he was going to get lynched when he got to Mississippi!

Baby then asked me, "Are you going to cut the wax?" Thinking that his emphasis was on "wax," I explained that we were going to cut onto acetate discs. He then explained he meant was I going to be at the controls. When I said yes, he remarked, "Oh, that's fine, that's what I wanted to know. Now I won't have anything to worry about." I thought to myself he must have me mixed up with Hugh Davis[9] or someone, but as long as he had confidence in my recording I didn't object.

Then Baby got serious for a few minutes and told how all his family had died young and how he didn't expect to live long. When talking, his actions and movements were remarkable; not only were they very rhythmic and dynamic but the looseness and control of all his muscles and entire body was really something to marvel at. I had no worries about how he would play with a "real New Orleans band" after all these years.

I tried to get Bunk to go by Dr Bechet's to get his tooth filed down. Bunk slipped out for a while to the corner saloon and then went to see Abby Williams about a room for the week. When he got back, he practiced in the front room, while Baby continued to talk and kept us all laughing. Bunk had his Joplin piano book out and was trying some of the rags like *Entertainer*

14

and *Easy Winners*. This may have been to impress Baby with what a fine sight reader he was. Later in the afternoon he played *Snag It* for a while and inserted some lovely long blue notes into the tune.

Baby had brought his sticks and wood block, but had forgotten to bring his bass-drum pedal. George had arranged for Baby to use Abby Williams's drum set that week. At about 5.30 pm, Abby came by and loaded the recording equipment onto his truck. Then we set off for the San Jacinto.

BUNK JOHNSON'S BAND
Rehearsal at San Jacinto Hall, 1422 Dumaine Street, New Orleans.
Saturday, July 29, 1944 (6.00–8.30 pm)

Bunk Johnson (tpt); George Lewis (clt); Jim Robinson (tbn); Lawrence Marrero (bjo); Alcide "Slow Drag" Pavageau (sbs); Baby Dodds (dms); Sidney Brown (sbs)(tuba*)

101 ?	(Note: Master numbers 101 to 104, 107 and 108 may have been used for	
102 ?	test recordings, but no discs have been found and no details	
103 ?	are are listed in Bill Russell's log.)	
104 ?		
105	There's Yes Yes in Your Eyes (no start)	AMCD-15
106	I Don't Want to Walk Without You, Baby (*)	AMCD-15
107 ?		
108 ?		
109	St. Louis Blues (*)	AMCD-8
110	Lowdown Blues (*)	AM V253. AM LP.647, Stv: SLP 128,
	("*Best Blues ever made, should issue*")	Dan: VC-4008, VC-7016, H 151**, AMCD-1

Note: *An extract from master 110 was issued on an EP anthology (Hirschsprung H 151) for use in Danish Public Libraries for educational study purposes

Bill Russell: When we arrived everyone seemed happy to see everyone else. Bunk was in his usual talkative mood and told everyone about California. We set up the recording machines. I decided to operate the better machine while my brother took care of the other, the one that I'd used in 1943. In some cases he got better results than I did. The caretaker was very helpful and found us tables, chairs and benches. We set up both microphones onto chairs about fifteen feet in front of the bandstand and plugged the machines into the light sockets. While we were setting up the machines, I told them they could rehearse a number. I remember thinking Bunk was in his 1928 pops mood and that he was even stronger than the previous year.

About 7 o'clock we were about ready. Bunk called for what I thought was *Mean to Me*, but it turned out to be *Your Lips Tell Me No, No, But There's Yes, Yes, in your Eyes*. Alfred Lion almost fell off his chair when Bunk hit the opening notes. They really swung that number and we made a short test of the first or second attempt. They wanted to hear the playbacks immediately and got quite excited about hearing themselves. Bunk would always say they wanted to hear it whenever I'd ask, but he usually didn't leave the stand and except for two occasions (the second spiritual on the Monday and the long blues on the Tuesday) made no remarks on hearing playbacks. As Alfred Lion said, "Bunk never made any remarks or suggested that they try a number over again after he'd made misses."

Especially at the early sessions, Baby always came down close to listen intently. He would concentrate on his own part and would occasionally yell, "Oh! Oh! I ain't gonna try that no more," when he heard one of his tom-tom breaks or something. George found he liked to listen best from the back of the hall, or at an angle of forty-five degrees from the speaker. Jim frequently came down from the stand to listen but never had anything to say.

We experimented with the tuba and bass positions and finally put the tuba behind Jim and the bass in front of the banjo.

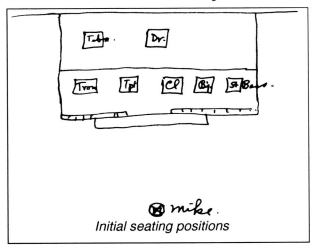

Initial seating positions

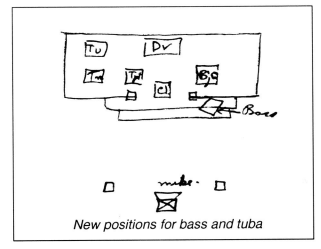

New positions for bass and tuba

The band tried *I Don't Want to Walk without You, Baby* and then possibly another tune, and then *St Louis Blues*, in which Bunk played the clarinet part on his trumpet. Not that he was trying to show off (he had played that once in San Francisco with the Lu Watters band), it was just a different variation from the normal way he played it.

Finally I asked if they'd like to try an original blues. Everything seemed ready to go when Bunk suddenly called me up to the stand and asked, "Are these records to sell?" I said I didn't think so as this was just a rehearsal and we were just doing a few tests. "Okay," he said, "I want to play *Lowdown Blues*," which he had recorded for World Transcription a couple of weeks before. Then he thought quickly and added, "These records won't be for radio transcriptions anyway, will they?" I really hadn't thought about this and didn't understand what he meant at first. It seems there was a tradition (if not an exact rule) that, if a number was cut for radio, it prohibited a musician recording that number again for anyone else for five years. When this was explained to me, I told him I didn't think they would ever be broadcast.[10] I didn't know what would happen to the records at that time. Maybe Blue Note might issue them, but I certainly didn't have any definite plans of issuing them myself. Bunk had signed a contract with the World Transcription people and he was right to ask about this. He wasn't as dumb as some people made out! Before I issued *Lowdown Blues* I cleared it with World Transcription so they wouldn't get mad at Bunk for seeming to break any agreement with them. Later, when the band got to New York in 1945, Decca and Victor wanted to record some of the numbers Bunk had made for me. They felt they had to ask me if I had any objections. Naturally I didn't, as I never had that sort of agreement with Bunk.

I let some of the numbers run a little long and usually didn't even try to give them a signal, since I decided it was better to experiment with the equipment and make this strictly a rehearsal. It was almost 8.30 pm and I knew some of the guys had jobs that evening. Jim Little had to go to his regular job and George and Drag had a job with Herb Morand.

16

By 9 pm we were all packed up and we decided to leave all the equipment in the little room at the end of the hall. As it was a Saturday night and most of the bands would be working, we went out to hear some music. We first stopped at the corner of Almonaster and Bourbon to hear Wooden Joe with his four-piece band. He soon played *St. Louis Blues*; very good, loud and rough and crude, with a real good old-time tone. Then we stopped by Luthjen's to hear Big Eye [Louis Nelson Delisle]. He wasn't playing much and Peter Bocage didn't sound too hot on trumpet. I can't remember who was playing piano that night [Benny Turner?], but I remember seeing Ernest Rogers on drums. We then took the St. Claude street car down to the Cadillac to hear Kid Rena for the first time. We got a table and stayed for about twenty minutes. The only attempt at a hot number was *G.I. Jive*. Walter Decou was on piano. Finally, we took the street car back to St. Bernard, where George and Slow Drag where working with Herb Morand and Walter Nelson (on amplified guitar) and a terrible drummer. George laughed how they would start out on a blues and end on a foxtrot. Morand really tried to hand out the jive and believed his brand of music was the best in New Orleans. However, he did play some more blues for me with his growling style. He also claimed that one of the numbers was "Just as Chris (Kelly) would play it." George was very bored and lifeless.

Apart from Wooden Joe's band the music seemed disappointing. I was sure that Bunk's band was about the best in New Orleans.

People have often accused me of trying to re-create some mythical New Orleans-type band that never existed. Certainly in the 1940s you never saw a six- or seven-piece band in any of the dance halls. Sometimes you might see five pieces, but mostly it was four. Bunk used to talk of how, in the early days, most bands were six or, if a violin was used, seven pieces. People also say that I forced George and the others on to Bunk. When we arrived in New Orleans in 1942, we didn't know who Bunk might want. On the Saturday night (June 6, 1942) we visited all the places where they had music to see who was playing. I went to see Big Eye but he was ill. He wasn't playing that night although they (Luthjen's) told him to sit on the stand with his clarinet just to make the band look bigger. I was hoping we might find someone like Johnny Dodds, but we never did. It was Bunk who mentioned George Lewis, although he got his name wrong at first. On trombone he mentioned Vic Gaspard, but he had retired by then. He knew Jim Robinson. Paul Barbarin and Johnny St. Cyr were approached, but didn't want to do it on account of the Union.[11] It was Bunk, with suggestions by the other musicians, who assembled the band.

When we made the Climax records the year before, we had a Saturday (May 15, 1943) rehearsal over at Edgar Mosley's house. He had been a member of various brass bands and had a tuba there. Jim Little happened to be going by the house and he heard them playing. He came in and wanted to play a number with them. He played *Two Jim Blues* and didn't get a cent for it. When the record was issued, I sent him $10, which maybe wasn't enough, but it was in proportion, as much as the others got for one number. So I thought we should hire him the next year. He was a good bass player too, as we know from the Sam Morgan records. He was a better bass player than Slow Drag for playing in tune. He hadn't been playing very much then, as he'd joined the church and wouldn't play dance jobs. Later on he did play with Celestin. We had him bring his tuba to the rehearsal and for first date. Bunk objected to the tuba; he said it was too heavy with the other bass. I'd asked Jim Little to bring his bass as well on Monday night, but thought that the tuba would be okay on a few numbers. When the three brass got going the band seemed pretty noisy and probably sounded a little like a brass band. Almost every New Orleans musician I ever talked to felt a string bass would swing a band more. Bunk wasn't prejudiced against the tuba (in a brass band you really need it) – in fact, he claimed his best instrument was the tuba.[12] On some numbers Jim Little played tuba with Slow Drag playing bass, but on most numbers we had them both play string bass.

On the Sunday (July 30), I was awoken at 7.30 am by Bunk yelling at the window about us young guys being still in bed when he was up. Later George agreed that Bunk probably hadn't been to bed on Saturday night. Bunk said he'd be back later to take us over to Algiers to see the parade, saying that he wanted to see Henry Allen [Red Allen's father], who was playing cornet again. After lunch we waited to see if Bunk was coming around, but he probably went home to sleep.

We went over to Algiers to see Jim playing with the Eureka. Al Landry was the leader, with Albert Walters, Albert Warner, Alphonse Picou, two saxes, snare and bass drum and Isidore Barbarin (on alto horn) in the band. On the ferry coming back, Jim told us that all the boys in the band wanted to record a couple of funeral marches for me, as I'd never had the chance to hear any of them and they wanted me to have the opportunity. I thanked him, but I didn't arrange anything as I didn't have any plans for recording a brass band that year.

George also had a six-hour picnic somewhere in Algiers, and then in the evening he worked with Herb Morand from 9 pm till 3 am. I thought he'd be tired for the Monday session. But New Orleans musicians seemed to get stronger the more they play. On the Thursday evening, when I stopped by Jim's house, he thought Sunday evening would be a good time to record. For, as he said, after playing a parade all day, "My lip would be getting good." But I was concerned about Bunk's cold and left the arrangements as they were. On the Monday, Bunk said his cold was getting better and said, "You didn't hear me cough that night in New Iberia, did you?" Evidently he must have caught a lot of colds in California.

That night we went by the San Jacinto to study the acoustics. We were considering hanging the microphone from the ceiling. Al was surprised to find Don Raymond's big band playing riffs with the same instrumentation as New York bands. We then went over to the Gypsy Tea Room. As we arrived Bunk came out of the bar. He was so drunk he could hardly talk, but remembered that he hadn't come by to take us over the river. He kept asking us to go inside and hear the band, but the doorman wouldn't let us in, as it was for coloreds only.

Most of the bars and places of entertainment were segregated at that time. Even amongst colored people there was segregation. One evening Bunk and George talked about the light Creoles (free mulattoes). Even though George was somewhat of a Creole, you could tell that both he and Bunk were treated as outcasts when they played in the Creole sections of town. Bunk said when he used to play for affairs at the Franzanne Club, or clubs that had people like Picou as members, they had rules that prevented Bunk (and other dark musicians) from getting off the stand or mixing with the guests in any way. George then told a story about playing at Creole functions and something about them having glasses for the lighter musicians and making him (and the other darker ones) drink beer out of the bottle. Bunk said he always called for a glass at Jim Crow saloons. George said that he got so mad once at the insulting discrimination that, at the intermission, he went out and got drunk and didn't go back. Bunk then told of how bad things were in New Iberia, which was far worse than in New Orleans.

On Monday morning Bunk had stopped by early and had undoubtedly been up all night again. I gave him $20 for his living expenses and begged him to get some rest. I also tried to persuade him to go and see Dr Bechet about his tooth, but he said it would probably take a long time to get fixed and he'd managed with it so far. I went with him when he wanted to get some bottles of beer. When we were alone I suggested that he shouldn't spend all his money on his friends as he'd needed money so badly last winter – adding that I wasn't trying to tell him how to spend his money. On the contrary, he agreed, I did have the right to tell him how to spend his money, as it was me, not his New Orleans "friends," he went to when he was broke. He said, however, that he didn't care how much money he made that week, as his wife had told him she'd be satisfied if he brought home $75. I told him, if we were able to make some good records, he'd be able to take home more than that. Although I had no plans to release the records at that time, I told him he should make over $150 that week and I'd send him more if they sold well. He suggested I should sell them "to Decca or no less than Commodore." He later also told the same thing to Al.

We waited for Baby Dodds to come around to George's before the session. He said he would be there. William and I went over about 6 pm and Bunk came shortly after. Jeanette [George's wife] had prepared some red beans and rice cooked with a lot of ham. All over New Orleans, people would have red beans and rice on Mondays. This was the traditional day for it, just like on Tuesdays everyone had gumbo. We got a big kick out of watching Bunk eat. At first he said he didn't want anything at all, then he said he would just take a little ham. Then he said he would take just a little rice to go with it. Then he began heaping up his plate and scraping the serving spoon clean. Then William's and Al's eyes almost popped out when he began emptying the pepper shaker over the red beans. The dish was just solid brown with pepper and seemed about a quarter of an inch thick on top. Al thought he was just doing it to show off. Bunk made some remark about liking a little pepper on his food, and ate it down without a gulp or taking a drink of water! He made us laugh when he talked about how it wasn't necessary for people to eat so much, while he stuffed down the heap of red beans, rice and meat.

JIM ROBINSON'S BAND
San Jacinto Hall, 1422 Dumaine Street, New Orleans.
Monday, July 31, 1944 (7.30–7.45 pm)

Jim Robinson (tbn); George Lewis (clt); Lawrence Marrero (bjo); Alcide "Slow Drag" Pavageau (sbs); Sidney Brown (sbs); Baby Dodds (dms)

201	I Can't Escape from You (issued as *San Jacinto Stomp*)	AM LP645, Stv: SLP 127, Dan: VC-4005, VC-7012, DALP2/1944, Seven Seas: MH 3026, Variety: REL ST 19146, Penny: REL ST 19146, AMCD-4

Bill Russell: When we got to the San Jacinto, Bunk wasn't there, so at about 7.15 or 7.30 pm we tried a number without him. It was the same number that George's trio had done the previous Thursday. They said it was called *I Can't Escape from You*, but it is not. It may be *You Can't Escape from Me*. This is a different number to the *I Can't Escape from You* that Bing Crosby had recorded. To avoid confusion, I've always put *San Jacinto Stomp* down as the title.

While the band was playing, Bunk must have got to the front door and, since it was carefully locked, he couldn't get in. He pounded on the door and finally William heard him and let him in. He seemed rather sore and complained about being locked out. I thought he sulked a little throughout the evening as he had very little to say. But since he didn't say much most of the weekend, I thought it was part of his usual quiet manner. Frequently Bunk would talk things over for a minute or two after we called for a number. Sometimes he'd spit out the opening phrases on his trumpet or whistle a little of it. During the week he became more talkative and got off on a story of some kind. He'd half stand up or turn to Baby: "And I said to

Joe . . ." etc, etc. Frequently I'd ask: "Are you ready?" and usually the answer would be: "Yes," but often he'd lean over to his trumpet case and pick up a cigarette and light it. I suppose he always wanted one lit so he could puff at it when he took a chorus off. I always gave him time for a few puffs before I started the machine. When I had it going, I'd call out: "Okay, anytime you're ready." Sometimes he'd do a reminder or even play or whistle lightly again. Then he'd give a very heavy stomp off using his whole leg as loud as the drums and they'd be off.

BUNK JOHNSON'S BAND
San Jacinto Hall, 1422 Dumaine Street, New Orleans.
Monday, July 31, 1944 (7.45–11.45 pm)

Bunk Johnson (tpt); Jim Robinson (tbn); George Lewis (clt); Lawrence Marrero (bjo); Alcide "Slow Drag" Pavageau (sbs); Sidney Brown (sbs)(tuba*); Baby Dodds (dms)

201½	Sister Kate (10" test)	Unissued
202	Sister Kate	Dan: VC-4016, VC-7018
203	Sister Kate	AMCD-2
204	Sister Kate	AMCD-3

Add Myrtle Jones (vcl)

205	Goodmorning Blues (test)	Unissued
205½	Goodmorning Blues (test)	Unissued
206	Goodmorning Blues	
	(issued as *Blue As I Can Be*)	AM LP647, Stv: SLP 205, Dan: VC-4008, VC-7016, AMCD-1
207	See See Rider	Stv: SLP 205, Dan: VC-4007, VC-7009, AMCD-1
208	Precious Lord Lead Me On (*)	Stv: SLP 205, Dan: VC-4007, VC-7009, Supraphon: 0 15 23972B, AMCD-12
209	My Life Will Be Sweeter Someday (*)	AM Book CD
210	My Life Will Be Sweeter Someday (*)	Stv: SLP 128, Dan: VC-4008, VC-7016, AMCD-3

Omit Myrtle Jones (vcl)

211	St. Louis Blues	AM V252, Stv: SLP 152, Revival (D) 001, Dan: VC-4006, VB 1003, VC-7006, AMCD-1
212	Tiger Rag	Dan: VC-4016, VB-1004, VC-7018, AMCD-17
213	Tiger Rag	AM V251, Stv: SLP 152, Dan: VC-4006, VC-7006, AMCD-3
214	2.19 Blues	
	(issued as *New Iberia Blues*) (*)	Stv: SLP 205, Dan: VC-4007, VC-7009, AMCD-17
215	2.19 Blues	
	(issued as *New Iberia Blues*)	AM V257, Stv: SLP 152, Dan: VC-4006, VC-7006, AMCD-1

Note: *Tiger Rag* and *New Iberia Blues* (masters 212 and 214) were intended for issue on Baby Dodds 4, but this LP was never released.

Bill Russell: At approximately 7.45 pm we started off with a 10" test of *Sister Kate*. I just got the middle 2½ minutes of it to check the balance. The two bass players were on either side of the band. Jim Little stood at the back (behind Jim) and Slow Drag at the front, beside George. Bunk made a few misses in all the takes and I remember saying to Al that it was a tough number to start on. However, he was powerful and there was a wonderful swing in the band.

Orin Blackstone came in and stayed until after the vocalist was through. John Hammond surprisingly showed up for a few minutes. He was still only a private in the "morale" service. He was able to arrange entertainments with both whites and negroes. Mrs Lewis and her sister and Shirley were also there, seeing how George hadn't shown up on Saturday night.

I'd tried to get Ann Cook for this session.[13] I'd tried the year before to get her to come to the Climax session to do a couple of numbers, but she didn't show up. George had taken me to find her, but she wanted too much money. She kept saying that Victor had paid her $100 to make two sides in 1929. I told her I couldn't pay her that. Although I'd paid all the guys about $20 in 1943, I later was able to give them an extra $10 or $15 when I sold some of the records to Blue Note. I think I might have offered her about $30, but on principle I couldn't offer her any more than that for two numbers, when all the other guys had worked all afternoon. I contacted her again for this session and was hoping she might show up. When I went with George, she was living in a two-room mobile home – although it had no wheels. It was pretty run down, in the "battlefield" area uptown from South Rampart. Although she was now in the church, George was a little afraid of her as she had a bad reputation from the old days. She always had some envelopes for her church contributions and it was difficult to leave without giving her some change.

George then suggested Myrtle Jones, who was a popular entertainer around New Orleans. George went and saw her at her home at 1402 St. Ann Street. She sang at one of the big nightclubs. George said she had also sung at the Lyric (or maybe the Palace) Theater.

She showed up at 8.30 or a little before, and waited while they did another take of *Sister Kate*. I asked her if she'd like to do a test of a blues. I rigged up a second microphone. She stood too far from the microphone on the first take, so I got her to move closer. The very first test has only George doing the interludes, so we sent Al up to ask Bunk if he would take some. The first 10" test has some talking at the end which sounds like Bunk yelling, "Too loud." We asked her if she wanted to make four regular sides for release and if $25 would be okay. She had never recorded before, and at first she thought we meant to sing the same song four times to have four copies. She was anxious to have a copy herself and I promised I would send her some. It was almost 9 o'clock and she said she had to be away by ten, but thought we should be through by then. We tried the blues again and she said the song was called *Goodmorning Blues*, but as it was very different from the standard version I thought I had better give it a different title (*Blue As I Can Be*). She didn't seem to know any other blues, only bits she'd heard on the juke boxes. So I suggested *See See Rider*, which went okay on the first take.

We tried a spiritual. She suggested *Precious Lord, Lead Me On* and after she rehearsed a chorus or two we cut it in one take, giving the band a signal for their last chorus.

I asked if she'd like to do another hymn. She couldn't think of another one straight away and it was almost 10 o'clock. George suggested his favorite – *My Life Will Be Sweeter Someday*. She had the words written out in a book. The first take didn't swing so well and George thought it would be better faster. After a couple of false starts we cut a good one. We had planned a routine of one orchestra, two vocal, two orchestra, two vocal, but the faster tempo permitted several extra choruses. After we played it back I paid her $25. She then said she had to rush off at 10.20 for a rehearsal, so I guess she must have been working somewhere.

I was never happy about her voice. It had a very metallic quality and I was sorry George suggested her. When Gene Williams heard the records, he called her "The New Orleans Billie Holiday." She was very pleasant – in her mid-thirties, short (about Baby Dodds's height) and medium build. She was really a nightclub singer rather than a proper blues singer.

About a year later I was sitting in George's yard talking with Jeanette and she suddenly mentioned "the singer on those records you made," and said, "George should have gone next door and gotten Cindy. She had a low mellow voice like Ma Rainey and could really moan the blues." This neighbor was not a professional singer, just an ordinary housewife, but Jeanette thought she could have sung a real low-down blues. I remember, later, seeing an advertisement for a club where Myrtle Jones was singing (this must have been after August 1945) and she was calling herself "The Atomic Bomb Singer." She must have thought that name would be good publicity.

Bunk seemed particularly pleased with the hymn, saying, "There's a record that Bill Colburn will put under his arm and carry all over San Francisco to play for everybody. They'll sell plenty in San Francisco." Bill used to carry Jelly's *Finger Breaker* [*Finger Buster*] record around with him to persuade people to buy it.

After things quieted down, I changed microphones and asked for *St Louis Blues*. The band were all ready and one take really did it. Then I asked for *Tiger Rag*, as they were going too hot for another slow blues at that time. Alfred Lion almost had a fit when he heard me ask for *Tiger Rag*. He carried on about it being a corny number, so I asked him if he'd ever heard Bunk play *Tiger Rag*. He'd only heard the New York bands race through it and was sure that Bunk would be no good on this number. Naturally, they were terrific. After it was all over, Baby Dodds came down beside Slow Drag and hung over the rails for a minute and groaned. Not that he was so exhausted physically, but he probably had never played that terrific in his life. Bunk just sat there as usual during the playback, without any apparent emotion. The clarinet breaks on what I thought was a solo sounded a little too soft, so I suggested George moved out a little. We then got what we all thought was an even better take. I thought that they would be worn out by then, so I asked if they'd like to finish with a slow blues and asked if they knew *2.19 Blues*. I recited the first verse but no one acted like they knew it until I mentioned Jelly. Bunk said, "*Mamie's Blues*," and I said, "That's it." I told the others that it was only an ordinary blues and Bunk knew the tune and it would be okay to go. We did two takes of the *2.19*, although it was quite a different motif than the one Jelly had used. I put it out as *New Iberia Blues*. Afterwards George said Bunk sounded just like Buddy Petit on this. A little later he thought it sounded more like King Oliver.

We finished up at about 11.45 and went home with George and Bunk, and Jeanette warmed up some red beans and rice. Al was exhausted, but William and I were full of pep. Al admitted it was the best music he'd heard in his life, but still wouldn't say that Bunk was the greatest.

Jim Little took his tuba and bass home and said he wouldn't be available again until Friday evening. I said I'd let him know in case we needed him. So our bass problem solved itself. Drag's old bass and Abby's drums were left at the San Jacinto.

On the Tuesday morning, Bunk came by shortly after 9 o'clock. After playing with Shirley [George's daughter], he left between 10 and 11 am, saying he needed to buy a hat. I had paid him $30 on Monday night. He said he knew a store down on Frenchmen Street, near the river or the Old Mint or someplace, and started in that direction. But after a few steps he turned around and went off in the opposite direction. He might have doubted the Frenchmen Street store was still there or thought of some other place, or else he had another idea. When George went to see him later that afternoon, he hadn't returned. I stopped by Abby's house on the way to the session, but Bunk still hadn't returned and his horn was still there. I expected he would be late, so we took our time setting up. George was about the last one there and said Bunk still hadn't arrived home.

At about 7.45 I decided to go out and look for him. I went down Dumaine to Dauphine, then to George's and on to Abby's, but Bunk still hadn't been home. Then I saw him staggering out of a bar around the corner on St. Philip. I said to him, "Let's get your horn. Everyone's waiting for you." He could hardly walk home, but he got his horn in a hurry. He hadn't got a hat and tried to tell me about all his old friends he'd seen that day. He mentioned Tom Albert, who ran a saloon in the back-of-town direction. He hadn't seen him since 1913. Abby Williams happened to drive up with some kid and told Bunk to get in the car. We soon got there and I gave Abby fifty cents. We rushed in and I tried to get things started. Bunk took his time at getting seated and some of them seemed pretty mad at Bunk. Al was really disgusted. Bunk got quite talkative and kept standing up and turning around to talk to Baby. Baby tried to ignore him but this made Bunk talk all the more.

BUNK JOHNSON'S BAND
San Jacinto Hall, 1422 Dumaine Street, New Orleans.
Tuesday, August 1, 1944   (8.15 pm–12.00 am).

Bunk Johnson (tpt); Jim Robinson (tbn); George Lewis (clt); Lawrence Marrero (bjo); Alcide "Slow Drag" Pavageau (sbs); Baby Dodds (dms)

385	I Love my Baby, my Baby Loves Me	Unissued
386	Honey Gal	AM Book CD
387	Ballin' the Jack	Unissued
388	Ballin' the Jack	Unissued
389	Ballin' the Jack	AM LP 643, Wolf: WJS 1001, WJS 1001 CD
390	Ballin' the Jack	Unissued
391	Bugle Boy March	Unissued
392	Bugle Boy March	Unissued
393	Bugle Boy March	Unissued
394	How Long Blues	AMCD-1
394½	How Long Blues	AMCD-8
395	Muskrat Ramble	Unissued
	("probably terrible – don't issue")	
396	Careless Love	Unissued
397	Careless Love	Dan: VC-4017, VC-7024
398	Careless Love	AMCD-8
399	Blues (8' 40". Recorded at 33⅓ rpm)	Dan: VC-4016, VC-7018,
	(issued as *Midnight Blues II*)	AMCD-8
	("very good throughout")	

Note: Master 385 has been listed as *My Baby Loves Me* in previous discographies.
Only the last 1' 44" of *Ballin' the Jack* (389) was issued on AM LP 643 and subsequently on Wolf WJS 1001 and Wolf 1001 CD.
Bill also notes that *Bugle Boy March* was based on *The American Soldier*.

Bunk and George outside George's house in 1942

Bill Russell: I wanted to get things started, so I went up and asked for *Everybody Loves my Baby*. Bunk (as near as I can remember) slurred, "I don't care about your baby, but I love my baby and my baby loves me," and he seemed to find that quite funny. I asked if they all knew the tune and they said they did. Bunk played a sort of intro or something, as if to remind them, and they all nodded. Even so, I didn't catch on that he had sprung a different tune on us. I wasn't too discouraged so long as he could still blow. I hoped he could work out of it and get control as the night wore on. But everybody, every single person in the room except me (and Bunk), was so disgusted and thought that no records could be made and it looked pretty hopeless to go on. However; I told someone that as long as I was paying for it, they should stay there and have a good practice anyway. It wouldn't do Bunk's lip any harm. I kept thinking of some of the San Francisco records he'd cut when he was a little drunk and hoped that we could get some great blues that night.

Bunk wanted to try *Honey Gal*, which went a little better. For one thing I was glad to get all these punk tunes out of his system on a night like this.

Then I asked for *Ballin' the Jack*. It wasn't too hot, but not too bad. However, it seemed that Jim (and maybe others) hardly knew the verse part. After the first take ran over five minutes, Baby Dodds took charge. After agreeing to leave the verse out, Baby suggested a traditional trombone part that he knew, with slides and long notes during the first part of the chorus. He sung them to Bunk and Jim. Bunk, who had been trying to teach Jim and the others the verse, immediately took up the notes that Baby had hummed and began pounding them right into Jim's ear with his trumpet. Jim looked annoyed but didn't say anything. The next take was better, and we tried it a total of four times. Sometimes Bunk would get quite loud and wild and would stand up and blow a series of high notes that almost knocked the needle off the volume meter. Frequently in this piece, as well as others that evening, he'd stand up, turn around and blow loudly out of the window behind Baby Dodds. As Rudi [Blesh] had once pointed out, it seems his imagination became more free and fantastic when he'd been drinking.

Between each number Bunk would have a lot of stories to tell and a lot of boasting. Baby would jive him right back and yell a lot of "Shut ups" at him, and a couple of times chase him around the room. Bunk continued to drink bottles of beer from the San Jacinto bar until finally I had William fix it with the kid (who worked the bar and brought the beer over to Bunk) to tell him he didn't have any more. Bunk was very calm and resigned about it: "No more?" he said, in a pitiful voice. Later, when William gave the kid a dollar for not selling any beer, the kid wondered what it was for. Before the last number or so, William figured that the other guys would be getting sore because they hadn't been allowed to have any beer either. We also thought it wouldn't make any difference by that time if Bunk did have some more. We told the kid to let them have it and he said, "What can I tell them why I have some now?" William said, "Just tell them you just got some more in." George came back at least once and said: "You won't get any recordings tonight," and seemed to hint that it would be better to pay everyone off and send them home.

George then suggested *Bugle Boy March* and at first took the opening "bugle call" on his clarinet, but after that Bunk took it. It lacked pep and the three takes served mainly as a rehearsal.

Generally they didn't play too many blues and I'd have to ask for a blues if I wanted to record one. Sam Charters used to think the only blues number I ever knew was *Careless Love*, as I kept recording it. Bunk had made a very good version with the Lu Watters band (as well as Kid Howard's record with George the year before), so I kept trying *Careless Love* on a few nights. In California, Bunk had played a chorus on *Careless Love* that I'd never heard him play before or since. I didn't like to ask him to play the same chorus and try to tell him what to play, but I was always hoping he might get into that chorus again.

Before that I'd asked him to try *How Long Blues*. This was more of a Chicago blues than a New Orleans blues. Leroy Carr had recorded it around 1930. No one knew it except Baby Dodds. So Bunk asked Baby to sing the melody. Bunk said in a sarcastic tone, "It sounds like a Cajun blues." That was the worst word he could think to call anything. New Iberia was Cajun country and he disliked the Cajuns intensely. He believed that they were far more prejudiced than the whites. They had treated him very badly and even tried to stop him from walking on the streets. When we took the early train into New Orleans in that year, I couldn't ride with Bunk; he had to ride in the front where all the smoke was (I had to go at the back in the white compartment). On the way over to the station, we passed a church at about 6 o'clock in the morning, and all the Cajuns were going to early mass. Bunk remarked, "They think they are Christians, but they're not, they're real evil people . . . you should see how they treat their maids the rest of the day."[14] They kept him in his place and there had been a riot in which several people had been killed in 1944. I didn't put *How Long Blues* out on American Music. When I heard it again in the early 1970s I didn't think it was too bad; in fact, it sounded better than I expected. I was going to put it out in Japan and I gave them a tape, but they never issued it in the end.

By this time Al had a tense headache and was pacing the floor. He'd been yelling for *Muskrat Ramble*, so I finally asked for it. It didn't go too good and we only tried it once. After it was over, he came back to the table and said he was really knocked out. He had a towel around his neck and an ice pack on his head. William and I razzed him and joked that it was Bunk who needed the ice pack, but perhaps he looked in a worse condition than Bunk.

Things didn't look very good that night. Finally, at about 11.45, Bunk had sobered up a little and, although the evening had been an almost total failure, I didn't want to give up. I told them I'd like to try an experiment, hinting that the night was a loss anyway. I told them about the speed attachment on the recording machine that enabled us to record at a very slow speed, and they could play for seven or eight minutes. I told them that I'd never tried it before but would like to see if it would work. Then I talked to George and Baby and especially Jim, telling them that they could just play anything, and anyway, that if Bunk got tired they could be featured more and take a couple of solos. I said that part loud enough so Bunk heard it. At about 11.50 we turned on the machine and they played a long, slow blues. When we played it back they were all fascinated to see the record revolve so slowly. When Al heard the playback he quickly got over his headache and became quite excited, saying, "That's worth $100." I said, "I hope so, 'cause it cost me a lot more than that." I paid everybody off and told them that I hoped that we would get something good the next night. After playing so well on Saturday night, Bunk hadn't done himself justice. I went home and counted all my money to see how many sessions I could afford to make up for the night's loss. William thought it might pay to hire a guy to follow Bunk around all day and guard him!

The next day we got up about 10 o'clock and learned that George had already been over to talk to Bunk. He must have lectured him and told him about letting me down after all I had done for him. I told George I knew Bunk too well not to expect one, or even two, bad nights. Very soon we played back all of the Tuesday night records, and decided to try and get Bunk to listen to *I Love my Baby* and one or two of the other sides, but he never came by till later.

About 1 o'clock I decided I'd better go over and guard Bunk before he could get away again. Bunk was cheerful and seemed to want to put the previous night's problems behind him. He had his trumpet and music out and had been demonstrating some of the Joplin rags for a soldier jazz fan who had come to see him. Then he got out his Melrose book (*40 Famous Blues*) and stood it up on his bed and proceeded to practice *Sidewalk Blues* and *Walking the Dog*. I believe he used a mute when practicing.

I stayed with him throughout the afternoon, not wanting to let him out of my sight. I'd taken some writing paper and envelopes along, so I used this as an excuse that I needed to write some letters. He then slept for several hours. After Bunk had been asleep for an hour or so, I was getting hungry (having only eaten some peaches that day) and decided to take a chance and sneak out to get something to eat. (I'd been prepared to go without any food in order to get him to the San Jacinto sober that night.) When I got back Bunk was still asleep. At about 5 pm Bunk woke. He didn't get up immediately and I didn't want to rush him. At about 5.30 I suggested we get something to eat at George's. He didn't seem very enthusiastic and dressed very slowly, still in sort of a daze. We got to George's about 6 and ate, and I left for the San Jacinto about 6.30. I got things set up and Bunk soon came in with George. Bunk was the first one in his seat that night and sat there waiting for the others.

BUNK JOHNSON'S BAND
San Jacinto Hall, 1422 Dumaine Street, New Orleans.
Wednesday, August 2, 1944 (7.00 pm–12.12 am)

Bunk Johnson (tpt); George Lewis (clt); Jim Robinson (tbn); Lawrence Marrero (bjo); Alcide "Slow Drag" Pavageau (sbs); Baby Dodds (dms)

401	When the Saints Go Marching In	AM LP.638, Stv: SLP 203, AMCD-8
	"should be issued as a second master some day"	
402	When the Saints Go Marching In	AM V252, Stv: SLP 152, Dan: VC-4006, VC-7006, AMCD-3
	"Very Good. Alright to be issued"	
403	Ballin' the Jack	Dan: VC-4016, VC-7018
404	Ballin' the Jack	Stv: SLP 205, Dan: VC-4007, VC-7009, AMCD-3
405	High Society	Dan: VC-4017 (cut), VB-1004 (cut), VC-7024 (cut) AMCD-3 (cut)
	"4¹/₂ mins, last minute should be issued. 2' 40" starting with clarinet solo, prob. best ever made"	
406	Darktown Strutters' Ball	Dan: VC-4017, VC-7024, AMCD-3
407	Darktown Strutters' Ball	AM V256, Stv: SLP 152, Dan: VC-4006, VC-7006, AMCD-8
408	Lord Lord You're Certainly Good to Me	Dan: VC-4016, VC-7018, AMCD-8
409	Lord Lord You're Certainly Good to Me	AM LP647, Stv: SLP 128, Dan: VC-4008, VC-7016, AMCD-3
410	Careless Love	Dan: VC-4016, VC-7018, AMCD-3
411	Careless Love	AM V258, AM LP 647, Stv: SLP 128, Dan: VC-4008, VC-7016, Tulane Alumni Fund: LH 15555/6, AMCD-1
412	Panama	Dan: VC-4016, VC-7018
413	Panama	AMCD-8
414	Panama	AM V255, Stv:SLP 128, Dan: VC-4008, VB-1004, VC-7016, Penny / Variety: REL ST 19146, AMCD-3
415	See See Rider	AM V251, AM LP.638, Stv: SLP 152, Dan: VC-4006 VC-7006, AMCD-1

416   Blues (9' 04". Recorded at 33¹/₃ rpm)   AM LP 638, Stv: SLP205, Dan; VC-4007, VC-7009,
                                                 AMCD-1

Note: Master 405 was intended for issue on Baby Dodds 4, and 413 was due for issue on Dan records; neither record ever appeared.
Master 416 is issued as *Midnight Blues* on AMCD-1.

Bill Russell: I wanted to record some spirituals, so we got started with *When the Saints Go Marching In*. A few minutes after 7 o'clock it went off without any problems and we made a second take, finishing a little before 7.30 pm. *When the Saints Go Marching In* had hardly been used then. The only record I'd heard of this was Louis Armstrong's (which had come out in 1938), but it had never caught on with the jazz bands.[15] When the American Music record came out they got a lot of requests for it when the band appeared in New York. When the customers applauded, they'd play the last chorus over again. If the applause continued, they would repeat the whole number over again sometimes as many as four times. Bunk didn't enjoy doing it over and over again, but as long as the public liked it he would play it. The other New York bands picked up on it and very soon bands all over the country started playing it.

I felt confident that we were in for a good evening, so we made a retake of *Ballin' the Jack* that had given us so much trouble the night before. It still didn't come out so good: for one thing, Jim had evidently forgotten the trombone part that Baby had taught him.

John Hammond and Scoops Kennedy came around and Al spent half the evening discussing his plan to record a date with some of the "modern" New Orleans men. He also wanted to record Irving Fazola with a band. Both would be Union dates in a radio studio, and he never did understand my lack of enthusiasm for his plans, even though he talked about using Baby Dodds in the "modern" band. I talked to John Hammond for a few minutes. He thought that these would be the best records ever made in New Orleans and I couldn't resist reminding him of the time he said Bunk would never play again.

We next tried *High Society* and Bunk tried to play the first part an eighth higher than anyone else and fluffed some of the notes. However, the last part (beginning with the clarinet solo) really went and was the most exciting version of *High Society* that I'd ever heard, with the last chorus even cutting the King Oliver version. The band really got going at the end and Bunk took a terrific break (based on the figures he's used in *Shine*, but terrific this time) that made Baby rush down as soon as it was over and pat Bunk on the back, saying, "Man . . . in there you must have run across Manuel." The next day, Bunk went to see Manuel Perez.[16]

Next I asked for *Darktown Strutters' Ball*. After a short try at the intro they were ready. It was another knockout, although possibly a little rough in spots, but Jim was really terrific and took some wonderful slides. We decided to try it again, just in case, and the second take we thought to be even better.

I think it was George who picked out *Lord Lord . . .*, and we ran this through twice. The first take was pretty good and Al seemed more impressed with this hymn than anything we'd tried all week. The way Bunk acted, he may not have known this tune. But if he hadn't played it before, he sure learned fast.

We then tried *Careless Love* again. Still some minor flaws and Bunk still didn't play his "San Francisco" solo, but it did have everyone taking solo choruses for a change. The second take was pretty good and I had thought of finishing with that number, but the band was going so good I decided we'd take a chance at *Panama*. Some people think I was crazy for trying to record *Panama* three or four times during the week. I still think of that wonderful version of

28

Panama we recorded for Jazz Man in 1942, when Bunk and Jim played so well together in that last chorus – those long blue notes, off-scale, bent notes as Johnny Wiggs called them. I had hopes that I would get a good *Panama* that I'd be 100% satisfied with. On the first take Bunk only got going with his long notes on the last chorus, so I arranged to give him a signal for the last two choruses. The next take was going great when, after a minute, Lawrence broke a string. He tried to repair it quickly and Baby tried to fill in more, but the take was ruined, even though Lawrence got back in for the last minute. We tried it once more and got a pretty good take.

Then I asked for a blues. No one but Bunk (and probably Baby) knew things like *Wolverine* or *Sidewalk Blues*. Anyway, I wanted a real blues. Baby had said any sort of "blues" would be okay, like *Look What a Hole I'm In*. I talked to Baby about how come they didn't seem to know, or want to play, a blues. Baby said, "You see, it's this way, our people have been raised with the blues and heard them all their lives . . .," and went on to imply that they didn't seem so special to them as to someone like me. He rather hinted that they were tired of the blues, or even wanted to get away from the blues. We finally settled for *See See Rider* and I told them that it made no difference that we had already recorded it on Monday.

The version of the long 33 1/3 *Blues* that we made that night was even better than the one the previous evening. When we finished, Bunk practically made the same remark as he had made on Monday evening: "There's a record Bill Colburn will put under his arm and carry all over San Francisco." We finished about 12.12 am and were all packed up by 12.30. Bunk wanted to go home with us and as soon as we got outside the San Jacinto I said, "Well, Bunk, tonight you really showed everybody how you can play." Bunk didn't say a word, but of course he knew what I meant. We all went down by the Gypsy Tea Room No.2. Bunk, Jim and Al had some drinks, and George, William and I had soft drinks. George called his daughter over from the gambling table, where she apparently worked, and introduced us.[17] Bunk was very talkative and left his trumpet on the floor against the wall. I kept a close watch on it. About 1 o'clock we all went to George's for something to eat and talked awhile.

Before I went down in 1944, I stopped off in Chicago to see Hugh Davis. He knew I had a machine that could record at 33 1/3 rpm and he warned me not to try any recording at the slow speed as it wouldn't be good enough fidelity. I would have trouble catching the higher notes. When I got back he was mad at me because I didn't get more low notes at the faster speed. He complained, "There's nothing below middle C." There may be a little "wow" here and there at the slower speed, but I'm glad I tried it and didn't take Hugh's advice. They were often reluctant to play a really "down-home" blues number. I usually asked for one at the end of a session and recorded it at 33 1/3 to get the extended playing time. At that time, no one foresaw the coming of the LP and I never thought they could ever be issued.

On Thursday morning (August 3) a singer came and asked for George first to see about recording. He said his name was George Guesnon and he said he'd made a few records for Decca. He told Al that he had been in Chicago just a few weeks before and hadn't been allowed to sit in for a certain guitarist on account of the Union. I tried to explain that the records were simply a hobby with me and that it was no big-time business; also we were concentrating on Bunk and the band all that week.

I soon ran around the corner to Abby's, but Bunk had gone off to buy a hat by that time. Throughout the afternoon I kept going by to check up and about mid-afternoon he came by George's with his new hat and also showed me where Dr Bechet had filed down his tooth that was broken. That day he also went to see Manuel Perez. He took a delight in telling (and showing) us just how Manuel walked, stiff and hunched over. Apparently Manuel was surprised that Bunk was still playing. Bunk must have told him what he had been doing and (according to Bunk) Manuel was impressed that Bunk could still do hard physical jobs, like field and longshore work. A couple of times that week Bunk would make us watch him demonstrate just how old people walk and then how he ambled along in a loose-jointed, relaxed manner. The previous year George had taken me over to see Manuel and we were able to talk awhile, but in 1945 Albert Glenny took Gene Williams and the photographer Skippy Adelman over to see him, but Manuel wouldn't let them in, saying he was "too sick to talk." Skippy was able to sneak a picture of Manuel which appeared in *Jazzways*.

Bunk said he was going home to rest (sleep), so I didn't worry about him. But beginning around 5.30 I went by several times to try and get him to come over and eat some chicken that Jeanette had fried in batter. He took his time getting dressed, as usual, and finally got there just after 6 o'clock.

George was afraid we were running out of tunes when he realized we intended to keep going for another night or two. But I told him we had still plenty of numbers and I worked a little that afternoon on a new list – trying also to remember the numbers we intended to try again. On Wednesday afternoon Bunk had shown me several lists of numbers (with all the keys listed) that he kept in his trumpet case. They were probably lists that he used in San Francisco to play at the CIO Hall. While he was asleep I copied most of them out and added some of these numbers to my own list. On Wednesday night Bunk had suggested that it might be better to play the tune just once, or have a list, just like "at a dance," and go right through them without repeats all the time. I don't know if he thought that the repetition of a number over and over, like *Panama*, tired them out or made them stale, or if he objected to reworking a number on successive nights, as we did with *Ballin' the Jack* and *Careless Love* on Tuesday and Wednesday. Anyway, I told him we'd try his idea.

Numbers copied from Bunk's list in 1944

Casey Jones	*Panama*
Sweethearts on Parade	*Weary Blues*
It's a Long Way to Tipperary	*St. Louis Blues*
Where the River Shannon Flows	*Maple Leaf Rag*
Over There	*Moose March*
Alice Blue Gown	*Pretty Baby*
Shine	*Baby Won't You Please Come Home*
You Are my Sunshine	*When the Saints Go Marching In*
Darktown Strutters' Ball	*My Buddy*
High Society	*Muskrat Ramble*
Fidgety Feet	*My Maryland*
Ole Miss Rag	*Kid Ory's Creole Trombone*
Stardust	*Milneburg Joys*
African Pas	*Sister Kate*

When Bill copied this listing he either had difficulty in reading Bunk's handwriting or, more likely, was unfamiliar with *Where the River Shannon Flows,* as this tune is listed as *The River Sharing Flowers*

BUNK JOHNSON'S BAND

San Jacinto Hall, 1422 Dumaine Street, New Orleans.
Thursday, August 3, 1944 (7 pm–approx. 11.30 pm)

Bunk Johnson (tpt); George Lewis (clt); Jim Robinson (tbn); Lawrence Marrero (bjo); Alcide "Slow Drag" Pavageau (sbs); Baby Dodds (dms)

501	Weary Blues	AMCD-1
502	Weary Blues	Dan: VC-4016, VC-7018, AMCD-2
503	Weary Blues	Dan: VC-4017, VC-7024, AMCD-8
504	Clarinet Marmalade	AMCD-8
505	Clarinet Marmalade	Stv: SLP 127, Dan: VC-4008, VC-7016, Seven Seas: MH3026, AMCD-2
506	Yes, Yes in your Eyes	AM V253, Stv: SLP 205, Dan: VC-4007, VC-7009, AMCD-3
507	Royal Garden Blues	AMCD-1
508	Royal Garden Blues	Dan: VC-4016, VC-7018
509	Streets of the City	AM LP 647, Dan: VC-4007, VB-1004, VC-7009, AMCD-8
510	Streets of the City	AM V256, Stv: SLP 203, SLP 128, Dan: VC-4008, VC-7016, AMCD-3
511	Maryland, my Maryland	AM Baby Dodds 3, Dan: VC-4013, VC-7015, AMCD-17
512	Sister Kate	Unissued
513	Sister Kate	AM V257, Stv: SLP 128, Dan: VC-4008, VC-7016, Variety: REL ST19146, Penny: REL ST19146, AMCD-8
514	Weary Blues	AM V258, Stv: SLP 152, Dan: VC-4006, VB-1004, VC-7006 AMCD-3
515	After You've Gone	AM LP 647, Wolf: WJS 1001, WJS 1001CD, AMCD-15
516	Alabama Bound	AMCD-12
517	Alabama Bound	Stv: SLP 205, Dan: VC-4007, VC-7009, Su: 0 15 23972B, AMCD-3

Note: Masters 501 and 507 were leased to Dan records but never issued.
Master 510 is incorrectly given as master 509 on Storyville SLP 128.
Master 514 was issued as *Shake It & Break It* on AMCD-3.
Masters 516 and 517 are listed in Bill Russell's log as *Alabama Bound*, although he agreed that the tune actually played is *I'm Alabama Bound*. To add further confusion, master 517 was issued on Storyville as *Alabamy Bound*.

Bill Russell: I made the unlucky choice of picking as the opening number *Baby Won't You Please Come Home*. They tried over a little of it, a chorus or two, and it sounded fine. Then Bunk stopped to straighten them out on the introduction. He played over his part and then showed George and Jim their parts. But Jim couldn't get his, which went something like this:

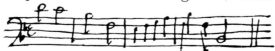

They tried it over and over. Jim almost got it. Then it started getting worse, and pretty soon he lost interest in it and didn't want to try it anymore. George sat there quietly for seven or eight minutes, then finally got up and went back to talk with Baby. I was afraid the whole evening would be wasted after what seemed like two hours (it was probably no more than ten minutes), so I went up and told Bunk and Jim that I thought they should try something else that they'd all know. I knew *Weary Blues* had a fool-proof introduction, which they all knew, so I suggested that. The first take was a little spotty; Jim was still weak, but George took most of the first breaks. I held back my signal for the final two choruses and let it run long at 4¹/₂ minutes (like *Panama* and *Careless Love*). The second and third takes turned out better, but I still wasn't real sure we had what I wanted. I decided we'd give it a rest and perhaps go back to it later.

Herb Morand came by and sat at the back. Al asked what he thought of Bunk, but Herb ignored the question and started asking Al how he liked his band.

We next tried *Clarinet Marmalade*. It started okay, but, again, Bunk wanted to stop to work out an introduction and played the harmony parts of all three instruments. George got his but Jim had trouble again. I sat down this time and resigned myself to fate. As Bunk played it over and over, mostly staccato notes in the third and fourth bars, it sounded corny and not as good as first played. However, when they put it together (and Baby filled up the staccato parts with some cymbals) it sounded wonderful. The first take went right off, but we moved George out in front and then got an even better take. George seemed very pleased with it and Al thought it was a knockout.

They then did *Your Lips Tell Me No, No, but it's Yes, Yes, in your Eyes*, which we'd done at the Saturday rehearsal. This didn't sound so hot after *Clarinet Marmalade*, so we didn't try it again. When I played it back later it sounded better. The full title was too long for the label so I put it out under the shorter title of *Yes, Yes in your Eyes*.

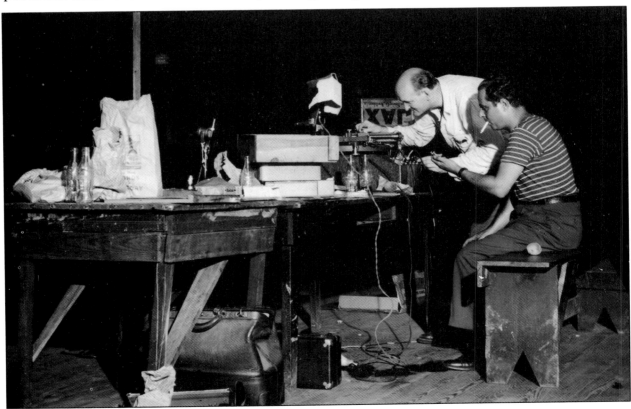

Bill at the recording machine and Alfred Lion timing a number – San Jacinto, 1944

Jim then had trouble again with the trombone break on *Royal Garden Blues*. No matter how hard he tried, he couldn't get it. Sometimes he would play it backwards, sometimes upside down. Later when they went to New York they had a rehearsal before they opened at the Stuyvesant. They tried this number again and still Jim had trouble with the break. Bunk tried to show him how it went on his trumpet but Jim still got the positions backwards. In the end Bunk got hold of his trombone and blew the break perfectly, showing him all the slide positions. Needless to say, this impromptu lesson didn't go down too well with Jim.

Next someone in the band must have suggested the hymn *We Shall Walk Through the Streets of the City*. Two takes were made, both good, although I thought at the time the tune might be a little monotonous to some people.

Once during the evening I had the recorder cutting and gave Bunk the signal to start, when he looked over and said, "Is that thing going up and down?" The piece of 16"-diameter light grey felt I had on the turntable had got turned up at one edge and it looked as if the turntable was wobbly. I told him it was okay. He never knew of the real problems I was having. On the Tuesday to Friday sessions I was having a problem with the needles. Often, when I wiped the disc cutter with cotton, it seemed to catch on a rough cut and occasionally there was trouble with some of the needles deflecting the thread the wrong way. On Tuesday I kept forgetting to pick up the needle before lifting the gear arm. So, starting Thursday, I had William remind me every time.

They all seemed to remember *Maryland* after Bunk had whistled part of it for them. Baby got very excited after we cut it and carried on about how strong Bunk's lip was, telling us that on parades they used several trumpets who would always share the *Maryland* bugle parts.

After retakes of *Sister Kate* and *Weary Blues*, Bunk suggested *After You've Gone*. It didn't seem very good and I didn't ask for a repeat.

Then the drummer from Don Raymond's orchestra came in and picked up the large cymbal from the drum set Baby had been using all week. I thought the cymbal belonged to Abby, but it seemed this guy really owned it. George came over to me very seriously and told me of the trouble we were in. Fortunately Abby was there and John Hammond was also there with his car. Abby said he knew where he could get another "big one." I used my nerve and asked John if he wouldn't mind going over with Abby to collect it. He very kindly went while Baby used a little 10" cymbal as they ran though one piece as a rehearsal. Soon John and Abby came back with a 14" or 16" cymbal.

I began asking for a blues, but without much luck. For a long time Bunk tried to think of *Tin Roof Blues*. He and Baby (and probably George) could remember the main part, but no one could remember the other section, and Bunk wouldn't try it without it. While Bunk was trying to figure out how it went I kept on suggesting other tunes, in the hope that they might all agree on one. Bunk then bawled at me, "Let us think about one tune for a while and we'll remember how it goes, but before we can think of it you keep naming more and more." So I held my tongue until they decided to abandon the number and then looked to me for a suggestion.

When they wouldn't suggest anything, I brought up the subject of *Alabama Bound*. First someone began to hum the regular Fletcher Henderson *Alabama Bound*, while I tried to explain that it was something called *Railroad Blues*. Finally I mentioned the words Jelly claimed to have written, "Don't you leave me here, but if you must go sweet mama . . ." It really registered with them and Bunk explained that there were three songs with similar titles to *Alabama Bound* – these two and also a possible third song of which I had vaguely heard before. They sang a snatch of it which went something like: "When you take that midnight choo choo to Alabama." Anyway, Bunk and some of the others, like Baby and possibly Jim, also remembered it and told how they used to play that piece at the Masonic Hall to entice the crowd to sing the words. When they played it they seemed not to vary the tune much at all and Al thought it was terribly monotonous and suggested we should cut it short. But I thought I should give them the benefit of the doubt and I let it run for four minutes. I went up to the stand and found some excuse to ask Bunk if they ever played more variations on that tune. Bunk said, "No, the tune never changes, only the words for every verse." I told them that the other take ran too long and we'd like to run it once more.

Al complained a lot, not only about *Alabama Bound*, but also about some of the numbers and the various timings during the latter part of the week. He also complained that "Bunk won't give the other guys a chance at all." I tried to find out what he meant and said I left it to them, they could do anything they want to. Then Al said, "Bunk plays all the time and always plays the lead. Why doesn't he let Jim or George have a chance sometimes?" I asked him if he thought he could change the whole system of New Orleans music, also if he thought that, after these guys had played a certain way all their lives, he could come down and teach them how to play in a week? One evening (probably the Friday) he complained that they (especially Jim) were making George do all the work. It happened at a time when Bunk quit for a rest, Jim did too, leaving George to carry the melody. On Friday evening Bunk made Jim and George quit so that all three could take solos in *Careless Love* and Al then complained about that. I should have told him off on several occasions, but decided to use diplomacy instead.

Bunk's Band at the San Jacinto Hall – Thursday, August 3, 1944: Jim Robinson, Bunk Johnson, George Lewis, Baby Dodds, Slow Drag Pavageau and Lawrence Marrero

Although it wasn't midnight, we decided to quit when we got through with *Alabama Bound*. That morning, William had brought some more film and flash bulbs, so we took two pictures with the guys with their shirts off, as it had been so hot. Then we took one more with them wearing their shirts. While we took the pictures, we had them play a little of *Alabama Bound* again.

Perhaps not trusting the seemingly erratic beer stocks of the San Jacinto bar from the previous night, Bunk had brought in some beer of his own this evening. He didn't drink too much and seemed in good humor, but I could see he was getting a little restless. We made some good sides and he generally played quite well, but not as well as he could play when he really wanted to.

We broke up about midnight and went home. I think the Gypsy Tea Room was closed that night. It seemed certain saloons would close on various days or at certain times because of the war-time shortage of beer.

Before I was able to leave the house on Friday morning (August 4) George Guesnon returned with a briefcase full of records and some acetates of his singing. I talked with him for a few minutes, but I thought I'd better go and check on Bunk, so I left him to Al and George. Al traded him a copy of *Jazzmen* for King Oliver's *High Society*, but he didn't convince Al that his acetates would sell "160,000 records."

I hurried over to Bunk's, and Mrs Williams [Abby's wife] said he'd gone up to (or near) Rampart Street to get his hair cut, which sounded bad to me. A few days before he'd spoken of some uncle (or relative) who ran a barber's shop uptown, and that possibly was it.

I went up to find Ann Cook, but no one was at home. I was told to see the lady in the restaurant on the uptown edge of the vacant lot, who turned out to be her niece. She said Ann had gone to pay some of her bills and I should have stopped by earlier, it being about noon at that time. She said Ann could still sing good, and I sat down at a table and wrote her a short note telling her to come around that evening and that I would pay her $35 for two songs. The niece had wanted to know how much money I was offering and for how many records.

I went back home, calling at Abby's on the way, but there was still no sign of Bunk. I went back to George's and sorted out the records we had made the previous night and got out some more blanks to take down to the San Jacinto. Finally, at a little after 4 pm, George (who was also worried) and I decided to start out and look for Bunk.

We went by Abby's once more, but no news. We then walked up St. Philip looking in all the saloons, and then took the Rampart street car to Canal. We kept our eyes open as we walked up South Rampart Street. George stopped and went into the Elite, but he wasn't there. I asked about a barber shop that was across Tulane, but George said it was just for whites. As we walked up on the lake side of South Rampart, George looked into a couple more saloons and a barber shop.

When we got about a third of a block from the Astoria Hotel, George said, "Do you see what I do up there?" It didn't take more than a few seconds before I saw Bunk out in front of the Astoria. He was leaning on a telegraph pole by the gutter and was swinging a fancy gold watch around in a circle (propeller style). It was attached to a heavy gold chain that was fastened to the buttonhole of his shirt. George stopped about fifteen feet before I got to Bunk (George never went around asking for trouble) and stood near the entrance to the hotel. I acted like I'd just happened to run across him, but there was no doubt he knew I was out looking for him and he didn't like it. He said he was waiting for some friend who was coming back in a minute. He looked towards the taxi that was waiting in front of him, saying that he was going over to the guy's house. I tried my best to persuade him to get into the taxi and go home to

George's for something to eat and told him that it would soon be time for the recording. He snapped back, "I'll be there," in a very annoyed tone, adding, "You came here with George and you can go home with George. I'm going with somebody else."

He told me all about his watch and seemed very proud of it, and had me look at it. He said he'd paid $30 for it and $6 for the chain at Finks. It was a yellow gold Waltham and probably a pretty good watch for the money if it was new, or in perfect shape. Bunk was probably not too drunk when he bought it and was not cheated on that account. He said they had a gold charm for $6 or $10 more and that he'd get it later. He then asked if I had any money. I told him that I'd waited for him to come and sign the check so I could cash it. He said he'd sent some money home that morning and added, accusingly, "And don't think I didn't."

I stood there and continued to talk and wait, even if I wasn't very welcome. Bunk continued to probe how I happened to come by there and then mentioned he'd seen Bob Lyons. He also talked about seeing the fellow who owned the Astoria [Beansy Fauria]. Then he noticed a young girl standing in front of the hotel and he really began to take on about her figure so much that I half expected him to go over and proposition her. When I'd almost given up he suddenly said, "Let's go over here and get the car." A street car had just gone by. I didn't want to take the chance that he might change his mind, so I suggested we take a taxi as there were several around in the block. We jumped into the taxi with George and told the driver to take us to 827 St. Philip. By that time Bunk was getting pretty vulgar in his talk, and amongst other remarks he began berating the taxi driver.

As we drove on he told the young taxi driver that he didn't know how to drive. I think the taxi driver knew pretty well Bunk was drunk, or he'd have stopped and pasted him.

We soon got home and Bunk wouldn't come in immediately. But as soon as he saw Shirley he was soon playing with her, chasing and being chased throughout the house. Meanwhile Jeanette heated up some food and started getting some coffee ready. Bunk had something to eat and at about 6 pm he sat down in the rocking chair and was soon asleep.

I didn't want to let him out of my sight, so I asked my brother if he would go uptown and see Ann Cook. He found her at home and she had got my note, but asked again how much cash she would get and for how many records. When William said $35 for two sides, she repeated the story that Victor had paid her $100 for just one side and how popular it was, and how they had to call out the police to keep back the crowds when the music stores put them on sale. William inquired if she still sang, so to prove it she sang part of a song she was due to sing at a funeral the next Sunday, or maybe the next day. She didn't sing too loud naturally, but William thought the quality of her voice was probably okay and would be alright when she got going. Ann didn't give any real indication if she would show up or not, but I had hopes. I think William suggested that she should phone me if she still wanted to sing. Al had been impressed when he heard my dub of her Victor record that I'd played him last Tuesday.

When it was time to leave for the San Jacinto Bunk was still asleep, so I told the others to go on and I'd bring Bunk as soon as I could. I mentioned Bunk's horn to George and wondered if we'd better get it and bring it back, so Bunk wouldn't need to stop by Abby's. George then offered to pick it up and take it on to the San Jacinto and I agreed. A few minutes after 7 o'clock I started waking Bunk up. He wasn't so hard to get up, but took his time, and it was about twenty minutes before he was ready to leave the house. He refused to take any coffee and wasn't very talkative. When we were all ready to leave I mentioned that George had taken his horn to the hall. Boy, was he mad! He snapped several times, "You shouldn't have done that . . . that's not a right thing to do . . . don't ever do that." We walked on but when we got to the corner he wouldn't to go any further and told me to go on. He said he had to go home to get some handkerchiefs and something else. I said I'd go back with him, but he wouldn't hear of it and insisted I go on. I saw he had no intention of moving until I went, so I had no choice. I took my time and continued to look back in the hope that he'd catch me up, but no luck. When I got to the hall I explained that Bunk would be along in a minute. When he didn't show up after ten minutes, I went over to George and explained the predicament and thought (after the business on South Rampart) that it wouldn't do for me to go back and get him again. I hated to ask George to run around and find Bunk, but it seemed the only thing to do. He didn't seem to like the job, but said he'd do anything for me and, if I wanted him to go, he'd do it. I told George to blame the trumpet business on me, if it helped. George took Lawrence and Slow Drag (and maybe someone else as well) and after about twenty minutes they all arrived back in a car with Bunk. They had found him in a bar on St. Philip Street, and after they had talked with him he eventually agreed to come without any fuss. I don't think he would have come unless they'd gone to find him.

BUNK JOHNSON'S BAND
San Jacinto Hall, 1422 Dumaine Street, New Orleans.
Friday, August 4, 1944 (8.00 pm–approx. 12.30 am)

Bunk Johnson (tpt); George Lewis (clt); Jim Robinson (tbn); Lawrence Marrero (bjo); Alcide "Slow Drag" Pavageau (sbs); Baby Dodds (dms)

601	Yes, Yes in your Eyes	Dan: VC-4017, VC-7024, AMCD-8
602	Ole Miss	Unissued
603	Ole Miss	Dan: VC-4017, VC-7024, AMCD-12
604	Ole Miss	Unissued
604½	You Are my Sunshine	Dan: VC-4017, VC-7024, AMCD-12
	When You Wore a Tulip	Unissued
605	When You Wore a Tulip	AM V255, Stv: SLP 152, Dan: VC-4006, VC-7006, AMCD-3
605½	Sugar Foot Stomp (1½" test)	Dan: VC-4017, VC-7024
606	Sugar Foot Stomp	AM LP 643, Stv: SLP 128, Dan: VC-4008, VC-7016, AMCD-1
607	Sugar Foot Stomp	
	(issued as *Dippermouth Blues*)	AMCD-8
608	Tishomingo Blues	Unissued
609	Tishomingo Blues	AMCD-1
610	Darktown Strutters' Ball	AMCD-12
611	Ballin' the Jack	AMCD-12
612	Careless Love	Unissued
613	Panama	Unissued
614	Blues in C (*Franklin St. Blues*)	AMCD-12
615	Blues (9' 05". Recorded at 33⅓ rpm)	Dan: VC-4017, VC-7024, AMCD-12

Note: Masters 607, 611, 612 and 614 were leased to Dan Records but never released.
The first take of *When You Wore a Tulip* was overlooked when the master numbers were assigned. When Barry Martyn and I checked through all the AM masters in October 1992, this master could not be found.
Masters 606 and 607 were both issued as *Dippermouth Blues* on AMCD-1 and AMCD-8.

Bill Russell: Before I could suggest any tune, Bunk had them off on *It's Yes, Yes in Your Eyes,* again. The first take was fairly good, so I asked for *Ole Miss Rag,* which George and Bunk had mentioned after the session on Wednesday while we were eating at George's. The first take was pretty good, but Bunk missed a little, so I asked for another cut, which was better. There was a little trouble with the thread so I claimed the cut wasn't so good and asked them to do it once more.

Next Bunk wanted to do *You Are my Sunshine,* which he announced as a Cajun number. It was on the radio all the time then and it was supposed to have been written by Governor Davis, who was a big-shot politician down here. I wouldn't have wanted to pay him any royalties and I thought of putting it out as *O Sole Mio.*

Bunk's next choice was *When You Wore a Tulip and I Wore a Big Red Rose.* Somehow he wanted to try it again and we made a better second take.

On Thursday night I'd done my best to get them to play *Sugar Foot Stomp.* At the time Bunk ignored the request, or acted like he didn't know it. George had been anxious to play it, so I again suggested it to Bunk. He seemed willing to try it, but wanted to play it in the key as written in the Melrose book – *40 Famous Blues.* George wanted to play it in the usual key the New Orleans bands normally used. They argued about it a while, with George rightly saying that the other key would make it harder for him. Finally Bunk relented and they played it in George's key, but Bunk didn't play the famous King Oliver chorus.

38

Orin Blackstone arrived, but Ann Cook never showed up. At about 9.30 there was a loud pounding at the window and the owner of the place came in, Beansy Fauria.[18] He was one of the free mulattoes, and so light that I thought he was white until Bunk told me. Orin said he was one of the richest guys in town and one of the biggest gamblers. He owned a lot of property, especially saloons and dance halls where gambling took place, and he also owned most of the slot machines in various bars. He was the fellow Bunk had met at the Astoria that he'd tried to tell me about. I believe he was the owner or part owner of the Astoria. Evidently Bunk had invited him to the session, and they did so much talking I couldn't get any work out of Bunk for fifteen minutes or so. Finally Beansy sent a man out to one of the saloons for a case of beer for the guys.

After Orin had listened to a number, Jim confided to him that he would have walked out earlier in the week if it hadn't been for the way I treated him and the others. Also Baby Dodds seemed a little discouraged for once and talked about the good beat they'd had earlier in the week. Baby, who was no longer drinking, told me, "You'll have to get that son of a bitch here sober if you want to make some good records," and tipped his head over towards Bunk. Baby admitted he used to do a lot of drinking himself, but added, "You never saw me too drunk to work, though." I explained to Baby that we didn't expect to get a good side every time, but let everybody try out anything they wanted and we'd pick out the best stuff to issue. Baby wandered back to his drum set shaking his head, perhaps a little annoyed with my lax attitude.

The first eight American Music 12" 78s – issued between March and April 1945. These records and the Stuyesant Casino appearance later that year introduced the band to a new generation of fans.

George suggested *Tishomingo*, but it sounded a little monotonous and the first take ran too long. The second take was better and I thought it might be okay to issue.

Then we tried the "dance set" idea of running through some numbers without repeating. I gave Bunk a slip of paper with four titles on it: *Darktown Strutters' Ball, Ballin' the Jack, Careless Love* and *Panama*. Bunk said they didn't need the list and I could just call them off. I explained that they were all numbers they knew as they had played them earlier that week. I really wanted to get some good takes of these numbers, but none of them seemed anything special, although they weren't too bad.

We went on to try to get some good blues, but no luck here either. Bunk called for a *Blues in C* which turned out to be the regular *Franklin Street* and no good. We then tried a 33 ⅓ *Blues*, but Bunk missed notes and, in general, it was no good.

I told everybody that we'd have one more final session on Saturday night, as no one had jobs for that evening. I know several could have had jobs that Friday playing for the prize fight that Massina was promoting, as it had been postponed from the Friday before.

During the evening, a young sailor came into the hall. I believe he was a trombonist and had been one of Bunk's pupils in New Iberia, but was now stationed at the naval base over in Algiers. When we were packing up for the evening, someone suggested that we all should go back to George's house for a meal. Bunk refused and said he was going out with the sailor. He said it in such a manner that I guess he preferred the sailor's company to ours. He also said he intended to go across the river the next day to see him. When I paid the others off, Bunk asked for his money and I told him that I would have to get the check cashed first and that I only had a few dollar bills left. After the session he told me about needing some money to pay Roger (the bartender) for drinks. So a minute later I asked Roger how much Bunk owed. He said $1.20, so I paid Roger. When Bunk asked for the money again a few minutes later I said that I'd just paid Roger. He was very sore that I'd paid it, instead of giving him the money to pay his bills. He said he was supposed to pay his own bills, and I just acted nonchalantly as if he was trying to thank me and said, "Oh, don't worry about that, we pay for all the drinks around here."

After he talked to the sailor, and various others, for about ten minutes (waving his watch around as he talked), he suddenly came over and said, "Let me have that change you have." I thought, naturally, by change he meant silver or the change from two dollars from Roger's bill. I started to dish out a handful of quarters and with great scorn he said that wouldn't do him any good. William also by that time was getting out some silver, so he asked William if that was all he had, and said, "You'll need more than that." He put his hand into his own pocket: "Let me help you," and began dishing out some silver to give William. It was really funny to see it in a way, but it made me mad (although I tried not to show it). I just explained that William wasn't going any place and that we didn't need any money. Bunk said he meant the five dollars in bills I said I had, so I dished out five single dollar bills that, fortunately, I had separated in my back pocket. Bunk then left.

We went on home and were all pretty sore about everything. It looked like Bunk had already started his weekend and was fed up with making records anyway. He didn't seem interested in co-operating anymore. As William pointed out, his attitude was having a bad effect on the other guys, who had all lost patience with him by now. This might mean that we probably wouldn't get any good records even if Bunk did show up and in good shape the next night. I figured he probably wasn't going to show up for that last night anyway. He was just fed up with too much recording and doing some of the numbers over and over again. I was fast coming to the conclusion that we would have to get another trumpet for Saturday. We laughed

40

about it and said it would be like the time they fired Bolden from his own band.

The next morning, George reported that Bunk had just got back to Abby's at 11 am without his trumpet and watch, adding, "He sure was sullen." George said, since Friday was a pay day, lots of young toughs hung around the bar-rooms that night, especially to rob guys. He told of seeing a couple of young kids grab a guy's purse and run from a saloon not long ago. When he saw him, Bunk just sat there rather dazed and gave the impression of a man who was trying to remember something. George was sure Bunk didn't know where his horn was.

Later that day, Jim said he'd seen Bunk at 10.30 am sleeping in the street, probably around St. Philip. He was sitting on a step or on a curb and his hat had fallen off. Jim stopped to pick it up and put the hat back on him and tried to get him home, but Bunk didn't seem to know who Jim was.

I talked with George about getting another trumpet. I hated even to think of it, for when you're going to replace the world's best, you're aiming downhill. George agreed it was a good idea. I'd hoped that I could record Kid Shots someday and asked George about him. George said he would be very good. I'd heard Shots on parades with the Eureka and I knew he was good. I remember he'd played a church dedication parade and played wonderfully. Some people watching started comparing him with Louis Armstrong. Shots was a very quiet, modest man, and when he heard this he got quite angry and told them off in no uncertain terms.

George and I went round to Shots's house about noon. He lived on Cleveland Street, near what they used to call the "Battlefield" at the back of Rampart Street.[19] When we got to the house, no one answered the door for a few minutes and it looked like we were out of luck. Then a woman came to the door and soon Shots came out, half awake. He had a job that night out at the Lake. I think he was playing with the young John Robichaux, who is now with our Ragtime Orchestra. The job was due to start about 9 o'clock, but he said he could be at the hall at around 5 for the recording. At first he wouldn't say much and I thought he possibly wasn't interested, but that was partly due to his lack of confidence. He explained he was afraid he might not know all the tunes we wanted to use. I assured him that there was nothing to worry about and we'd only use tunes he knew and wanted to play.

Then the problem was to tell everyone the change of time, so I tried to get round to tell all the guys to be there at 4.30 pm so that we could start at 5. We then discovered that we didn't know where Baby Dodds was living. George thought it was about the 2800 block of Louisiana Avenue, near Broad. We went up there and walked around various streets, trying to find where Baby lived. We thought it might be somewhere near Howard Street, as Baby had mentioned something about a hospital and mentioned Howard Street.

We were having no luck and George suggested going across the street to ask at the house where he thought "Happy" lived. We knocked at the house and the woman said "Happy" lived next door. I told George that I'd heard "Happy" was dead, but he reminded me that there were two "Happys" – a "Red Happy" and a "Black Happy" – and this was "Black Happy" Goldston.[20] He came to the door and invited us in to sit down. He said he worked in the shipyard most of the time these days. George implied that "Happy" didn't do much in music anymore but probably still played drums okay. "Happy" knew that Baby was in town, but hadn't seen him and couldn't tell us where he lived. He told us to go down to see Tom Benton,[21] who lived a few doors down, and he could probably tell us where Baby lived. He then said he'd walk down to Benton's with us and apologized for not being dressed up. One of Tom's many daughters came to the door and called him. He was rather tall and not very heavy and almost reminded me of Bill Johnson, except that he was lighter than Bill. He wore a hat and seemed rather dignified, although something about him confirmed George's belief that he was a hard drinker. Tom pointed out the house where Baby was living and insisted on walking us down there with "Happy." Tom told us he used to play piano and guitar with Celestin, then he knocked on the door. Baby was glad to see both of them and we all went in and sat down for about ten minutes. Baby said that Tom Benton was his old-time pal and they always used to go out to get drunk together. I would think that "Happy" was about Baby's age and that Benton was a little older, perhaps in his fifties. We told Baby that we'd like to get started early, about 5 o'clock. I was surprised he didn't remember who Shots was, but he said he'd probably recognize him when he saw him.

We got to the hall about 4.30 and set up. When the guys arrived, we went out into the back yard and took some pictures. Shots was introduced to Baby and we got under way about 5.20.

KID SHOTS NEW ORLEANS BAND
San Jacinto Hall, 1422 Dumaine Street, New Orleans.
Saturday, August 5, 1944 (5.20–8.00 pm)

"Kid Shots" Madison (tpt); Jim Robinson (tbn); George Lewis (clt); Lawrence Marrero (bjo); Alcide "Slow Drag" Pavageau (sbs); Baby Dodds (dms)

701	I Can't Escape from You	
	(issued as *San Jacinto Stomp*)	Dan: VC-4015, VC-7017, AMCD-2
702	High Society	Dan: 4015, VC-7017, AMCD-4
703	High Society	AM LP 639, Stv:SLP 201, Dan: VC-4004, VC-7007, AMCD-2
704	In Gloryland	AM LP 645, Stv: SLP 127, Dan: VC-4005, VC-7012, Seven Seas: MH 3026, AMCD-2
705	In Gloryland	AM 530, Gazell: 1035, Stv: SLP 203, Dan: VC-4015, VC-7017, AMCD-4
706	Uptown Bumps	
	(issued as *Bucket's Got a Hole in It*)	AM 529 (cut), AM LP 645, Stv: SLP 127, DLP2/1944 Dan: VC-4005 (cut), VC-7012 (cut), Gazell: 1035 (cut), Penny: REL ST 19146, Variety: REL ST 19146, AMCD-2
707	Everybody Loves my Baby	Dan: VC-4015 , VC-7017, AMCD-2
708	Baby Won't You Please Come Home	Dan: VC-4015, VB-1005, VC-7017, AMCD-2
709	Shots Blues	
	(issued as *Dumaine Street Drag*)	AM 530 (cut), AM LP 645, Gazell: 1035 (cut), Stv: SLP 127, Dan: VC-4005, VC-7012, Seven Seas: MH 3026, AMCD-2
710	When You and I Were Young Maggie	AM 529 (cut), AM LP 645, Stv: SLP 127, Dan: VC-4005, VB-1003, VC-7012, Gazell: 1035 (cut), S.S's: MH 3026, Penny: REL ST 19146, Variety: REL ST 19146, AMCD-2
711	Sheik of Araby	AM LP 645, Stv:SLP 127, Dan: VC-4005, VB-1005, VC-7012, AMCD-2

Note: *Uptown Bumps, Dumaine Street Drag* and *When You and I Were Young Maggie* were faded in for shorter playing time on the 10" AM 78s and Gazell issues. The more familiar title was used for the complete version master 706 when issued on AM LP 645 and on all subsequent reissues.

"Kid Shots" Madison before the session

Bill Russell: George quickly took over the leadership and picked the first number, *I Can't Escape from You.*[22] After rehearsing about two or three choruses, they played it right off the first time and we didn't repeat it. I went up to congratulate Shots and tell him he was going great. They all wanted to hear the record and paced around the hall while they listened. When Shots went by I asked for *High Society.* He looked uncertain: "I'm not much of a *High Society* man, but we can try it." Shots knew it alright and the first take wasn't too bad. For the repeat we moved George out in front a little and the next take sounded very good.

After *Gloryland* they chose *Bucket's Got a Hole in It.* One take was all that was needed and it had a good rock to it.

Then we got on to the "baby" numbers: After *Everybody Loves my Baby,* they tried *Baby Won't You Please Come Home,* then Al suggested *I Found a New Baby,* but none of them seemed to know that piece at all.

Then I asked Shots about playing a blues. He looked very uncertain and warned me, "I'm not much of a blues man." We went ahead anyway and he did a real low-down blues, which sounded wonderful. I put it out as *Dumaine Street Drag.*

The two American Music 10" 78s and (right) the 10" LP label from the session

43

Slow Drag had told me a couple of times that *When You and I Were Young Maggie* was a good number. Since he hadn't put in a request all week I couldn't refuse him. When he brought it up for the second or third time, they agreed to try it. Once was enough and it was as good as anything they'd played so far.

Shots had mentioned *The Sheik of Araby* a few minutes before. It was about 7.45 and he said he thought he ought to be going, as his nephew was due to stop by and take him on to his job. I'd counted on him staying until about 8.30, but since we had several good takes I didn't mind. But knowing he liked *The Sheik of Araby* I asked him to do it for a final number. It really went and seemed like the hottest of the evening.

William had the camera lights ready and we snapped the band in a hurry.

After Shots had left, I told them we would quit early that evening, but this would be a good chance to try over a couple of numbers with just clarinet and trombone.

JIM ROBINSON'S BAND

San Jacinto Hall, 1422 Dumaine Street, New Orleans.
Saturday, August 5, 1944 (8.00–9.30 pm)

Jim Robinson (tbn); George Lewis (clt); Lawrence Marrero (bjo); Alcide "Slow Drag" Pavageau (sbs); Baby Dodds (dms)

712	"Quintet Blues" (issued as *San Jacinto Blues*)	AM LP 639 (cut), Stv: SLP 201, Dan: VC-4004, VC-7007, Jz Con: JCC 102, AMCD-2
713	Ice Cream	AM V254, AM LP 639, Stv: SLP 201, DA LP 2 /1944, Dan: VC-4004, VB-1003, VC-7007, Jz Con: JCC 102, AMCD-2
714	Farewell Blues (issued as *San Jacinto Blues No.2*)	Stv: SLP 127, DA LP 2 / 1944, Dan: VC-4005, VB-1005, VC-7012, Seven Seas: MH 3026, AMCD-4
715	Talking: Baby Dodds, George Lewis, Jim Robinson, Lawrence Marrero, Slow Drag Pavageau, Alfred Lion, Bill Russell, William Wagner and Abby Williams	Dan VC-4015, VC-7017 (cut), AM Book CD (slighty edited)

Bill Russell: At the parade in Algiers the Sunday before, as I walked over to the beer joint with Jim, he stuttered out a story of how he had a little hymn and that he'd like to make a special record (presumably for home use) with just trombone and rhythm. I said that would be fine, but since I only had glass records with me, I said it would be better if I made him a copy on metal later. Jim thought that would be fine, then we could both have a copy.

On Thursday evening I'd mentioned this again when he was there early, but he said he'd prefer a full band accompaniment. On Friday, when Bunk wasn't too hot, I did my best to get him to play his number. He must have played a few phrases, maybe for George, and when I went back a little later he said they'd decided that the number was too slow. I didn't want to insist too much and thought we could get it the next night, or sometime when the others weren't all there. So Saturday I asked him again for the spiritual or anything that he wanted to play, but for some reason he acted like he didn't want to do his spiritual and didn't suggest anything. So I suggested they play a blues to feature Jim. He played okay, but George sounded better because he played some phrases from *Burgundy Street*. I then asked George if he'd like to think of something that would feature him. George had played *Ice Cream* on one of his trio records the previous week and wanted to try it again. With no rehearsal George stamped it in. It really floored us when Jim really cut loose and stole the show. We played it back with much excitement and Jim later hinted to George that he only played like that because Bunk wasn't there.

When I put it out, I didn't ask anybody but just put Jim Robinson's name on the label. That really pleased him and he would often carry the record around with him to show people. He was proud of it.

After they had put their instruments away, I asked if they'd mind making a talking side. They seemed interested and gathered around the microphone. Baby took charge to get things livened up. They got quite a big kick out of it, especially all of Baby's jive, and they enjoyed it even more hearing it played back.

William insisted on taking some pictures of Al and me with the recording set-up. At first Al objected to posing with the ice pack (à la Tuesday), but finally saw the funny side and agreed. We took our time packing up and looking around, so that nothing was missed. We left four boxes in the storeroom but managed to carry everything else.

As usual the fellows took their time leaving and we didn't get out till about 10 pm or a little later. They usually went into the bar and got a few iced drinks after the sessions. Roger always kept Cokes, beer and ice in a little refrigerator in front of the bar, so throughout the evening we had something cool. Occasionally someone would open the door and a bottle would fall out and break on the floor.

In general, the San Jacinto had been a nice convenient place in which to work and record. On a couple of nights we could hear a radio and loud footsteps in the living quarters on the floor above, but generally it was fairly quiet and few people bothered us. It may have been a little too "live" as far as the acoustics went, but probably we couldn't have done any better elsewhere. At least we had the run of the place and could take our time.

We took our time getting home with the heavy luggage and talked all the way, deciding we were lucky to have got so much good stuff when a hundred things could have gone wrong. And we had Bunk on record for three nights at his best.

When we got home we took it easy and ate, and talked about the forthcoming *Esquire* publicity and concert and what it might mean. I warned George not to expect to be voted the world's favorite clarinetist, but if *Esquire* went with the concert idea in New Orleans, they would have to have him, Bunk and Jim play. George said he didn't care about the contest, but if he got his chance he was "sure gonna make it hot for somebody!" I mentioned the difficulty in keeping Bunk straight if they got a chance to play. Jeanette said she could take care of that. She said she'd have Bunk stay there and sit at the front door with a gun. She'd then tell Bunk, "Now if you want to go out that's okay, but as sure as you step across this doorway, this gun is going to go off."

That evening I'd vaguely heard a rumor that Bunk had asked Abby Williams (or someone) if they wanted him at the San Jacinto that evening and he was told no (maybe by George). On the other hand it seemed like Abby had tried to get him to go.

The next morning, William and I went up to the San Jacinto to collect the rest of the boxes. When we returned George had been around to see Bunk and he didn't seem to know where his trumpet was; he'd told Abby something about leaving it with some people back-of-town. George was sure he'd either lost it or pawned it. William and I wondered if we shouldn't go to the police in case it was stolen or turned up in a pawn shop.

George suddenly volunteered the opinion that Bunk had something on all the younger men. He didn't say much but he expressed it very well. I remember he said, "Bunk had a certain spirit and a certain way of playing that the younger fellows seem to have lost, something that no one else has any more today." He implied that this certain quality must have been present in some of the older men he'd heard, perhaps Oliver and Keppard and probably Buddy Petit. He went on, "It is something you feel when you play with him that the others don't have." I don't know if this thought occurred to him after playing with Shots the night before, or in anticipation of his job that evening, working with DeDe Pierce.

After eating Sunday dinner, we went over to Algiers about 1.30 pm to catch the parade that Shots had told us about.

When we got home, Bunk was sitting in the kitchen talking to George and Jeanette. I hadn't seen him since Friday night, but he acted like nothing had happened. He mentioned about the record we'd made last night and I wasn't quite sure if he'd lost track of time or if he was still drunk or not. Although I tried to treat him coolly at first, he was so friendly that I couldn't help but warm to him. He had a new stiff-brimmed straw hat from his son's in the Ninth Ward. He mentioned how expensive food was when he had taken a chicken for Sunday dinner to his son's (or possibly step-son). Bunk never mentioned his trumpet once. He started to ask about Shots but stopped short, and I was glad to ignore the remark. I hardly really believed he'd said "Shots," but later George said he heard "Shots" too. Pretty soon, however, he did come right out and ask about the talking record we'd made. Evidently Abby Williams had told him we had a lot of fun making it. He said he hoped to hear the details, as Abby must have mentioned Baby Dodds's part in it. I simply said that Baby had jived around and we had got his "Aw shucks" on the record. I then quickly changed the subject.

That night, Abby Williams had a job at a lawn party on Touro Street, between Urquart and Marais. George, Slow Drag and Lawrence, and a trumpet player called "Jean,"[23] had been booked to play. Later in the evening Bunk sat in for a few numbers.

AMERICAN MUSIC
by
BUNK JOHNSON'S BAND
ON 12-inch VINYLITE* RECORDS

No. 251   Tiger Rag
          See See Rider

No. 252   St. Louis Blues
          When The Saints Go Marching In

No. 253   Lowdown Blues
          Yes Yes

No. 254   Ice Cream (Jim Robinson's Band)
          Burgundy St. Blues (Geo. Lewis)

No. 255   Panama
          When You Wore A Tulip

No. 256   Darktown Strutters' Ball
          Walk Thru The Streets Of The City

No. 257   Sister Kate
          New Iberia Blues

No. 258   Careless Love
          Weary Blues

Price $1.75 each

AM Records
647 MEANS AVENUE - PITTSBURGH 2, PA.

*Vinylite is the new high-grade flexible plastic, with minimum surface noise, as used for radio high-fidelity transcriptions.

AMERICAN MUSIC Records

A wonderful collection of new records . . . brilliant. relaxed . . .

VOGUE

Really stupendous . . . They sound better with every hearing . . . The group playing is superb.

DOWN BEAT

As real American music they belong in every record collection.

N. Y. HERALD-TRIBUNE

- - - - - - - - - - - - -

AM Records
647 Means Avenue
Pittsburgh 2, Pa.

Enclosed find $................, for which send me, postpaid, the American Music records checked below.

☐ 251   ☐ 255

☐ 252   ☐ 256

☐ 253   ☐ 257   (NAME)....................................

☐ 254   ☐ 258   (ADDRESS)................................

The first American Music catalog with an order form on the reverse

Bill Russell: I recorded all the 1944 sides for issue on 12" records because I thought maybe Blue Note might be interested, as they specialized in 12" records. Although Al was there all week, he never expressed any interest in releasing the records and I never brought the matter up – we never discussed any deal. I was glad I recorded the 12" sides, even though, on one or two numbers, the band was ready to quit earlier. But a lot of people then didn't want to fool with 12" records and many of the jazz record stores wouldn't stock them. The next year I stuck to 10" records. *Burgundy Street Blues* had been a 12" and sold well. I think I might have had this pressed two or three times (maybe around a 1000 copies of the 12" were pressed). When I re-pressed it again around 1946, I put it out on 10" 78. It just fitted. Some of the Kid Shots numbers I put onto a 10" 78 had to be faded in.

Note: The 1944 12" 78s with a "V" before the release number indicate that those records were on pressed vinylite. Later some of these 12" records were re-pressed on shellac.

New Orleans, 1945

Bill Russell: I believe I first heard Wooden Joe in 1942. There were three saloons right off Almonaster, about three blocks towards the river on Marais Street. I remember old man Glenny playing in one of them with his three-string bass. Kid Clayton was in another and I think I heard Wooden Joe in the third place. I heard him again in 1943 where he was working at Graffanini's Beer Parlor on the corner of Tulane and Claiborne, the area where the Charity Hospital is now. He had a four-piece band. I think Louis Keppard was the guitar player, and might have also played banjo. John Casimir played clarinet and I think Albert Jiles was the drummer. Wooden Joe was on trumpet and occasionally doubled on clarinet. I went in there one Saturday night (May 29, 1943) and, as I entered, he was playing *Tiger Rag*. I'd never heard anything so powerful; I thought I was going to be blown right out of the place. He had so much drive, yet everything he did seemed effortless, with that easy relaxed swing that all the best New Orleans horn men must have had. I knew straight away that I wanted to record him as soon as I could. I didn't have time to do it in 1944, so on the first day I was down in 1945 (Sunday, May 6) I set out to find him again. I heard he was playing at the Shadowland and I found it on Washington Street, back of Dryades. It was quite a fancy place with the colored people arriving in evening clothes. The boss wouldn't let me in, as it was for colored only, but he said he would call Wooden Joe out after the next number. Wooden Joe came out and remembered me okay, and I explained that I was down in New Orleans to record him. I arranged to go over to his house on Tuesday to talk things over. He said he was always at home, adding that he "had no place to go." I explained that they wouldn't let me in, so he told me to "wait a while and I'll play a number for you." He went back and cracked down on the blues, and, boy, it was the hottest blues I'd heard since Bunk's *Lowdown Blues*. It honestly seemed like the most powerful blues I'd ever heard. After about three choruses there was a vocal (the drummer, Joe later told me) which was very good and reminded me of Jelly. Joe's lip seemed more powerful than ever and there was a solidness and substance to his tone that I'd never heard outside of Bunk (or perhaps Oliver, Keppard or Louis on record). After the blues, I waited a minute to see if he'd come out, and in a few seconds out he came. I told him how pleased I was and how I thought we could make some wonderful records.

I then went over to see Albert Burbank at the Pleasure House and returned to the Shadowland about midnight. The photographer Skippy Adelman[24] and Gene Williams had been at the Pleasure House and came back with me to see Wooden Joe. When we got there Joe had just finished.[25] He tried to line up his four-piece band for a photograph but two of them had already left, so Skippy took some shots of Joe with his hat on and holding his trumpet case as he talked with me.

On the Tuesday (May 8) I went over to see Joe at about 5 o'clock. We talked a while on his front porch and he hoped he could use his regular band (trumpet, clarinet, drums and banjo) for the recording and said what a good singer his drummer was. I also wanted to record Albert Burbank, and when I mentioned him to Joe he said that was okay, but he gave me the impression that he would rather have worked with George Lewis. (In 1943 Joe told me that George could "run anybody in town" – meaning that he thought he was the best.) But he said he was glad to be able to work with Burbank, Jim, Lawrence or anyone else I mentioned.

I asked his advice on a bass player. He suggested Glenny. Then I asked him about Austin

Young, who had played so well with Bunk in 1942. Joe said: "Yes, he plays wonderful bass," and told me he was at the Cadillac with Kid Rena's band, with Picou and Walter Decou. He said Austin Young had been a wonderful trombonist. I wondered if Young or Glenny had a good instrument. I tried to tell him Jim Little's story about Glenny's home-made bass and I had an idea that he had made it himself. Joe thought Glenny didn't even own a bass and always borrowed one. He said Glenny would be able to play good bass as long as he lives, since he didn't need to depend on a lip.

I asked Joe to think of some good tunes that he would like to play. I discovered he liked spirituals (he was getting religious) and he mentioned some numbers he'd like to do, like *Lead Me On*. He then gave me the phone number of his next-door neighbor, so I could call for him as soon as the date was fixed.

I decided, before I came down that year, that I wanted to record Albert Burbank. I first heard him when I spent a month in New Orleans in 1943. While I was there Memorial Day came up,[26] which most of the southern colored people celebrated. The night before Memorial Day I went down to a little village below Chalmette, called Franzenville. It was a small colored community of about a couple of hundred people. (Ann Cook had originally come from there.) George Lewis had a job somewhere else that weekend, so I went down with Lawrence Marrero, Burbank, Harold Antoine on drums and "Sambo" Joseph – who played pretty good trumpet. They were playing a dance. They played a set and Burbank didn't seem anything special and I wasn't too impressed. Then a local band drove up on the back of a wagon and began to play outside. The local band (Johnson's Serenaders) also had a dance about a couple of blocks down the street and tried to steal Burbank's customers. When the other band started to play, Burbank perked up. He went into *Dippermouth Blues* and sounded almost like Johnny Dodds. He was inspired and played the best I ever heard him in my life. So I knew I had to record him.

Gene just couldn't understand my enthusiasm for Burbank. When Gene saw him at the Pleasure Club that Sunday (May 6) Burbank didn't sound too hot, and Gene said, "Is this your great clarinet player? He's just as corny as Kaiser." I must admit I'd heard him play a lot better, but at least he had a strong big tone. He was leading a four-piece band of trumpet, clarinet, piano and drums. His regular trumpet player, Percy Humphrey, wasn't working with him that night and he didn't want Skippy to photograph him with the non-Union musicians in his band.

Unlike Wooden Joe's band, Burbank had been used to working mainly for white audiences. The Pleasure Club had been for whites only until the night before, but there had been some trouble and I think the boss had lost his license. So the night we were there it might have been under new management, as it was for blacks now.

After I left Joe's house I caught the Galvez bus and hurried over to Burbank's. I almost walked right by the house, when I saw his wife and daughter sitting out on the steps. He invited me in the front room and we talked about the recording. He mentioned that he would like to record a Creole song that was quite popular and that he'd like to sing it. This was *Eh, La-Bas*, that I'd heard him do at dances. He also mentioned that he'd like to record numbers like *High Society* with his trio someday. When I mentioned bass players, he said he'd be happy to work with Glenny or Slow Drag but didn't seem to know Austin Young at all.

Around 8 pm Albert Burbank came over to George's house and called me out. He acted like he didn't want to come in and I thought he had something confidential to say, so I didn't invite him inside. I remembered that Jeanette had told me that there seemed to be a little jealousy between him and George. It seems if Albert had a job that he couldn't make he would try to get them not to hire George. I'm sure George never had any bad feelings towards Albert.

Wooden Joe and Albert Burbank outside the Artisan's Hall before the session

All Albert wanted to say was that the band he had been working with across the river, Elton's band, would be playing tomorrow night [Wednesday] and, since that would be his last job with them, he thought I might want to go and hear them. It was an eight-piece band and he mentioned to me that his trumpet player, Percy Humphrey, would be working with them and I ought to hear him too. They were due to play from 8 till 12 am at the Rose Room in Marrero and Albert said it would take about an hour to get there.

While we were talking, George came to the door and made us come in. We soon got out the records as I wanted Albert to hear Bunk. He seemed quite impressed, and when I was out of the room George made him listen to *Burgundy Street Blues*. George was really proud of that record and played it for everybody, every chance he got.

Since Albert played so well at Wooden Joe's session, Gene thought part of the improvement might be due to his having heard Bunk's and George's records.

After Albert left, Lawrence, Slow Drag and Jim came round. We played all last year's records as they sat in the yard. They all got a kick out of hearing themselves again and especially hearing Baby. They remarked that it was Baby who shouted on *Ice Cream*, and they'd almost forgotten about the tuba on *Lowdown Blues*. I mentioned briefly that we hoped the band could go to New York.

I was still uncertain who to use on bass for Wooden Joe's session. George said that Austin Young should have another bass by now, as his old bass wouldn't have held together all this time. Gene remarked that Young would be glad of the work as he'd heard that Kid Rena's band had just been fired from the Cadillac. It seems a white band had been hired, after only Austin Young and one other musician had shown up on Monday.

I asked Drag about the bass he was going to get for $45, and he said that it had just been sold. George told Gene that he "didn't see why Drag hadn't gotten it as he had the money saved up." George and Lawrence remembered a bass that Morris had. Burbank or someone else had mentioned Joe Morris earlier that day. They told how when his mother had died he got religious and joined the church and gave up music. He had played with George's band at a USO dance and maybe with Big Eye's band at the Economy Hall. Lawrence made Drag go over with him to see the bass, and in about twenty minutes they hurried back saying they could get it for $90. Drag asked me for an advance of $45 to help him pay for it. They soon came back with it and George opened all the front doors to get it in. It was a little larger than Drag's old bass and looked in perfect condition. The original price had been $125 to $150 and Drag thought it was much better than the $45 one he'd missed out on. He said it was good enough to take to New York or anyplace else, but it was too good to take to the country dances. He was so crazy about it that he kissed it and said he was going to take it to bed with him. I believe his wife was still in California.

After everybody had left, we discussed the New York proposition with George for about half an hour. I said how they'd all have to stick together and how Bunk would be almost essential to make it go right. George agreed this was right. Earlier he had mentioned to Gene that if the whole band couldn't go he would like to go with "a three-piece band."

The next morning (Wednesday, May 9) Gene and I went to Union Station to meet Baby Dodds. He was due in at 9.15 am on the Panama Limited, and we almost missed Baby when he came down a different platform. We didn't recognize him at first in his brown winter suit. As he led us through the colored waiting room, I mentioned that I'd hired Abby's drums again. He said the set was okay, but he didn't think Abby knew how to tune them up. Baby had brought a packet of sticks, his wood block and a small clamp for the tom-toms.

I told him that I'd like to use him on the Wooden Joe date and he seemed disappointed at first. When I said that Bunk would be in on Saturday and the whole gang would be getting together for dates next week, he cheered up. I mentioned Austin Young and Slow Drag's new bass. He recalled all the fun he'd had working with Slow Drag and how much he was looking forward to seeing him again. When I mentioned Jim, Baby hoped he wouldn't have a "fight" with him again, referring to the night he suggested a different trombone part for *Ballin' the Jack*.

Since the San Jacinto Hall was already booked for a couple of functions and they had started opening the bar every evening, I had to look elsewhere to record. George had mentioned the Artisan's Hall and thought it had a fine sound. He thought we could get it every night and it shouldn't cost more than $5 or $6, as it was no more than $10 for a dance. On the Tuesday, I suggested to Lawrence that he might enquire about it on one of his delivery trips, if George wasn't able to see Beansy.

On the day of the session (Thursday, May 10), I called at the *Times Picayune* office to see Orin Blackstone. He talked about how he'd like to give up his newspaper job and open a record shop. I then went to see Kid Howard, but his wife said he worked every day till 4 o'clock.

We got to the Artisan's Hall about 4.50 pm and George helped me unload and set up. I put the fruit juices in a bucket of water in the back room. The caretaker (who was married to Big Eye's sister) was named Baptiste and turned out to be an uncle of Buddy Petit. They all lived in a building at the back of the hall and Big Eye had a small room upstairs. We talked to him about Buddy. He seemed to think he was a wonderful musician but didn't try to glorify him. Baptiste said that Joe Petit (Buddy's stepfather) lived right across the street from the hall – in fact, he was out there clearing up his yard. Before I knew it, he came across the street in his old sweatshirt to have his picture taken. I forgot all about him being deaf and, according to Rudi Blesh, speaking only Creole. His accent was very thick, but I could make him out okay. We talked about Buddy: "Yes, I raised Buddy," he said. He came in and talked to Wooden Joe and the others and stayed all evening.[27]

Joe Petit "in his old sweatshirt"

WOODEN JOE'S NEW ORLEANS BAND

Artisan's Hall, 1460 North Derbigny Street, New Orleans.
Thursday, May 10, 1945 (5.45 pm–12.00 am)

"Wooden" Joe Nicholas (tpt); Albert Burbank (clt & vcl); Lawrence Marrero (bjo); Austin Young (sbs)

800	Weary Blues	
	(issued as *Shake It and Break It*)	AM LP 640, Stv:SLP 204, Dan: VC-4010, VC-7014, AMCD-5
801	St. Louis Blues	Dan: VC-4022, VC-7019
801½	Eh, La-Bas (test of vocal)	Unissued

Add Jim Robinson (tbn)

802	Precious Lord, Take my Hand	
	(issued as *Lead Me On*)	AM LP 640, Stv SLP 204, Dan: VC-4010, VC-7014, AMCD-5
803	Careless Love	AM LP 640, Stv SLP 204, Dan: VC-4010, VC-7014, AMCD-5

Add Josiah "Cié" Frazier (dms)

804	Tiger Rag	AM Book CD
805	Careless Love	Dan: VC-4022, VC-7019
806	Weary Blues	
	(issued as *Shake It and Break It*)	Dan: VC-4022, VC-7019
807	Original Blues	
	(issued as *Artesian Hall Blues*)	Stv: SLP 204, Dan: VC-4010, VC-7014, AMCD-5
808	Tiger Rag	Stv: SLP 204, Dan: VC-4010, VC-7014, AMCD-5
809	All the Whores Like the Way I Ride	Dan: VC-4022 , VC-7019, AMCD-5
810	Eh, La-Bas	Unissued
810½	Eh, La-Bas (test)	Unissued
811	Eh, La-Bas	Dan VC-4022, VB-1003 & VC-7019
812	Eh, La-Bas	AM LP 640, Stv: SLP 204, Dan: VC-4010, VC-7014, AMCD-5
813	Up Jumped the Devil (test)	Unissued
814	Up Jumped the Devil	Stv: SLP 204, Dan: VC-4010, VC-7014, AMCD-5
815	Up Jumped the Devil	Unissued
816	Up Jumped the Devil	Dan: VC-4010, VC-7014
817	Don't Go Way Nobody	Dan: VC-4022, VC-7019, AMCD-5
818	Don't Go Way Nobody	Stv: SLP 204, Dan: VC-4010, VC-7014
819	I Ain't Got Nobody (incomplete)	AM LP 640, Stv: SLP 204, Dan: VC-4010, VC-7014, AMCD-5
820	I Ain't Got Nobody (incomplete)	Dan: VC-4022, VC-7019
821	I Ain't Got Nobody	part on AM LP 640, Stv: SLP 204, complete on Dan: VC-4022, VC-7019

Note: While "Artisan's Hall" is the correct spelling, AM LP 640 used the phonetic spelling (*Artesian Hall*) on the cover. Storyville SLP 204 issued master 807 as *Artesan Hall Blues*.
Master 819 has the final bars of 821 spliced on.

Bill Russell: As soon as I got inside the Artisan's Hall and somebody whistled, I knew the acoustics were bad, so we opened all the windows, restroom and cloakroom doors. Wooden Joe was about the first musician to show up at about 5 pm (the time the rehearsal was set for). Austin Young, Lawrence and Burbank arrived within a few minutes and I took some pictures of Joe and Albert outside before the light went. I knew Jim was going to be a little late, but would be ready to work without eating when he got there. At 5.40 Baby Dodds hadn't arrived, so George and I thought we'd better have the guys run through something to keep them interested. Wooden Joe was playing a few notes by himself and was anxious to get going, so I said, "Let's try something." I didn't know what tune they were going to play until Joe stomped off *Weary Blues*, which they called *Shake It and Break It*. They were sitting in a straight line with the microphone clamped onto the back of a chair about 15 feet away, slightly to the right of the string bass. The acoustics were so bad I even thought about moving the band up to the balcony.

Wooden Joe really cut loose right from the start and really scared Gene. He had too much volume but he wasn't causing the "distortion". *Shake It and Break It* was very good, but I didn't think we could ever use it, as we could hardly hear the band properly for the echo. I moved the mike back and we took off any extra clothes we had, like sweaters and jackets and things we had wrapped around the records, and hung everything over chairs to absorb the sound. The doors and windows were already open so we invited people in from the neighborhood to come in, as people absorb sound too.

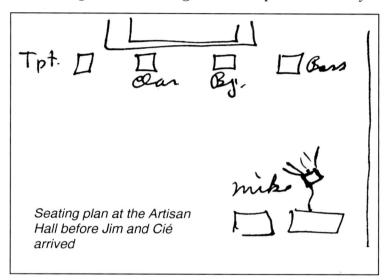

Seating plan at the Artisan Hall before Jim and Cié arrived

I was afraid we wouldn't be able to use *Shake It and Break It* and I was surprised that it sounded as good as it did. Burbank sounded fine on *Shake It and Break It*, but on *St. Louis Blues* Gene thought he sounded pretty corny again, as he had when he heard him on Sunday night. Then we tried a short test of Burbank's vocal number. After that, Jim came in and they did *Lead Me On* and *Careless Love*.

The drums I had rented from Abby Williams were all set up, but Baby still hadn't arrived. At about 6.30 I asked George to phone him, but he couldn't get an answer. I guessed he was on his way so we decided to take time off for supper about 7 pm. Quite a few people were there listening, including Burbank's whole family. While we had this intermission, Baby phoned and asked if we could do the recording tomorrow and, if so, he would be willing to work all day if necessary. I tried to explain that everyone was waiting for him and told him to get over as soon as he could and quickly hung up. I told everyone again he was on his way, but I didn't really believe it myself anymore. After about another half hour, I got a call from his niece saying Baby had had some kind of accident and wouldn't be able to make it at all. So I called George over and asked if he and Abby could go up to Baby's and either pick him up or find out what was wrong.

About that time Lawrence Marrero suggested his cousin, Cié Frazier, and said he was a good drummer. He said he was in the navy band over in Algiers and lived only a few blocks away from the hall. At about 9 o'clock Lawrence came back with Cié, who was still in his naval

Wooden Joe's Band recording at Artisan's Hall:
Jim Robinson, Wooden Joe Nicholas, Cié Frazier, Albert Burbank, Lawrence Marrero and Austin Young

uniform. When Cié sat at the drums, he discovered that Abby didn't even have two sticks that matched, only three beat-up old short ones. So I sent Gene back to George's house to get Baby's pair from last year. In recent years, Cié was about the only decent drummer around, but then he was playing with a fourteen- or fifteen-piece naval band and he was used to pounding like crazy. He played too loud (like a rock 'n' roll drummer) and the band sounded a lot better before he came. What we should have done was to get George to play drums. He could play drums pretty good, like Kid Thomas.

On *Tiger Rag* (804) Cié was hitting the drums far too loud and I had to ask him to take it easy. During this number Joe really let go towards the end, and let loose a chorus that seemed to shake the whole building. We moved the mike back thirty to thirty-five feet from the band, but the room was so alive that it didn't make much difference.

During the evening both Lawrence and Jim kept yelling at Joe to play softer, but actually his volume didn't really affect the distortion. Lawrence laughed about the time when he used to be a member of Joe's band. Once they had a dispute how Joe played a certain melody and finally Lawrence got out the music to show Joe how he always played this one phrase wrong. After that Joe never hired him for a job.

After the slow *Original Blues* (807), George arrived back with the news that Baby had fallen and sprained his right arm.

George seemed more worried than I was about the hall, and felt bad having recommended it. He was rushing around, talking over numbers and making himself very useful. Gene said he'd make a better recording director than me.

I asked Joe about some of his favorites and any original tunes he might have. The subject got around to the songs they used to play in the district, like *Wind and Grind* and *All the Whores Like the Way I Ride*. He said he had an original arrangement to *Wind and Grind* which was similar to *Kiss my Fucking Ass*, but he suggested we use the politer title of *Up Jumped the Devil*. Burbank then reminded me of *Eh, La-Bas* which he wanted to sing. I got the second microphone set up on a couple of chairs in front of the band and switched over to the Federal amplifier. The balance wasn't bad so we cut another test on the same blank (810). The next take (811) ran a little short – 2 minutes 10 seconds – and the third take (812) was the best. Then Joe wanted to do *Up Jumped the Devil* and we tried that a few times, but I was still worried about the echo. After *Don't Go Away Nobody* it was almost midnight, so I asked if they could try one more, perhaps a slow blues again. Joe seemed slow to make suggestions so I asked Jim. When Joe blew softly the first phrase from *I Ain't Got Nobody*, I turned around and asked if he had got something; he just said, "That's it." The first take sounded fine but ran too long and the stylus went over the edge of the record. Skippy got excited about Jim's playing on this and wanted to take some pictures as a trade for a dub of the record.

Only one Wooden Joe 78 was released during the 1940s. His reputation and power had to wait until 1952 until the LP was issued.

The next day, when I played Baby the Wooden Joe records, he innocently remarked how much better the ones were before the drummer arrived. He explained that he wasn't trying to run down the drummer, but not everybody knew how to fit into a band and "balance" it. He said the first two numbers sounded fuller, "no holes," and "were more together," adding that a band need not be big to sound full. However, when we got to *Careless Love* (803), Baby found something wrong: "A different rhythm, they're crossing." He explained how Lawrence and Austin Young were playing different rhythms and weren't together. I believe one of them might have been playing a pattern too fast or in double time, and someone wasn't necessarily hurrying. Maybe Baby looked down on Wooden Joe a little as he was limited and played most things in B flat. Jim Robinson (who often didn't get along too well with Bunk) admitted later that Wooden Joe had played everything in the same key and that made it harder for him as certain pieces were better in other keys, and added, "At least Bunk always picks the right key for each number." I'm not trying to knock Wooden Joe, he was one of my favorite musicians, but he was limited as to the keys he could play in.

On Saturday morning (May 12) Gene and I went over to Union Station to meet Bunk. The 10.30 train pulled in on time, but we couldn't see Bunk. After checking the colored waiting room and the street outside we thought he must have missed the train, so we waited for the next one, but he wasn't on that either. While we waited we had some breakfast in the depot restaurant, and, after an hour, went back to George's.

At about 1 or 1.15 pm, Bunk popped his head around George's door. He was carrying his trumpet case, suitbox and straw hat and had his coat over one arm. He was sweating and said that he'd walked all the way from Union depot, stopping on the way to see friends. He had been on the 10.30 am train, but had gone down by the side of the depot and across the street to a hamburger stand.

Bunk had ordered a new set of teeth, so when he arrived I suggested that we should go and see Dr. Bechet as soon as possible. We walked over to Dumaine and Dauphine and got on the Dumaine bus, transferring at Claiborne to the St. Bernard bus, and walked down to Dr. Bechet's office (1402 St. Bernard Avenue). Just before we went in, I handed Bunk the $150 that Gene had given me, so that he could give it to Dr. Bechet. He seemed glad to see us and was just finishing another patient. He had Bunk sit in the dentist chair for a few minutes while he tried the new set. Bunk wasn't satisfied with the upper plate and asked to have the top edges cut down just a little. Bunk carefully got out his old grey plate and compared it with the new red plastic. While Dr. Bechet was talking, Bunk fell asleep within two minutes, sitting in the straight chair by the window, with the curtains blowing across his face. After about ten minutes we woke Bunk up and he tried the teeth again. He seemed to find the gold clasp that Dr. Bechet had made to fit around his loose tooth a little painful, but acted like it was okay. Dr. Bechet polished up the plates and Bunk seemed all set to go.

On the way to the Esplanade bus, I told Bunk that I hoped to do the brass band date the next week and we discussed the instrumentation he would like to use. He said he never used more than nine men on a parade: two cornets, clarinet, trombone, alto and baritone horns, tuba and two drums. I asked him about how many saxes he would like to use and kept a straight face. I knew what his reaction would be. "No saxes," he said. "All the saxes are no good." I'd already discussed saxes in brass bands with George and Jim, and their ideas on what makes a good brass band were the same as Bunk's.

When we got back to George's house, Bunk got out his horn to warm up. George had mentioned *Old Folks Home* (*The Old Folks at Home*, otherwise known as *Swanee River*) would be a good tune to record. Bunk then played an arrangement of *Swanee River* that was beautiful; it must have been one Bill Colburn heard him play. He played with a full tone and modified the fancy concert variations in a way that sounded as if he'd written the piece. However, when he played the *Swanee River* that night and on Monday for the recording, he used a different idea and stuck to his usual lead rather than the florid variations. We later set off for the dance date that Lawrence had got for Bunk and George at Pointe à la Hache.[28]

When Bunk warmed up, the acoustics in George's house sounded far better than the Artisan's Hall, so Gene and I agreed that I should use it for the rest of the week. In many ways this proved to be a mistake, as the sound was not always good and everyone was so cramped-up in that small room.

On Monday (May 14) George cleared out the middle room. The bed and springs had been put out in the yard and one of the wardrobes had been moved towards the back wall. At about 3 pm most of them had arrived and they started to rehearse. After trying one of Bunk's favorite pops (*Don't Fence Me In*), they played a boogie-woogie number for Slow Drag so he could try out his new bass (later titled *Slow Drag's Boogie Woogie*). The problem came when Bunk wanted Jim to play a boogie-woogie figure. No matter how many times he tried, Jim couldn't get it. Jim must have tried it either on his own or with Bunk twenty to thirty times. Bunk tried to teach him note by note. Sometimes he'd almost get it, but then next time it came out different. Bunk had plenty of patience, but it was really getting on everyone's nerves. I hoped they would try another number, but Bunk was determined to make him learn it. Once, when

George came into the front room, I suggested he told Jim to tongue each note so he wouldn't be tempted to slur some of them. He was getting the figures mixed up and upside down. Fortunately Baby arrived, and as he hadn't seen Bunk yet they had to have a reunion and talk for a while, which broke things up. Baby's nephew, Dent, whom Johnny had taught clarinet, borrowed George's clarinet for a few minutes. He hadn't played for years, yet he didn't sound too bad. George was no longer playing his metal clarinet and sounded a little flat on some numbers with his new instrument.

They all ate a little and shortly before 5 pm everything was set up to record. Abby's drums were set up in the corner and Baby used an ordinary chair to sit on. At first I tied the microphone onto the back of a chair out in the kitchen. Then Bunk thought it would be better to have it in the same room as the band, so I tied in on top of the door and it remained there all evening.

During the evening there was some slight adjustment in their positions. Sometimes Bunk and Jim would shift to the side and at other times both of them, and George, would turn to face the microphone more. Depending on how the playbacks sounded, Lawrence and Drag also moved a little. The acoustics in the room seemed to be a little too live and the highs were too thin. We hung a few blankets on the open side-doors and stacked the big mattress from the yard up in the corner.

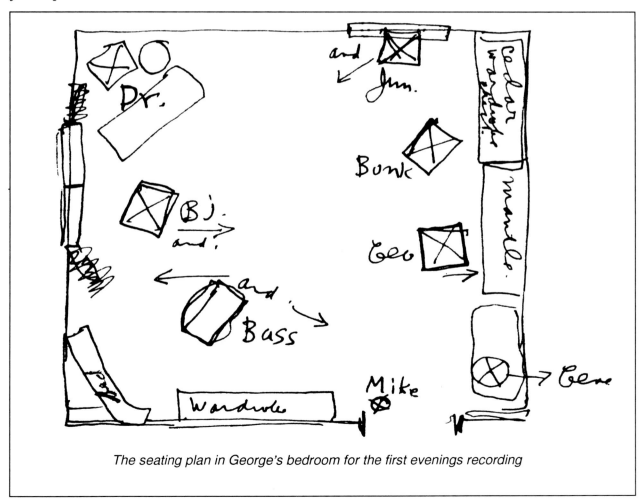

The seating plan in George's bedroom for the first evenings recording

58

BUNK JOHNSON'S BAND

George Lewis's home, 827 St. Philip Street, New Orleans.
Monday, May 14, 1945 (5.00–10.00 pm)

Bunk Johnson (tpt); George Lewis (clt); Jim Robinson (tbn); Lawrence Marrero (bjo); Alcide "Slow Drag" Pavageau (sbs); Baby Dodds (dms)

822	Don't Fence Me In (test)	Unissued
823	Sister Kate (test)	AMCD-12
824	(a) Sister Kate (test)	Dan: VC-4018, VC-7020, Jz Con: JJC.78
	(b) Swanee River (test)	Unissued
825	Swanee River	Stv: SLP 202, AMCD-6
826	Swanee River (drum solo)	Baby Dodds 1, Dan: VC-4013, VC-7015, AMCD-17
827	Swanee River	Baby Dodds 1, Dan: VC-4013, VB-1003, VC-7015, AMCD-17
828	Swanee River	AM 512
829	All the Whores Like the Way I Ride	AM LP 644, Stv: SEP 401, Wolf: WJS 1001, WJS 1001 CD, AMCD-6
830	All the Whores Like the Way I Ride	Dan: VC-4018, VC-7020, Jz Con: JJC.78
831	Snag It	
	(issued as *827 Blues*)	AM LP 644, Stv: SEP 401, Wolf: WJS I001, WJS 1001 CD, AMCD-6
832	Snag It	Unissued
833	Snag It	AMCD-12
834	Margie	Dan: VC-4018, VB-1003, VC-7020, Jz Con: JJC.78, AMCD-6
835	Margie	AM 511, Wolf: WJS 1001, WJS 1001 CD, AM Book CD
836	Runnin' Wild	AM 512, Stv: SLP 202, Dan: VC-4009, VC-7011, AMCD-6
837	You Always Hurt the One You Love	AM LP 644, Stv: SEP 401, Wolf: WJS 1001, WJS 1001CD, AMCD-15
838	I'm Making Believe	AMCD-15
839	Amour	Dan: VC-4018, VC-7020, Jz Con: JJC.78, AMCD-15
840	The Sheik of Araby	Purist PU 7, Stv: SLP 202, NoLa LP6, NoLa TC 006, Dan: VC-4009, VC-7011, AMCD-6

Bill Russell: Bunk picked *Don't Fence Me In* to run over for the first test. After *Sister Kate* I requested *Swanee River*, and we decided to try for a 10″ side. Bunk said he'd prefer to have Gene give them a signal before the final chorus rather than judge the time themselves. But often when Gene did give the signal he failed to see it, or possibly paid no attention to it when he did see it.

Abby had fixed a big square pad on the outer head of the bass drum, which couldn't be removed. Baby had objected to this and couldn't figure out why Abby had it on, but of course anyone who knew Abby didn't need an answer. Baby said it was like playing without any bass drum. So when, during the second take of *Swanee River*, my best needle gave out, I asked Baby to try a solo to see how it sounded. I offered to pay for a new head if he wanted to take it off, but Baby thought that as we had the band "balanced" it would be best to leave it.

George suggested *All the Whores Like the Way I Ride*. The first take went on too long, so we tried it again and got one at 2 minutes 55 seconds.

While Gene went down to the corner shop with his basket of bottles, we listened to the playbacks. When Gene got back with the cold drinks, they were trying Bunk's suggestion of *Snag It*. I was pleased that they were suggesting numbers and I stayed out in the kitchen to keep out of their way. Baby had the idea that the "wax" (as he called it) was very expensive, as some studios charged $10 for each cut. When Bunk and George asked if I had plenty of records (blanks) I assured them I had and they could suggest anything they would like to try. The actual cost of a 12" glass-based acetate blank was less than a dollar in 1945.[29]

When they were working on *Snag It* (*827 Blues*), Bunk told Gene that every time he played this number he thought of Joe Oliver, but, except for the trumpet solo, the performance sounded more like a Bunk's blues than a Joe Oliver blues. When they rehearsed it, Bunk always seemed to hurry the last part of the cadenza. But, as he had also played it this way with Sidney in Boston, I assumed it must have been intentional. When we came to cut it, Bunk didn't seem to rush the phrase as much and it sounded okay, although it was too long for a 10" side. Gene had given Bunk the signal before the last chorus, but that started a long discussion by Bunk as to what was a chorus. He explained that George's twelve-bar solo was really half a chorus and a second chorus was needed to complete the idea. I didn't want any argument to start, so I accepted his word for it. Later Gene asked George about this and George thought that twelve bars of a blues was a chorus, but he didn't want to say Bunk was wrong.

The second take of *Snag It* ran 2 minutes 53 seconds, which was okay for length, but Bunk messed up the cadenzas. I asked if they wanted to try it again but Bunk said, "No, it was okay," and it wouldn't be any use to play it over again as it wouldn't be any different. Next they did *Margie* and I said to Bunk, "I know how you can play that one." They really stomped it off and the time ran for 3 minutes 40 seconds. I said to Gene that this was a 12" band, as it looked like they couldn't cut their performances down for a 10" record. We kept on trying. Baby thought that the first take was the better one and everybody began to relax. They walked around as they listened, but Bunk, apart from going out into the yard for the toilet, didn't move from his chair all night.

About 9 pm I made my third and final request of the evening. *Runnin' Wild* had gone so well at the dance on Saturday night and it went just as well here. Bunk almost jumped the gun on me, but luckily I had the cutting head in my hand when I heard him stomp off, and I dropped it right on. When I played it back I had less than a full silent groove to start. The pickup slid into the first note, but the performance was so good that I couldn't ask them to repeat it.

Bunk suggested they tried *You Always Hurt the One You Love* as a fox-trot and not, as originally written, a waltz. It went so well at 2 minutes 52 seconds that we didn't need a second take.

Then Bunk said, "I want to do *Make Believe* (*I'm Making Believe*) with just Lawrence, Baby and Drag." It was a beautiful performance. Bunk was getting in his little runs with the most beautiful tone imaginable. After about three choruses, George and Jim came in for the final chorus. I'm not sure if Bunk signalled for them to come in, or they just wanted to get in on the act, but it made a very effective close. During the playback everyone marvelled at the beauty of Bunk's tone and Baby would shake his head and smile when Bunk hit those low notes. Bunk as usual sat motionless, looking down without any expression or staring straight ahead.

George asked for *Amour* which had been one of his favorites for months. At 3 minutes 45 seconds it was too long for a 10", and didn't seem anything much at the time.

It was getting near 10 pm and I was afraid that the neighbors would start complaining about the noise. Even Jeanette had been concerned that the Sisters, two houses down the street, would object. I had hoped we could start at 4 pm and finish around 8 pm. However, Jeanette relayed to us how much the neighbors were enjoying the music. I didn't want to wear everyone out. We had at least half a dozen good numbers and, with eighteen masters, we had cut more sides than any single session the previous year. I was glad to make up for the problems of Thursday night as I didn't think, at the time, I would be able to use any of the Wooden Joes. So I said, "Let's cut one more and really quit." Bunk then called and started playing *The Sheik of Araby*. It clicked right off and as they sat listening to the playback I asked them if they would pose for a couple of photos. I got them to sit closer together and Gene fixed up the flash bulbs. Then they ran through two or three choruses of the *Sheik of Araby* while I photographed.

Slow Drag Pavageau, Lawrence Marrero, Baby Dodds, George Lewis, Jim Robinson and Bunk Johnson

We finished up just after 10 pm and, by the time everyone had left, it was almost midnight before we got the recording equipment all packed away in the front room, took down the drapes over the doors, etc., and refurnished the bedroom for George and Jeanette.

It was too late to ask Jeanette to fix anything to eat, so Gene and I went down to the little Italian delicatessen on the next block of St. Philip. We got a couple of fancy fat cheese sandwiches and walked down Royal Street to Ursuline. I had the master list with me and, as we sat on some steps eating, we discussed the numbers.

I'd been generally pleased with the session, but I could see problems ahead. Bunk and Jim hadn't hit it off and the whole band sounded rather sour and didn't seem to be as together as it had been the previous year.

George didn't go to work at Smith's Coffee Dock No. 2 that week and usually slept until almost noon. Jeanette was a light sleeper, but no noise could ever awake George. When he eventually awoke, we discussed the possibility of Bunk showing up that evening. I remembered last year's Tuesday night and wasn't very optimistic. George and Jeanette thought Bunk had reformed and pointed out his perfect behavior so far. They thought he had learned his lesson after the January 17 concert (*Esquire* magazine's concert featuring Louis, Bechet, Henry Allen Sr. and Bunk, at the Municipal Auditorium),³⁰ when he had stayed with George overnight. Bunk had gone to a party at the Gypsy Tea Room. Either at the party, or more likely afterwards, Bunk claimed that all of his money had been stolen. The next day Bunk had to go up to the National Jazz Foundation and beg his fare home.

George didn't know what they paid Bunk, but I believe he said the rest of the band (five guys) got $90 for the date, which included the Union initiation fees. I believe the initiation fee was about $12 per man; I guess they probably had about $6 each left.

On Sunday, Jim had mentioned *Rosa Lee Rag* and hummed a little of it. George and the others decided it was probably *Rose Leaf Rag*, but when Bunk heard some of them play the bit they knew on Monday evening he said it was one of the strains of *Sunflower Rag*. On Monday night they had talked about coming in early to learn *Sunflower Rag*. (Jim had also mentioned that *Climax Rag* was a good one to play, but his accent was so thick that I thought he said *Columbus Rag*.) At about 10 pm, someone suggested *Sunflower Rag* again, but they agreed that it would be better to wait and work it out the next day. I really dreaded them starting out on it, but when Bunk had played a few snatches of it and Jim had played a little of the trombone part, it sounded good and could be a fine number. The part Jim and George had known turned out to be only the trio part, but Bunk agreed just that much might make a good number. I got all the recording gear organized early on Tuesday, but no one showed up especially early for a rehearsal.

Bunk arrived about 5 pm. He looked hot and tired and not particularly happy. He had been down to see his daughter, and although he seemed sober enough he was in a grumpy mood and didn't want to eat anything at first. Finally we got him to eat a plate of rice and meat out in the yard, at the little table where Jeanette washed the dishes. Bunk then went to the toilet and stayed there a long time, as if he was sick or something. When he finally came in, he fooled about for a while and eventually got his trumpet case, but he seemed so tired and bad tempered that I wish I'd suggested that he went into the front room and slept awhile. It would have been better to have recorded some trio or quartet sides – *Ice Cream* type of sides. But he got out his horn and sat down ready to play. He seemed quite disagreeable and was very talkative. He kept talking continuously to and about everybody. At times he didn't seem to be talking to anybody in particular, but it was just as though he was talking in a trance. It was all done in a dead-pan manner, just like a comedian trying to attract attention with a constant patter of wisecracks. I couldn't tell if he was trying to be funny or if he really meant it. It usually sounded as if he really meant it. He rattled off a long monologue once that was pretty good. The general theme was that Lawrence should be working on his furniture wagon, Baby ought to be back in Chicago where he belongs, Drag should be painting his house, the soldiers should all stay in their camps where they belong. (Bunk had overheard a remark I made that Ed Rubin would shortly be round from his camp to hear the session.) I don't know how the rest of it went – probably that Jim should be at his shipyard and perhaps Gene should be back in New York, etc. Anyway, he wished everybody would get out of there and go on home and tend to their business.

BUNK JOHNSON'S BAND

George Lewis's home, 827 St. Philip Street, New Orleans.
Tuesday, May 15, 1945 (5.30–approx.10.30 pm)

Bunk Johnson (tpt); George Lewis (clt); Jim Robinson (tbn); Lawrence Marrero (bjo); Alcide "Slow Drag"
Pavageau (sbs); Baby Dodds (dms & vcl *)

841	The Sheik of Araby	AMCD-12
842	Carry Me Back to Old Virginny	AMCD-15
843	Marie	Unissued
844	Don't Fence Me In	Unissued
845	Careless Love	Unissued
846	Willie the Weeper	AMCD-12
847	"Vocal Blues" (*)	Unissued
848	"Vocal Blues" (*)	Unissued
849	"Vocal Blues" (*)	
	(issued as *Listen to Me*)	AM 514, Baby Dodds 3, Dan: VC-4013, VC-7015, AMCD-17
850	Sweet Georgia Brown	AMCD-15
851	High Society	Unissued
852	High Society	Dan: VC-4018, VC-7020, Jz Con: JJC.78, AMCD-17
853	Shine	Dan: VC-4018, VC-7020, Jz Con: JJC.78, AMCD-12
854	Make Me a Pallet on the Floor	Unissued
855	Slow Drag's Boogie Woogie	Dan: VC-4018, VC-7020, Jz Con: JJC.78, AM Book CD
856	Slow Drag's Boogie Woogie	Unissued
857	Slow Drag's Boogie Woogie	Unissued
858	Make Me a Pallet on the Floor	AM Book CD
859	Maria Elana	Unissued
860	Maria Elana	AMCD-15

Bill Russell: At last they got started and Bunk announced and wanted to play *Rum and Coca Cola*. I'm certain this is what he said, but it might possibly have been some other late pop tune. However, the music came out as *The Sheik of Araby*, the tune they had finished up with the night before. The next day George laughed about how Bunk called one number and they played another. The performance didn't compare with the other night anyway.

We had quite a time to stop Bunk talking and get on with another number. I thought it best, at that moment, to suggest tunes which I had heard them do. I asked for *Carry Me Back to Old Virginny*, which they had played last Saturday night at the dance. Bunk paid no attention to Gene's signal and kept playing until it ran over the edge of the blank. I decided not to waste another blank on another take of the tune at that time. During the playback, Bunk fell sound asleep in his chair, his head dropped forward and a little to one side. I thought we would never get him awake for the next number. The rest of the gang were sitting pretty disgusted and sore at him by that time. They were doing plenty of talking about him. They kidded him unmercifully, especially Baby, who got pretty hot with him. At times Baby would say, "George, what did you do with that watch you had, the one you were swinging around like this?" George would say, "Baby, I don't remember what I did with that watch . . ." Later on Baby would repeat the question, saying that he took it to the repair man, etc. They also kidded Bunk about a lot of things. At times Bunk would ignore them or make a smart answer back.

I looked up my dance list again and suggested *Marie*, which had gone so well last Saturday. They got the time down to 2 minutes 45 seconds okay, but for some reason the performance seemed very weak. When they ended the piece, Bunk immediately began fussing about the tune being no good: "None of those pieces or songs that have girls' names are really any good." He mentioned *Sweet Sue, Dinah* and two or three more. So we didn't try that over again either.

We let him pick the next one and he called for *Don't Fence Me In*. He missed the signal on this, but it was no good anyway.

Ed Rubin had arrived, and while we were chatting Drag came out into the kitchen to suggest we get some olives for Bunk. Drag thought it would sober him up. Ed went out and got a jar, but Bunk refused to eat any of them. He knew the purpose in getting them and was probably pretty annoyed at our motive. He then delighted in going round for the next half hour asking everybody to have an olive, telling them how good they would be for them! I could see Lawrence getting mad and biting his lip to keep from yelling at Bunk. Later he said he was so mad that, if Bunk had been his own age, he would have gotten up and busted him in the head. I guess he would have done, as he'd been a former prize fighter. Its just as well Bunk was older. Jim had hardly anything to say. He had been the first one there, arriving around 4 or 4.30 pm, and then left and came back an hour later. He sat in the back, silent, rather discouraged and disgusted looking.

Someone, probably Bunk, next suggested *Careless Love*, so we cut it and it seemed like a fairly good performance, although the next day George rejected it along with all the other sides made that night. Before the last note died away, Baby yelled out, "I want to know who wrote that. I've heard a lot of different ideas on it. Lonnie Johnson told me he wrote it." Bunk scoffed at that idea and said, "I don't know who wrote it or where it came from. But it was here when I got out of school in 1894." Baby remarked he'd just wondered for his information, since Lonnie had told him. Bunk thought that he was trying to pick an argument and said, "All I'm telling you is that the song was here when I got out of school." I believe he said that his sisters had sung it at that time.

Bunk mentioned *Willie the Weeper*. Possibly they had played it at the dance on Saturday night, so they were willing to try it. Bunk had to explain that there was a minor strain and he played it all through for them once or twice. He got them to try the minor section and didn't think that the full band needed to run though the whole piece. When we cut it, the change to the minor section was pretty rough. At the playback the next day, George thought that the minor section should be first, but Gene explained that Louis [Armstrong] and everyone played it as Bunk had organized it. On some folk songs, like *Carry Me Back to Old Virginny* or perhaps *Swanee River*, Bunk altered the usual form and always repeated the first section. This possibly fooled some of the other musicians too, who seemed not to expect this repeat.

Things were not going well and I told them we might as well fool around and have some fun. Baby Dodds wanted to do a vocal. He was a pretty good singer and sang a blues on *Listen to Me*. I tried to get Bunk to sing and told him I'd rig up an extra microphone for him. I suggested *Down by the Riverside*, which he'd sung so well in San Francisco, but he simply pointed towards the drums and said, "Baby's our singer."

Ed Rubin suggested *High Society*. The first take was pretty bad, but the second was a little better. Bunk then complained that New Orleans bands couldn't play *High Society* the way it should be played. He then asked for *Shine*, which went fairly good but maybe not good enough to issue. I tried again to get Bunk to sing *Down by the Riverside* or *Ballin' the Jack*, but no luck. He would just refer me to Baby.

64

Two or three times we took time out for playbacks – we had plenty of time that evening. Bunk would slip out the side door and go up to Johnnie's at the corner of Dauphine. I suppose Gene wasn't bringing in his basket full of beer fast enough, although after every other piece Gene seemed to run up to the corner.

After about ten minutes, when Bunk was gone, the guys started working on the boogie-woogie number again, but left out the trombone bass figures they had worked out the day before. George rehearsed Drag on it and it sounded good. When Bunk got back he wanted to try it too. I was all set to record, but just as they started Bunk yelled, "Don't record this" in a threatening voice. So I stopped the motor and went to sit in the front room to hear the run-through. The band somehow got going in a terrific groove. Baby, Drag and the rhythm were really stomping like crazy. Bunk was riffing as he does on boogie-woogie numbers, and it was good, effective riffing. The big kick was that Jim cut loose (as he hadn't all week) and really jazzed up the piece, using a lot of hand in the bell effects. They went on and on, probably for five or six minutes at least. It would have been too long to get on a record, but I was sure sorry I hadn't sneaked a cut of it. They were really stomping, and as soon as they finished, Bunk shouted, "Did you get that?" Ed Rubin and I could have killed the guy! I asked them to play it again and switched to 33⅓ rpm in case they got into that groove again. It ran for 4½ minutes but the performance had no life at all: it was mainly a lot of monotonous riffs, with Bunk sounding as though he was imitating Louis. I switched back to 78, but the other takes were no better. Before we started the last take I asked Jim if he couldn't cut loose again. He said Bunk had just bawled him out for playing too loud and too much. Jim seemed at a loss for what he was supposed to do. I told him just for once to disobey Bunk and cut loose, as once the number started there was little Bunk could do to stop him.

Drag was very excited about having a number named after him and came out to the kitchen half a dozen times afterwards to be sure I'd promised that the title would be *Slow Drag's Boogie Woogie*.

Before we'd started, Bunk took me on to one side and asked if I could stop Jim playing lead. It seems there was a good deal of friction between Jim and Bunk, more of course on that Tuesday night. During the week Bunk complained to me a couple of times that Jim played too loud. He said Jim's horn was right in his ear and that was all he could hear sometimes. I suppose I should have done something, but I didn't want to make matters worse. Bunk also complained that Jim should get a tutor book and take it to Vic Gaspard[31] to learn the positions.

Jim later complained to me that Bunk held him back too much and kept telling him to play softer, adding that the reason he played *Ice Cream* so well the year before was that Bunk wasn't there to hold him back.

After the boogie number they tried *Pallet on the Floor* again, but it was not as good as it could have been. I was resigned to not getting any good numbers that night and told them that we'd better finish, but Bunk wanted to try *Maria Elana*. Lawrence had been annoyed with Bunk all evening, and on the second take he hit the banjo string so hard that it broke. That really finished off the evening.

Bunk stayed around after the others had gone, still talking. Somehow the talk got around to Jim again, and Bunk, evidently with "the band going to New York" in mind, mentioned Sandy Williams again and then J. C. Higginbotham as a fine example of a good trombonist. After a harrowing evening I decided for the first time in my life to give Bunk an argument. I think this surprised Bunk and he and George laughed about how Higginbotham, at the *Esquire* concert, drank all day and had a quart of whiskey at the concert and another quart in his trombone case. As Bunk put away his trumpet he perked up and began telling me a lot of good tunes (*Dardanella, I'll Walk Alone, Over the Rainbow, Dark Eyes, On a Coconut Island, Till We Meet Again, I'm Afraid to Go Home in the Dark*, etc) that they should try at the next session.

During the previous weekend we had all agreed that Wednesday (May 16) would be a day off from recording. I felt it had been a mistake in 1944 to try and record Bunk for five consecutive nights. In view of the wasted Tuesday session I was glad we had made this arrangement and hoped everybody would do better on the Thursday.

I had talked to George about making some more "trio" records and we all agreed that we'd have been better off concentrating on this rather than trying to make the records with Bunk on the Tuesday night. George, like most New Orleans musicians, never talked about a trio or quartet – it was always a three- or four-piece band. So George arranged to have Drag and Lawrence come around before Bunk arrived. Soon after 3 pm we were ready and before 4 pm we were cutting.

GEORGE LEWIS 3-PIECE BAND
George Lewis's home, 827 St. Philip Street, New Orleans.
Thursday, May 17, 1945 (3.45–4.30 pm)

George Lewis (clt); Lawrence Marrero (bjo); Alcide "Slow Drag" Pavageau (sbs)

| 861 | Hindustan | Dan: VC-4015, VC-7017 |

Ricard Alexis (sbs) replaces Pavageau

| 862 | Hindustan | Stv: SLP 201, DA LP 2 / 1944, Dan: VC-4004, VB-1005, VC-7007, Jz Con: JCC 102, AMCD-4 |

GEORGE LEWIS 4-PIECE BAND

Alcide "Slow Drag" Pavageau (sbs) replaces Alexis; add Baby Dodds (dms)

| 863 | Ciribiribin | Dan: VC-4015, VB-1005, VC-7017, AMCD-4 |

Bill Russell: The first title I didn't even recognize, which was *Hindustan*. Drag was a little too soft and George stood out too much.

At about that time Drag must have had to go home, and when I wasn't looking Ricard Alexis, who must have come in the side door, slipped into Drag's place. He asked if he could play and I said, "Okay, go ahead," so he stood in for another take. I didn't pay him anything at the time. He just wanted to play and wouldn't have expected anything, but I think I gave him $10 later on. It turned out a better take than the one Drag was on. Then Drag returned and Baby Dodds arrived, so George got them to play *Ciribiribin*. All we could hear was the rhythm section on the playback and George was really covered up.

Before we'd really got any decent trio or quartet records, Bunk arrived, so I thought I'd better get him involved before he disappeared.

BUNK JOHNSON'S BAND

George Lewis's home, 827 St. Philip Street, New Orleans.
Thursday, May 17, 1945 (5pm–7.10 pm)

Bunk Johnson (tpt); George Lewis (clt); Lawrence Marrero (bjo); Alcide "Slow Drag" Pavageau (sbs);
Baby Dodds (dms); Ed "Noon" Johnson (vcl*)

864	Vocal - "Jap song" (*)	Unissued
865	Vocal Blues (*)	
	(issued as *Noon's Blues*)	Dan: VC-4018, VC-7020, Jz Con: JJC.78, AMCD-12

Add Jim Robinson (tbn)

866	Do Right Baby (*)	AM 511, Wolf: WJS 1001, WJS 1001 CD, AM Book CD
867	Lonesome Road	Dan: VC-4018, VC-7020
868	Lonesome Road	AM LP 638, Stv: SLP 201, DA LP 2 / 1944, Dan: VC-4008, VC-7016, Jz Con: JJC.78, AMCD-6
869	Milneberg Joys	
	(issued as *Golden Leaf Strut*)	Dan: VC-4018, VB-1004, VC-7020, Jz Con: JJC.78
870	Milneberg Joys	AMCD-12
871	The Cat's Got Kittens (*)	Dan: VC-4018, VC-7020, Jz Con: JJC.78, AMCD-12
872	My Old Kentucky Home	Dan: VC-4018, VC-7020, Jz Con: JJC.78
873	My Old Kentucky Home	AM 514, Stv: SLP 202, Dan: VC-4009, VC-7011, AMCD-6
874	Milneberg Joys	
	(issued as *Golden Leaf Strut*)	AM LP 644, Stv: SEP 401, Wolf: WJS 1001, WJS 1001 CD, AMCD-6

Note: The number played to accompany the "Jap Song" (master 864) is *Down in Jungle Town*.
Although "Milneberg Joys" is generally accepted as the correct spelling, the tune was copyrighted on
October 10, 1925, as *Milenberg joys* (sic).

Bill Russell: Then this singer turned up . . . I didn't know his name at the time, but George later told me he was called Edward "Noon" Johnson. He said that he just wanted to hear his voice on a record, to see how he sounded. George had told him to come around, and he was related to Jeanette. He wanted to do a couple songs with the band, and as we were just fooling around at that time I said okay. It seems the first number was one of his topical specialities; it was an anti-Japanese propaganda song. One line went something like ". . . go over there and kill all those yellow rats." If there ever was a down-trodden race it was the southern negroes who'd had the hell knocked out of 'em down here. How could a black man (they don't like the term "negro" these days) do a propaganda song about killing off another race just because they were yellow? If you kill someone because they're supposed to be yellow, what about all the black guys in George's house? What was supposed to happen to them?

On the side of a mountain on one of the Pacific islands they'd painted a fifteen-foot high sign saying "Kill Those Yellow Rats." There were pictures of this in all the papers – I guess it was part of the war propaganda – and this guy must have seen that. I was pretty disgusted by it all. "Noon" Johnson was something of a "folk" singer down here. When Preservation Hall opened, Larry would sometimes hire him with a trio.

The first take of *Lonesome Road* ran too long and finished right up to the edge of the blank. On the next take Bunk saw Gene's signal and we got a good number.

The only time during the week that Bunk wanted to try a tune over again was after the first take of *Milneberg Joys*. I believe they got two silent breaks in a row, and when I played it back Bunk immediately began talking it over with the guys so they wouldn't mess it up again.

Before I knew it, the vocalist was up at the mike crooning again. We made a quick cut (*The Cat's Got Kittens*). As it was getting around 6.30 pm, with only one or two decent sides, I was getting tired of fooling around. I rather blamed George for inviting the guy there. I complained to George that we'd better get on before Wooden Joe arrived. He reacted very calmly and said quietly, "Okay, we're waiting on you."

Albert Burbank arrived before 7 pm and soon Wooden Joe arrived. Bunk hadn't seen Joe for about fifteen years or more and they recalled meeting in Port Arthur. Bunk mentioned the show they were both with.

I decided it might be a good time to call for *Milneberg Joys* again and it turned out to be a good performance. At 7.15 pm we turned things over to Wooden Joe.

ORIGINAL CREOLE STOMPERS
George Lewis's home, 827 St. Philip Street, New Orleans.
Thursday, May 17, 1945 (7.15 pm– approx. 8.30 pm)

"Wooden" Joe Nicholas (tpt); Jim Robinson (tbn); Albert Burbank (clt); Lawrence Marrero (bjo); Alcide "Slow Drag" Pavageau (sbs); Baby Dodds (dms)

| 875 | Eh, La-Bas (vcl Burbank) | AM 513, Stv: SLP 203 (part), AMCD-5 |

Joe Petit (tbn) replaces Jim Robinson

876	Maryland, my Maryland	Unissued
877	St. Louis Blues	Unissued
878	St. Louis Blues	Dan: VC-4022, VC-7019
879	St. Louis Blues	Dan: VC-4022, VC-7019, AMCD-5
880	Careless Love	AMCD-17

Bill Russell: I had arranged for Wooden Joe and Burbank to come over to play with Bunk's rhythm section, as I wasn't sure I'd be able to issue any of the records that we'd cut at Artisan's Hall due to the echo.

For the remake of *Eh, La-Bas* I used the one microphone, as we had for "Noon" Johnson. Burbank got up just a couple of seconds before his vocal. Then, when he finished, he turned his back on the microphone and started playing before he got back to his chair.

About then, Joe Petit arrived with his trombone and we took a few minutes off while he talked to Bunk and everyone.

Rudi Blesh had talked to Joe Petit the year before and Joe had told him he'd like to make a record some day. Rudi told me this and I thought it was worth trying. Joe Petit lived across the street from the Artisan's Hall, and while we were setting up for Wooden Joe's session there he came over, and I talked about him making a record. He seemed very keen, but I didn't get around to doing it that evening. So when I arranged for Wooden Joe to make some numbers at George's house, I told Joe Petit to come over.

Some years earlier he'd lost his front teeth and he'd hardened his gums so he could continue playing. Joe Petit took his time setting up, and when I asked him what he wanted to play he said *My Maryland*. Wooden Joe stomped off and Petit wasn't doing too good. At first we couldn't tell if it was his lip, his ear, or if he'd just forgotten how to play. Anyway the prospect of making a good side with him didn't look too promising. The funny thing was that he was so deaf that he didn't know what key they were playing in. When they began, he was in one key and they were in another. Albert caught on to this straight away and signalled to Joe to change keys. But it took Joe a couple of choruses before he realized that Albert had switched to "Old Man" Petit's key. We played the record later for George. He thought it was the funniest thing he'd ever heard in his life.

Rather than ask for *Maryland* over again, I asked if they had another tune they'd like to try and someone suggested *St. Louis Blues*. Petit was much better on this and at least he'd gotten into the right key. Gene was much impressed with Burbank's clarinet chorus, which was entirely different from the "traditional" solo he used the week before. During the next two takes Joe Petit's lip seemed to be coming back and he came in pretty strong as he took the lead motive on the Black Butts "Jogo" strain (as Jelly called it).

By this time, Joe Petit was beginning to feel at home. Although he hadn't played since the last Mardi Gras Carnival in 1941, he was swinging away, his shoulders rocking and the entire upper part of his body doing a dance. In the old parades he must have been really a sight.

The funniest part of the whole evening was during the first or second take of *St Louis Blues*. "Old Man" Petit was sitting there blowing, and all of a sudden the slide flew right out of his hand and landed in the middle of the floor. I didn't see it fly off, although I could tell something had happened. When I looked into the room, there was the old man, bending over to pick up the slide and hurry back to his chair. The guys didn't dare laugh even though they thought it so funny. Lawrence Marrero wanted to laugh but, having a long chin and a barrel chest, pressed his chin right down on to his chest so he couldn't open his mouth to laugh! Baby Dodds (who was sitting next to Petit) tried hard not to laugh out of respect for the old man and pressed his lips together tightly to keep a straight face. Dent, Baby's nephew, was sitting with his wife, by the door, and he couldn't restrain himself and was doubled over with laughter.

The luckiest part of the evening was that Jim wasn't there, as it was his trombone. Joe's trombone was pretty beat up, so when Jim went over to the corner saloon he offered Joe the loan of his trombone. Jim was always very careful with his instrument – he always kept it in perfect condition. He'd spend a lot of money to have it regularly checked over at Werlein's and would never normally leave it out of his sight. Anyway, he let Joe borrow it and I was glad Jim wasn't there. When Jim came back, he never knew what had happened to his trombone.

I'd been prepared to finish with Joe Petit after the second take of *St. Louis Blues*, but he wanted to try it again. After the third take, I tried to get Jim back for another *Eh, La-Bas*, but the old man kept saying, "I can play another one," and "I'm not tired." He really was enjoying himself and I couldn't get rid of him.

So after *Careless Love* I went over and thanked him so much that he had to quit. I paid him the $10 I'd promised him and he soon went home.

As he walked out, Baby went into one of his dramatic and serious orations. "Man, you've got history on that wax. You've got something there that no one else got – that's history." More than anyone else, Baby had understood just why I'd bothered to record Joe Petit. Baby then mentioned how Joe had been a great player years ago when he and others were nobodys and not even good enough to play with him.

To many of the other fellows there, who had stayed in New Orleans and seen dozens of great musicians come and go without any particular fuss, Joe Petit probably was just another trombone player.

In the 1950s I planned to put out a short extract of his playing on the fourth Baby Dodds LP that never materialized. In the end I let them be put out in Japan, so people could hear what he sounded like.

Bunk and George later talked about how Joe Petit had been a pie vendor on the riverfront near the Canal Street boat landing. When he had pies left at night, instead of selling them off cheap, he would take them home and feed them to his horse. Bunk had a good time laughing about his horse and how he kept it in the back yard. Joe had only a very narrow passage between the houses for the horse to leave the yard. One evening the horse had eaten so many pies that it got stuck when it tried to wander down the passage. The horse didn't seem too well and during the night it died and slid under the house. The next day Joe had a tough time getting the horse out from under his house! Bunk also laughed about when they once put soap on Joe's slide where it leaked in a couple of places. Joe never blew the spit out of his horn, so when he had played, soap bubbles came out of his horn.[32] I think he must have been something of a comedian in the old days, but everybody seemed to have a great respect for him. In his prime he played valve trombone and led the Olympia band.

ORIGINAL CREOLE STOMPERS
George Lewis's home, 827 St. Philip Street, New Orleans.
Thursday, May 17, 1945.

"Wooden" Joe Nicholas (tpt); Jim Robinson (tbn); Albert Burbank (clt); Lawrence Marrero (bjo); Alcide "Slow Drag" Pavageau (sbs); Baby Dodds (dms)

881	Eh, La-Bas (vcl Burbank)	Dan: VC-4022, VC-7019
882	Eh, La-Bas (vcl Burbank)	Unissued
883	Up Jumped the Devil	Dan: VC-4022, VC-7019
884	Up Jumped the Devil	Dan: VC-4022, VC-7019
885	Up Jumped the Devil	AM 513, AM LP 640, Stv: SLP 203, AMCD-5
886	Eh, La-Bas (vcl Burbank)	Stv: SLP 203 (part)

Note: Masters 875 and 886 were spliced together for the Storyville issue.

Bill Russell: Afterwards we remade *Eh, La-Bas* and *Up Jumped the Devil*, as I thought I'd better try and get a cleaner recording than the Artisan's Hall versions. I kept asking for *Eh, La-Bas*, hoping that Burbank could recapture the spirit when I'd heard him play it at a dance.

Jeanette, who evidently had never heard Wooden Joe cut loose, was afraid he was going to blow her roof off, he was so loud. Gene wondered if it wasn't really true, as some had reported, that Joe really was as strong as Bolden. When Jeanette was talking to Gene about his big tone after the session, George said, "Oh, he wasn't loud tonight," which was true. Lawrence said he and Jim yelled at him so much to "keep it down" that he didn't blow so loud.

I paid Wooden Joe and Burbank $15 and thanked them for coming back and making the two sides.

When Burbank arrived, he had called me aside and said if it was just a question of money he would be glad to get his trio and work for nothing and I could pay them if the records went well. I told him I would hate to ask him to do that, but thanked him for his gracious offer and assured him that I would use him again someday, with other groups.

Earlier we heard that Big Eye Louis Nelson had a hemorrhage that day, and his brother-in-law (Batiste) had come by to ask George if he could take Big Eye's place at Luthjen's at the weekend. But as we didn't know how long the brass band date would take on Saturday, and George already had a job for Sunday, he had to decline. George then told Burbank about Big Eye and Albert said he'd go by and see Mrs. Luthjen. Since he was out of a job anyway, he'd be glad to fill in for Big Eye.

While Wooden Joe was playing, Bunk had sat listening to a few numbers and seemed raring to go, probably to show what he could do after all the guests. So, after a short break, we got going again.

BUNK JOHNSON'S BAND

George Lewis's home, 827 St. Philip Street, New Orleans.
Thursday, May 17, 1945 (Approx. 9.00–11.00 pm)

Bunk Johnson (tpt); George Lewis (clt); Jim Robinson (tbn); Lawrence Marrero (bjo); Alcide "Slow Drag" Pavageau (sbs); Baby Dodds (dms)

887	Lady Be Good	Purist 8, Dan: VC-4018, VC-7020, NoLa: LP 6, NoLa: TC 006, Jz Con: JJC.78, AMCD-12
888	Old Grey Bonnet	Dan: VC-4018, VC-7020, Jz Con: JJC.78, AMCD-12
889	Ballin' the Jack	Unissued
890	Indiana	AMCD-15
891	The Waltz You Saved for Me	AMCD-15
892	When You and I Were Young Maggie	AMCD-15

Bill Russell: Several times I'd asked Bunk and the others what they wanted to play and a few times they suggested things. But Bunk would usually say, "Anything you want. It makes no difference to me." So this time I asked for *Lady Be Good*, which Bunk had been featuring since Boston. Everybody hit it hard and it seemed to be a wonderful performance. Next, Jeanette asked for *Put on your Old Grey Bonnet*. They didn't need to try over a chorus, or intro, but stomped it right off. I told Jeanette she sure knew how to pick them.

About that time, George's right ear gave out. Bunk had been blowing in it all week and George said he couldn't hear anything in it, so he moved over in front of Lawrence and the bass drum, and more or less faced Bunk. Then Bunk complained that Jim had been blowing in his ear drum, so they all shuffled around a little, with Bunk facing the microphone more.

Someone, maybe Gene, suggested *Ballin' the Jack*, and I made one more attempt to get Bunk to sing, but he quickly waved aside my request and said Baby was the band's singer. The performance wasn't so hot anyway.

It was after 10 pm and most of the guys had been there since 4 o'clock, so I knew we had to quit soon and had a chance for only a couple more numbers. It seemed no one knew *Michigan Water* except Baby, who at least knew some of the words. Bunk also acted like he'd never heard that it was a Tony Jackson tune. So I asked about *Take it Away*, which they either didn't want to play or didn't know so well.

I asked Bunk if he wanted to play *Stardust*, as his lip seemed to be in very good shape. He made an excuse to go with me into the kitchen. He then explained, so the others couldn't hear, that *Stardust* required the right, and varied harmonies, and it was a number that they'd have to work out, and perhaps even use a piano. After hearing some of Drag's and Lawrence's work on a few numbers that week, I knew Bunk was right, so I dropped the idea in a hurry.

It was too late to try *Sunflower Rag*, so I asked them to try *Indiana*, which I figured out couldn't miss. However, somehow it didn't turn out as good as other performances I'd heard Bunk give.

So it looked like we had one more request before the band "dissolved." It was a tough choice with a dozen good tunes left on my list, but I'd got a bunch of fine takes already that night, so I couldn't complain. I decided to gamble on a novelty, which would be nice to have even if it didn't come off. So I went over and asked Bunk, "How about playing a waltz like you did at the dance the other evening?" (Pointe à la Hache – May 12). I suggested a first-half waltz and then stomp off the last half. Baby grunted that he hadn't played a waltz in a long time. I mentioned *The Waltz You Saved for Me* and, after talking it over, they decided that no half-way signal was necessary. It went quite well, although Gene thought the change to the fox-trot wasn't very smooth. The thing that worried me most was George's out-of-tune clarinet. All week he'd been using the old wooden one, which must have been a good deal lower than the metal one he'd used for the past two years. The flatness was noticeable much of the time, especially on the slow waltz, where he'd tried to play accompanying figures around and above Bunk's lead.

I was ready to call it a night, but then the guys didn't seem to want to quit and Bunk wanted to play *When You and I Were Young Maggie*. So I said, "Let's cut one more and quit," as it was then close to 11 pm. It went fine, and after the "ear" business it seemed to cheer them up, as we played it back while they packed up.

Before they left, I reminded them of the brass band date in George's back yard the next day. Jeanette's brother-in-law had been chopping down the grass and weeds and cleaning up the yard all Thursday in preparation for the event.

Before the last few numbers, I went in and made a speech about how all the guys may think I sounded like a crook, but I'd been too busy that day to go to the bank and could they wait until the next day for that night's payment. They all yelled, "Oh, forget it," and "That's okay." My real motive was to ensure that Bunk would be there for his brass band date.

Earlier in the week I'd talked with Bunk about the brass band and asked him what instrumentation he wanted to use. Some of the bands, like the Eureka, always had three trumpets, and the Union had a rule that you had to use a minium of ten players. The bands would often use three trumpets, two trombones, two saxes, bass and snare drum, and sousaphone – usually not a clarinet any more. Bunk felt that saxophones had no place in a New Orleans band. When I asked him about saxophones, he felt insulted. He didn't know I was really kidding.

We'd already agreed that most of Bunk's regular band would be used, but we needed a few extra men. Bunk said George would know best who to get on baritone and alto horn and tuba. He also refused to name a second trumpet, but said anybody we wanted would be okay so long as they were good. When George and I asked if Shots would be okay, he said yes, or anyone else. George said that Shots was about the only one who could play a good second trumpet part. Bunk mentioned if we got Shots that they could trade around, playing lead and second trumpet.

For baritone horn George had said there was only one good player available: he was Adolphe Alexander, who had recently got out of the navy. He was playing sax at the Budweiser Dance Hall, which was a tough job with long hours, but he thought he could get a substitute for the afternoon. When I saw him he said he only had a small baritone horn but he could probably borrow a larger one for the record date. George also suggested "Old Man" Barbarin [Paul's father] for alto horn. George said Barbarin couldn't march anymore but thought he was still the best in the city.

Joe Howard and Jim Little had been suggested for tuba. George felt that Jim Little played too much "trumpet" on the tuba and most of the guys seemed to think "Red" Clark would be best. When I went around to see him he was out working, but his wife let me into their one-room apartment at the back of Dryades. It was a terrible place and she apologized a lot for it, but said it was all they could find to live in the past two or three years. She said he used to play trombone with the Eureka and used to do some dance work, but didn't like "jazz." I told her about the date and she gave me his phone number. When I later spoke with him, he said he'd be glad to make the date.

I asked Bunk if he wanted to use two or three trumpets. "No," he said, "We don't need three trumpets" (he used to play parades where he was the only trumpet in his younger days).

He said, "If you have three trumpets, two of them are always up and one is down." I thought he meant two played up high and one played low. But what he meant was, when one is down, he's loafing, and two are up playing. I'd been prepared to book twelve or thirteen musicians if Bunk wanted them, but he said he only needed nine men. Baby Dodds said that they "only needed to use eight or nine pieces in the old days – although some of the more organized bands, like the Excelsior, often used twelve pieces." Jelly used to say: "Those eight or nine men used to make more noise than a forty-piece band." Baby had also said, "When those bands of only nine men began to play, you'd wonder how in the world a nine-piece band could play the music those fellows played. If we would have a larger band, someone was going to loaf."

After the session on the Thursday, Bunk decided he wanted some Chinese food and rice. He had got there too late to eat that day and was probably pretty hungry. We thought we'd better stick with him and not let him out of our sight, so the three of us walked up Dauphine talking about the session and Wooden Joe and Joe Petit. Gene said how he'd gone to hear Lawrence Toca on Sunday night and repeated George's story that Toca played something like Buddy Petit. Bunk said, "I never heard Toca, but I know he's not as good as Buddy." The way he said it left no doubt that Buddy was something special.

We soon passed a cafe that advertised "Musicians' and Entertainers' Headquarters," and Bunk and Gene made some remark about that. Evidently it wasn't one of Bunk's hangouts and he didn't seem interested in going inside. It catered for the Bourbon Street colored entertainers and there was jukebox music coming out of the place.

We marched up Bienville, where the Chinese restaurant was, and looked in. It was for both colored and white, but it had the well-known segregation partition. There were no real secluded booths, as in some Chinese restaurants, or we would have gone in the colored side. Across the street was another restaurant, but it was for coloured only, so we knew we couldn't be served there. Bunk stood on the corner a few minutes, looking and making appropriate comments on how ridiculous the situation was.

We crossed the street and walked downtown a block. There was another colored place, but it was mainly a saloon. We decided to look for a hamburger stand, or anything, on the next corner.

At the next corner we were back at the "Entertainers' Headquarters," so we had no choice but to go in. The back part was a little lunch room where five or six stools lined the lunch counter. Bunk and Gene ordered some fried bologna and I got cheese, all on toasted buns.

It was about 1 am and we were only a couple of blocks from the Pig Pen on Burgundy Street.[33] Shots was working there with Picou, in a four-piece band. We stood outside for a minute but we could hear no music. As it was a white-only club, they elected me to go in and negotiate Bunk's entry. I walked in through the bar room and into the club room, where the band was sitting on a small bandstand, drinking. Shots and Picou recognized me as I walked towards the stand in the almost empty room. I asked Picou if there was any way in which Bunk could get in and hear them. Picou said, "Sure, just come down to the side door down there." I hurried over and pushed open the side door and yelled at Bunk and Gene, who were down about ten feet away, talking, and didn't even see me at first. We all went back in and they all seemed to be glad to see Bunk. Picou had just quit Kid Rena at the the Budweiser. The girl pianist, Sadie Crosby, was the leader and they introduced her to Bunk. He knew the drummer Charlie Sylvester, who was from Bunk's territory in the Irish Channel. Charlie said Bunk had taught him and his brother. Bunk had to sit on the stand behind Shots, as Gene and I stood in front of the band. Most of the time they talked and drank, but about every ten or fifteen minutes they'd play one or two pieces, usually requests for a late pop tune like *Tea for Two*, *Honeysuckle Rose* or *This Heart of Mine*. Occasionally, one of the girls, or even a customer, would get up and sing. The girls all hung around waiting for customers and another four or five had customers all lined up – a soldier and sailor or two, and a couple of civilians.

Before long the boss came in and gave the band a packet of cigarettes each, and Bunk asked me for some change so he could buy a carton of Kool. Sadie said the boss was pretty good and let them finish at 2.30 am if business was slow.

Soon Bunk was half asleep, and occasionally sound asleep, in his chair behind Shots. Every few minutes, Sadie would collect a few dimes from each of the guys and empty the kitty, and come back with a half-pint bottle (marked rum), a couple of cakes and a beer or two for Sylvester. Then they all filled their glasses. Bunk didn't seem too interested in drinking, although he grabbed a quick one now and then. Gene asked if the green-colored liquor really was rum and Picou said no, they only used that bottle at the bar to get it filled with whiskey.

Ricard Alexis came by and invited Bunk and all of us over to the Famous Door where he was playing. George had warned me to keep Bunk away from Alexis, as he'd get Bunk drunk. However, he seemed a nice guy, very friendly and polite, so I said we hadn't time that night, but promised him I'd try to go over before I left town.

We had hopes of getting Bunk home about 2 am. Gene was so tired and sleepy he could hardly stay awake. But they said the floor show would be on in a few minutes and we ought to stay for that. Bunk had acted sleepy too, as if he wanted to go home or perhaps stop by Alexis's place, so we were trying to get him out. But the girls were already going to the dressing room and Jackie, their MC, had made her announcement over the PA speaker, so Gene and I reluctantly took a table in the corner near the band for the floor-show.

They turned off the neon lights around the edge of the room and switched on a small spotlight. The show featured a couple of singers and two fake striptease dancers and, thankfully, was soon over. Gene was really tired by now and wanted to go home, but Sadie kept insisting that we and Bunk should stay.

When the job finished about 3.30 am we tried to get Bunk to come home with us, but he said Sadie had invited him to a party at her house and he felt he ought to go. I reminded Bunk and Shots that they had a recording date at 3 pm that day and gave Bunk quite a lecture about being in shape for it. I said I hoped he wouldn't come in all tired, like he did on Tuesday night, when he fell asleep after the first number, and the effect it had on the other guys. Bunk acted like he wasn't listening to my spiel, but the next day Gene thought that it might have done some good. Gene was practically asleep and Alexis came back and offered to drive us home, while everyone else piled into Picou's car to go to Sadie's party. Gene and I figured that Bunk wouldn't show up later that day and talked over the possibility that we would need to get another trumpet player. Shots had not gone to the party so we figured he would show up and we wondered if we should get "Fernandez" or maybe Wooden Joe. We didn't get to bed until about 5 am, and we later learned that Bunk didn't get in until about 7.30 that morning.

I got up about 10.30 am and went uptown to get some bills changed. I hurried back to talk to George about getting another trumpet player. But, lo and behold, when I got back about 12.30, there was Bunk out in the back yard washing out his horn. He was running water through it and proceeding to get it all cleaned, oiled and shined up so he could show off good when the band got there. He couldn't have had more than four hours' sleep and said he'd been up early to phone his step-daughter Emily Mae, who was attending Xavier University. She was coming over to see the session and he wanted to be ready for her.

It seemed to make a lot of sense to try and record the brass band out of doors. George's back yard wasn't that big, but big enough for the purpose. After we'd eaten, we took a few more chairs out in the yard and cleared the long bench. We tried to get the clothes lines up higher and out of the way. Then I got a step ladder and clamped the microphone onto it.

Lawrence must have taken the afternoon off and brought down his bass drum and cymbal before 2 pm. Mr. Barbarin was one of the first to arrive, and soon they were all there, except Jim, who came about ten minutes after the others but got there about one minute after 3 pm. Bunk talked to some of the fellows, mostly in the house, and we started to take pictures of groups. I believe the drums were the first, then the alto and baritone horns, etc, finally the trumpets and George, then the whole band. We had to do a lot of trading and borrowing of caps for the small group pictures, in order to get some of them to match. The drawing I made at the time is about how they lined up at the start [see opposite page].

BUNK'S BRASS BAND

Back yard of George Lewis's home, 827 St. Philip Street, New Orleans.
Friday, May 18, 1945 (3.15–7.30 pm)

Bunk Johnson, "Kid Shots" Madison (tpt); Jim Robinson (tbn); George Lewis (E-flat clt); Isidore Barbarin (alto horn); Adolphe "Tats" Alexander Jr. (baritone horn); Joseph "Red" Clark (sousaphone); Lawrence Marrero (bs dm); Baby Dodds (sn dm)

893	When the Saints Go Marching In	Dan: VC-4019, VB-1003, VC-7023, AMCD-17
894	When the Saints Go Marching In	AM 102, AM LP 643, Dixie LP 107, Stv: SLP 202, Dan: VC-4009, VB-1003, VC-7011, Murray & Hill 927942, AMCD-6
895	Just a Closer Walk with Thee	Dan: VC-4019, VC-7023
896	Just a Closer Walk with Thee	AM LP 638, Stv: SLP 202, Dan: VC-4009, VC-7011, AMCD-6
897	Didn't He Ramble	Dan: VC-4019, VB 1004, VC-7023
898	Didn't He Ramble	AM 103, Dixie LP 107, F'ws: FP 57, FJ 2803, SLP 202, Col: CL 2104, C3L-30, JC3L-30, CBS: BPG 62234, Dan: VC-4009, VC-7011, Col (J): SL 1199C, Pogo Plattan 101, AMCD-6
899	Just a Little While to Stay Here	Dan: VC-4019, VC-7023, AMCD-17
900	Just a Little While to Stay Here	AM 101 (cut), AM LP 643, Dixie LP 107, Stv: SLP 202, SLP 203, Dan: VC-4009, VC-7011, AMCD-6
901	Nearer my God to Thee	Dan: VC-4019, VC-7023, AMCD-17
902	Nearer my God to Thee	AM 102, AM LP 643 (cut), Baby Dodds 1, Dixie LP 107, Stv: SLP 202, Dan: VC-4009, VC-7011, AMCD-6
903	In Gloryland	AM 101, Baby Dodds 1, Dixie LP 107, Stv: SLP 202, Dan: VC-4009, VB-1004, VC-7011, AMCD-6
904	St. Louis Blues	Dan: VC-4019, VC-7023, AMCD-6
905	St. Louis Blues	Dan: VC-4019, VC-7023
906	Maryland, my Maryland	Dan: VC-4019, VC-7023, AMCD-17
907	Bye and Bye	Dan: VC-4019, VB-1004, VC-7023, AMCD-6
908	Maryland, my Maryland	Dan: VC-4019, VB-1004, VC-7023, AMCD-6
909	Tell Me your Dreams	AM 103, Baby Dodds 1, Dixie LP 107, Stv: SLP 202, Dan: VC-4009, VB 1004, VC-7011, AMCD-6
909a	Happy Birthday to You	Dan: VC-4019, Dan VC-7023, AMCD-6

Note: On AM 102, *Saint's Go Marching On* is printed on the label and *When The Saints Go Marching In* is printed in the booklet accompanying the album containing the three 78s. All subsequent reissues carried the latter title.

It has often been suggested that AM 102 (*Nearer my God to Thee*) may have used master 901. Although a few bars of the opening drum beats are missing on AM 102, this is undoubtedly master 902.

Bye and Bye (master 907) was intended for Baby Dodds No.4, which never appeared.

Happy Birthday to You (master 909a) was recorded for Gene Williams's birthday.

The session was "dedicated to the memory of Hoyte D. Kline." [34]

Bill Russell: Finally everything was set and I asked if they'd try something so I could make a test. Bunk, or someone, picked *When the Saints Go Marching In*. I experimented with the settings, as it seemed to be overcut. I moved the step ladder back and they tried it again. It went well and lasted about 2 minutes 20 seconds, but at that time I had never any intention of using that number for release.

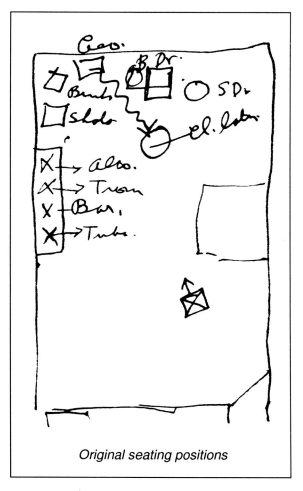

Original seating positions

The balance of the band seemed pretty good just as they were sitting, but possibly George's clarinet didn't come through so good, or he was having trouble getting adjusted to it. Later he volunteered the information (when someone else was discussing changing instruments and forgetting for a minute what they were playing) that, when he started out that day, he didn't feel at home on the E-flat clarinet. He hadn't played it since the Sunday before and said during the first few numbers he almost forgot which clarinet he was playing and which key to play in, etc. So we had him move out a little from in-back of the trumpets and in front of the bass drum.

I then asked if they'd try a real funeral march, with the drums muffled, and play just as they do at funerals, with roll off and everything. Baby had been wondering if he'd remember how all the parade beats go, not having played a funeral for twenty-five years.

I asked if they could play *Flee as a Bird* and, surprisingly, a couple of guys acted almost as though they'd never heard of it. I believe Shots was one who didn't know it and I know Clark was the other. Clark explained he wasn't so good at "faking." About that time, he slipped about twenty band cards out of his pocket, obviously some of the Eureka parts. I was too busy to look at them to see if they were complete sets or just tuba parts. When I told him I had some band parts to *Flee as a Bird* and other funeral marches, he wanted to see them. So thinking there might be a possibility of some of them using the *Flee as a Bird* parts, which I wanted very badly to record, I went in the front room and dug out my Robichaux band music from under the chest of drawers.

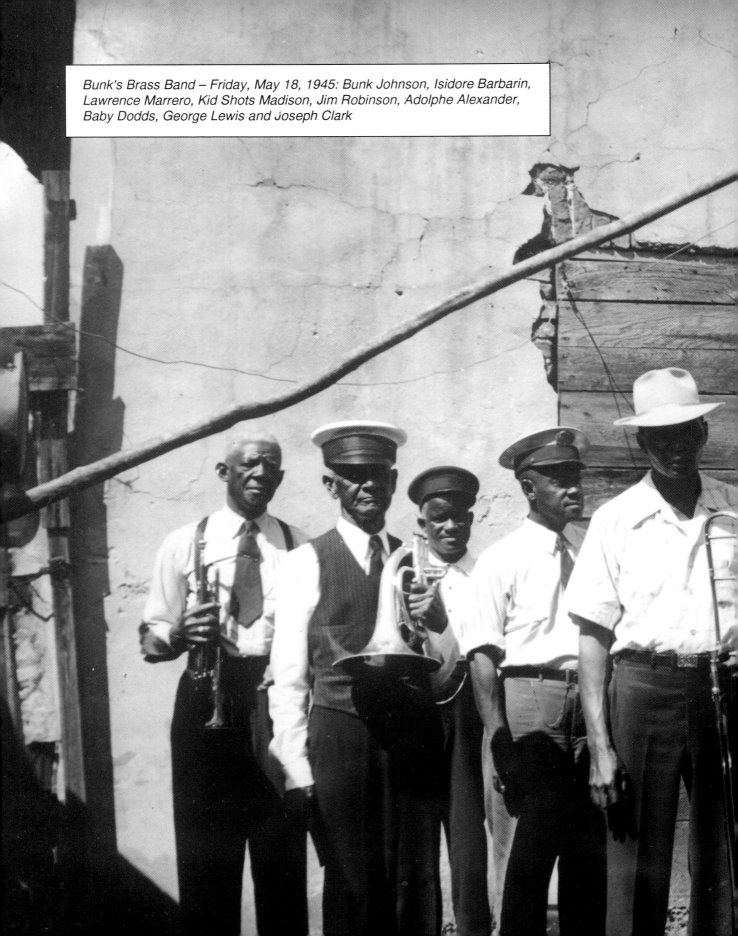

Bunk's Brass Band – Friday, May 18, 1945: Bunk Johnson, Isidore Barbarin, Lawrence Marrero, Kid Shots Madison, Jim Robinson, Adolphe Alexander, Baby Dodds, George Lewis and Joseph Clark

We looked over them in the kitchen, but there were only about half a dozen parts to *Flee as a Bird* – not the right ones anyway. I quickly realized that none of the written parts could be used and that we'd never get anything at all recorded if we got Bunk teaching them all to read the parts. So as soon as possible I put the music away and asked if they'd just play any funeral march. George or someone suggested *Just a Closer Walk with Thee*.

Baby then threw off his snares and started with a slow muffled dead march, Lawrence came in with his bass drum and the whole band wailed away at a very draggy tempo. It was the most peculiar band music I'd ever heard. They played in a rather full and, perhaps at times, strange harmony. The E-flat clarinet wailed and stood out quite prominently. At the end of phrases only the snare drum and E-flat alto horn continued a slow rhythmic figure. That feature of the performance sounded a little thin to me and later, when I checked with George and others to see if the record sounded exactly like a real funeral, they said that the performance, alto, rhythm, etc, were all "just right."

For this number and the rest of the session, I cut onto 12" blanks. The first take of *Closer Walk* took about 4 minutes, but the performance was slow and I doubted that I could get a 10" record out of it. I didn't ask them to cut it short and let them run 4 minutes on the second take.

I knew we'd better stick to old, familiar tunes after the *Flee as a Bird* episode and they were all glad to try *Didn't He Ramble*, which they played in 6/8 time. The first take ran 4 minutes and I decided that we would be better to stick to a 10" side on that tune. I'd hoped everything could be done on 10" in order to sell the brass band idea at all.

About this time Gene suggested reshuffling the band, moving the tuba back and the trumpets more to the front [see right]. Bunk seemed to want to stay where he was and said the band, and the playback, sounded okay and had plenty of lead. So we just moved the sousaphone forward and the mike back a little more, and shaded it so the sun wouldn't hit it so much.

It was very hot: George would run for shade after each number and Baby did his best to shade himself with his handkerchief over his head. I got Bunk and Shots to move around and face the microphone a little more and later on Clark faced his bell more towards the

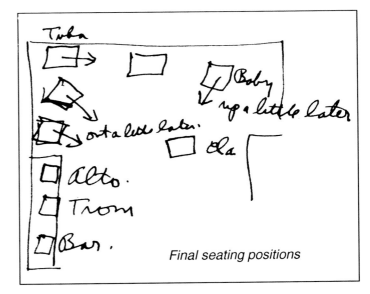

Final seating positions

microphone. I wondered if there was enough snare drum and kept moving Baby up and over, so he wouldn't seem to be behind the toilet as we kept moving the microphone back. But Baby kept saying how his part sounded okay on the playbacks. Gene thought the bass drum was too loud and caused some distortion and possible overcutting. But I wanted to be sure and have plenty of bass drum in it and the band sounded fine that way. As the sousaphone and baritone were not very prominent, I didn't mind hearing a little extra bass drum.

Next I thought a faster hymn would go well and I took my list of possible tunes out into the yard to talk it over. Someone didn't know George's tune *Lead Me Saviour* (Bunk had mentioned this a few days before also) and no one at all seemed to know Bunk's suggestion of

Come Ye Disconsolate. So I told them to pick something. George, or maybe a couple of the other guys, suggested *Just a Little While to Stay Here.* This time Bunk spoke up and said he didn't think he knew the tune. I was quite sure he'd heard George's record of it, but probably he had never played it. When I acted like that tune was out, Bunk began saying, "Oh, I'm only <u>one</u> in the band. If all the others say that they know it . . ." At first I wasn't quite sure just how he meant it. Perhaps he was saying, "Oh that's alright to play a tune I don't know. I'm just the leader. I don't count." But I soon decided he really meant that it was alright and that he could fake his part okay. In any case, we had to try *something.* I asked him if he'd try it anyway, and reminded him that after the first chorus he'd know the tune better than any of the others.

Shots took the lead to start with. It ran a little long at 3 minutes 22 seconds. On the second take, Baby started as usual with a couple of rolls for Lawrence to come in, but nothing happened. Baby gave him a dirty look and started on his taps again, sounding as though he was really mad and beating much louder. This time Lawrence came in okay and the band got going good.

At first I'd fade out the drums at the end gradually, but after a few masters I decided to leave the drums up fairly full and give a quick fade out and wait until the final masters were dubbed ·before worrying about proper fade outs. I usually added a little volume after the last band notes so the drums could be heard clearly. I also had the volume up a little higher than normal at the start, until the bass drum came in.

Then I asked if they would try another funeral march, and they picked *Nearer my God to Thee.* The first take was good, but we ran again and got a fine 3 minutes 5 seconds take to the end of the band, or 3 minutes 23 seconds to end the snare drum taps.

Shots took the lead in *Gloryland,* with Bunk playing second. This may have been one of the other tunes that Bunk hadn't played. It went fine first time, so we didn't try another take.

Someone in the band decided that *St. Louis Blues* was next. It almost looked like they were picking the tunes we had recorded last year. Although we had picked six tunes that I had recorded in 1943 and 1944, during the week we had played sixteen tunes that I had already recorded since 1942.

The parade bands evidently liked to swing *St. Louis Blues* in march tempo, but I was afraid that some of the dance band fans wouldn't like a brass band version as well as AM 252. But it was a very good performance. The full brass, E-flat clarinet and bass drum gave it quite a different sound. Towards the end, Shots came in with some fine trumpet work, then Bunk came in and finished up with some good high-note work. I faintly remember that Lawrence objected to the tempo of the first take, so we tried it again with a faster tempo. The performance was a different style. Shots and Bunk were featured in about the same order, but their parts (especially Bunk's) were entirely different.

Baby had been talking about *My Maryland* all week and requesting it, so we tried it. Gene thought that Bunk's "bugle" solos were a little weak (before Shots came in at the end) and he thought Bunk should have left it to Shots to play them. After the session Baby said he'd enjoyed *My Maryland,* but thought that last year's band version was better. The first take went a little long; when Gene gave the finishing signal, only the trumpets seemed to get it and the others kept going. However, it gives a fine varied effect (like a soft trio section) when you hear the strong lead tones supported by the low brasses.

The previous Sunday, all the parade bands had used *Bye and Bye.* This seemed to be a favorite of all the parade bands then. Before we started, Joe Clark asked how much longer we would be playing. It was about 6.45 and he spoke about a job he had that evening. Then Tats and Shots mentioned about their jobs. Just then, Abby came into the yard asking for his drums soon for his night's job. It wasn't really a case of mutiny as they had all worked pretty hard. But even though they'd been in the hot sun, we hadn't been there as long as some of the other evenings, so I told Joe Clark we'd quit as soon as we'd run through a couple more tunes and we wouldn't have to fool around trying them first. I said we ought to be through in half an hour, or by 7.30 at the latest. He seemed a little peeved and said he'd have to go and phone his people and tell them he'd be late. He had a job driving for some white folks every night.

While Clark was gone, I talked to the other fellows. Someone said Tats had to go home to get his sax to take to his job at Budweiser. But when I talked to him, he said it was okay as he had his sax with him. I asked Shots again what time his job started. The previous day he had said 9 pm, but now added that he'd like to go home and eat first, if he could. I told him we could get some steak for him if they'd wait a little longer. I then assured Abby that I'd personally carry his drums around to his job and I guaranteed to have them there by 8 pm.

At about 4.30 pm, Bunk's daughter and a school friend from Xavier University arrived. They came in at the side gate between numbers. I was busy at the time and didn't see them. Gene had met Emily Mae in New Iberia in 1942, but I had not seen her, as when I visited Bunk last year she was in Mississippi or Alabama, taking a summer course in physical culture. When I did see them I thought they were some of Baby's folks. Then Bunk introduced the two girls to me, saying, "Meet Miss Johnson" (or probably Miss Thomas). I had no idea who they were until ten minutes later Gene said something about Bunk's daughter. I woke up then and hurried over to talk to her and her friend and explain that I'd just realized who she was. She said she would only be in New Orleans for about a week or so, as their school would be finishing for the summer. I then explained to Bunk that I hadn't realized who Emily Mae was.

NEW ORLEANS PARADE

An Album of Six Marches by

BUNK JOHNSON'S
BRASS BAND

101—In Gloryland
    Just A Little While To Stay Here

102—Nearer My God To Thee
    When the Saints Go Marching In

103—Tell Me Your Dreams
    Didn't He Ramble

Left: the four-page booklet that accompanied the three 78 records in Bunk's Brass Band album

Below: the album's gummed label and record labels

NEW ORLEANS PARADE

Six Marches by

BUNK JOHNSON'S BRASS BAND

AMERICAN MUSIC RECORDS
647 MEANS AVE.
PITTSBURGH 2, PA.

83

After Emily Mae had been there for about half an hour, Bunk came over to me and asked if he could have some of his money, to give to her. I went into the front room and got Bunk his $60 from under the scarf on top of the chest of drawers. Jeanette had heard Emily Mae say she needed $50 to pay back her friend a debt, so I hoped Bunk had given her $50 out of his $60. Later the girls asked Gene who it was I kept calling Baby. Whenever we were ready to start I'd yell, "Okay, Baby, we're ready," or "It's cutting, Baby."

There was quite a crowd who had come in to hear the band. Picou had said he would drop by, but he never made it. Jeanette's brother-in-law (the singer from the previous day, "Noon" Johnson), as well as Abby and some other people I didn't know, sat on the bench boxes and chairs near the doorway. Several times I had to caution them to keep quiet, especially at the end of pieces, but some of their talk got on the records.

We came very near getting a wonderful sound effect near the end of one piece, possibly the *Tell Me Your Dreams and I'll Tell You Mine*. The title didn't sound so promising, but it was getting near the quitting time of 7.30. I checked it with Bunk to make sure it was okay with him and then told them, "Okay, go ahead." It turned out to be a fine performance, and Clark was bearing down a little more on his sousaphone. I'd often expressed doubts during the session that he wasn't loud enough.

As I was ready to put the machine away I could tell the guys had something up their sleeve, and George came running in to ask if I had another blank, as there was something they wanted to try. Before I could get the blank on the turntable, they started on *Happy Birthday to You*. It was Gene's birthday. George and Jeanette had known it, but not me. The band stood in a sort of circle in the middle of the yard and played. When they saw that I didn't get it, they played it over again, so I could record it. For the last couple of numbers we had moved the microphone back all the way, and had it clamped on the shutter of the kitchen widow. During

Eugene Williams and Bunk – New York, 1945

the last part of the song, Jeanette leaned out of the window and yelled, "Happy birthday!" She tried to get everybody to yell and sing. She almost died when she heard herself yelling on the playback. They had got Gene a big, fancy, iced birthday cake and no one was in too big a hurry to get home before they ate a piece of the cake.

Clark said he wished Remy[35] could have heard that last pop number, and hoped I could record the Eureka sometime, as they had a lot of good marches all worked up. Baby and Bunk were talking about how my machine must be pretty good to pick up a band playing out of doors that way. It seems before the session they had been very skeptical about it picking up any music out of doors.

The session had been pretty good, but I wished we could have got down some of the better funeral marches. It was interesting to see how Shots and Bunk often wanted the other to play lead, as they both preferred to play the second trumpet part.

After the session, Shots said he was tired. He said he didn't want to play again that night, so he asked Bunk if he would like to take his place at the Pig Pen. Shots was pretty smart: he knew on Friday nights the job ran from 9 pm until 7 am the next morning. I don't know if Bunk was aware of this, and he didn't need the money, but he was keen to do it. So after recording all week and getting hardly any sleep Thursday night, he did a five-hour brass band session, then went on that night for a nine-hour job at the Pig Pen with Picou. The next night, he did a 4½ hour job with George! Bunk had a strong lip. He used to say, "If I could just play a couple of more hours, I'd be alright. My lips are just getting good and hard."

On the Saturday night I went down river near the Ship Island Canal [Violet] to hear Bunk, George, Andrew Morgan, Lawrence and Slow Drag work with Abby Williams (Kid Williams's Happy Pals).[36]

On Sunday afternoon (May 20) Baby left for Chicago on the Panama Limited. That night George had a quartet job with Slow Drag, Lawrence and Abby at the Old Loyalty Bar at Gov. Nicholls and North Rampart. We got there about 11 pm and got a table by the door.

The boss must have waived his rule ("No Stags Allowed" was painted over the door), as a few white soldiers were already in there. The place was very small (25 feet x 30 feet) with about ten tables. The band sat in a corner on a small recessed platform about six inches high. This acted like a shell and made the band sound twice as loud as normal. George's tone sounded very big. There were probably no more than a dozen people in there, but when a few people danced it made it seem crowded.

They sounded really good in there, although a couple of times Lawrence had trouble with the harmonies. Abby played so soft that we didn't really notice him.

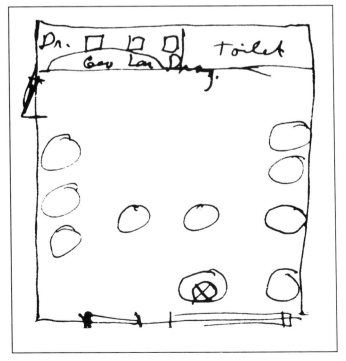

Interior of the Old Loyalty Bar

85

As we hadn't been able to get any decent trio records made on Thursday, George suggested we should record some more sides the next day.

I requested *La Marseillaise*, but George said they'd have to work that out at home. Their *Hula Lou* (which I put out as *New Orleans Hula*) was one of their very best numbers and had a real blues quality. *Over the Waves* was also played beautifully. At about 12.30 am we all walked home.

The next day (Monday), Gene and I took Bunk up to the station for him to catch the early morning train back to New Iberia. We talked about taking the band to New York and Bunk said no contract was necessary with the guys, and they'd just have to stick together if the band was going to be a success.

Before we started with the "trio" records, George insisted that I didn't need to pay him, so long as I gave Lawrence and Slow Drag something. But I said, if he recorded, then I would have to give him something.

GEORGE LEWIS'S 3-PIECE BAND

George Lewis's home, 827 St. Philip Street, New Orleans.
Monday, May 21, 1945 (7.30–10.00 pm)
George Lewis (clt); Lawrence Marrero (bjo); Alcide "Slow Drag" Pavageau (sbs)

910	Lead Me Saviour	Dan: VC-4015, VB-1003, VC-7017
911	Lead Me Saviour	Stv: SLP 127, DA LP 2/1944, Dan: VC-4005, VB-1005, VC-7012, Seven Seas: MH 3026, AMCD-4
912	Over the Waves	AM 639, Stv: SLP 201, DA LP 2/1944, Dan: VC-4004, VB-1003, VC-7007, Jz Con: JJC 102, Sup: 0 15 23972B, AMCD-4
913	Over the Waves	Dan: VB-1005, VC-4015, VC-7017, AMCD-4
914	La Marseillaise	Dan: VC-4015, VC-7017, AMCD-4
915	New Orleans Hula	Dan: VC-4015, VC-7017
916	New Orleans Hula	AM 639, Stv: SLP 201, DA LP 2/1944, Dan: VC-4004, VC-7007, Jz Con: JJC 102, AMCD-4
917	This Love of Mine	Stv: SLP 201, Dan: VC-4004, VB-1005, VC-7007, Jz Con: JJC 102, AMCD-4
918	St. Philip Street Breakdown	AM 639, Stv: SLP 201, DA LP 2/1944, Dan: VC-4004, VC-7007, Jz Con: JJC 102, AMCD-4
919	Old Rugged Cross	Stv: SLP 127, Dan: VC-4005, VB-1005, VC-7012, Seven Seas: MH 3026, AMCD-4

Note: The remaining three titles on AMCD-4 are *Careless Love* (112), *Just a Little While to Stay Here* (115) and *Just a Closer Walk with Thee* (116). These are alternative takes to the issued Climax numbers of May 16, 1943. These titles were previously issued on Mosaic MD3-132.

Bill Russell: By 7.30 I had set up the recording equipment in George's kitchen. George was keen to get going and after he had yelled at Drag a few times they were ready. The first number (*Lead Me Saviour*) had been on the brass band list.

Jeanette might have suggested *Over the Waves*. She always called it "The Singing Clarinet." The number was based on an old Mexican waltz. For the World's Cotton Centennial Exposition (1884–5) in New Orleans, the famous seventy-piece Mexican Cavalry Band used it as their theme song when they played concerts at the Mexican Pavillion every day. The number had been published, in Mexico, as *Sobre Las Olas* by Junentino Rosas. During the World's Industrial and Cotton Centennial Exposition, Hart's piano and music store on Canal Street published over eighty Mexican compositions and titled this one *Over the Waves*. (Grunewalds and Werleins also published some Mexican music with English titles.) In the 1950s it also became a hit as *The Loveliest Night of the Year*.

Next they tried *La Marseillaise*, which they had rehearsed while Gene and I were at Jim's, but it didn't seem to go so well so we didn't repeat it. The *Hula* was much better, and when I asked George if that was the same as they'd played at the Climax rehearsal (at Ed Mosley's house in 1943), when they put the *Farewell to Thee* quote in, he said, "Yes." When he played it this time, he put the *Farewell to Thee* quote in again.

A little before 10 o'clock we were all through, and, although no one expected to be paid, I gave each of them $10 and promised that if any of the sides were released I would pay them more. Jeanette never did get the record of her blues. The week before, she insisted she was going to sing, but just wanted George, Baby, Lawrence and Drag to accompany her.

The next day I caught the 8.45 am train to New Iberia to stay with Bunk for a couple of days before returning to Pittsburgh.

Jeanette Lewis and Shirley (1943)

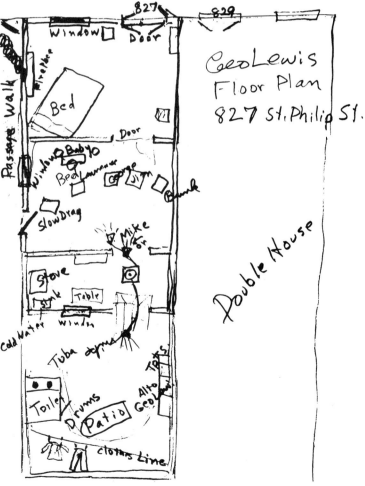

Plan of George Lewis's house showing where the various recordings where made

LOS ANGELES, 1946

Bill Russell: Dink Johnson's real name was Oliver ("Ollie") Johnson, though no one ever called him that. He was the youngest of five or six brothers, three of whom became musicians. The bass player, Bill Johnson was the oldest brother and his sister "married" Jelly Roll Morton.[37] I knew Dink had been the drummer with the Original Creole Band and the clarinetist on Kid Ory's Sunshine records, but I didn't know he was also a pianist until Bill Colburn told me.

When Jelly moved out to Los Angeles in November 1940 (he died there the following July), Bill took the next bus down from San Francisco to see Jelly, who was staying with Dink and his wife Stella. At first Bill didn't know who Dink was, except that he was probably related to Jelly in some way. Dink would kid Jelly that he couldn't play any of those fast pieces that Art Tatum or Teddy Wilson could play. This would make Jelly really mad. Jelly would shout, "I can play you something those guys can't play," and he'd play *Finger Breaker* (that was Jelly's title – Dave Stuart called it *Finger Buster* when he put out the record). One day, after Jelly had been talking all day and telling Bill how good he was, Dink sat listening and said nothing. When Bill was leaving, Dink saw him to the door and said, "Don't you believe all that bullshit he's been giving you. I can play better piano than he can, any day!" Jelly laughed; he thought that was the funniest thing. Jelly had taught Dink some pieces and helped him with his playing. Dink had a wonderful beat, but he was no Jelly. Dink gave Bill a business card which advertised "Dink's Place," which he passed on to me.

Dink behind the counter at "Dink's Place"

88

Dink's wife Stella had recently got religion and she was having a tough time with Dink's drinking. When he got drunk she'd get mad at him and call the police to have him locked up! He would write to me, saying, "I'm all tanked up," meaning he was in jail again, and he would put as his address "Tank 6," or whatever jail he was in at the time.

He seemed to have spent a good part of his life getting in and out of trouble, and usually a girl was involved. He once told me of a fight he had in a nightclub. This guy (as Dink insisted) mistook him for his wife's lover, and started throwing bottles at Dink. As he was trying to escape between two cars he fell and broke his leg, but, still dodging the bottles, Dink got to his feet and grabbed the man and held a knife to his neck. Then the guy's wife threw a bottle at Dink, but it missed him and it hit her husband in the face, breaking into pieces. When Dink finally got to hospital the doctors wanted to amputate his leg, but Dink refused.

There was also an incident in Mexico when some guys grabbed him and (fearing that they were bandits) he took a swing at them. They were really soldiers and they came at him with a bayonet that almost killed him. When the police got him he had to buy them all a drink to stay out of jail, and he spent the next six months playing at that saloon to pay off the debt

He always claimed that there was some divine providence looking out for him, or he'd have been killed many times. For this reason, he would never have a spiritual on the jukebox in his cafe. When I saw him in 1947, his left-hand knuckles were busted after he'd shielded his eyes to stop a beer bottle. Dink had then shot the guy in the leg and he had to be bailed out of jail by one of his brothers.

When I went to Los Angeles in March 1946, Dink still had his little restaurant with a bar. It was called "Dink's Place," otherwise known as "Musicians Cafe" (4229 Avalon Blvd). It was situated right next to the minor league ball park, Wrigley Field. He did most of his business after ball games, when people would flock in there to get a drink. He only had a license to sell beer and wine, so he used to bootleg whiskey in a room at the back. While I was there in 1947, his drinks license was due to be suspended for fifteen days. For some reason this license was in Bill Johnson's name. He once told me that he'd "always lived outside of the law," as he never had much time for the law. In the back room he had a little kitchen. One day he was showing me how it was set up when, all of a sudden, he had a gun in his hand. He used to keep it in a pan hanging on the wall. He had a whole row of pans hanging, but he knew which one contained the loaded gun, in case of trouble. He thought the police would never think to look there if he was raided.

I helped him buy a piano for $50. He wanted it because it had a very high keyboard which came to about the middle of his chest." [38]

DINK'S GOOD TIME MUSIC
Unknown studio, Los Angeles.
Saturday, March 16, 1946

Dink Johnson (pno, vcl); "Louis Gonzales" (Bud Scott, gtr); "Jose Mendoza" (Ed Garland, sbs)

Tracks cut onto two 16" red aluminium Audiodiscs at 33$\frac{1}{3}$ rpm, outside start — 85 line per inch.

Master disc 1, side 1 (AM master numbers)

1–1	Stomp de Lowdown	920	Unissued
1–2	Stomp de Lowdown	921	Dan: VC-4021, VC-7025
1–3	Stomp de Lowdown	922	Unissued
1–4	Stomp de Lowdown	923	Unissued

| 1–5 Stomp de Lowdown | 924 | Dan: VC-4021, VC-7025 |
| 1–6 Stomp de Lowdown | 925 | AM 515 (a & b), Stv: SEP 390, Dan: VC-4021, VC-7025, AMCD-11 |

Master disc 1, side 2
2–1 "Blues"

| (issued as *So Dif'rent Blues*) | 926 | AM 515 (a), AM 516, Stv: SEP 390, Dan: VC-4021, VC-7025, AMCD-11 |

Master disc 2, side 1

| 3–1 Grace and Beauty | 927 | AM 515 (b), Dan: VC-4021, VC-7025, AMCD-11 |
| 3–2 Grace and Beauty | — | Unissued |

Master disc 2, side 2

| 4–1 Take your Time | 928 | AM 516, Stv: SEP 390, Dan: VC-4021, VC-7025, AMCD-11 |

Bill Russell: I thought of just recording some piano solos, but Dink wanted to record with a bass and guitar. So I thought of the best rhythm section in Los Angeles – Bud Scott and Ed Garland from the Ory band. Dink wasn't in the Union, and while Bud Scott wanted to do it he was afraid of what the Union might say. Montudi didn't care about what the Union might think, as he was an executive in the Union, so he figured they couldn't touch him. In order to protect Bud and Tudi, if I was asked, I always gave a couple of Mexican names.[39] I hired a studio and the session was through in about three hours.

New York, 1946

Bill Russell: The first time I saw Don Ewell was when he sat in with Bunk's band for the final set at the Stuyvesant Casino on Bunk's birthday (Thursday, December 27, 1945). At that time a Yugoslavian organization [American Committee for Yugoslav Relief] was working on a benefit concert at the Town Hall (January 1, 1946), with Bunk's band, Clarence Williams, Albert Nicholas, Red Allen, Sister Ernestine Washington and others. Orson Welles was going to be the MC and Don also had a feature spot on the program. That Thursday, this Yugoslavian organization put on a party for Bunk at the Stuyvesant.

At the Town Hall concert, Don played in a trio and went over big with the audience. Bunk, as usual at concerts, didn't play to his best and seemed to have little enthusiasm. I remember Gene thought he sounded like "Old Man" W. C. Handy when he played. I guess Handy was a halfway-decent straight trumpet player, but, as Jelly said, "He never played no jazz."

When Bunk re-opened at the Stuyvesant Casino (April 10, 1946), Don took Alton Purnell's place and Kaiser Marshall had taken Baby Dodds's place. The Stuyvesant management [Sam Augenblick] didn't want Lawrence Marrero after Hodes had only used a six-piece band. Art Hodes had a band in there between Bunk's two engagements.[40]

I saw Bunk's band the week after they opened and everything seemed to be okay. I tried to get over to New York as often as I could. One afternoon (Wednesday, May 15) Gene and I were eating in his kitchen and Bunk was in his room, with the bathroom mirror, practicing *In the Gloaming*. The band also played it that night. By that time, Alphonse Steele had replaced Kaiser, who had become unreliable with his drinking. Bunk asked me to arrange a train reservation for him and Maude back to New Iberia on June 3, as the band was due to finish on May 31. The Stuyvesant management had offered to extend his contract for four nights a week, but Bunk felt most of the fellows were hoping to get another engagement without him, under George's leadership. Then he started on how they were not interested in improving themselves and how George and Jim left their instruments over at the hall all the time. He said, "Jim should be blowing around the house as I do every day, trying to get a better tone and work on scales, but no; Jim just takes up each night where he left off the night before, playing the same rough stuff." He then talked about the possibility of bringing a new band back in the fall. Then I brought up the idea of recording just trumpet and piano, some "folk" tunes such as *In the Gloaming*. Bunk said that would be a good idea, but that drums could also be used, then added, "*Gloaming* is a fine tune, also *I'll Take You Home Again Kathleen* and *Where the River Shannon Flows*."

Later I went over to where Don was staying at Matt Cobb's at 146 W. 23rd St. He was brought down by the news that the band was definitely closing on May 31, since he'd hoped he could stay all summer and work out his local 802 card. Don mentioned that he had been trying to follow Bunk's ideas more rather than "imitate" Jelly so much. Don didn't go over to Gene's or try to see Bunk much off the job, having learned in the army that it's better not to mix with your boss if possible.

When I next went to New York (Tuesday, May 28), things had got pretty bad. About the Friday before, with only one week to go on the contract, there had been so much hard feeling that Bunk had told them that, since they didn't like him, he also didn't like them and didn't like them to live with him. He'd just discovered some more of their plotting to come back to New York without him, using Kid Howard. I guess he never told them that he intended to come back without them!

91

Gene asked me if I had decided anything about recording. He told me that, two or three days before, he had talked to Bunk about recording. Milt Gabler had spoken to Gene (and Bunk too, I believe) about making some records for his Commodore label, but using, instead of Bunk's band, an all-star band. Bunk had suggested using Sidney Catlett, but Gabler said, "No, George Wettling," and Bunk said someone like Simeon on clarinet, if he's in town. But Gabler said, "No, Pee Wee Russell," and so it went. Of course, Bunk made up his own mind not to record for him, although Gabler was still counting on going down to the Stuyvesant to talk it over. But Bunk told Gene the only thing he'd be interested in doing would be some records with piano and drums.

A couple of nights later (May 30), the band played *Ja-Da* and *River Shannon* as well as *Gloaming*. The next night (Friday, May 31) was the closing night at the Stuyvesant. Before he got ready to leave I finally asked him about making the trumpet–piano records after the band closed. He said yes, it was a good idea, but he also wanted to use a drummer. Among the pieces he mentioned were *Gloaming, Kathleen* and *Poor Butterfly*. When I said I didn't know *Poor Butterfly*, he gave me a long lecture about not knowing it.

The funniest part of the whole closing evening was the next to the last number, when Bunk called for *In the Gloaming*, stomped off, then fell off asleep that quick that he didn't even get his horn up to play a note. George tried to play the lead but didn't know the tune that well. Don admitted the next day that there were a couple of chord changes in the bridge that he was also unsure about.

The next day at noon (June 1) I went up to 23rd Street to talk to Don about the recording date, which was set for Monday night, June 3rd, since Bunk and Maude couldn't get train reservations for New Orleans until June 5th.

When I got back to Gene's I talked to Bunk, and he said, if Al Steele couldn't make the records for any reason, we could pick up some other (or perhaps, any other) drummer for the date. He really wanted a drum, but if none was available he'd use Pops Foster on bass. I asked how many rehearsals, if two would be enough, and he said one would be all that was needed. The rehearsal was later set up for 1 pm Monday at the Stuyvesant.

That evening Al Steele called up. He suggested using a bass player, a good friend of his (Gladstone Thomas) who "played just like Slam Stewart." I told him Bunk wanted to use guys he'd been working with regularly, but I would tell him anyway. Of course Bunk wouldn't even consider it, and said that if he'd use any bass, it would be Pops Foster.

On Monday (June 3) Bunk had been awake since 5 am with the light turned on, sitting up in bed waiting to catch a mouse who had disturbed them. Maude was really afraid of mice and one had woke them up, chewing on something, so Bunk turned on the light and sat on the edge of the bed watching for it, but it never came back. That morning he went out and bought two traps.

I got to the Stuyvesant a little before 1 pm, for the rehearsal. Bunk was in the bathroom practicing and washing out his horn. I helped Al Steele move his drum set upstairs to the ballroom.

While Al set up his drums, I went downstairs to the street to look for Don. Bunk thought he might be in the 141 Club across the street, but he wasn't there. I had phoned Matt Cobb at 12.40 and he said Don knew about the rehearsal, so I wasn't worried. Just at 1 pm, when Bunk came down to the door to look, Don and "Sister Kate"[41] came along.

We all went upstairs. The bandstand had been moved over to the side of the hall, where it had been on the opening night in September. Bunk set up his trumpet case on the platform floor as a music stand, and he sat in a chair down on the dance floor level. Al set up only his bass and snare drum, one cymbal and hi-hat, but didn't bother to set up his tom-toms. Don was handicapped by the lack of a music rack on the piano, and bad light, until we moved the piano around. The hall had been halfway cleaned up from a wedding the night before; the white tablecloths were still on the tables. The sun was shining quite brightly through the upper ceiling window, and almost blinded Don.

They got started about 1.15 on *I'll Take You Home Again, Kathleen*. After trying it over once, Bunk decided we'd better time it, so I got out my watch. Bunk planned about five choruses with Don taking the third, but it ran about five minutes, with each chorus taking about a minute. Don worked out a little two-bar intro and asked me if I thought a simple chord style was okay. I told him it sounded okay to me, but he shouldn't ask me how to play!

Bunk then tried *Kathleen* with three choruses, and it ran about 3 minutes 12 seconds. So they tried it a little faster. Bunk told me to get some paper and write down the number of choruses (three) and mark "brighter tempo," so they'd be sure and get it okay on a 10" side.

Next was *In the Gloaming*. Bunk had asked me what to try next; I told him it made no difference to me, that he was the boss and could play anything he wanted.

Bunk was using a copy of "Everybody's Favorite Community Songs," and Don had the "Twice 55" book and the Feist blue book called "Merrily We Sing." Bunk once started to refer to a certain line, so I decided to run out and try to get another copy each of the Favorite book and the Feist blue book, so they both would be able to play from the same music. He then called for *Poor Butterfly* next and I wanted to look for that music, so I ran over to 4th Avenue to the Orpheus Music Shop, picked up the two song books and got back in three or four minutes – or so it seemed. Maude thought I'd just run downstairs. They were trying *Oh You Beautiful Doll* when I came in.

Don asked Bunk if he knew *You've Got to See Mamma Every Night*, and they tried that one next. It was terrific, with Bunk taking several *Cornet Chop Suey* breaks that made Don and me burst out laughing. They worked out a routine of seven choruses, with the piano taking choruses number three and five, and breaks in all choruses except the first, second and last. The seven choruses ran for 2 minutes 59 seconds. Between numbers Bunk himself would try other tunes in the Everybody's book, such as *Aloha*. He also asked Maude about this time to keep a list too, and while I was writing out cards with the address and time of recording for all the guys, I neglected to keep time once. That made him mad and he bawled me out.

Then I mentioned to Bunk that on Saturday he'd suggested *Massa's in the Cold, Cold Ground* (he'd said that it had the "blues effect"). Each chorus ran one minute, so they planned to take three, with piano on the second. Bunk played his part of *Massa* in the key of E. Later he said another key might be better. The key in the book (D) was okay "for singing," but "for dancing" another key would be better.

I ran out to get the music to *Poor Butterfly* and also went to Fischers' to try to get *Porto Rico* and *Riverside Rag*. By the time I got back, "Sister Kate" had brought Coca Colas for everybody and a bottle of beer for Don.

Bunk tried *River Shannon* and I got out the music. It ran much too long at first, and Bunk decided they'd just take "two full choruses," with the piano coming in for sixteen bars, then Bunk on the last sixteen. We didn't time this, but it seemed pretty short.

During the rehearsal I'd mentioned Don's suggestion, *Nellie Gray*, but Bunk said he wanted to use numbers that hadn't been recorded. *Sweet Lorraine* and *White Wash Man* came up and Don tried a few bars once, but evidently Bunk didn't want to try it.

Before we left Bunk made me copy all the titles, timing and routines for him, and Maude also had a list. It was about 3.30 when we quit, and as Al had packed up his drums Bunk chatted by the outside door for a few minutes with Sam Augenblick and Menschel, the owner of the Stuyvesant.

I had told everybody where the recording would be, and the time – 7 pm at John Cieferskor's Studio (which was also known as Arts Recording Studio) in the Aeolian Hall on 57th Street. This was just across the street from Carnegie Hall.

While Al Steele waited for a taxi out on the street, I talked with Sam and Menschel a few minutes and paid Sam $5 for the use of the Stuyvesant. They asked about Kid Ory's band and I told them it was a fine band – that it was probably in San Francisco now, and could be booked through MCA.

Don, Bunk and Maude had little or nothing to eat that day, so said they would get a good dinner. Al had called up Henry Allen during the rehearsal. He had planned to meet Henry about 6 pm, but I think he decided to see him earlier – or perhaps go home and eat. On the way up in the taxi, Al mentioned that the last time he'd been at Aeolian Hall it was on 42nd Street, and Fats Waller was recording. Al was about 49 years old, I believe, and his son was in the ground crew of the air force and would be home soon. He still planned to go to Baltimore early next morning, and said he might go on to Canada later that spring.

I got up to 57th Street a little before 4 pm and got everything unloaded quickly. I talked for a while to John Cieferskor. He agreed a studio shouldn't be too dead. (His looked okay, with carpet the main deadening material.) He also agreed to one microphone, as far away as possible. (In his studio, about fifteen feet away would do the job best.)

I went on home, after stopping at Decca to worry Gene for a few minutes. I got off the bus about 5 pm. Bunk and Maude were about through with their dinner; Bunk had some meat and plenty of rice, as usual. He had said he didn't want to sleep before recording.

About the first thing he said to me was, "Well, I committed murder this afternoon." I didn't know what he meant, so he explained that he'd killed the mouse. When he arrived home, it was sitting in the sun on his window sill. He showed how it turned its head to look at him and then went back to sleep. Maude had already come into the room, and ran for cover as Bunk got a broom and hit the mouse. He demonstrated how it quivered and how he pushed it out of the window.

I heated up some soup while we talked. Maude had some cherry ice-cream, which she'd gotten at the drugstore on the way home from the Stuyvesant, but Bunk didn't eat any. A little after 6 pm, Bunk went into his room to get ready, but it was about 6.40 before we went downstairs, and then it took five minutes to grab a cab. We went right up Fifth Avenue and made good time for that hour of the evening – all the buses worried Bunk, though. About a dozen were in sight up the avenue, although not more than two or three per block, but Bunk said they looked just like a big circus parade the way they all lined up. He also didn't like it when they passed one another and blocked the entire street. At 56th Street we turned left and went around the block to get to 57th.

We got into the studio about three or four minutes before seven. Cieferskor and Gene were already there, and Al was just starting to unpack his drums; when he opened one case something slipped out and a cymbal made a lot of noise. Bunk later said he thought Al had had a drink, or he wouldn't have made all that noise.

We looked at the piano, a full concert grand. Bunk had Al hit "A" for him (after I had left the room) so he could tune up.

Don still wasn't there. About 7.10 I began to get worried and decided to go downstairs. About a minute after I got down on to the street, Don and "Sister Kate" jumped out of a taxi and ran in, much excited, trying to explain that they'd left in plenty of time, 6.40, but had gotten the wrong subway (express to 72nd Street)! I told them I wasn't mad, but they'd better have a good story ready for Bunk. They should have taken the BMT, not the IRT! Don was pretty nervous about it all. Bunk didn't say anything, but he was rather cool to "Sister Kate," who tried to tell Bunk he shouldn't say anything.

Cieferskor was going to have Bunk and Don sitting either side of the drums, but I asked Bunk if he would rather sit in the middle, which, of course, he did. So Bunk picked up his chair and they all moved back against the wall. Don opened up the top of the Steinway.

Cieferskor asked them to try something so he could hear the balance over his speaker in the control room. Bunk had them try *Lady Be Good*, which sounded very fine. He had a big high floor-microphone in the corner, right by the door to the control room, and, what we didn't know, another microphone on the table hooked in. They were marked "Bruno Velocity." The relative balance of the three instruments sounded pretty good, so we decided to go ahead and cut, although the tone on the speaker sounded too loud or overloaded to me, and a little distorted and rattly.

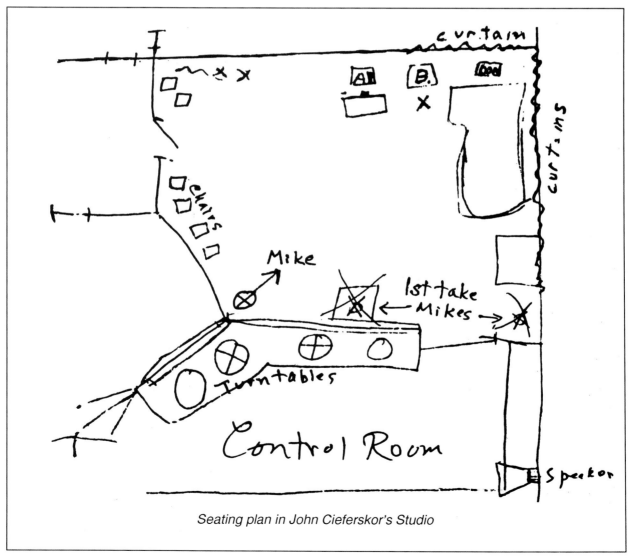

Seating plan in John Cieferskor's Studio

BUNK'S 3-PIECE BAND

Cieferskor's Studio, 29 West 57th Street, New York.
Monday, June 3, 1946   (7.00–10pm)

Bunk Johnson (tpt); Don Ewell (pno); Alphonse Steele (dms)

929	In the Gloaming	Dan: VC-4021, VC-7025, AM Book CD
930	In the Gloaming	AM 520, AM LP 644, Stv: SLP 202, Dan: VC-4009, VC-7011, AMCD-15
931	I'll Take You Home Again, Kathleen	AM 520, Dan: VC-4021, VC-7025, AMCD-15
932	You Got to See Mamma Ev'ry Night	AM 519, AM LP 644, Stv: SLP 202, Dan: VC-4009, VC-7011, AMCD-15
933	Beautiful Doll	AM 519, Dan: VC-4021, VC-7025, AMCD-15
934	When the Moon Comes over the Mountain	AM 517, Stv: SLP 203, Dan: VB-1004, VC-4021, VC-7025, AMCD-15
935	Where the River Shannon Flows	AM LP 644, Dan: VC-4021, VC-7025
936	Where the River Shannon Flows	AM 517, Dan: VC-4009, VC-7011, AMCD-15
937	Ja-Da	AM 518, AM LP 644, Stv: SLP 202, Dan: VB-1004, VC-4009, VC-7011, AMCD-15
938	Poor Butterfly	Dan: VC-4021, VC-7025
939	Poor Butterfly	AM 518, Dan: VB-1003, VC-4021, VC-7025, AMCD-15

Bill Russell: The first tune was *In the Gloaming*, which sounded okay, but a little dead to me, compared to the rehearsal. Bunk appeared to be rather mad, sulking, and untalkative, and in his usual "Uncle Tom" recording mood: "Anything you say." I tried to get him out of it by telling him that he was the boss.

I stayed out of the studio entirely, after talking over the routines each time before the takes (when Bunk would ask me what was on my notes from the afternoon). When Bunk was ready to go, I'd go into the control room and either I would tell Cieferskor that Bunk was ready to cut, or he'd wait till Bunk gave him the go-ahead sign. Then John (Cieferskor) would start the turntable. When he got the cutter into a 9½-inch diameter with a silent groove, he would wave to Bunk to stomp off. Often there were three or four dead grooves before they got going, but everything went on, luckily.

I thought we had decided earlier that John was to cut the regular 10" masters ready for processing, and the safeties, at 78 rpm, but to be prepared for longer cuts on them if necessary. That evening they had quite a discussion as to whether Mrs. Cieferskor, who ran the "safety" turntable, should cut at 33⅓ rpm or not. (About six of the masters were delivered to Muzak for processing on 13⅓-inch blanks, and two were cut on 16".) So we decided again that Mrs. C. should cut the safeties (or "standbys," they called them) at 78 on 12" blanks, starting near the outside.

After playing back *Gloaming* (929), Gene, who was keeping the master list data and checking the time with a stop watch, happened to overhear the Cieferskors mention something about having the second microphone on. He tipped me off at once and I had quite an argument with Cieferskor, who (after having agreed to one microphone, that afternoon) claimed it was necessary to pick up the piano properly and said that the high one was just for the trumpet. I asked him what he would do if he had a whole orchestra in there; then we asked him to try it with just one microphone and compare the results. We had the band try something again and the tone cleared up when he faded out the second microphone. So now, since they'd messed up the microphones when Bunk played *Gloaming* before, I asked him to try once more.

Maude had been listening in the second studio, but I told her the music didn't sound natural there, so finally she moved into the cutting room and sat beside Gene. He said she seemed to enjoy it and remarked a few times during the evening that she really liked the way Bunk played a number.

The next one was *Kathleen*, which went okay on the first take.

When I asked Bunk once, after the first or second master, if he was satisfied with that take, or if he wanted to try it again, he said he wanted to go on to a new tune and to get them all over with – not to fool around all night on one tune. Now he didn't seem to want to waste time hearing playbacks, but I could tell the others all wanted to hear them and I thought doing so might help them, so after the first couple of tunes we played back all the takes, except the long *River Shannon*.

When he said he wanted to try *Mamma* next, his voice was pleasant, and I was glad he would liven things up a bit with a tune like *Mamma* after the delayed start and rather strained beginning.

They evidently had a little mix-up on starting signals, as Cieferskor never even got his machine running, but we didn't stop them. Fortunately they got mixed up on the breaks and number of choruses, and it ran too long anyway, so we had a perfect excuse to try it again. After we talked over the routine, someone had the final drum break mixed up with the routine of *Beautiful Doll*. The second try went very well, but several of us thought the first try had been better, and I was sure neither take came near the afternoon rehearsal try. It was about this time that Bunk suggested they try *Ja Da* and *The Moon Comes over the Mountain*. But the next tune was *Beautiful Doll*, which "Sister Kate" had been yelling for. It went fine on the first take. They talked over the routine and Bunk had to bawl Al out for trying to explain it at the same time. Then he said, "Let's not all talk at once; let one man explain it."

Someone suggested trying the whole thing then, but Bunk said, "No, we'll save time and just rehearse the final chorus, with a drum break." When I said, "The time came out just right on the first take, at 2 minutes 59 seconds," they all seemed pleased, and Don said, "It seemed a lot shorter than three minutes, but it was sure fun to play."

Bunk called for *The Moon Comes over the Mountain*, and we called in Gene to time one piano chorus; it worked out that there would be time for just four choruses. We weren't sure if they'd make it with a piano intro, so I asked Mrs. C. to be sure to get it all on, and she cut at 33 ⅓ rpm. All of *The Moon* just barely made it in 3 minutes 11 seconds – one more second and it might have been too long.

Next was *River Shannon*, and it did run much too long, at 3 minutes 52 seconds. I was all set to open the studio door at three minutes to try to stop them, but they were all set for the piano chorus, so I let it run, for a 12" take, if necessary. The master on Mr. C's machine was, of course, no good, but Mrs. C. got it all on her 12" blank.

They talked it all over once again and had it straight at last by playing straight through the music, as published, twice. Bunk startled us by starting out again on *The Moon Comes over the Mountain*. At home later, when I kidded him about it, he said that there had been so much discussion about the routine on *Shannon* that his mind had been distracted. *Shannon* went okay the next time, in 3 minutes 7 seconds – a fine performance.

Next was *Ja Da* and Bunk again had Gene and Don time one chorus. As Gene said later, these trial piano choruses sounded pretty bad and beatless without drums, but possibly Don wasn't really trying, or maybe he was just reading the music straight. There was time for five choruses, and Bunk and Don decided they would have two piano choruses.

Later on I mentioned to Bunk that *Ja-Da* went fine for the trio, when it is usually regarded as an orchestra piece. Bunk said, "Oh, it was sure to be good, anything like that that has the 'blues effect'."

They had the first six sides a little before 9.30, in about 1½ hours of actual recording, so I asked if they wanted to make it eight sides before they did *Ja-Da*. There were still twenty minutes left for one more, so Bunk called for *Poor Butterfly*.

On the first take a couple of Bunk's notes on the first chorus seemed weak, and Gene and Maude and others agreed they had better try it again. Since there was plenty of time left, I went into the studio and explained that, although there weren't any "misses" in that take, a couple of notes sounded weak, as though Bunk had turned away from the mike or something, and that some people would say he's an old man and sounds weak. Bunk said, "Sure, I'll try it again, but it's a 'soft' piece." The second try turned out fine. Don said he wished Louis could hear some of these records when we were listening to some of the tests.

It was 9.57 when we finished playing back the last number and everybody packed up. I paid Bunk $280 for the recording and $8 for the rehearsal. Al and Don got $140 each and $4 for the rehearsal. This included 2 cent advance royalty to Bunk and 1 cent each for Al and Don, for each record sold. Although the session hadn't been done through the Union (as none of my recordings ever were), everybody got more than the Union scale for the session.

When we got back, we were all hungry. I thought Bunk would go right on into the kitchen, but he wanted to change his clothes first, as he was wearing his good dark blue suit. We talked a few minutes in Bunk's room and he remarked how easy it was to make good records when all the musicians were good. He said if they had used George Lewis and Jim Robinson they would still be there trying to play those simple songs that everybody should remember from school. He then went into an "argument" against big bands, which were so noisy and hard to work with. (Gene and I both thought that by a big band he meant seven pieces or so.)

Bunk said, "The best band Louis ever had was when he had the Hot Five, and Louis knows it." When I told him he was going to revive his Hot Five, Bunk laughed, seeming to

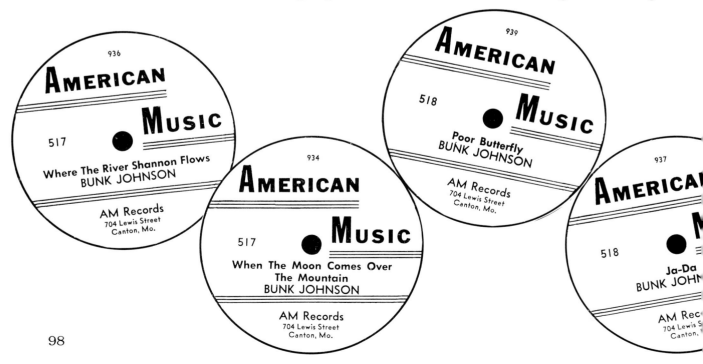

think Louis never would.

Bunk then went on to say he'd like to enlarge that evening's trio to five pieces sometime and try some more records – with Albert Nicholas and Pops Foster added. He said Nicholas would know just what, and how, to play in such a group, and would add no complications to the outfit since he could read, learn quickly, and already knew what to do.

Gene and I cooked up a little soup and beans, etc, while Bunk and Maude stayed out in the kitchen. I finally talked Bunk into coming in to warm his rice. Bunk went to bed early, but I was still too happy to sleep for a while, after planning and thinking about these records for the last eight weeks.

Bunk's tone was really strong that night. Once or twice, when I opened the studio door while they were playing or rehearsing, his tone was so loud that it almost hurt my ears. His lip had evidently healed up entirely. On Saturday, when I'd asked him how his lip was, he rubbed it and pointed to a very narrow streak about a quarter of an inch long near mid-left of his upper lip. It had been cracked a couple of weeks before and now it looked almost healed. He'd said, "If that heals up, my tone will be as clear as a bell."

The next day Bunk went over to the Stuyvesant to see Sam, but he later told us that nothing had been decided to bring him back in the fall. It seems Sam wanted to tell Bunk who he should have in his band. Bunk, of course, didn't like that, and told Sam if he hired Louis Armstrong they wouldn't tell him who to have, and anyway he didn't tell Sam how to run his business. It seems Sam didn't like Don Ewell and would have preferred Art Hodes.

Bunk spent Wednesday morning (June 5) packing up his trunk and suitcases, while I went over to Muzak to deliver eight of the nine masters I wanted processed. Bunk had so much luggage that he and Maude took as much as they could in their taxi and Gene and I followed with the rest in another cab. I said goodbye to Bunk and Maude at Penn Station at 5.25 and I then went to see Cieferskor to pick up the last of the masters and dubs. That night I caught the 12.45 train back to Pittsburgh.

PITTSBURGH, 1947

GEORGE HORNSBY

Phifer Recording Productions, 5611 Pennsylvania Avenue, Pittsburgh.
February or March 1947

George Hornsby (pno solo)

940	"Unknown title"	Unissued
941	Jesus Gave Me a Little Light	Unissued
942	Jesus Gave Me a Little Light	Unissued
943	Jesus Gave Me a Little Light	Unissued
944	Jesus Gave Me a Little Light	Unissued
945	Jesus Gave Me a Little Light	AM 521
946	I'll Tell It	Unissued
947	Yes, They Tell Me	Unissued
948	Jesus Never Fails	Unissued
949	I Know it Was Blood	AM 522
950	Trees	Unissued
	Bye and Bye	Unissued
951	Bye and Bye	AM 521
952	My Soul Loves Jesus	AM 522
953	I Need Jesus	Unissued
954	Bye and Bye	Unissued

Note: *Just a Closer Walk with Thee*, *Old Rugged Cross* and two other unidentified numbers were also recorded, but not assigned master numbers. The four missing master numbers following 954 and the next AM session (starting at 959) were probably reserved for these extra titles.

This was the least successful of all the American Music sessions and Bill Russell was always reluctant to discuss it. Having listened to all of the above masters I can confirm that the playing is of a poor standard and there are no plans to issue any of the above tracks in the AMCD series.

The following information on George Hornsby is taken from Bill's stencilled biography that was enclosed with the records.

George Hornsby was born in Mobile, Alabama, in 1912. He moved to Pittsburgh when he was four and was educated in the public schools. His father was a quartet singer and his interest in music developed early. When he was nine he took up piano, and at nineteen began playing with the Regals of Rhythm and Harlemites, with whom he broadcast. His own "Fess Hornsby Orchestra" toured Pennsylvania and Ohio. Since 1939 he has devoted his time to religious work, teaching piano, presenting a weekly radio program, "Modern Hymnology," and as an accompanist to travelling vocal groups. At present, Elder Hornsby is organizing his own Church of the Good Shepherd in Pittsburgh.

LOS ANGELES, 1947

Bill Russell: When I went to Los Angeles in 1947 (September 30–October 27) Dink was living in Santa Barbara by this time. He had separated from Stella and had no one to pester him about his drinking. He still had his cafe next to the baseball park. We'd talked about the possibility of his making a one-man band record (clarinet, piano and drums), as he'd always said how he'd like to do this after hearing Sidney Bechet's one-man band record [*The Sheik of Araby* – Victor 27485]. I went by Dink's that evening and he seemed glad to see me. He shut off the jukebox and got down to business, playing and singing several numbers like *Pigeon Walk*, *Las Vegas Stomp*, *Jelly Roll Blues*, *Frisco Dreams* and a long vocal blues. There was a ball game that evening, so things got pretty busy after 7 o'clock and I soon left.

By Friday (October 3) Dink said he'd be ready to try the one-man-band piano part on Monday. He was still very business-like and seemed to be in fine piano form, but he hadn't played much on clarinet.

DINK JOHNSON
Associated Studios, 1032 North Sycamore Avenue, Hollywood.
Monday, October 6, 1947 (6.30–7.30 pm)
(Cut onto a 17¼" acetate at 33⅓ rpm)

Dink Johnson (pno solo)

Side A:	1-1	Pigeon Walk	Unissued
	2-1	Rag Bag Rag	(Used for piano part of master 965)
	2-2	Rag Bag Rag	Unissued
	2-3	Rag Bag Rag	Unissued
	2-4	Rag Bag Rag	Unissued

Bill Russell: When we got to the studio I asked him to try a warm-up number, and he played and sang *Pigeon Walk*. It wasn't a very satisfactory take as the vocal was rough and hoarse. Dink had been over at his son's place the previous evening for a chicken dinner. Later they had a party over at Dink's Place and Dink had entertained them until his voice gave out. When we got down to the piano part for the one-man band, he seemed confused at first as to how long to leave for the clarinet breaks. After we were through, Long (the engineer) made two 12" dubs for Dink to practice the clarinet part with.

When I got back to Dink's and tried to play the records, I found that he only had an old pre-1915 hand-wound phonograph. The tone arm was stuck and wouldn't track and the spring motor was too weak to drive a 12" record. I took it home and got it going eventually.

He got out his A clarinet. It was in poor condition as he probably hadn't touched it in years, and he had no reeds. At first he couldn't get his clarinet in tune with the piano, but after pulling out one of the sections a quarter of an inch he got it in tune. He complained that every time he got a good reed, a musician would steal it. He even accused Albert Nicholas of stealing his reed when Nick "had depped for him for a few minutes." I doubted this story, as Nick had told me when he'd brought Alfred Lion down to see Dink the previous year Dink wouldn't even play for them, saying he had an exclusive agreement with me.

Every few days I'd go out and buy him the best reeds I could find. He'd try one and it wouldn't be right, so he'd cut off the end and scrape it down until it was wafer thin. After about half an hour, the reed would be useless, so he'd throw it away and start on a new reed until he found one that was just how he wanted it. Thinking about those records he made with Ory in June 1921, I asked him when he got started on the clarinet. He surprised me by saying he only took up the clarinet after hearing Larry Shields on the Original Dixieland Jass Band records, so that must have been after 1917. When he practiced (which wasn't very often) there were so many squeaks that I was doubtful if we would ever get a decent take, but he said he had to make the one-man band record as he'd told so many people he was going to do it.

When we got to the studio, we helped Dink set up his drums. I don't think he practiced on the drums at all – maybe he felt he didn't need to.

DINK JOHNSON
Associated Studios, 1032 North Sycamore Avenue, Hollywood.
Tuesday, October 17, 1947 (5.45–9.30 pm)

Note: "Side B" was cut onto a second 17½" acetate at 33⅓ rpm.

Dink Johnson (drums added to piano of *Rag Bag Rag*, side A, take 2-1)

Side B: 2-1	Rag Bag Rag	(used for piano/drums version of master 965)
2-2	Rag Bag Rag	Unissued
2-3	Rag Bag Rag	(used for clarinet/piano/drums version of master 965)

Bill Russell: Take B-1 sounded pretty good to me, even though the drums sounded a little loud. But Dink, who had been hitting them very hard, insisted they should be even louder, so we turned up the drums on the next take.[42] He sounded awfully good with his rather complicated drum taps and fast short rolls, etc. After replaying the last two takes, Dink chose to use the third take for the clarinet part.

Dink Johnson (clarinet added to *Rag Bag Rag*, side B, take 2-3)

Note: The "Side C" tracks were made on the reverse side of the "Side A" disc and cut at 33⅓ rpm

Side C: 2-1	Rag Bag Rag	AM Book CD
2-2	Rag Bag Rag	Unissued
2-3	Rag Bag Rag	Unissued
2-4	Rag Bag Rag	Unissued
2-5	Rag Bag Rag	Unissued

Bill Russell: After a warm-up trial, he cut the C-2-1 take without a squeak, but, as he admitted, he was taking it easy, being afraid he'd "cut a pig." The second take seemed better, with a beautiful tone in the low register, but when we started to play it back the disc had thread tangle in the first part. We cut another right away, but Dink had trouble with his reed and there were a few squeaks. On the next take Dink messed up the first clarinet break, although the rest of it seemed to be the best take so far. Take 5 was really bad, full of squeaks, so we decided to give it a rest and switch to some piano and vocal numbers.

Side C: 3-1 "Blues"   (Master 964 - issued as *Yeah Man*)
        4-1 "Blues"   Unissued
        5-1 "Blues"   Unissued
        5-2 "Blues"   (Master 966 - *So Dif'rent Blues*)

Bill Russell: On the first take he had his eyes closed when I waved to him to signal the final chorus, so I waved him "out" again after that chorus and he spotted me and quickly finished with a bang and a flourish. He complained about the baby grand in the studio and about the records being so short that he couldn't get all his ideas in. He also didn't like the idea of an introduction (which he'd always included before), so we asked him just to do it naturally, as if he was at home. He started off the next take with no introduction at all, and we had to cut him off in the middle of the final piano chorus, when he'd planned at least another couple of vocals. On take 5-1 he got impatient and raced through it in two minutes without an introduction or coda, trying to get everything in. It was 9 pm and Dink began hinting he ought to get back to open up, as there was a ball game that night. So we decided to try one more piano/vocal number. This seemed slightly better and contained some different verses.

We still hadn't got a good take of the clarinet part, so I persuaded Dink to have one final go.

Side C: 2-6   Rag Bag Rag   (issued as master 965)
        2-7   Rag Bag Rag   Unissued

Bill Russell: When he'd been playing the clarinet on the earlier takes he sat on his drum chair, but he seemed to play better when he fooled around between takes standing up, so I suggested he might try standing. Take 2-6 had a squeak, but Dink felt that this might be the best so far. He had one more try standing nearer the speaker, but the clarinet was too soft as he kept turning away from the microphone.

He seemed quite pleased with the one-man band record, but said a couple of times that he was sorry he couldn't play the clarinet like he used to in the old days. He wanted me to leave him the number of the studio so he could have people call them up if they doubted he'd made the record.

Before I went to Los Angeles that year, I had this idea to find the trombonist Ash Hardy and record some trombone piano duets with him and Dink. Ash was born in Texas around 1897, but had lived in Los Angeles most of his life. His father had been a bandleader and had taught Ash reading and harmony before he allowed him to take up cornet. In the early 1920s, Dink (dms) led a band which included Ash (cnt), Wade Whaley (clt) and Jelly at the US Grant Hotel in San Diego. (They got fired when Jelly wouldn't play without crossing his legs.) Ash had organized a band for Jelly's funeral, but when they got to the church the priest wouldn't allow them to march to the graveyard. He'd lost his lower right leg jumping on a street car and was now helping a guy called Walter on his shoe-shine stand. When I finally met him and explained I wanted to record him with a pianist (à la Ike Rogers and Henry Brown) he was enthusiastic and suggested Buster Wilson. When I told him Buster was in San Francisco with Ory, he suggested Dink. As he no longer had a horn, I offered him an advance and he got a trombone with a mute from a pawn shop for just under $50. Dink and he started to practice and it sounded good, then they started to argue and the rehearsal finished without anything being resolved. They had a couple of more rehearsals. Sometimes it sounded promising, but then they'd start to fight over how numbers should be played. When they started accusing one another of stealing tunes from each other, I really couldn't see how they could ever work together. Ash still wanted to do the session and "didn't want to let me down," but as Buster Wilson wouldn't be back from San Francisco before I had to leave I couldn't see how we could do it.[43]

I still wanted to do one more session with Dink. A couple of days before, I'd played him Jelly's "General" album and he got quite interested in the records and felt that he could sing better than Jelly and maybe play a few similar pieces if I could get a studio. He couldn't believe that they were all under three minutes until I timed each one for him. He finally chose five numbers and played each over twice, while I timed them.

DINK JOHNSON
Studio & Artistes Recording, CBS Building, Sunset Boulevard, Hollywood.
Thursday, October 23, 1947 (8.00–10.10 pm)

(Cut onto two 16" master discs at 33$\frac{1}{3}$ rpm)

Dink Johnson (pno solo)

Side 1 - 1st cut:	The Stella Blues	Issued as master 960
2nd cut:	Indian Rag	Unissued
3rd cut:	Indian Rag	Unissued
4th cut:	Indian Rag	Issued as master 959
Side 2 - 1st cut:	Frisco Dreams	Unissued
2nd cut:	Frisco Dreams	Issued as master 961
3rd cut:	Las Vegas Stomp	Issued as master 962
4th cut:	Jelly Roll Blues	Unissued
Side 3 - 1st cut:	Jelly Roll Blues	Issued as master 963
2nd cut:	Indian Rag	Unissued
3rd cut:	Indian Rag	Unissued
4th cut:	Indian Rag	Unissued
Side 4 - 1st cut:	"Vocal Blues"	
	(issued as *Dink's Blues*) Issued as master 967	

When the best takes were selected they were assigned the above master numbers and issued as follows:

959	Indian Rag	AM 525, Wolf: WJS 1001, WJS 1001 CD, AMCD-11
960	The Stella Blues	AM 524, Stv: SLP 155, AMCD-11
961	Frisco Dreams	AM 526, Wolf: WJS 1002, WJS 1002 CD, AMCD-11
962	Las Vegas Stomp	AM 524, Stv: SLP 155, AMCD-11
963	Jelly Roll Blues	AM 525, Wolf: WJS 1002, WJS 1002 CD, AMCD-11
964	Yeah Man	AM 523, Wolf: WJS 1002, WJS 1002 CD, AMCD-11
965	Rag Bag Rag (pno & dms version)	AM 523, Wolf: WJS 1002, WJS 1002 CD
965	Rag Bag Rag (clt, pno & dms version)	Stv: SEP 390, AMCD-11
	Rag Bag Rag (clt, pno & dms version)	AM Book CD
966	So Dif'rent Blues	Unissued
967	Dink's Blues	AM 526, WJS 1002, AMCD-11

Note: A second version of *So Dif'rent Blues* from the October 17 session (Side C, track 5-5) was assigned the master number 966, but never issued.

There are three different versions of *Rag Bag Rag*. AM 523 and WJS 1002 are from B-2-1 with piano and drums only, while the drum take on Storyville SEP 390 and AMCD-11 is from B-2-3 and has the additional clarinet part from C-2-6. Masters B-2-3 and C-2-1 have been used on the enclosed AM Book CD version.

Bill Russell: He wanted to name the first slow blues after his wife Stella, as she had asked him to put her name on one of the numbers (*The Stella Blues*). Although they were separated, he was due to see her that weekend.

On *Indian Rag* he seemed to be nervous and had trouble getting started, but the third take turned out okay.

The first take of *Frisco Dreams* sounded good, but too much of Dink's vocal was missing. So the engineer added a second microphone by the keybooard for the next take.

During *Jelly Roll Blues*, Dink had his eyes shut when I tried to give him the signal. I hoped then it would run about four minutes for a 12" master, so I let him finish when he was ready, which he did at 3 minutes 35 seconds. After the playback he said he'd forgotten to put in the trill interlude. He told me how he'd learned *Jelly Roll Blues* while Jelly was out of town, and when Jelly returned he couldn't believe that Dink had learned it so fast. On the next take Dink really loosened up and did a lot of singing and jiving which he'd never done before. The engineer said the record was too long which really disgusted Dink. Dink said no one could make records that way: he was just getting warmed up and had lots of ideas of new parts and things to put in, then he was signalled to stop. We told him that would be okay and asked him to try again on *Indian Rag*. But by that time he'd forgotten what else he wanted to put in the earlier take. He seemed to play it with more pep, but stopped without a signal after two minutes.

We were figuring to quit about 9.50 when Dink said he wanted to try a final blues. His eyes were again shut for the final chorus signal, but he managed to finish at three minutes. Later, when he found out I couldn't use *Pigeon Walk* from the earlier session, he wished he'd known, as he'd have liked to make it again. He considered this one of his better numbers.

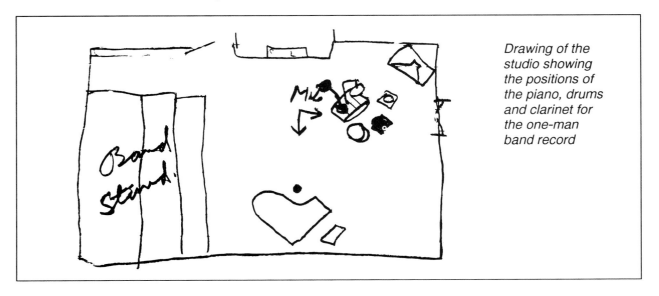

Drawing of the studio showing the positions of the piano, drums and clarinet for the one-man band record

St. Louis, 1947

Bill Russell: On the way down to record Bunk in 1942, I stopped off in St Louis (June 4 and 5) to look around and see what music was left. The first morning I arrived, I got in at Union Station (which was up on Market Street about the 1600 block; that's sixteen blocks west of the river); the old "district" had started just about there. I walked up north through the "district" (which wasn't there anymore) to Chestnut. I was trying to find the old saloons that Tom Turpin ran. There's still some confusion as to what was called "The Rosebud" (2220-22 Market Street) and "The Hunting and Shooting Club." There was one of his old saloons that I found on Market Street, about 23rd Street. Eventually, I stopped at a restaurant around 23rd Street (it was called something like Jefferson then). It turned out that it was run by a fellow called Johnson, who was married to Edith Johnson. She had recorded for Paramount in the 1920s and I knew of her from her records. He'd once owned a record store and had been a distributor for Paramount Records. He said the name of his record store was "The Pastime Record Store," and claimed that Artie Matthews named his *Pastime Rags* after his record store.[44]

He told me where Bob Hampton was playing, and I knew of him as the composer of *Cataract Rag*. Hampton was working way downtown in the theatrical section, just across the road from the old Grand Opera House (then called the Grand Theater), a "burlesque" theater that was still running. All that section has been torn down since, and was not far from the big arch that was erected for the St. Louis World's Fair. Hampton was playing in a saloon – Bonnie's Coconut Grove (517 Market Street, between Broadway and 5th or 6th Street) about four blocks from the river. Jelly had talked about when he went to St. Louis around 1912. He mentioned Turpin, Matthews, Joplin and especially Chauvin as being about the best in the city. He also mentioned Bob "Hamilton." I guess even Jelly's memory let him down for once. Jelly said that he had played "pretty good piano." When I heard him, he played nicely and may even have had a drummer there with him. I guess I'm about the only one of the jazz collectors who ever saw him and talked with him, as he was dead when others went down there later.[45] I went to his home (3135 La Clede, on the third floor), in a poorly furnished attic room. His home was near Compton, two doors from Small's Sandwich Shop. He was asleep when I arrived, having worked the night before. He told me about Fate Marable, who had recovered from his stroke and was well. Also that a New Orleans band was on the excursion boats that year (1942). He also told me about James Scott, who had died in 1938 while working for the Jenkins Music Company in Kansas City. Hampton said he "gave" Artie Matthews the *Weary Blues*. When I asked him to play some rags for me, he said that he "didn't play rags anymore" as he "couldn't play 60 or 45 degrees, let alone 90 degrees." I didn't know what he meant and I didn't like to ask at the time, but I think he meant the angle at which he could extend his fingers. Joplin's rags only need about a twenty-degree angle.

I went back again in 1943, and I hadn't heard of Charlie Thompson until I got down there. I went back again in December 1947 after I'd moved to Canton, Missouri, in the spring. Canton was only about 140 miles north of St. Louis. At that time Charlie Thompson was living on the second floor of 3001a Lawton Blvd. His "Charlie Thompson's Bar" was at 3005 Lawton Blvd.

Although he had a piano in a little room at the back, he said he hadn't played that much in the last couple of years. He had a weekend job at Sauter's (1033 Lemay Ferry) working with a drummer. Previously he had worked at Coconut Grove after Hampton. He told me he was the composer of *Lily Rag* and *Sweet and Low*, which had been sold outright to Wurlitzer for piano rolls. He said he'd been at Sauter's for about two years. Thompson said Louis Chauvin was born in St. Louis and he also told me about Artie Matthews, who was then in Cincinnati. Charlie Thompson had been born in St. Louis and was fifty one years old at the time. He said the *St. Louis Tickle* "originated right here in St Louis" and was taken to Chicago and published.

When I asked about recording him, he mentioned a recording place he'd seen on Delmar in the 4100 block, but I couldn't find any studio near there. He then recommended the Zanzibar [a nightclub?] at 3100 Cardinal, near Pine and Olive. He said he would be ready to record at three days' notice. He suggested that Tuesday would be the best day, between 1 and 4 pm. He asked me to get Tom Turpin's *Harlem Rag*. He was much interested in the *Record Changer* article with his picture in it, and showed it to his wife, Tams. He said that there were many good non-Union musicians in St. Louis who could record. He mentioned his singer again, and insisted she was very good and mentioned the possibility of using a small group on his records. He readily agreed to record four tunes for $100, and I left $10 advance.

A few days later I went back to see Charlie Thompson at 1.15 pm (December 29). He was up, although he had been sick with sinus trouble. He said he was all set to go. When I asked if he'd picked the tunes, he asked me how many I wanted him to "punch." When I said four, he

said he'd make one record with *Lily Rag* and on the other side his blues. For the other, he'd like to do a couple of songs with his singer, Maude Lee. He mentioned one number with a recitation in the middle. I just hoped she was good, and was quite disappointed that he did not want to play a Joplin number or a Turpin rag – although I'd wanted to record the singer as well. I was also interested in a friend of his who had recorded *Act Right* on a home recorder. He said he had a date to meet the guy up at the Musicians' Protective Association last week, but the guy hadn't shown up. He thought the acetate would be good enough to issue. I explained that it would be doubtful if the record had been played a lot.

We had arranged to meet Miss Lee at her home on Pine Street, where he had been practicing. She looked over his music and acted like she hadn't known Tom Turpin was a composer. Charlie praised Artie Matthews, who had arranged *The Lily* for publication. The piano was a little out of tune, especially in the upper half of the keyboard, but was generally in good condition. Charlie Thompson though the action was as good as a grand.

He tried *The Lily*. The third try went to 3 minutes 20 seconds, and he thought they could make it. He explained that the song should be a jukebox hit. When he got on to the blues, he had Maude singing just any words for two or three choruses. She acted like she didn't know any blues at all, although he said she used to sing the blues with him. He then tried his own blues, which turned out to be a fast boogie-style number, with a complicated bass part that he seemed rather proud of. He spoke about getting his pieces copyrighted, although he wasn't afraid that anyone would copy them. While he was playing, Maude shouted a couple of things like: "Oh play it, Mister Thompson." This seemed to encourage him, and for the fourth side he suggested another rag. It sounded pretty good, but after 1½ minutes he finished it off suddenly and said another blues would be better.

CHARLIE THOMPSON

Technisonic Recording Laboratories, 818 South Kings Highway Boulevard, St. Louis.
Tuesday, December 30, 1947 (1.00–3.00 pm.)
3 sides of 16" acetates at 33⅓ rpm

Charlie Thompson (pno), Maude Lee (vcls *)

Side 1 - cut 1:	The Lily	Unissued
cut 2:	The Lily (*Lily Rag*, given master number 968)	AMCD-11
cut 3:	Fast Blues	Unissued
cut 4:	Fast Blues *(Derby Stomp*, given master number 969)	AMCD-11
cut 5:	You Left Me out in the Rain (*)	Unissued
Side 2 - cut 1:	You Left Me out in the Rain (*)	Unissued
cut 2:	Delmar Rag (given master number 970)	AMCD-11
cut 3:	Slow Blues (*Lingering Blues*, given master number 971)	AMCD-11
cut 4:	The Lily	Unissued
Side 3 - cut 1:	The Lily	Unissued
cut 2:	Dub of side 1, cut 2 (Lily Rag)	
cut 3:	Dub of side 1, cut 4 (Derby Stomp)	
cut 4:	Dub of side 2, cut 2 (Delmar Rag)	
cut 5:	Dub of side 2, cut 3 (Lingering Blues)	

Note: Side 3, cuts 2–5, contained the selected "cuts" to be used for mastering. When Bill got back to Canton, he discovered that the dubbing of the selected tracks onto Side 3 had been overcut by the studio and could not be used. When asked to re-dub, the studio claimed to have lost the original "Side 1" and "Side 2" masters. Many years later these were discovered and returned to Bill.
Thus three of these numbers were recorded again the following year and all four were recorded again in 1949. This last session produced the issued American Music 78 rpm titles.
The titles issued on AMCD-11 were copied directly from the re-discovered masters using sides 1 and 2.

Bill Russell: It was a good studio with good equipment, but when I took the disc (Side 3) to Hugh Davis for mastering he couldn't use it. He said they were all overcut. You can make out the piano, but it doesn't sound too good. I didn't get back the first two discs for a long time, so we later went back to another studio and he re-made some of the titles.

CHARLIE THOMPSON

Technisonic Recording Laboratories, 818 South Kings Highway Boulevard, St. Louis.
Monday, August 4, 1948 (1.00–3.00 pm)

Three sides of 16" accetates at 33¹/₃ rpm.

Charlie Thompson (pno, vcl); Bessie Madison and Maude Lee (vcls where noted)

Side 1 - cut 1: The Lily (*"no good"*)   Unissued
        cut 2: The Lily (*"no good"*)   Unissued
        cut 3: I Had to Lose You   (*"test cut - song by Bessie Madison"*)   Unissued
        cut 4: I Had to Lose You   (*"song by Bessie Madison"*)   Unissued
Side 2 - cut 1: I Had to Lose You   (*"okay"*)   AMCD-11
        cut 2: I Gave You the Sunshine (*"vcl Maude Lee & Charlie Thompson"*)   Unissued
        cut 3: I Gave You the Sunshine (*"Thompson thought this the better take. Timing better"*)
Unissued
Side 3 - cut1: Derby Stomp (*"no good"*)   Unissued
        cut 2: Delmar Rag (*"no good"*)   Unissued
        cut 3: Weary Blues (*"vcl by Bessie Madison"*)   Unissued
        cut 4: Weary Blues (*"vcl by Bessie Madison"*)   AMCD-11

Note: The full title for *I Had to Lose You* was *I Had to Lose You to Learn That You Were Meant for Me.*
No regular master numbers were assigned to any of the above titles.
Except for the above information and comments in the recording log, Bill Russell could recall little about
this session and no session notes could be found.

New Orleans, 1949

Bill Russell went to New Orleans again in 1949 (Tuesday, June 28–Monday, July 25) to record for American Music. Although he had visited the city a couple of times since 1945, this was to be his final trip to record using his own funds. In 1951 he returned with Alden Ashforth and David Wykcoff to help them record Emile Barnes with DeDe Pierce and Kid Thomas. (They also recorded George Lewis with the Eureka Brass Band, which Bill declined to issue for cost reasons.) These sessions were organized by Alden and David, with funds from Alden's father. The results of the Emile Barnes and Kid Thomas sessions were then offered to Bill for release on American Music.

The 1949 sessions marked a new method of recording for Bill. Although wire and tape recorders had been commercially available for a number of years, the fidelity of the earlier machines left a lot to be desired. By the late 1940s, however, high quality recordings could be achieved from portable equipment using magnetic tape. Having endured so many problems in trying to record musicians on acetate discs, Bill was happy to accept the loan of John Steiner's reel-to-reel tape machine. Armed with an instruction manual, a dozen or so boxes of high-grade tape and his usual undaunted optimism, he boarded the train for New Orleans.

The following sessions are listed in "reel" order. The "master" numbers shown in brackets after certain titles are those given at the time of the 78 issue. The titles issued on American Music LPs were not given separate master numbers.

Bill Russell: I got into New Orleans early on Tuesday (June 28). As Orin Blackstone's record shop opened at 9.30 am, I left the tape recorder with him while I looked for a room. I soon found one at 924 Bienville Street. Bob Matthews played me the tape of Wooden Joe with Raymond Burke that he recorded in May.[46] About 7 pm I called up Albert Burbank and Wooden Joe and arranged to see them. Burbank still worked for the Southern Railroad and seemed to have no regular music work. Since Mardi Gras he had worked at Luthjen's when Big Eye was sick for several weeks.

I went around to Wooden Joe's house and asked him about musicians that he would like to make some records with. He suggested Israel Gorman, Big Eye or Picou for his dates. He mentioned that he once studied, or learned, from Big Eye. Wooden Joe said that Big Eye had been taking it easy for the last few years, but he could "make him play." He mentioned that Big Eye had not played as well since changing from his C clarinet to a B-flat model. When I mentioned drummers, he suggested Albert Jiles, whom he had often worked with. He said Ernest Rogers didn't seem to play in the right style anymore. "At one time he used to hit the bass drum too loud; now you can't get him to hit it loud enough." On guitar, he suggested St. Cyr or his regular guitar player, Louis Keppard, and thought Albert Glenny was still the "strongest" on bass. When I put these ideas to Big Eye, he objected at first. Big Eye wasn't trying to boast, or act high class, but he said of Keppard: "He wasn't like his brother – he wasn't in the class of us." He classed himself with Freddie Keppard. He also objected to Albert Glenny and Albert Jiles. Big Eye preferred people like Ernest Rogers, who kept a steady beat.

I was interested in recording Big Eye with a band of his own choice. He was still working weekend jobs at Luthjen's, with Charlie Love, Louis Gallaud and Ernest Rogers. He seemed to be playing better, yet I had a feeling that it might be my last chance to record him.

Before I went down to New Orleans in 1942, I stopped off in Chicago to see Jimmie Noone.

111

He wasn't supposed to mix with the clientele, so I went around the back and talked to him through an open window. We talked about possible clarinet players whom Bunk might want to use, and he thought Big Eye would be about the best choice. When I got down to New Orleans, we went to Luthjen's on the Saturday before the session (June 6, 1942) to see Big Eye. He had been sick and couldn't play, but the owners had insisted that he should sit on the stand holding his clarinet so the band would look bigger! When we were working on the book *Jazzmen*, I saw Jelly Roll in 1938 and asked him about all the old time musicians. He said, "There were three great clarinetists in the old days in New Orleans: George Baquet, Tio (the young Lorenzo Tio) and Picou." I asked him about Big Eye and he said, "Big Eye wasn't really first class; he couldn't read" (that would knock him out with Jelly). Then he said, "And beside that, he's a whiskey head." Jelly didn't like people who drank on the job. Big Eye had stomach ulcers, which was probably caused by the alcohol in his system.

Natty Dominique told me a story of when Big Eye was working with Manuel Perez at the Economy Hall. One night Perez couldn't make the job, so he sent his pupil Natty Dominique along in his place. Natty was just a young kid at the time and when he walked in Big Eye called out, "Look who Manuel's sent. Some young dumb kid!" This hurt Natty's feelings. Big Eye looked down on him because he was just a little kid. Then Natty told of how, later, he played real well for Big Eye and was accepted by him. Big Eye was certainly one of the better clarinetists, even if he didn't read.

Wooden Joe and Big Eye had mentioned Louis Nelson as a good trombonist, so the next day (Wednesday, June 29) I went by Louis Nelson's home to talk with him. He said he'd be happy to make the dates, but every Tuesday at 8 pm, he rehearsed with a forty-piece band at the Tulane Club under Mr. Pritchard. In the daytime he was enrolled for a baking course under the GI Bill of Rights.

I hadn't decided where I was going to record and I went to look over the New Hall on Derbigny, but it was too large.

Over the past year Maude had been writing to me, telling of Bunk's illness, so I phoned her to say I was coming out to New Iberia the next day.

I caught the mid-day train (Thursday 30) and, as I approached Bunk's door, I couldn't help remembering how tidy Bunk had kept the outside, as it looked so neglected now. When I arrived he was slumped in a chair and looked very weak. He recognized me and I sat with him a while, but all he would say was, "There's nothing to talk about." He uttered a few other words, but it was difficult to make it out, as I could hardly hear what he said under his mumbles.

Bunk had talked to the doctor the week before and wanted to know how he was. Maude said he hadn't talked to anyone since. After the doctor had been, he'd told Maude, "You can give my trumpet to Bill Loughborough – or to David Bell; he plays too, maybe he'd want it." When Maude told me this, I said I didn't want to think about that. Bunk was sleeping in his chair and I pointed to him and said, "There's the only one I want to hear play that trumpet." I told Maude not to give up any hopes, even if Bunk had, and there could always be a miracle to save him.

Maude said the first stroke (possibly November 2) hadn't paralyzed him, but the second stroke (November 24) had paralyzed his left side. The past month, Bunk had even lost interest in his mail. Before he had always been anxious to get it and dictate answers. But lately Maude would ask him should she reply, and he would just say, "Tell them hello and best regards."

Emily Mae was there and was due to travel to Washington the following week. It was an important job interview, but she feared she'd have to cancel it if Bunk got any worse. Maude was resigned to the worst. She had been with Bunk for twenty-two years.

That night I slept on the floor by Bunk's bed and the next morning I washed him and gave him a shave. It was sad how soft his lip had gone since he'd been unable to play. After I had got some shopping in for Maude, I felt there was nothing else I could do for the moment. I hated to leave him.

I caught the afternoon train back to New Orleans and that evening (Friday, July 1) I went by Luthjen's to hear Big Eye and to Manny's Tavern (Benefit and St. Roch) where George was playing. The next day I heard Johnny St. Cyr in a four-piece band, including Eddie Richardson from the Eureka, but I was not too impressed with them. Then I went over the river to Westwego to hear Alvin Alcorn, Jim, Israel Gorman, Charlie Hamilton and Batiste Moseley at the Gay Paree.

On Monday (July 4), at about 3 am, my landlady woke me saying a telegraph girl had just phoned. I got up and went out to phone Emily Mae. She had cancelled her trip to Washington, and said Bunk was not expected to pass the night. Then I went over to the Roosevelt Hotel at about 4.30 am to phone Maude. Bunk was still alive. I felt pretty depressed, but thought it better to go ahead with the Wednesday and Thursday record dates I'd arranged. I phoned Maude again on Tuesday; he was still alive, but mostly unconscious.

On Wednesday (July 6) I went by George Lewis's. Over ice-cream and cake, Mrs. Lewis told me gravely that Bunk must be dead: "Slow Drag had a dream the night before and Bunk had said to him, 'Come and pack your trunk, we're going on a trip; we're going to New York.' Drag was worried, as he hadn't been feeling too well himself lately."

I took the recording equipment over to Wooden Joe's house and set it up. Big Eye soon arrived. He was smartly dressed and said he felt okay. Louis Nelson and Glenny then arrived, followed by Keppard and then Jiles. Although it was Wooden Joe's date, Big Eye more or less took charge of the rehearsal, being the senior musician. He kept trying to get Glenny and Keppard to tune up. He'd sound a note on his clarinet and call "higher" or "lower." Eventually he got them halfway in tune and we finally decided to try a number or two.

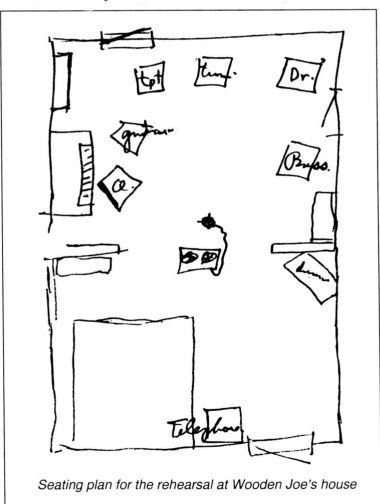

Seating plan for the rehearsal at Wooden Joe's house

REEL 1:

WOODEN JOE'S BAND

Rehearsal at Wooden Joe's home, 2138 Painters Street, New Orleans.
Wednesday, July 6, 1949 (7.00–9.00 pm)

"Wooden" Joe Nicholas (tpt); "Big Eye" Louis Nelson Delisle (clt); Louis Nelson (tbn); Louis Keppard (gtr); Albert Glenny (sbs); Albert Jiles (dms)

1	Shake It and Break It		Unissued
2	Shake It and Break It		Unissued
3	Holler Blues	("Fairly good to use")	AM LP 640, Stv: SLP 212, Dan: VC-4012, VC-7013, AMCD-7
4	Holler Blues	("Not good")	Unissued
5	Pallet on the Floor	("slow') (neither v. good")	Unissued
6	Pallet on the Floor	("faulty)	Unissued
7	Creole Song (*Ai-Ai-Ai*)		Unissued
8	Creole Song (*Ai-Ai-Ai*) ("not so bad, vocal too soft") Unissued		
9	B-Flat Blues		AM LP 646, Stv: SLP 212, Dan: VC-4012, VC-7013, AMCD-7
10	Leaning on the Everlasting Arm ("Pop on radio; possibly theme song")		AMCD-7
11	You Made Me What I Am Today		AM LP 646, Stv: SLP 212, AMCD-7
12	Creole Song		Unissued

Bill Russell: Wooden Joe asked for *Shake It and Break It*, which turned out to be the usual *Weary Blues*. It didn't sound so good. Next came *Pallet on the Floor* played rather slowly. Wooden Joe said it was okay to play it either fast or slow. For the repeat, Big Eye wanted to pitch the tempo faster, like Buddy (Bolden) used to play it. After *Creole Song*, in which Wooden Joe had sung, I suggested they might play a spiritual. (Wooden Joe had suggested a title or two when I talked to him earlier.) My request must have astonished Big Eye. He looked hard at me, "What? Play a spiritual!" They tried Wooden Joe's suggestion of *Leanin'* (*Leaning on the Everlasting Arm*), which he said was used on a religious radio program all the time. The others didn't seem to know it too well. Louis Keppard particularly wanted to sing *You Made Me What I Am Today*. He sang it in a very dramatic fashion with all the movements, just like an old-time vaudeville singer. The whole band seemed to enjoy this number more than most. It ran quite long and Big Eye played some nice clarinet.

The room seemed crowded with musicians and furniture, and it wasn't possible to move the microphone back any further into the other room.

During the evening we tried moving Big Eye up a little closer and moving Wooden Joe farther back, but the balance never did sound very good.

The trombonist, Louis Nelson, evidently didn't feel so good after the 4th of July holiday down in the Delta country. His stomach was still upset, and he stuck to soft drinks when we sent Joe's grandson across the street to get refreshments during the intermission.

There were several people on the porch, but little noise. Thankfully the street outside the house was closed off due to repairs, so we didn't get any traffic noise. It was very hot and we used a large window fan between pieces. By 9 pm we were ready to quit. I wasn't happy about the acoustics and tried to think of somewhere else where I could record. I took the Gentilly bus down to Herb Otto's on Bourbon Street and looked over his house, kitchen and courtyard, but decided the street noises were too loud for recording. I was also doubtful about using Orin Blackstone's store, which would also be crowded.

The next morning I decided we had better try and use Wooden Joe's large back yard. The boys suggested putting tar paper down, as they did at lawn parties, but Joe and I said no, as it wouldn't make any difference. I played over some of the tape again for Joe.

I went to see Big Eye in the afternoon. I asked him if we should try to get St. Cyr to come that night on some excuse, but Big Eye said not to bother, as they would get along somehow. He was still annoyed with Keppard and said, "He never did get that thing in tune last night," and ". . . hated to keep after him all the time, to tune his guitar up." I said I'd do what I could and asked him to remind him also. I asked Big Eye's advice on the tunes and mentioned the spiritual to him. He thought for a moment: "You'd better use *Bye and Bye*." He really was a man of few words (as far as I knew him), but there was always the impression of a lot of thought behind everything he said. With just a word or two and a knowing nod or a roll of his eyes, he seemed able to understate a lot.

Later in the afternoon I went to Orin's, and when I returned home at 5 pm there was a telegram waiting for me. As soon as I saw the New Iberia postmark I knew what it was, even before I opened it. I waited until after 6 pm (on the way to Wooden Joe's) before phoning Maude. She hoped I could come out to New Iberia as soon as possible, before the noon train. She said she'd wait to go to the funeral home and make the burial arrangements until I got there. I told her I'd try to get an earlier bus before that train. I then went on to Wooden Joe's, but didn't mention the bad news to anyone until after the session.

We set up in the back yard and Joe's folks helped him run a light cord out there. A radio was going in Joe's relatives' home next door, so instead of setting the band up against the house I set them up in the other corner of the yard.

We were a little late getting started and it was getting dark, but by 7.30 pm we started on a blues.

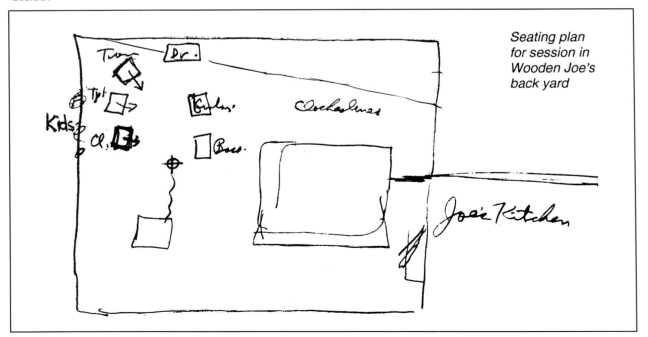

Seating plan for session in Wooden Joe's back yard

REEL 2:

WOODEN JOE'S BAND
Wooden Joe's back yard at 2138 Painters Street, New Orleans.
Thursday July 7, 1949 (7.30 –10.30 pm)

"Wooden" Joe Nicholas (tpt); "Big Eye" Louis Nelson Delisle (clt); Louis Nelson (tbn); Louis Keppard (gtr); Albert Glenny (sbs); Albert Jiles (dms)

1	Holler Blues	(*"not so good"*)	Unissued
2	March		AMCD-7
3	March		Dan: VC-7026
4	Bye and Bye		Unissued
5	Bye and Bye		Unissued
6	Bye and Bye		Unissued
7	Bye and Bye		Unissued
8	Creole Song		Unissued
9	Creole Song		Unissued
10	Creole Song		Unissued

(*"Intermission while reels were changed"*)

REEL 3:

1	Bunk's Blues	Unissued
2	Bunk's Blues	Dan: VC-7026
3	Creole Song	
	(issued as *Ai-Ai-Ai*) (977)	AM 534, Wolf: WJS 1002, WJS 1002 CD, AMCD-7
4	Creole Song ("vocal louder OK")	Dan: VC-7026
5	Bye and Bye	Unissued
6	Bye and Bye (979)	AM 536, Wolf: WJS 1002, WJS 1002 CD, AMCD-7
7	Bye and Bye	Dan: VC-7026
8	Holler Blues	Dan: VC-7026
9	Holler Blues (976)	AM 534, Wolf: WJS 1002, WJS 1002 CD

(*"About 4¹/₂ min left on reel 3"*)

Bill Russell: Up to the intermission, none of the numbers sounded too good and I was getting a little worried. It was often difficult to keep the kids sitting on the fence quiet. Some of the neighbors often peeped over the fence to see what was going on. About 9 pm we took an intermission and sent the kids out to get some soft drinks, 7 Up. Big Eye asked for a Jax beer. Burbank arrived and I even thought of asking him to stand by in case Big Eye was sick anytime.

After the intermission I asked for a blues. Everyone was in good spirits, and when they heard the playback Wooden Joe said, "That sounds like some of Bunk's stuff." I later gave it the title of *Bunk's Blues*. The first take of *Creole Song* was better than the one the previous

AMERICAN MUSIC 977

534

Ai Ai Ai (Creole Song)

WOODEN JOE'S BAND

AM Records
704 Lewis Street
Canton, Mo.

AMERICAN MUSIC 976

534

Holler Blues

WOODEN JOE'S BAND
With Louis Delisle

AM Records
704 Lewis Street
Canton, Mo.

AMERICAN MUSIC 979

536

Bye and Bye
WOODEN JOE'S BAND
With Louis Delisle

AM Records
1637 N. Ashland
Chicago 22

evening, although when Wooden Joe came to the microphone to sing he often turned towards Glenny and Keppard. Wooden Joe's daughter was supposed to sing a spiritual, but I forgot to ask her. We finished about 10.30 pm, and I told them about Bunk dying that afternoon.

The next morning (Friday, July 8) I caught the 7 am bus to New Iberia. Maude and Emily Mae were there, with Maude's sister, Georgia Dickson. After the funeral, I returned to New Orleans on Sunday.

When I got back, I went to see Al Burbank. He suggested Percy Humphrey (as he had in 1945) or "Fernandez" [Albert Walters] as good trumpet men. He said most of the Eureka men were not in the Union. I wasn't sure about this as I'd seen Shots and Picou working together, and Richardson and St Cyr. Burbank said he was in the Union, but he never had any problems if he worked a non-Union job. I asked him about taking Big Eye's place (when Big Eye was sick) at Luthjen's. He said he never had any trouble, as they never advertised and the Union delegates never got around to such places. He seemed more concerned about the pay on parades. We talked about trombonists and he suggested Eddie Pierson. I then went to see Percy Humphrey, but he said his insurance work would keep him busy until the end of the month. Burbank then suggested Herb Morand. The previous month, Morand had made some tapes for Bob Matthews. I'd heard these the week before and I thought it was a fine idea. I went with Burbank to find Morand. He lived at the back of St. Philip (1728), behind Claiborne. He said he would be happy to work as he wasn't doing too much then.

I had wanted to use Herb Morand in 1943 for the Climax session and I was surprised when George wrote to me and suggested Kid Howard. I'd never heard of Kid Howard, so the night I got in I went down to hear him at the Harmony Inn, where he was working with a three-piece band. I then planned to use two trumpets on some numbers and then some with either Morand or Howard. Herb Morand dropped by at the rehearsal at Edgar Mosley's house and said he might try to make the session, but he wouldn't promise. Later he took me outside and said, "Don't mix me up with those guys" – like George Lewis and Jim Robinson – "I'm a recording artist!" He had recorded a lot in Chicago for Decca, in the 1930s. He didn't mean, "Don't put me with them." He meant, "Don't confuse me as only being in their class." He didn't intend to be spiteful; it was just his attitude. George was, more or less, his regular clarinet player the following year and was probably the best thing in the band.

I went around to see Big Eye (Tuesday, 12 July) and we talked about trombonists. He said that Louis Nelson was a good man, although he drank. He also mentioned Eddie Pierson and Bill Matthews, but pointed out that Matthews was working six nights a week from 9 pm. Big Eye said he had been responsible for getting Bill Matthews to switch from drums to trombone.

When I asked him about rags, he said *Maple Leaf Rag* would have to be worked out from the parts. He might have mentioned that he didn't think Wooden Joe would be able to play them and suggested that his regular trumpet player, Charlie Love, would be the better man for the dates under his name. We talked about other numbers like *All the Whores . . .*, and he suggested it would be nice to use the old version: "You know, there were three sections to that piece and I can remember only one part." I was hoping he might remember the other parts. I asked him about using Luthjen's for the recording. He said that he'd ask about it, but I would have to talk to Mrs. Luthjen myself. George Lewis had told me that her oldest son, Joe, really ran the place. I also asked about Artisan's Hall, but Big Eye said he wasn't sure what they would rent it for. I told him I'd paid $10 in 1945. Big Eye didn't offer any encouragement, saying he only lived there and that they kept it padlocked most of the time.

Luthjen's (2527 Marais) was also known as "the old folks home," as it catered mainly for the older white dancing crowd. "Old Man" Luthjen, a German, had died and left the place to his wife. I took the bus to Almonaster and saw Mrs. Luthjen at about 4.30 pm. I explained that I'd like to record the band on their night off, from about 7 pm until 10 pm, and also hire the place for an hour (or an hour and a half) on another night for a rehearsal. She didn't understand what I was trying to explain. At first she thought I wanted her to hire some extra men. I went over it again and explained it the best I could. She didn't seem too impressed with the idea and said she would have to talk it over with her son and that I would have to come back the next day.

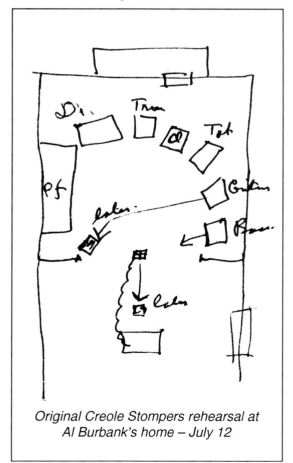

Original Creole Stompers rehearsal at Al Burbank's home – July 12

That night we scheduled a rehearsal at Albert Burbank's house. At 7 pm I was all set up, so that we could finish early in time for Louis Nelson to go to a band rehearsal at the Tulane Club. Herb was the first one there and all ready to go to work. Soon Jiles and Nelson arrived and then St. Cyr in his old truck, "Caldonia." Young didn't get there until after 7.30. I'd tried to phone him, but his party line was always busy. The friend who had promised to bring his bass down didn't show up and he had to get a taxi at the last minute.

We set up in Burbank's front room. The fan in the mid room worked fine and it was quite cool all evening. No tunes had been decided before the session, although I'd asked Albert to think over some. The night before he'd suggested *Creole Song* and even hummed it, but decided for some reason it would not be ideal – perhaps it needed a special accompaniment that some relative had played on the piano. His son also had a *Creole Song* in mind. Burbank was wondering about the copyright on *Eh, La-Bas*. He thought that Ricard Alexis had sent it in for copyright, so he also sent a copy in some time ago.

118

REEL 4:

ORIGINAL CREOLE STOMPERS
Rehearsal at Albert Burbank's home, 2129 Lapeyrouse Street, New Orleans.
Tuesday July 12, 1949 (7.30 pm start)

Herb Morand (tpt); Louis Nelson (tbn); Albert Burbank (clt); Johnny St Cyr (gtr); Austin Young (sbs);
Albert Jiles (dms)

1	Some of These Days	Unissued
2	Tin Roof Blues (issued as *B-flat Blues*)	AMCD-9
3	Nobody's Sweetheart Now	AMCD-9
4	Eh, La-Bas (vcl Burbank)	AMCD-9
5	South	AMCD-9

Bill Russell: Burbank suggested *Some of These Days* for the opening number. After rehearsing his suggestion of *Tin Roof Blues*, I asked for *Nobody's Sweetheart*, which he'd played so well at carnival time. But after playing it Burbank said he didn't remember it very well.

The day before I'd asked Nelson to keep in mind any tunes he'd like to try, but he never suggested anything. When Burbank requested *South*, Nelson seemed unsure of it. St. Cyr had brought some amplification equipment for his guitar, but didn't use it that night. After five numbers we called it quits. I paid everyone $5 for the rehearsal and gave Austin Young $2 for his taxi expense. Burbank's son and nephew had been out and got some drinks and shortly afterwards Nelson left for his own rehearsal.

Original Creole Stompers
Albert Jiles, Louis Nelson, Herb Morand, Austin Young, Albert Burbank, Johnny St. Cyr

(Session added to Reel 4)

ORIGINAL CREOLE STOMPERS
Albert Burbank's home, 2129 Lapeyrouse Street, New Orleans.
Wednesday July 13, 1949 (7.00 –10.30pm)

Herb Morand (tpt, vcl); Louis Nelson (tbn); Albert Burbank (clt); Johnny St. Cyr (gtr); Austin Young (sbs); Albert Jiles (dms)

6	I Can't Escape from You	AM Book CD
7	Sheik of Araby	AMCD-9
8	Baby Won't You Please Come Home	Unissued

REEL 5:

1	Baby Won't You Please Come Home	Dan VC-7026
2	Baby Won't You Please Come Home (974)	AM 532, Stv: SLP 203, AMCD-9
3	Tin Roof Blues	AMCD-9
4	Tin Roof Blues	Dan: VC-7026
5	Some of These Days	Unissued
6	Some of These Days	
	("Moved mike further back into next room")	Unissued
7	Some of These Days	
	("Still distortion from electric guitar")	Unissued
8	Eh, La-Bas ("Without electric guitar")	Unissued
9	Eh, La-Bas (980) ("OK to issue")	AM 535
10	Milneburg Joys	Dan: VC-7026, AMCD-9

REEL 6:

1	Some of These Days (981)	AM 535, AMCD-9
2	B-Flat Blues	Dan: VC-7026
3	B-Flat Blues (975)	AM 532, AM Book CD
4	Baby Won't You Please Come Home	Unissued
5	The Sheik of Araby	Dan: VC-7026, AMCD-9
6	High Society	AMCD-9

Bill Russell: Although Burbank had virtually called all the numbers during the rehearsal, at the actual session Herb Morand was intent on taking charge. Before we got started, he suggested using some of his own material, like *If You're a Viper*. I wasn't too keen on the idea and I didn't encourage him. (It was really Burbank's date, and I didn't want to tie up any of Morand's material, as his name wouldn't be on the label.) Even so, before each number Herb Morand would sit and think for a moment and then tell them how many choruses they should take "to make it come out right." If anyone expressed surprise, he would remind them that he hadn't spent those years with Decca for nothing.

They warmed up with *I Can't Escape from You*. This (like *Climax Rag*) seemed to be a favorite warm-up number for many New Orleans bands. Herb then sang on *Baby Won't You Please*

120

Come Home. He stood at the back of his chair for some of his trumpet solos, and on *B-flat Blues* he used a coconut shell for a mute.

Earlier they'd talked about *Nobody's Sweetheart* and *Dippermouth Blues*, but in the end they choose *The Sheik of Araby*.

When we were all finished, St. Cyr suddenly said he wanted to do "his number" – some sort of guitar solo. Before we could set up, Albert Burbank asked to do *High Society*, which he said would be some "Lagniappe." It ran quite long, and even though there was a lot of enthusiasm in the playing it probably wasn't anything that I would issue.

At about 10.45 pm everybody was packed up and leaving. Johnny St. Cyr and I told Herb Morand how much we had enjoyed his playing. For a moment he seemed to be at a loss for words, then he turned towards Johnny St Cyr and said, "I am honored to have the chance to record with one of the real pioneers." Then turning to me he added, modestly, "I'm not really one of the pioneers, you know." Johnny replied, "You may not be one of the pioneers, but, man, you sure played like one." He was very pleased to be told that. He had been very easy to work with and certainly wasn't an objectionable person. But, like Big Eye, I guess he thought he was in a higher class than many New Orleans musicians. Johnny St. Cyr was another musician that I had tried to record earlier. I'd had him in mind for Bunk's Jazz Man session, but he was afraid of what the Union might say and declined. Most of the band (except probably Young and Jiles) were in the Union, but since I'd assured most of them that I wouldn't be putting their names on the label, they didn't seem to be too bothered. I got the impression that even if the Union had asked them about the records, they wouldn't have been too worried about what the Union might say.

On Thursday (May 14) I went to see Mrs. Luthjen. She said she didn't like the idea of Big Eye recording there, making some excuses about the neighbors and patrons wanting to come in. I was really annoyed about this after Big Eye had worked there for so many years. Then I went to Louis Gallaud's house on St. Anthony Street, near Perseverance Hall. He was working at the GI school during the day. His piano was in poor shape, as many of the keys stuck.

I was still looking for somewhere to record, so I went to Grunewalds, Werleins, and then finally to the Godschaux Buildings (where Rudi Blesh had recorded the brass band in 1946). The piano looked good, but Harvey and Orin Blackstone had said that their work was not so good and had "too much shrill."

I wanted to record Big Eye with Gallaud, as they worked so well together at Luthjen's. I went to see Karl Kilinski's studio. He had a good piano and was very helpful and didn't mind if I used my own tape machine. When I told Big Eye we could use his studio, he said using St. Cyr and Young and a piano "would make the rhythm too heavy," and added, "You know we used to play without pianos all the time in the old days."

On Sunday night I went by Luthjen's and everyone was ready for the rehearsal the next night. It was raining hard and I caught the bus down to Canal and stopped to talk to Ray Burke and Monk Hazel outside the Famous Door for a few minutes. Burke had joined the Union two weeks before in order to play with George Hartman's band on Bourbon Street. He was also substituting for Lester Bouchon in Sharkey's band while Lester had an operation.

On Monday afternoon (July 18), while walking downtown, I met Wooden Joe, on his way uptown to see Keppard. Joe had a wedding job the next Saturday and wanted Keppard to play guitar.

Big Eye's Band recording at Dr. Nelson's home – July 18

It rained again later that afternoon, but I'd got over to Dr. Nelson's home early to get everything set up. Louis Nelson wasn't home yet, which worried me a little. Soon Rogers and Young came in with their big instruments, and then Charlie Love. They laughed at Big Eye not being there, as he'd ordered the others to be early so they could finish the job and get away earlier. Soon after Big Eye arrived, and then St. Cyr, but still no Louis Nelson. When he did finally come, he looked as if he'd been drinking and straight away went and sat in the back of the house for a while.

I put the tape recorder on the piano bench and placed the microphone on a small stool I'd taken from the dresser. Dr. Nelson's folks stayed in the back room and kindly covered the telephone with pillows during the recording.

REEL 7:

LOUIS DELISLE'S BAND
Rehearsal at Dr. George Nelson's home, 1421 Touro Street, New Orleans.
Monday, July 18, 1949 (7 pm start)

Charles Love (tpt); "Big Eye" Louis Nelson Delisle (clt); Louis Nelson (tbn); Johnny St. Cyr (gtr); Austin Young (sbs); Ernest Rogers (dms)

1	Black Cat on the Fence	Unissued
2	Black Cat on the Fence	Unissued
3	Black Cat on the Fence	Unissued
4	South	
	(issued as *Pork Chop)*	AM Book CD
5	Clarinet Marmalade	Unissued
	Tests by gtr and bass	Unissued
6	Clarinet Marmalade	Unissued
7	Dinah	Unissued
8	Basin Street Blues	Unissued
9	Basin Street Blues	Unissued

Bill Russell: Big Eye called for *Black Cat on the Fence* and said this was a number by Charlie Love. There was a little trouble getting the trombone part right, especially on the intro and coda, but Big Eye didn't seem to mind too much. Big Eye then suggested *Pork Chop* (*South*). They tried it only once and it ran 2½ minutes, promising to be okay for the next night. Big Eye then called for *Clarinet Marmalade,* which rather surprised me as he'd said he'd use numbers that everybody hadn't recorded. Big Eye reminded me that I'd once suggested *Dinah* – which I'd liked when I heard them play it at Luthjen's about two weeks before.

During the intermission they had drunk a little beer. Big Eye had a bottle of Jax and Louis Nelson kept to soft drinks. Big Eye didn't seem too discouraged that Nelson had been late and not in good form. He smiled and quietly said to me, "You can't expect to do too much with a trombone that's drunk."

Afterwards I paid them each $5 for the rehearsal and everybody soon left, except Austin Young, who stayed to talk with Dr. Nelson awhile.

The next morning I was a little concerned about Louis Nelson, but glad we'd only been having a rehearsal and not a real session. In the early afternoon I went up to see him and he seemed fine. I hadn't taken any pictures the night before, so I took one of him sitting at his mother's piano. He said she had been a good pianist. (In recent years Louis Nelson has been a real gentleman and about the best trombonist around. But like a lot of younger musicians in those days, he liked to drink, although I don't think he ever missed a job through being too drunk to play.)

I then went by Wooden Joe's and discussed his session for later that week. Joe was keen to have George Lewis on the date, so I went to talk to George, but he was out. I talked with Jeanette for a few minutes and got some ice-cream soda for Shirley.

Every evening it seemed to rain, but it never cooled the temperature. Fortunately Dr. Nelson had a large fan in the bedroom, which we would sometimes forget to turn off before the music started. It was very hot and sometimes I helped to fan the guys between numbers. The tape machine also got very hot, and I could hear an audible hum during the playback on some of the numbers. I began turning the machine off whenever possible, and even fanning it, to cool it down. After we finished the previous evening I took the tape over to Herb Otto's, but it sounded okay when I played it on his machine.

Everybody was about on time and we started around 7 pm.

REEL 8:

LOUIS DELISLE'S BAND

At Dr. Nelson's Home, 1421 Touro Street, New Orleans.
Tuesday 19 July 1949 (7.00 pm start)

Charles Love (tpt); "Big Eye" Louis Nelson Delisle (clt); Louis Nelson (tbn); Johnny St. Cyr (gtr); Austin Young (sbs); Ernest Rogers (dms)

1	Black Cat on the Fence	Dan: VC-7026
2	Black Cat on the Fence (982)	AM 537, AM LP 646, Stv: SLP 212, Dan: VC-4012, VC-7013, AMCD-7
3	South	Unissued
4	South (issued as *Pork Chop*) (986)	AM LP 646, Stv: SLP 212, Dan: VC-4012, VC-7013, AMCD-7
5	Clarinet Marmalade	Unissued
6	Clarinet Marmalade ("not good")	Unissued
7	Clarinet Marmalade (983) ("Prob. best take to issue")	AM 537, AM LP 646, Stv: SLP 212, Dan: VC-4012, VC-7013, AMCD-7
8	Clarinet Marmalade ("not good")	Unissued
9	Clarinet Marmalade	Unissued
10	Clarinet Marmalade	Unissued
11	Basin Street Blues	Dan: VC-7026

REEL 9:

1	Basin Street Blues (972 & 972a)	AM 533, AM LP 646, Stv: SLP 203, Dan: VC-4012, VC-7013, AMCD-7
2	Dinah	Unissued
3	Dinah (973)	AM 533, AM LP 646, Stv: SLP 212, Dan: VC-4012, VC-7013, AMCD-7

Add William Tircuit (vcl)

4	Basin Street Blues	AMCD-7

Note: The AM LP 646 version of *Clarinet Marmalade* is the same as on AM 537, except that a different clarinet and guitar chorus has been spliced from two of the other takes.

124

Big Eye's Band – July 19:
Johnny St. Cyr, "Big Eye" Louis Nelson, Charlie Love, Louis Nelson and Ernest Rogers

Bill Russell: Big Eye started with *Black Cat on the Fence* again and the second take sounded very good. There was no trouble with the intro and coda. Charlie Love laughed and explained that *Black Cat on the Fence* was only the polite title they told the girls when they asked the name of the piece.

The second take of *South* also seemed okay. Very often Big Eye would run over a little of a number before I recorded, to remind them of the tempo. Afterwards, he always wanted to hear everything played back and sat motionless, with the clarinet bell resting on his knee, listening intently. I always made a point of asking him if he was satisfied with the number before going on to a new piece.

Clarinet Marmalade gave them a little trouble. Some takes ran too short, so a guitar solo was suggested to lengthen the piece. Big Eye seemed to think it was a good idea, and when they tried it he yelled to St. Cyr, "Take two." After six takes of *Clarinet Marmalade* they tried *Basin Street Blues*, which came out pretty good. Big Eye was fairly satisfied with it, but I asked for another try.

Then Big Eye asked how many numbers we had, and I said four, but would also like to try *Dinah* as an alternative number. After the first take he seemed to be getting anxious to end the session, saying they couldn't do *Dinah* any better. I told him it was a good idea to have a second take as a "safety." I also mentioned that the second take of *Basin Street Blues* (at the rehearsal) turned out better than the first. He acted doubtful and said, "Did you think so?"

The session went off smoothly, in spite of the trouble with *Clarinet Marmalade,* and didn't take the three hours that I'd expected. We stopped for a break right after *Dinah* and I took some pictures. For these, Big Eye went over and sat between St. Cyr and Love. We almost forgot about the vocal on *Basin Street* that Nelson's son-in-law wanted to do, so I asked Big Eye to try it once more, just for him. It ran quite long and he sang in a Billy Eckstine crooner style. He was only a foot away from the mike, yet he could hardly be heard. Big Eye yelled, "Sing out." I paid all the guys $33 and Big Eye $50. I also gave Rogers and Young an extra $1 for their taxis.

The guys were in no big hurry to leave, and St. Cyr made a very emotional speech about how "I've know this man (Big Eye) for forty years and I've never seen him frown. I don't believe he ever gets mad." Big Eye, as usual, was very quiet during the evening, but very business-like and efficient. He didn't seem to plan any arrangements – perhaps because Love, Rogers and he had worked so much together, they felt they didn't need to. Yet some of the numbers (such as *Dinah*) were played quite differently at Luthjen's. Big Eye never seemed to waste much time tuning up, nor do I remember him having any reed trouble. When he took a solo, I pointed the microphone towards him. Sometimes, if he was bearing down, he would lean over and point his clarinet towards the microphone.

That night there was a notice about Bunk's death in the *New Orleans Sentinel* and a piece about Bud Scott dying in Los Angeles in early July. All the guys seemed interested.

On the way home I walked by George Lewis's to ask if he would be available on Wednesday and Thursday for Wooden Joe's session. The house was dark and I didn't want to wake him if he was in bed.

The next morning (July 20) I started out early and met George coming up Dauphine Street, about a block from his house. He seemed a little embarrassed, and more cautious than usual when I asked about recording and rehearsing that night. He said he was afraid to do it on account of the Union. It seems that a day or two before Kid Howard had asked him if he was going to record, and he'd told him he "didn't know anything about any recordings." He mentioned he'd had a lot of trouble when they did the brass band date for Rudi Blesh [1946]. Joe Howard and Isidore Barbarin hadn't been in the Union and he'd had a lot of trouble from the Union, but managed to talk himself out of it. He said he wished he could have played, as he needed the money.

After I'd left George, I decided I'd better try and get Ann Cook. I'd been asking Wooden Joe and everyone if they knew of any good, experienced female blues singers. Wooden Joe had a couple of ideas, but he hadn't seen any of them for several years, and, since they were probably now married, it would be impossible to trace any of them.

I'd already fixed up Young and St. Cyr for the session the night before, so I got the bus to Canal and walked down to the Southern Railroad offices. Burbank was cleaning up the hallway and he got permission to take some time off to talk to me. We both went out to the company's railroad yard and found Albert Jiles. They were both glad to be able to work the session and said they would be there for the rehearsal.

I went up to see Wooden Joe and talked over the session with him. He suggested *Any Rags*, an old song, that he would like to sing.

I then went uptown to look for Ann Cook. The trailer camp, on South Rampart and Julia, looked different from my earlier visits, but the little restaurant was still operating. I went in and asked if Ann Cook still lived around there. A young boy took me to a saloon nearby, and there one of Ann Cook's nephews gave me her new address – 2227 Thalia Street. Luckily, she was in and she remembered me. She said the reason she hadn't come in '43 and '44 was that I hadn't offered her "any money." She told me again the exact amount that Victor had paid her to sing with Louis Dumaine. I told her I was hardly in a class with Victor and I could only pay her $50 for two sides. I also asked her about blues again, but she said at once, "No, I belong to the church now, I don't sing no blues." I knew there would be no chance of getting her to come to a rehearsal, so I told her about my plans for Thursday. She said she had a church meeting that night, so if I wanted to record her we should start at 7 pm. She said her songs shouldn't take long and she still could get to her meeting in good time. I wrote down Burbank's address and gave her some money for the taxi. I said I would send her a dozen copies of the record, and if she wanted to sell some more to her congregation she could have them for half price – 50c each. She thought about this for a few seconds, but said that there wasn't enough in it for her and she wouldn't be interested in that. I still wasn't convinced she would ever show up.

REEL 9 (continued)

WOODEN JOE'S BAND
Rehearsal at Al Burbank's home, 2129 Lapeyrouse Street., New Orleans.
Wednesday, July 20, 1949 (7.00 pm start)

"Wooden Joe" Nicholas (tpt & clt*); Louis Nelson (tbn); Albert Burbank (clt); Johnny St. Cyr (gtr); Austin Young (sbs); Albert Jiles (dms)

5	Up Jumped the Devil	Unissued
6	Up Jumped the Devil	Unissued
7	Up Jumped the Devil	Unissued
8	Some of These Days (*)	Unissued
9	B-flat Blues (*)	Unissued

REEL 10:

1	Any Rags	AMCD-5
2	Any Rags	Dan: VC-7026
3	Climax Rag	Dan: VC-7026
4	Clarinet Blues (*)	AM LP 640, Stv: SLP 204, Dan: VC-4010, VC-7014, AMCD-5
5	Clarinet Blues (*) (issued as *Clarinet Blues No.2*)	AMCD-5
6	Clarinet Blues (*)	Unissued
7	Any Rags	Unissued
8	Any Rags	Unissued
9	Any Rags	Unissued

Note: Due to the reel and take number (10-4), *Clarinet Blues* has sometimes been listed as *10-4 Blues* in some discographies.

Bill Russell: We got started with the rehearsal at 7 pm. After a few tries of *Up Jumped the Devil*, I asked Joe if he could try a clarinet number. He suggested *Some of These Days*. It didn't sound especially good, and since I already had a pretty good version by Morand I asked him for a blues on the clarinet. They played a long (five-minute) *B-flat Blues*, which sounded pretty good. Joe said, afterwards, that he hadn't touched the clarinet for a long time. When they did *Any Rags*, St. Cyr took the vocal. He remembered the old tune and said it was based on the "street cry" of the junk peddlers. This had also been mentioned as a "Bolden number" by Rudi once. Wooden Joe had talked about *Climax Rag* a day or two before. They rehearsed it once, but it didn't sound too promising. I told them about my meeting with Ann Cook and my doubts. Burbank and Jiles said they would try and look up some other singers, in case Ann Cook didn't come.

The next morning I rang Burbank to see if he'd located anybody. He suggested Myrtle Jones, whom I'd recorded in 1944. That afternoon I went back to see Ann Cook. She started out by saying she had talked to her manager and he'd said $50 wasn't enough. He thought she should have $65 I told her I didn't think she needed to give him a cut, or involve him, since I had gone direct to her. She seemed to back down on the manager talk and said he wouldn't get any commission. But before I left she asked again for $65. I offered her $55 to show that I'd pay her as much as possible, but that was all I could manage. I acted like I didn't expect her to come, but she said, "Oh, I'll be there alright." She then sang the two songs she had selected. I'd already given her more than enough for the taxi, but I gave her a little more and told her to be there by 7 pm.

Just in case she didn't show up, I went by Myrtle Jones's house (now living on Robertson Street). She was keen to record, after I'd mentioned $25. I explained about Ann Cook and said I would phone her at 7.30 if Ann Cook hadn't arrived.

I got to Dr. Nelson's early, and Burbank, St. Cyr and Young were already there. Promptly at 7 o'clock, a taxi drove up and out stepped Ann Cook. She was really all dressed up – a big flowered print dress and a large fluffy broad-brimmed hat, decorated with flowers. She entered looking like she owned the whole town, although I later found out that she'd borrowed some of the clothes from a neighbor. As I began to take some photos of her, she noticed some artificial flowers in a vase on the piano, so I took one of her holding the bouquet. Unfortunately she was wearing her glasses, and when I had the film developed, the flash had reflected in her lenses and ruined the photo.

REEL 11:

ANN COOK with WOODEN JOE'S BAND
Dr George Nelson's home, 1421 Touro Street, New Orleans.

Thursday, July 21, 1949 (7.00–8.45 pm)

"Wooden Joe" Nicholas (tpt); Louis Nelson (tbn); Albert Burbank (clt); Johnny St. Cyr (gtr); Austin Young (sbs); Albert Jiles (dms); Ann Cook (vcl)

1	Where He Leads Me, I Will Follow ("slow funeral march rehearsal")	Unissued
2	Where He Leads Me, I Will Follow	Unissued
3	Where He Leads Me, I Will Follow	Unissued
	Bob Matthews (dms) replaces Jiles	
4	Where He Leads Me, I Will Follow	Unissued
	Albert Jiles (dms) replaces Matthews	
5	The Lord Will Make a Way, Somehow	Unissued
6	The Lord Will Make a Way, Somehow (978)	AM 536, Stv: SLP 204, Dan; VC-4010, VC-7014, AMCD-5

Bill Russell: Wooden Joe hadn't arrived, but since I'd stressed getting started promptly I thought we had better go ahead and try a song. They started to work out *Where He Leads Me, I Will Follow*. Ann thought it could be sung as a slow funeral hymn, in the manner of a dead-march – one heavy bass drum beat on the first beat of each bar and the snare taps on the other three beats. Either Ann's tempo was unsteady, or she'd leave out a beat now and then, and often at the end of a line. When Joe arrived we tried it again, but Jiles and Young got mixed up several times and everybody got very confused. They even tried leaving out some of the subordinate beats on some of the other takes, but nothing worked. So I suggested we tried her other song. *The Lord Will Make a Way* seemed to go better, but the first try was still unsatisfactory. It was now 8.30 and Ann Cook was getting restless. She told everybody how her Victor date with Louis Dumaine had taken "so many minutes." She seemed to think that every take she had done had been okay. She finally agreed to try the song once more, but remarked "I'm tired," and that she wanted to go. She then surprised everyone by starting the second take in a different key. Burbank spotted the change straight away, but Wooden Joe seemed slow to pick it up. The rest of the band switched as soon as they could. When we played it back she said, "That's good enough," and, no matter how I begged her, she refused to sing it again. I paid her $55 and gave her the taxi fare home.

When she sang, she turned halfway towards the band and held the microphone close. At first she seemed intent on "teaching" the band her numbers. She seemed to remember Wooden Joe and St. Cyr and was generally very pleasant with everybody. When she had gone, St. Cyr thought she had a good voice, but he said she wasn't a good musician, as she couldn't keep time.

Johnny St, Cyr and Albert Burbank at the July 21 recording session at Dr Nelson's home

REEL 11 (continued)

WOODEN JOE'S BAND
Dr George Nelson's home, 1421 Touro Street, New Orleans.
Thursday July 21, 1949 (9.15–approx. 11.30 pm)

"Wooden Joe" Nicholas (tpt & clt*); Louis Nelson (tbn); Albert Burbank (clt); Johnny St. Cyr (gtr); Austin Young (sbs); Albert Jiles (dms)

7	Up Jumped the Devil	Unissued
8	Up Jumped the Devil	Unissued
9	Up Jumped the Devil	Unissued

REEL 12:

1	Blues (*)	Unissued
2	Blues (*)	Unissued
3	Blues (*)	Unissued
4	Any Rags	Unissued
5	Any Rags	Unissued
6	Sugar Blues	Unissued
7	Sugar Blues	AM Book CD
8	Seems Like Old Times	
	("*Boots Young vcl. for Dr. Nelson*") AMCD-5	

Note: On *Seems Like Old Times* the opening clarinet chorus was overcut and has been edited out on AMCD-5.

Bill Russell: After a few beers and time for the machine to cool off, we got started again. I suggested a few numbers like *Wind and Grind* or *Pork Chop*, but it always came out as *Up Jumped the Devil*. Several takes ran short and it was getting late. Wooden Joe always kept his clarinet on a chair beside him, so I asked him to try a *Clarinet Blues*. When he played his clarinet chorus, he would stand and move nearer Burbank's chair. The first take ran too long for a 10" 78, but was better than the next two tries.

The tape machine began to heat up again and I could hear some distortions on playback. *Any Rags* seemed to drag along, and we even played back the rehearsal version to check the tempo. I hoped that *Sugar Blues* might come through as a good number, but it didn't. The guys were getting restless and the tape recorder was about shot, so we quit.

Even with the problem of Ann Cook's numbers and the recording machine trouble, I hated to give up. The next day, Wooden Joe mentioned he thought some of them had been unreasonable about the length of the session, saying that they would have to work far harder (and twice as long) at a dance job, and for a fraction of the money.

Although Wooden Joe had lost most of his power, it had been good to record him again and talk with him. Some years earlier he had the tendons cut in his lower right arm. This meant he couldn't bend the fingers of his right hand, and he played the clarinet (and trumpet) with his fingers straight.

Wooden Joe, Louis Nelson and Albert Jiles at the July 21 recording session at Dr Nelson's home

I still wanted to get a good picture of Ann Cook. So a few days later (Monday, July 25) I went up to her house to take some more photos of her without her glasses. She sent a little girl over to her mother to ask if she could borrow a dress, and got all dressed up. I took some photos of her in her yard. She said she wanted her name on the records as: "Ann Cook of the Greatest St. Matthew No. 2 Baptist Church," and got me to write it down. As I took the photos, she held her mouth stiffly and pulled in her lips so they would look smaller. Jelly used to tell how a lot of negroes were sensitive about their large lips. He always considered (being a Creole) that he had nice lips.

I went around to see Big Eye, to say goodbye. He told me he was 68: "You know I always thought I was older than Bunk." I asked him about recording next time and how I hoped to have some of the Red Back Books. He replied: "I might not be here next time." I told him he was looking better than he had been in years, but he said he didn't feel very well. He died within a few weeks [August 20].

Dr Bechet thought that Big Eye was in his seventies and older than Picou. Some of the books say Big Eye was born in 1885, the same year as King Oliver, but that would have made him 64 when he died. I'm sure Big Eye knew how old he was. But, whatever his age, I know Bunk was older.

132

Ann Cook photographed in her borrowed dress – July 25

Montgomery, 1949

Bill Russell: At Mardi Gras time in the 1940s, a washboard band would come down to New Orleans and play in Jackson Square. They played for tips or whatever they could get. They called themselves the Mobile Strugglers. Most of them came from Montgomery and a couple of them were from Mobile. There weren't any jug or washboard bands in New Orleans, so after they'd been coming two or three times, I decided to record them. When I went down for Mardi Gras in 1949, I spoke to the leader and arranged to go to Montgomery later that year.

On the way down to New Orleans in 1949, I stopped off in Montgomery, Alabama (Monday, June 27). The guys were all waiting for me, but two of the fellows hadn't come over from Mobile and the washboard player was out of town. The leader, Paul Johnson, warned me that most of them were unreliable, but they could play with any size group. They played *St. Louis Blues*, then a march (probably *Billboard March)* and *Fattenin' Frogs* with a vocal by Lee Warren. I then went to see James Fields (the band's violinist) in Mobile, about recording. I arranged to record them on my return from New Orleans in a month's time.

Before I left New Orleans, I thought I'd better remind them again I was coming. So, on the Monday (July 25), I sent a telegram to Montgomery to remind Paul Johnson, and one to Mobile, to their violinist James Fields, saying that I would be in Montgomery the next day.

When I arrived I had to wait for James Fields to come over from Mobile, but the regular washboard player (Tyler Jackson) was in jail that week, so we had to go ahead without him. The size of the band varied as to who was available, and they told me they sometimes used Orlan Crenshaw and W. Broad (gtrs), both from Mobile. Other musicians like Tim Finley (gtr) and Tyler Jackson (washboard) were from Montgomery. James Fields was the oldest musician at 62. Paul Johnson was 58 and the others were probably in their thirties and forties.

REEL 13:

MOBILE STRUGGLERS
James Fields's barn, 105 East Washington, Montgomery, Alabama.
Tuesday, July 26, 1949 (7pm–10pm)

James Fields (vln); Lee Warren (vcl, mandolin, bjo and "streamline bass"), Paul Johnson (leader/manager, gtr, sbs and "streamline bass"); Charles Jones (vln), Wesley Williams (sbs)

1	Cornfed Indiana Gal	AMCD-14
2	Cornfed Indiana Gal	Unissued
3	Cornfed Indiana Gal	Unissued
4	Cornfed Indiana Gal	Unissued
5	Memphis Blues	Unissued
6	Memphis Blues	Unissued
7	Memphis Blues (984) (*"vcl by Fields – OK to issue"*)	AM 104, AMCD-14
8	Indiana Rag	Unissued
9	Indiana Rag (*"OK to issue"*)	AMCD-14
10	Don't Bring Lulu	Unissued

REEL 14:

1	Don't Bring Lulu	AMCD-14
2	Don't Bring Lulu	Unissued
3	Billboard March	Unissued
4	Billboard March ("OK")	AMCD-14.
5	Fattening Frogs for Snakes ("vcl by Lee")	Unissued
6	Fattening Frogs for Snakes ("vcl by Lee")	Unissued
7	Fattening Frogs for Snakes ("vcl by Lee")	Unissued
8	Fattening Frogs For Snakes (985) ("vcl by Lee")	AM 104, AMCD-14
9	Original Blues ("vcl by Fields")	Unissued
10	Original Blues ("vcl by Fields – OK to issue")	AMCD-14

Note: The remaining titles on AMCD-14 are by the Louis James String Band (originally issued on Mono LP 11) and recorded by Reg Hall in 1965.

Bill Russell: They started off with two violins, guitar, banjo and string bass, although a couple of them switched instruments during the session. The "streamline bass" that you see in the picture is made from a tub with a string attached to a pole. The only time this was used was during *Indiana Rag* and both Paul Johnson and Lee Warren took a turn on it during the different takes. Wesley Williams played the regular bass on all the numbers. They also tried *St. Louis Blues*, *66 March* and another rag, which I didn't record.

As it was a different sort of band to the type of thing I had been putting out, I decided not to use the black-on-yellow label. So, for this record, I changed the color to black type on a blue label. I don't think I had more than a hundred records pressed.

CHARLIE THOMPSON

Unknown studio, St. Louis.
Tuesday, August 2, 1949

Charlie Thompson (pno); Bill McCall (dms)

REEL 15

1	The Lily Rag	Rejected
2	The Lily Rag	(given master no. 968a)
3	The Lily Rag	(given master no. 968b)
4	Derby Stomp	(given master no. 969b)
5	Derby Stomp	Rejected
6	Lingering Blues	(given master no. 971b)

REEL 16

1	Delmar Rag	(given master no. 970b)
2	Delmar Rag	(given master no. 970a)

The session was also recorded simultaneously onto disc, the "a" takes at 78 rpm on 12" discs and the "b" takes at 33⅓ rpm on to a single disc. It is from the "a" source that the takes were mastered.

	The Lily Rag (two-minute test at 78 rpm)	Unissued
968a	The Lily Rag	AM 527
969a	Derby Stomp	AM 527
	Derby Stomp (not on tape)	Unissued
970a	Delmar Rag	AM 528
971a	Lingering Blues (not on tape)	AM 528
cut 1:	The Lily Rag (968b)	Unissued
cut 2:	Derby Stomp (969b)	Unissued
cut 3:	Lingering Blues (971b)	Unissued
cut 4:	Delmar Rag (970b)	Unissued

Note: This session is a remake of the earlier December 30, 1947, recording in which the dubbed final disc was overcut by the studio. The same master numbers for each title have been used.

Bill Russell: The drummer was Bill McCall. He told me he came from New Orleans and he had played with Big Eye and others. This was the third time that I'd tried to record Charlie Thompson, so I got it on tape as well as disc in case anything went wrong this time.

Below: two 1949 American Music handbills

American Music

BUNK JOHNSON'S
latest and best records

No. 517   Where the River Shannon Flows
When The Moon Comes Over
The Mountain.

No. 518   Ja-Da
Poor Butterfly

◆

Four Solos

by the outstanding Pittsburgh Pianist

GEORGE HORNSBY

No. 521   Jesus Gave Me A Little Light
Bye and Bye

No. 522   I Know It Was The Blood
My Soul Loves Jesus

10-inch Records, Price $1.05 each
Add 25c per package for shipping postpaid

AM RECORDS
704 Lewis St., Canton, Missouri

AMERICAN MUSIC

Bunk Johnson
517—River Shannon—Moon Over The Mt.
518—Jada—Poor Butterfly
519—Got To See Mamma—Beautiful Doll
520—In The Gloaming—Kathleen

Original Creole Stompers
513—Eh, La-Bas!—Up Jumped The Devil
(Featuring Wooden Joe Nicholas & Albert Burbank)

Dink's Good Time Music
515—Stomp de Lowdown—Grace & Beauty
516—So Dif'rent Blues—Take Your Time
523—Rag Bag Rag—Yeah Man
524—Las Vegas Stomp—The Stella Blues
525—Jelly Roll Blues—Indian Rag
526—Frisco Dreams—Dink's Blues

Charles Thompson
(Real St. Louis Music)
527—The Lily Rag—Derby Stomp
528—Delmar Rag—Lingering Blues

10-inch Records—$1.05 each

Bunk Johnson's Band
251—Tiger Rag—C. C. Rider
252—St. Louis Blues—Staints Go Marching In
12-inch Vinylite Records—$1.75 each

10-inch Records—$1.05 each
A M RECORDS
704 LEWIS STREET, CANTON, MO.

CHICAGO, 1953

NATTY DOMINIQUE'S CREOLE DANCE BAND
Saber Room, Darbell Springs Hotel, 8900 W. 95th Street, Chicago.
Monday, September 28, 1953

Natty Dominque (tpt); Preston Jackson (tbn); Darnell Howard (clt); Ralph Tervalon (pno); Sam Casimir (gtr); Bill Settles (sbs); Baby Dodds (dms)

In the Shade of the Old Apple Tree	Unissued
Sweet Georgia Brown	AMCD-18

Bob Matthews (dms) replaces Baby Dodds

I'll Never Be the Same	AMCD-18

Baby Dodds (dms) replaces Bob Matthews

Rehearsal Blues	AMCD-18
Blues (issued as *Chicago Slow Drag*)	Baby Dodds 2, Dan: VC-4013, VC-7015
	AMCD- 18
You Are my Silver Star	Unissued
You Are my Silver Star	AM Book CD
You Are my Silver Star	AMCD-18
You Are my Silver Star	Unissued
In the Shade of the Old Apple Tree	Unissued
In the Shade of the Old Apple Tree	AMCD-18
Careless Love	AMCD-18
Careless Love	Unissued

Note: Two tape machines were running when *Chicago Slow Drag* was recorded (and possibly other numbers). John Steiner's machine had a microphone in front of the whole band, while Bill Russell operated the machine with the microphone adjacent to Baby Dodds's drum outfit. Both versions were issued on Baby Dodds No. 2 (Bill Russell's tape being titled *Slow Drag No. 2*) while only John Steiner's tape was issued on Dan VC-4013 and VC-7015.

The first take of *You Are my Silver Star* was recorded on John Steiner's machine, while the second take was recorded on Bill Russell's machine – now moved to a different position. It is not known which machine (or both) was used on the other takes. As all the takes have different timings, these are different takes and not the same takes recorded on two different machines. In total, five reels of tape were used, between the two machines.

Bill Russell: This was the regular band that Natty was using at the time, except that the clarinetist was Volly De Faut. I never did like his playing, too thin, so I got Darnell Howard for the recording. Natty was one of the nicest men you could ever wish to meet. I recorded a lot of interviews with him and I still have all his letters.

Natty Dominique's band recording at the Saber Room: Bill Settles, Natty Dominique, Ralph Tervalon (partly hidden), Preston Jackson, Darnell Howard, Baby Dodds. Sam Casimir is not shown.

DANCING
to
NATTY DOMINIQUE'S
CREOLE DANCE BAND
featuring

VOLLY DE FAUT   PRESTON JACKSON
JASPER TAYLOR   BABY DODDS
BILL ANDERSON   RALPH TERVALON

introducing
THE SLOW DRAG
NEW ORLEANS' OLDEST and
CHICAGO'S NEWEST RHYTHM

EVERY SATURDAY NIGHT
STARTING MARCH 22, 1952

●

THE FRENCH QUARTER
of
THE MIDNIGHT SUN
1531 NORTH CALIFORNIA AVENUE

8:45 to 1:30 A.M.   ADMISSION $1.50 Incl. Tax

NEW LOCATION
FOR
NATTY DOMINIQUE'S
CREOLE DANCE BAND
FEATURING

Odell Rand   Baby Dodds   Sam Casimir
Jasper Taylor   Preston Jackson
Bill Anderson   Ralph Tervalon

THE SLOW DRAG DANCE SERIES
New Orleans' Oldest and
Chicago's Newest Rhythm Rage

Saturday Nights, April 5th and 12th
9:00 TO 1:30

Admission $1.50 Incl Tax
FOR RESERVATIONS PHONE AL 2-2436

Rainbow Gardens
1959 West Armitage Ave. (at Damen)
2000 NORTH AND 2000 WEST

Natty Dominique,1953

Two10" LPs of Natty Dominique were planned but never issued.

NATTY DOMINIQUE LP 1
Side A: Talk (Early History)   8 minutes
      Rehearsal Blues (from 9/28/53)   3 minutes 8 seconds
Side B: Talk ("Be Original & Sunset Cafe")   8 minutes
      Mute Demonstration (Conn, Long and Cup) 3 minutes 32 seconds

NATTY DOMINIQUE LP 2
Side A: Talk (Kelly's Stables)   7 minutes 30 seconds
      Silver Star (extract from first take from 9/23/53) 3 minutes 30 seconds to 4 minutes 30 seconds
Side B: Talk (Advice to Students)   9 minutes
      Demonstration of "Apple Tree"   2 minutes 55 seconds

The tapes for the above LPs have now been assembled by Barry Martyn and will be issued as part of AMCD-18.

In addition, a fourth Baby Dodds l0" LP was planned but never issued. This was an ambitious project that involved the release of an extensive booklet and a 16 mm movie film to accompany the record. The booklet was based on the Baby Dodds interviews referred to below and this fascinating document is to be included in Bill's unfinished *New Orleans Style* book – shortly to be completed by Barry Martyn and myself. The music examples were to be taken from previous American Music recordings (master numbers shown), and further extracts from the Baby Dodds interviews. Details and timings are as follows:

BABY DODDS No.4

Side A: Talk on High Society	38 seconds
High Society (extract of master 405)	2 minutes 35 seconds
Talk on Tiger Rag	9 seconds
Tiger Rag (master 212)	4 minutes 15 seconds
Talk on Spanish Blues	10 seconds
St. Louis Blues (extract of master 878)	1 minute 53 seconds
Talk on Uptown Blues	22 seconds
St. Louis Blues (master 214)	3 minutes 5 seconds

Side B: *MOVIE ACCOMPANIMENT*
Scenes: Parade music   (Bye and Bye - Brass Band)
Funeral music   (dead march drums)
Snare drum & press roll   (also in slow motion)
Bass drum (foot pedal technique, also in slow motion)
Cymbals
Over entire drum set foot & tom-tom solo
Drums are musical instruments (using timpani drums by arrangement with Moe Asch)
"Light Hands - That's my Secret," music by Natty Dominique's Band

Bill Russell's design and text for the proposed cover:

BABY DODDS No.4

HIGH SOCIETY – TIGER RAG
DOWNTOWN BLUES – UPTOWN BLUES

Baby discusses the proper tempo for some well known **New Orleans favorites**, which are played by **Bunk's Band**. The spanish account of the **Creole Blues** is illustrated by **Joe Petit's Imperial Band**, with Albert Burbank and Joe Nicholas, the negro **Uptown Style** is by **Bunk's Band**.

AMERICAN MUSIC RECORDS 1637 N. ASHLAND AVE. • CHICAGO, 22

Note: The extract of *High Society* (master 405) contained only the last four choruses. The "Spanish" *Downtown Blues* was an extract from *St. Louis Blues* (master 878) and the *Uptown Blues* was the last 6 choruses of the previously issued *New Iberia Blues* (master 214). The text for side B is as above. The 16 mm film still exists.

BABY DODDS TALKING & DRUM DEMONSTRATIONS

Baby Dodds (drum solos and talking)

Baby Dodds - Drum demonstrations	Baby Dodds 1,	Dan: VC-4013, VC-7015, AMCD-17
Baby Dodds - Drum demonstrations	Baby Dodds 3,	Dan: VC-4013, VC-7015, AMCD-17
Playing for the benefit of the band	Baby Dodds 3,	Dan: VC-4013, VC-7015, AMCD-17
Explains his part in "Chicago Slow Drag"	Baby Dodds 2,	Dan: VC-4013, VC-7015

Note: The above are extracts from twelve reels of Baby Dodds interviews and drum demonstrations that Bill Russell recorded between 1952–54.

Bill Russell: Most of these tapes are not dated. I used to stop by at Baby's house at 51st Street sometimes, after I had finished work at a factory on the South Side of Chicago (at about 110th Street).

142

SESSIONS NOT RECORDED BY BILL RUSSELL, BUT ISSUED ON AMERICAN MUSIC

Recorded by John Steiner and Hugh Davis for their "S & D" label

TUT SOPER & BABY DODDS
Jack Gardener's House (Studio B), 503 West Aldine, Chicago.
Monday, January 31, 1944

Oro "Tut" Soper (pno & vcl*); Baby Dodds (dms & vcl#)

13144- 1	Oronics No.1	Unissued
13144- 2	Butter & Egg Man No.1 (*#)	Unissued
13144- 3	Butter & Egg Man No.2 (*#)	Unissued
13144- 4	That's a Plenty	Baby Dodds 2
13144- 5	Oronics No. 2	Unissued
13144- 6	It's a Ramble	S.D. Records 5001
13144- 7	Right Kind of Love (*)	Unissued
13144- 8	Thou Swell	S.D. Records 5001
13144- 9	Keeping Myself for You	Unissued
13144-10	Stardust Stomp	S.D. Records 5000
13144-11	Oronics No.3	S.D. Records 5000
13144-12	Tea for Two (drum novelty)	Baby Dodds 2, Dan: VC-4013, VC-7015

It is believed that all the above titles were originally cut onto a single 16" disc at 33⅓ rpm.

Recorded by Jack Stanley

BUNK JOHNSON
Coffman Memorial Union Auditorium, University of Minnesota, Minneapolis.
Friday, May 3, 1947

Bunk Johnson interview	AM LP 643 (part),
	Purist LP (no number) (complete),
	Paragon PLE-M 102 (complete)

Kid Thomas and Emile Barnes sessions recorded by Alden Ashforth and David Wyckoff

Alden Ashforth: David Wyckoff and I were both students at Harvard and we decided to quit college and go and live in New Orleans. We both planned to get jobs down there and find out as much as we could about the music. In the first week of December 1950, we went to Chicago to see Bill Russell. Although we were due to rise to leave for New Orleans at six the next morning, we stayed up till 4 am talking and listening to his unissued material of Bunk and Wooden Joe. He hadn't released any of the Artisan Hall Wooden Joe numbers then, and I thought they were wonderful. But Bill had no plans to issue them because of the extremely live acoustics, which he called "distortion" – we disagreed. I sensed that he felt since Bunk had died it was the closing of a chapter and he had no intention of doing any more recordings. Some of his Bunk Johnson 12" 78s had gone out of print and he felt some of the unreleased stuff was too long for a 10" 78. He had no interest in 12" 78s anymore and he also doubted that the LP had a future. He did, however, suggest certain musicians we should investigate. Among them was Kid Thomas.

In the early spring of 1951, I began taking clarinet lessons from George Lewis and we soon became friendly with the whole band. Lawrence Marrero, and also Slow Drag, lived nearby. I would often see Lawrence sitting on the stoop at 907 Burgundy and I'd join him and talk. One day he suggested that I should telephone his cousin Emile Barnes, but he made me promise that I would never mention this to George Lewis as there was some "bad blood" between Emile Barnes and George. "Meely" often played in a pickup band at "Fump and Manny's" (the F&M Bar at 4841 Tchoupitoulas). It was usually Abby Williams's job, and, besides Meely, there'd be George Guesnon on amplified guitar (which Meely hated) and Toca (with whom Meely liked to work) or Clayton or, if he was sober, Howard. One night they couldn't get a trumpet so they got Burbank. It was wonderful hearing them both passing the lead between them. Meely used to say that when bands stopped using the violin as the lead instrument, it was the clarinet that first took over lead with the cornet still playing second.

In the Spring of 1951, I struck a bargain with my father who wanted me to resume my studies at Harvard. I agreed to go back to college in the fall if he would give me enough money to buy a tape machine and to record one Union session. He also agreed to send an allowance for rent and food, and by economizing I was able to divert much of that toward funding a couple of non-Union sessions as well. (Earlier, when I couldn't find work, I'd learned that I could eat on as little as 38 cents a day.) Although David Wyckoff did not contribute directly to the financing of the sessions, he was in on all the planning and decision-making, and we agreed that the sessions would always be considered jointly sponsored.

The question was who to record. George Lewis had the best band in New Orleans. Percy Humphrey had just taken over after Talbert's death. It was the most exciting band I had, and ever have, heard. But Doc Souchon had just recorded them, so we thought of recording one of the regularly organized brass bands, either the Tuxedo or the Eureka. Because of its modernistic trumpet section the Tuxedo was stylistically inconsistent, so in the end it just had to be the Eureka.

I wrote to Bill about which tape recorder to purchase and he suggested several models, but thought the best was the Magnecord PT-6, which cost about $600, and the Shure Unidyne microphone. As Bill knew where to do the best deals for this type of equipment I took the bus up to Chicago to see him. Bill got quite excited by the project and agreed to come back with me to New Orleans for the session. It was the first time he'd been back since Bunk died. Two classmates of mine drove from Harvard University to meet up with me in Chicago, and after a great night on the town, with Bill taking us to hear Lee Collins and others (J. Lee Anderson and Barbara Reid were also along), they drove Bill and me and the equipment to New Orleans. As we approached New Orleans, Bill was getting more and more agitated. I remember him leaning out of the window and pounding on the roof with his fist and shouting, "Faster, faster . . . got to get to New Orleans!"

After Bill had returned to Chicago we thought we had better experiment with the tape recorder, so we set up a trial session with Emile Barnes at our apartment, which came out (heavily edited) on Folkways in 1983. This was with George Guesnon, Lawrence Toca, Harrison Brazley, Albert Glenny and Cié. It was only meant to be a rehearsal for a later session and no one got paid. We had problems with the sound and the "refreshments" (i.e. drinks) when we took a break. I'd bought soft drinks, beer, and, unfortunately, a bottle of Seagram's Seven Crown blended whiskey — for which Lawrence Marrero, who had come along as a non-playing guest, scolded me. Toca consumed most of the whiskey, which ruined much of his playing after the break.

We felt obliged to use all of the same musicians on what was to be the paid session, but we also wanted to record Kid Thomas and Billie and DeDe Pierce; however, I really couldn't afford three sessions. George Guesnon was at that time reluctant to play the banjo and (as is well documented) tended to want to dominate things. He wanted to take a couple of solos (usually the same solo) on everything. So we figured that he would be better on a Kid Thomas session (as no one ever told Thomas what to do), and Billie could provide the chord instrument instead of a banjo in the band we'd rehearsed with earlier. Also, as Toca proved he could be unreliable, we thought that having DeDe there to play some numbers would ensure that it would not be a wasted session.

When I wrote to Bill to tell him of our plans, he wrote back that he would bring down a marvelous new microphone (the Stephens condenser-type, from Costa Mesa, California) that he could borrow from E. D. Nunn.

It was Bill who arranged for the band to record at the Karl Kilinski Violin Studio at 315 St. Charles Avenue. Kilinski was an old violin friend of his and he got the studio for next to nothing.

EMILE BARNES NEW ORLEANS BAND
The Karl Kilinski Violin Studio, 315 St. Charles Avenue, New Orleans.
Thursday, August 30, 1951

(Recorded on six 7" reels at 15 ips)

Emile Barnes (clt); Lawrence Toca (tpt on "a" tracks); DeDe Pierce (tpt on "b" tracks); Harrison Brazley (tbn); Billie Pierce (pno, vcl on "c" tracks); Albert Glenny (sbs); Josiah Frazier (dms)

REEL 1:

1	Shake It and Break It (a and c)	Unissued
2	Shake It and Break It (a and c)	Folkways: FA 2463, Topic 12.T 55, AMCD-13
3	Lonesome Road (b and c)	Folkways: FA 2465

REEL 2:

1	Lonesome Road (b and c)	AM 641, Stv:SLP 164 (part), Barrelhouse (no number), Dan: VC-4011, VC-7010, Jz Con: JJC 40, AMCD-13
2	Panama (a)	AMCD-13
3	Eh, La-Bas (b and vcl)	AM 641, Stv: SLP 164, Barrelhouse (no number), Dan: VC-4011, VC-7010, Jz Con: JJC 40, AMCD-13

REEL 3:

1	Hindustan (a and b)	Stv: SLP 164, Barrelhouse (no number), Dan: VC-4011, VC-7010, Jz Con: JJC 40, AMCD-13
2	Hindustan (a and b)	Unissued
3	DeDe and Billie's Blues (b and c)	AM 641, Barrelhouse (no number), Stv: SLP 203, Dan: VC-4011, VC-7010, AMCD-13

REEL 4:

1	DeDe and Billie' s Blues (b and c)	
	(issued as *Billie's Blues No 2*)	Stv: SLP 164
	(issued as *DeDe and Billie's Blues No 2*)	AM Book CD
2	Careless Love Blues (a and c)	AM 641, Stv: SLP 164, Barrelhouse (no number), Dan: VC-4011, VC-7010, Jz Con: JJC 40, AMCD-13

REEL 5:

1	Careless Love Blues (a)	AMCD-13
2	Tout de Moi (b and DeDe vcl)	AM 641, Stv: SLP 164, Barrelhouse (no number), Dan: VC-4011, VB-1003,VC-7010, Jz Con: JJC 40, AMCD-13
3	St. Louis Blues (a and c)	AMCD-13

REEL 6:

1	St. Louis Blues (a, b and c)	Stv: SLP 164, Dan: VC-4011, VC-7010, Jz Con: JJC 40, AMCD-13
2	Some of These Days (a and b)	AMCD-13
3	Ciribiribin (b)	AMCD-13

Note: On the above recording log, Bill Russell circled *St. Louis Blues* (reel 6, title 1) and wrote "Good." This number may have also been considered for inclusion on AM LP 641.
In 1953, Bill wrote of plans to issue this session on a 12" LP, adding *DeDe and Billie's Blues* (4-1), *Hindustan* (3-1), *St. Louis Blues* (6-1) and *Panama* (2-2) to the 10" LP.

Alden Ashforth: The numbers were chosen by asking some of the musicians individually what each would like to play. Toca selected *Shake It and Break It* and wanted to play *Careless Love* in his Chris Kelly style. Meely chose *Hindustan* and Billie *Lonesome Road*. DeDe wanted to do *All of Me*, and it was Bill who suggested that he might sing a chorus in Creole patois. I wanted Meely to try again the so-called Larry Shields solo on *St. Louis Blues* that he'd done at the rehearsal, but we never did get a good take of that. It was arranged for Toca to play on certain numbers and DeDe on others, and I never expected that the two trumpets would play together, but Toca joined in playing harmony in sixths and thirds, in the old style without prompting.

The opening number (*Shake It and Break It*) caught us by surprise as we didn't expect a vocal, and Billie had been used to just shouting out the words at Luthjen's when she felt like it. So Bill, who was handling the microphone (he wouldn't let any else touch it at that stage), simply took it over to Billie for the second take, with me handling the Magnecord.

On the first take of Billie's blues number, it seemed that DeDe was upset by her unexpected lyric about marital infidelity, and he quickly switched from B-flat to E-flat, probably to ruin the take. Billie caught on to this right away and switched, then Brazley and finally Barnes picked up the change of key. When it was over Meely was angry, and we decided to do another take, but we always thought that the first was definitely better.

There was a little blank tape left on the last reel; it looked like enough for another, short take. *Ciribiribin* was a wonderful number and everybody was playing well. Then I noticed that we were running out of tape. In the middle of Brazley's solo I shouted for them to "go out" and they all came in right away; we just made it.

Right: Billie, DeDe and Albert Glenny during the recording

Below: Harrison Brazley, Cié Frazier, Lawrence Toca, Billie Pierce, DeDe Pierce, Emile Barnes and Albert Glenny

(The mask just visible on the far wall is a life mask of Beethoven.)

Alden Ashforth: Ruben Roddy (of the Eureka) was a regular member of Kid Thomas's band and he told us where, in Algiers, we could hear Kid Thomas play. We had a lot of difficulty getting to hear him. After the ferry ride, the bus dropped us off at the wrong place. We had some problems when we hitched a lift, and decided to make a dash for it when the car stopped for a red light. After walking a while and asking directions we thought we were hopelessly lost when finally we heard a trumpet in what we thought was the next block. Actually it turned out to be about five blocks away! We had been unprepared for such a powerful sound, and we were overwhelmed by Thomas's playing that evening.

Kid Thomas – Hope Hall, September 3

One afternoon I went over to Thomas's home to talk about the session. I asked him about playing with Meely Barnes. He said he had often worked with Meely in the old days and would be happy to play with him again. He knew I wanted a full band and insisted on Bob Thomas and Babe Phillips, adding, ". . . if he still plays." He also insisted that we record at Hope Hall, which was near where he lived. Meely was also happy to work with Kid Thomas and suggested using George Henderson, whom he had often worked with, and whom we had heard at Luthjen's. Although Henderson had a tendency to speed up during a number, I thought that having Guesnon in the rhythm section would keep things steady.

I knew Bob Thomas personally, as he and I had often wound up on the same bus on the way to work. Although the buses were segregated we would stand on either side of the dividing sign and talk. Babe Phillips I didn't know. Thomas gave me his address; it was way uptown, and when I got there I found this one-eyed ancient-looking character holding a baby. I asked if it was his grand-daughter and he looked offended: "No, it's my *daughter!*" He said he hadn't played in a long time, but eventually he got out his ancient three-string bass and plucked a few notes.

Although the tape machine was housed in two carrying cases, they were large and heavy. On the evening of the recording, Bill, David and I took turns in carrying the heavier section. About every block we had to put it down and rest. Hope Hall was a long rectangular box-like wood building with a large room and a raised bandstand at one end, and a smaller adjacent room. We first set the band up in the larger room but the sound had too much echo. The smaller room was better, but it had no power outlet. So we had to leave the tape machine in the large hall and run a cable into the smaller room to the microphone. Bill offered to look after the tape machine and I looked after the microphone and gave the musicians their signals.

Bob Thomas, Kid Thomas, Emile Barnes, George Henderson, George Guesnon and Babe Phillips

KID THOMAS ALGIERS STOMPERS
Hope Hall, Homer and Verret Street, Algiers.
Monday, September 3, 1951

(Recorded on six 7" reels at 15 ips)

"Kid Thomas" Valentine (tpt); Emile Barnes (clt); Bob Thomas (tbn); George Guesnon (bjo and vcl*);
Joseph "Babe" Phillips (sbs); George Henderson (dms)

REEL 1:

1	Bucket's Got a Hole in It	AM Book CD
2	Bucket's Got a Hole in It	AMCD-10
3	Panama Rag ("might cut 1 bjo chorus")	AMCD-10
4	Sister Kate	AMCD-10

REEL 2:

Harrison Barnes (tbn) replaces Bob Thomas

1 Blues   Unissued
2 Blues (*)
   issued as *Come on Down to New Orleans* AM LP 642, Stv: SLP 212, Barrelhouse (no number),
                                            Dan: VC-4012, VC-7013, AMCD-10
3 Blues (*)
   issued as *Come on Down to New Orleans No. 2* Stv:SLP 203, AMCD-10

REEL 3:

1 St. Louis Blues   Unissued
2 St. Louis Blues   AM LP 642, Stv: SLP 212, Barrelhouse (no number),
                                  Dan: VC-4012, VC-7013, AMCD-10
3 Sweet Georgia Brown   Unissued
4 Sweet Georgia Brown   AM LP 642, Barrelhouse (no number), Dan: VC-4012,
                                  VC-7013, Wolf: WJS 1002, WJS 1002 CD
                                  AMCD-10
5 Bucket's Got a Hole in It   AM LP 642, Stv: SLP 212, Barrelhouse (no.number),
                                  Dan: VC-4012 & VC-7013, AMCD-10

REEL 4:

1 Panama Rag   Unissued
2 Sister Kate   AM LP 642, Stv: SLP 212, Barrelhouse (no number),
                                  Dan: VB-1003, VC-4012, VC-7013, AMCD-10
3 Kid Thomas's Boogie Woogie   Unissued
4 Kid Thomas's Boogie Woogie   AM LP 642, Stv: SLP 212, Barrelhouse (no number),
                                  Dan: VC-4012, VC-7013, AMCD-10

REEL 5:

1	Careless Love Blues	AM LP 642, Barrelhouse (no number), Dan: VC-4012, VC-7013, Wolf: WJS 1002, WJS 1002 CD, AMCD-10
2.	Some of These Days (Guesnon, ampl gtr solo)	AMCD-10
3	Sunny Side of the Street (Guesnon, ampl gtr solo)	AMCD-10

REEL 6:

1	Marie	Unissued
2	Marie	Unissued
3	Marie	Stv: SLP 212, AMCD-10
4	Panama Rag	Stv: SLP 212, AMCD-10

Note: *Marie* (reel 6, take 2) was incomplete, lasting only 1 minute 45 seconds. Take 3 was noted for possible inclusion on AM LP 642.

Alden Ashforth: I thought it was strange when Bob Thomas arrived for the session all dressed up. He had assumed we would just be making a couple of 78s and had accepted an engagement for later that evening.[47] He played on just three tunes (plus an extra take of one) and left after about thirty minutes. Everybody then started suggesting other trombone players. There was a pay phone in the lobby and, armed with a pile of nickels, we began telephoning around. Joe Avery and Harrison Brazley were both out and others we tried couldn't do it. David ran down to the local store for some more nickels, but after about an hour we still hadn't got a trombone player. Then Meely suggested Harrison Barnes, who lived nearby. He answered but he said he was no longer playing. We really didn't want to go ahead with a short band, so Meely and one of the others (Guesnon, I think) went over to see Harrison Barnes to try and persuade him to change his mind. After about half an hour they came back with him.

Guesnon had never met Babe Phillips. He was greatly amused from the start by this old man and immediately parked himself next to him. When Guesnon began playing stop-time

Harrison Barnes and Emile Barnes

151

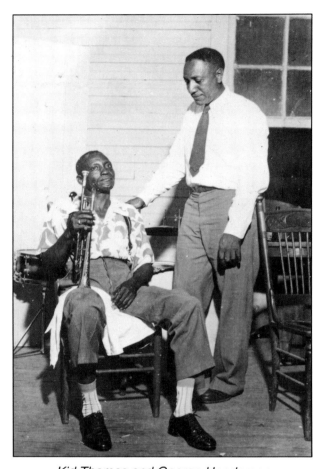

George Guesnon and Babe Phillips   *Kid Thomas and George Henderson*

choruses on the first blues take, it confused Phillips, and Guesnon started shouting encourage-ments to him. Bill thought this sounded good, and Guesnon needed no persuading to work this into a take of a later number. After a few takes Thomas became aware that Guesnon was trying to hog the solos, so he began to exert his authority. But Guesnon was never one to miss a chance to project himself. I had asked the musicians to remain silent for five seconds when they'd finished a number, otherwise their voices might not be able to be edited out. Naturally Guesnon couldn't resist the opportunity offered, and right after the last note of the boogie number, he called out, "This one I got to hear, Mister Russell, this one I got to hear." He'd been itching to play the amplified guitar all evening, so eventually Thomas agreed to this for two tunes. On the first he turned the volume up for his solo so high that it distorted. On the second he was persuaded to use more tasteful levels.

Guesnon had no title in mind for the blues he sang, so Bill called it *Come on Down to New Orleans* when he later selected the tracks he wanted to use.

We wanted Bill to start issuing records again and we offered him all the material we had recorded. He immediately declined the Eureka session, saying he could never afford to reimburse me for the high Union-scale costs,[48] but said he would think about the others. After about a year he wrote to say he would like to issue material from the Barnes session with

Alternative photograph from the Kid Thomas session – September 3, 1951

DeDe and from the Thomas session, but that he couldn't afford to compensate me for the session costs. I replied that this didn't matter and suggested if he made money out of the records he should give some to the musicians as a bonus. When I asked him for the master tapes back in 1985, he gave me his carefully documented accounts and how much extra each musician had been paid. It seemed like Guesnon had been back every few weeks for more money. ("I know you must be making a million bucks out of that record, Mister Russell.") He also reminded me that he had never paid me for the use of the tapes and insisted that he reimburse me not only for the original amount but for interest accrued over the intervening years, and taking into account inflation. All of this he had carefully calculated. By this time all of the musicians had passed away, but David took part of the money to Meely Barnes's widow as a goodwill gesture.

Baby Dodds, Art Hodes and Darnell Howard recording, November 5, 1953

Recorded by John Steiner for his Paramount label

ART HODES TRIO
Phil Atwood's home, Winnetka, Illinois.
Thursday, November 5, 1953

Darnell Howard (clt); Art Hodes (pno); Phil Atwood (el.bs); Baby Dodds (dms)

112253-1a	Slow and Easy Mama	Paramount CJS112, Baby Dodds 2, Dan VC-4013, VC-7015
112253-2c	I Know That You Know	Paramount CJS112
112253-3a	Baby Food	Paramount CJS112, Baby Dodds 2
112253-4a	Sweet Georgia Brown	Paramount CJS112

Note: I asked John Steiner why this was billed as a trio, when four musicians were present.

John Steiner: Since Phil was not on the contract, we felt it best to omit his name and otherwise ignore his slight presence (with his approval) on the issued Paramount 10" LP. There was another session besides the one you have listed for these titles. The same titles were re-recorded with the same personnel on November 22, 1953 [issued on Jazzology J-113]. On both sessions, no other titles were recorded, but other takes and partials may exist. Both sessions were taped.

Recorded by Joe Mares

BRUNIES BROTHERS DIXIELAND JAZZ BAND

Buena Vista Hotel, Biloxi, Mississippi.
Exact date unknown –1957

Abbie Brunies (tpt, vcl); Merritt Brunies (valve tbn); Jules Galle (clt);
Eddie James (pno); Tony Fountain (sbs); Joe Wentz (dms)

Zero	A-LP 651
Tin Roof Blues	A-LP 651
Till We Meet Again	A-LP 651
Let Me Call You Sweetheart	A-LP 651
That's a Plenty	A-LP 651
It's a Sin to Tell a Lie	A-LP 651
Over the Waves	A-LP 651
Jazz Me Blues	A-LP 651
Angry	A-LP 651

Note: As this was a non-Union session, Joe Mares felt he could not issue it on his Southland label and Bill agreed to its appearing on American Music. Although Bill did carry stocks of the LP, it was sold mainly by Joe Mares through his regular Southland distributors. Joe Mares confirmed that there were no additional titles or alternatate takes recorded.

PARAMOUNT RECORDS ISSUED ON AMERICAN MUSIC

JOHNNY DODDS with Tiny Parham   (Recorded 1927)
635   Loveless Love   (Paramount 12483)   AM V-1
634   19th Street Blues   (Paramount 12483)   AM V-1
(Issued in 1947. The "V" was omitted from the second pressing and *Loveless Love* was re-titled *Careless Love*)

JOHNNY DODDS with Blythe's Washboard Band   (Recorded 1926)
2541   Bohunkus Blues   (Paramount 12368)   AM V-2
2542   Buddy Burton's Jazz   (Paramount 12368)   AM V-2
(Issued in 1947. The "V" was omitted from the second pressing)

FREDDY KEPPARD with J. Dodds   (Recorded 1926)
956   Stock Yards Strut   (Paramount 12399)   AM 3
955   Salty Dog   (Paramount 12399)   AM 3
(Issued in 1948. *Salty Dog* is take 1. The original Paramount issue was *Freddy Keppard's Jazz Cardinals*)

LOVIE AUSTIN'S SERENADERS with Dodds & Ladnier (Recorded 1926)
957   In the Alley Blues   (Paramount 12391)   AM 4
958   Merry Makers Twine   (Paramount 12391)   AM 4
(Issued in 1948. The original Paramount issue was *Lovie Austin and her Blue Serenaders*)

156

MA RAINEY with Her Georgia Band   (Recorded 1926)
451 Soon This Morning (Paramount 12438) AM 5
452 Don't Fish in my Sea (Paramount 12438) AM 5
(Issued in 1949)

MA RAINEY with Lovie Austin's Serenaders (Recorded 1924)
1703 Those Dogs of Mine (Paramount 12215) AM 6
1704 Lucky Rock Blues (Paramount 12215) AM 6
(Issued in 1949)

OLLIE POWERS' ORCHESTRA   (Recorded 1923)
1502 Play That Thing (Paramount 12059) AM 7
IDA COX with Tommy Ladnier   (Recorded 1923)
1509 Blues for Rampart Street (Paramount 12063) AM 7
(Issued in 1949. *Play That Thing* is take 3. The original Pararmount issue was *Ollie Powers Harmony Syncopators* and the reverse Ida Cox number was *I've Got the Blues for Rampart Street*).

JABO WILLIAMS   (Recorded 1932)
1404 Jab Blues (Paramount 13141) AM 8
1407 Pratt City Blues (Paramount 13141) AM 8
(issued 1949)

Note: The titles and master numbers shown are those printed on the American Music label. Only AM 2, 6, 7 and 8 bear any similarity to the original Paramount master numbers.
AM 9 was also mastered but never issued – Henry Brown & Ike Rodgers: Twenty-First Street Stomp / Henry Brown: Henry Brown Blues. (Both from Paramount 12825)

157

Dink's Good Time Music

No. 515 - Stomp de Lowdown

Grace & Beauty

No. 516 - So Dif'rent Blues

Take Your Time

Original Creole Stompers

(Featuring Wooden Joe Nicholas and Albert Burbank)

No. 513 - Eh, La-Bas !

Up Ju

Bunk Johnson's

("sensation of the year"-

No. 511 - Margie

Do Right Baby

10 inch Records, Price $

Add 25c per package f

A M REC

647 MEANS AVE.

LP
33⅓
638-A

BUNK
PLAYS THE BLUES
San Jacinto Hall
N.O. 1944

AMERICAN MUSIC
AM Records
1637 N. Ashland
Chicago 22

AMERICAN MUSIC

BUNK JOHNSON
518—Jada—Poor Butterfly
519—Got To See Mamma—Beautiful Doll

ORIGINAL CREOLE STOMPERS
513—Eh, La-Bas!—Up Jumped The Devil
532—Baby Won't You Please Come Home—B-Flat Blues

LOUIS DELISLE'S BAND
533—Basin Street Blues—Dinah

DINK'S GOOD TIME MUSIC
515—Stomp de Lowdown—Grace and Beauty
516—So Dif'rent Blues—Take Your Time
523—Rag Bag Rag—Yeah Man
525—Jelly Roll Blues—Indian Rag
526—Frisco Dreams—Dink's Blues

CHARLES THOMPSON
527—The Lily Rag—Derby Stomp
528—Delmar Rag—Lingering Blues

KID SHOTS' NEW ORLEANS BAND
529—Uptown Bump—Maggie
530—Dumaine St. Drag—In Gloryland

GEORGE LEWIS
531—Burgundy St. Blues—Closer Walk

Reissues From Paramount Records
Licensed by The N. Y. Recording Lab.
3—KEPPARD—Salty Dog #1—Stock Yards Strut
4—AUSTIN—In The Alley Blues—Merry Makers
5—MA RAINEY—Soon This Morning—Don't Fish
6—MA RAINEY—Lucky Rock Blues—Those Dogs
7—POWERS—Play That Thing #3—COX—Rampart St.
8—JABO WILLIAMS—Jab Blues—Pratt City Blues

10-inch Records—$1.05 each
A M RECORDS
704 LEWIS STREET, CANTON, MO.

LP
33⅓
638-B

BUNK
PLAYS SPIRITUALS
In New Orleans
1944-45

AMERICAN MUSIC
AM Records
1637 N. Ashland
Chicago 22

AMERICAN

BUNK JO

517—River Shannon—Moon O
518—Jada—Poor Butterfly
519—Got To See Mamma—B
520—In the Gloaming—Kath

ORIGINAL CRE

513—Eh, La-Bas!—Up Jump
(Featuring Wooden Joe

DINK'S GOO

515—Stomp de Lowdown—
516—So Dif'rent Blues—Ta
523—Rag Bag Rag—Yeah
524—Las Vegas Stomp—T
525—Jelly Roll Blues—In
526—Frisco Dreams—Dink

Reissues From

Licensed by T

FREDD

with

3—Salty Dog (No. 1

LOVIE AUS

with

4—In The Alley Blue

10-inch

A M

704 L

AMERICAN MUSIC RECORDS

Long Playing - 33 1/3 - Microgroove -
10 inch-red vinyl - $3.85

638 - BUNK JOHNSON - BLUES & SPIRITUALS
(with Geo. Lewis, Jim Robinson, Baby
Dodds, etc.) 5 numbers including a
nine minute Blues, Saints Go Marching,
& Closer Walk (Bunk's Brass Band).

639 - GEORGE LEWIS - IN THE FRENCH QUARTER
Ice Cream, Burgundy St. Blues, Over The
Waves, High Society (with Kid Shots),
lip St. Breakdown, and two

OE'S NEW ORLEANS BAND - A NITE
IAN HALL (with Burbank, Jim
, etc.) Shake It, Careless
ad Me On, Eh La Bas, & 3 more

NES & HIS NEW ORLEANS BAND
ie and De De Pierce. Creole
Blues.

MUSIC
N
ountain
oll

OMPERS
vil
l Albert Burbank)

MUSIC
Beauty
Time

Blues

ount Records
ecording Lab.

PARD
dds
Stock Yards Strut

ERENADERS
adnier
Makers Twine

—$1.05 each

CORDS
anton, Mo.

AMERICAN MUSIC

LONG PLAYING RECORDS

638 BUNK JOHSON - BLUES and SPIRITUALS

New Orleans band with Geo. Lewis, Jim Robinson, Baby Dodds. 5 numbers, including a nine-
minute Blues, Saints Go Marching In, and
Closer Walk With Thee (Bunk's Brass Band).

639 GEORGE LEWIS-IN THE FRENCH QUARTER

AMERICAN MUSIC
LONG PLAYING RECORDS

638 BUNK JOHNSON—BLUES and SPIRITUALS
New Orleans band with Geo. Lewis, Jim Robinson,
Baby Dodds. 5 numbers, including a nine-minute
Blues, Saints Go Marching In, and Closer Walk
With Thee (Bunk's Brass Band).

639 GEORGE LEWIS—IN THE FRENCH QUARTER
Burgundy St. Blues, Ice Cream, Over The Waves,
High Society (Kid Shots), St. Philip St. Breakdown,
and others.

640 WOODEN JOE—AT ARTESIAN HALL
New Orleans Band with Albert Burbank and Jim
Robinson. Shake It, Careless Love, Lead Me On,
Eh La Bas, and others.

641 EMILE BARNES & HIS NEW ORLEANS BAND
With Billie and De De Pierce. Creole Songs and
Blues.

643 THIS IS BUNK JOHNSON TALKING
Buddy Bolden's Style, illustrated by trumpet and
whistling, with piano by Bertha Gonsoulin. Parades,
Tony Jackson, Pete Lala's, Dago Tony's, music by
brass and dance bands.

644 BUNK—1945-1946
The New Orleans Band playing 827-Blues and 3
other pieces. The New York Trio in Jada, Got To
See Mama Every Night, etc.

645 GEORGE LEWIS with KID SHOTS
Band with Dodds, Robinson, Slow Drag, and Mar-
rero. Bucket's Got A Hole In It, Dumaine Drag,
Gloryland, Sheik, others.

646 BIG EYE LOUIS NELSON DELISLE
New Orleans Band with St. Cyr, Charles Love, etc.
Dinah, Clarinet Marmalade, Basin Street Blues,
Black Cat, B-Flat Blues and 3 more numbers.

647 BUNK JOHNSON—1944
The New Orleans Band in Careless Love, Streets of
The City, Lowdown Blues, Lord You're Good To Me,
etc.

648 DINK'S GOOD TIME MUSIC
Trios, Piano and vocal solos, One-man band. Stomp
de Lowdown, Jelly Roll Blues, Rag Bag Rag, Stella
Blues, Krooked Blues, Cannon Ball Rag, Yeah Man,
Frisco Dreams.

D-1 BABY DODDS—NEW ORLEANS BRASS BAND
Parades and Funerals—talk and music. Demon-
stration of tom-toms, rims and shells. Sewanee
River (Bunk's band and drum solo).

D-2 BABY DODDS with NATTY DOMINIQUE'S BAND
6-minute Blues, Tom-Tom "foot" solo, Trios.

D-3 BABY DODDS—"Playing for the benefit of the band"
Discussion of the drummer's job. Demonstration of
cymbals and other traps. Listen To Me, My Maryland.

D-4 BABY DODDS—NEW ORLEANS STYLE
Uptown and Downton Blues, Tiger Rag, High
Society. 16-mm. movie accompaniment.

★ ★ ★ ★ ★

10-inch, 100% pure red vinyl LPs — $3.85
AMERICAN MUSIC RECORDS
600 CHARTRES   NEW ORLEANS 16, LA.

159

LISTING OF AMERICAN MUSIC RELEASES

12" 78s

BUNK JOHNSON'S BAND
213	Tiger Rag	V-251
415	See See Rider	V-251
211	St. Louis Blues	V-252
402	When the Saints Go Marching In	V-252
110	Lowdown Blues	V-253
506	Yes, Yes in your Eyes	V-253

GEORGE LEWIS,
LAWRENCE MARRERO, SLOW DRAG
95	Burgundy St. Blues	V-254

JIM ROBINSON'S BAND
713	Ice Cream	V-254

BUNK JOHNSON'S BAND
414	Panama	V-255
605	When You Wore a Tulip	V-255
407	Darktown Strutters' Ball	V-256
510	Walk Thru the Streets of the City	V-256
215	New Iberia Blues	V-257
513	Sister Kate	V-257
411	Careless Love	V-258
514	Weary Blues	V-258

10" 78s

BUNK JOHNSON'S BAND
866	Do Right Baby	511
835	Margie	511
836	Runnin' Wild	512
825	Swanee River	512

ORIGINAL CREOLE STOMPERS
875	Eh, La-Bas!	513
885	Up Jumped the Devil	513

BUNK JOHNSON'S BAND
872	Kentucky Home	514
849	Listen to Me	514

DINK'S GOOD TIME MUSIC
925	Stomp de Lowdown	515
927	Grace and Beauty	515
925	Stomp de Lowdown (new pressing)	515
926	So Diff'rent Blues (new pressing)	515
926	So Dif'rent Blues	516
928	Take Your Time	516

BUNK JOHNSON
936	Where the River Shannon Flows	517
934	When the Moon Comes Over the Mountain	517
937	Ja-Da	518
939	Poor Butterfly	518
932	You've Got to See Mamma Ev'ry Night	519
933	Beautiful Doll	519
930	In the Gloaming	520
931	I'll Take You Home Again, Kathleen	520

160

The American Music / Paramount issues are listed on pages 158 and 159

10" LPs

AMERICAN MUSIC by BUNK
Blues and Spirituals

LP 638

416	Blues
415	See See Rider
401	When the Saints Go Marching In
896	Just a Closer Walk with Thee
868	Lonesome Road

AMERICAN MUSIC by GEORGE LEWIS

LP 639

912	Over the Waves
916	New Orleans Hula
955	Burgundy St. Blues
918	St. Philip St. Breakdown
703	High Society
712	San Jacinto Blues
713	Ice Cream

A NITE AT ARTESIAN HALL
with WOODEN JOE'S NEW ORLEANS BAND

LP 640

800	Shake It and Break It
803	Careless love
802	Lead Me On
812	Eh, La-Bas
819/21	I Ain't Got Nobody
885	Up Jumped the Devil

AMERICAN MUSIC by EMILE BARNES

LP 641

V-2	Tout de Moi
IV-2	DeDe and Billie's Blues
II-3	Eh, La-Bas
II-1	Lonesome Road
IV-2	Careless Love Blues

AMERICAN MUSIC by KID THOMAS

LP 642

III-5	Bucket's Got a Hole in It
II-2	Come on Down to New Orleans
IV-4	Kid Thomas Boogie Woogie
V-1	Careless Love Blues
III-4	Sweet Georgia Brown
III-1	Saint Louis Blues
IV-2	Sister Kate

"THIS IS BUNK JOHNSON TALKING,
explaining to you the early days of New Orleans"

LP 642

—	Bunk talking about Buddy Bolden (Part of Jack Stanley's interview)
11 (3)	Pallet on the Floor (part) Bunk talking and whistling (1942)
12 (3a)	Pallet on the Floor
13 (3b)	Pallet on the Floor
894	When the Saints Go Marching In (part)
4	Bunk talking about Funeral Parades
902	Nearer my God to Thee (part)
900	Just a Little While to Stay Here
8	Maple Leaf Rag (part)
1	Bunk talking about Tony Jackson
5a	Baby I'd Love to Steal You
389	Ballin' the Jack (part)
3	Bunk talking about Pete Lala's and Dago Tony's Tonks
606	Dippermouth Blues

BUNK 1945 –46

AMERICAN MUSIC
by GEORGE LEWIS with KID SHOTS

AMERICAN MUSIC
by BIG EYE LOUIS NELSON DELISLE

BUNK NEW ORLEANS 1944

American Music Records LP 647

BABY DODDS No.1

—	Demonstration
826	Swanee River
827	Swanee River
903	Over in Gloryland
902	Nearer my God to Thee
909	Tell Me your Dreams

BABY DODDS No. 2

	Tea for Two
	That's a Plenty
	Baby Food
	Slow & Easy Mama
	Chicago Slow Drag
	Chicago Slow Drag #2

BUNK NEW ORLEANS 1944

LP 647

509	Streets of the City
409	Lord, You're Good to Me
411	Careless Love Blues
110	Lowdown Blues
515	After You've Gone
206	Blue as I Can Be

BABY DODDS No. 3

—	Playing for the benefit of the band
—	Demonstration
849	Listen to Me
511	My Maryland

The three Baby Dodds covers are reproduced on page 142. For details of the 12" Brunies Brothers Dixieland Band LP – see page 157.

Compact Discs

BUNK JOHNSON
"THE KING OF THE BLUES"

AMCD-1

415	C.C. Rider
110	Lowdown Blues
211	St. Louis Blues
206	Blue as I Can Be
606	Dippermouth Blues
416	Midnight Blues
501	Weary Blues
215	New Iberia Blues
411	Careless Love
394	How Long Blues
507	Royal Garden Blues
609	Tishomingo Blues
207	C.C. Rider Blues

GEORGE LEWIS with KID SHOTS

AMCD-2

703	High Society #2
704	Gloryland #1
95	Burgundy Street Blues
706	Bucket's Got a Hole
713	Ice Cream
712	San Jacinto Blues
711	Sheik of Araby
709	Dumaine Street Drag
710	When You & I Were Young, Maggie
701	San Jacinto Stomp
707	Everybody Loves my Baby
708	Baby, Please Come Home

with Bunk's Band

505	Clarinet Marmalade
203	Sister Kate
502	Shake It & Break It

BUNK JOHNSON 1944

AMCD-3

213	Tiger Rag
510	We Will Walk Through the Streets #2
204	Sister Kate #2
409	Lord, Lord, You Sure are Good to Me #2
406	Darktown Strutters' Ball #1
605	When You Wore a Tulip
410	Careless Love #3

506	There's Yes Yes in your Eyes
210	My Life will be Sweeter, Someday
514	Shake It & Break It
414	Panama #3
517	Alabama Bound
405	High Society
404	Ballin' the Jack
402	When the Saints Go Marching In

GEORGE LEWIS – TRIOS & BANDS

AMCD-4

918	St. Philip Street Breakdown
912	Over the Waves
914	La Marseillaise
916	New Orleans Hula
862	Hindustan
863	Ciribiribin
201	San Jacinto Stomp
705	Gloryland #2
702	High Society #1
714	San Jacinto Blues #2
94	Ice Cream
92c	Life Will Be Sweeter
919	Old Rugged Cross
911	Lead Me Saviour
917	This Love of Mine
913	Over the Waves #2

George Lewis N.O. Stompers / Climax session

122	Careless Love
115	Just a Little While
116	Closer Walk

WOODEN JOE NICHOLAS

AMCD-5·

800	Shake It & Break It
802	Lead Me On
803	Careless Love
812	Eh, La-Bas
814	Up Jumped the Devil
807	Artesian Hall Blues
808	Tiger Rag
817	Don't Go Away Nobody
809	All the Whores
819	I Ain't Got Nobody
X-1	Any Rags
XI-6	The Lord will Make a Way
X-4	Clarinet Blues

X-5	Clarinet Blues #2
XII-3	Seems Like Old Times
885	Up Jumped the Devil
879	St. Louis Blues
875	Eh, La-Bas

BUNK'S BRASS BAND and DANCE BAND
AMCD-6

903	Gloryland
900	Just a Little While to Stay
896	Just a Closer Walk with Thee
898	Didn't He Ramble
909	Tell Me your Dream
908	My Maryland
904	St. Louis Blues
907	Bye & Bye
902	Nearer my God to Thee
894	When the Saint's Go Marching In
909a	Happy Birthday
836	Runnin' Wild
834	Margie
868	Lonesome Road
825	Swanee River
873	Kentucky Home
874	Milneberg Joys
831	827 Blues
829	All the Whores
840	The Sheik of Araby

BIG EYE LOUIS NELSON DELISLE
AMCD-7

973	Dinah
I-9	B-Flat Blues
983	Clarinet Marmalade
I-11	You Made Me What I Am
972/972a	Basin Street Blues
982	Black Cat on the Fence
986	Pork Chop
I-3	Holler Blues
IX-4	Basin Street Blues
I-10	Leaning on the Everlasting Arm
X-11	March
977	Ai Ai Ai
979	Bye and Bye

(Herbert Otto's live recording at Luthjen's– 5/14/49)

| — | Shake that Thing |
| — | Rose Room |

—	Tiger Rag
—	Eh, La-Bas
—	Shake that Thing (reprise)
—	Tin Roof Blues
—	Weary Blues

BUNK JOHNSON 1944
(2nd Masters)
AMCD-8

109	St. Louis Blues
509	Walk Through the Streets
513	Sister Kate
408	Lord, Lord, You Sure Been Good to Me
407	Darktown Strutters' Ball #2
398	Careless Love
601	Yes, Yes in your Eyes
503	Weary Blues
413	Panama
607	Dippermouth Blues
504	Clarinet Marmalade #1
394½	How Long Blues
401	Saints Go Marching In
399	Midnight Blues #2

HERB MORAND 1949
AMCD-9

IV-7	Sheik of Araby
981	Some of These Days
IV-2	B-Flat Blues
Iv-4	Eh, La-Bas
vl-6	High Society
974	Baby Won't You Please Come Home
IV-3	Nobody's Sweetheart
IV-5	South
V-3	Tin Roof Blues
V-10	Milneberg Joys
V1-5	Sheik of Araby

(Herbert Otto's live recording at Mama Lou's – 5/21/49)

—	Panama
—	Tin Roof Blues
—	Exactly Like You
—	St. Louis Blues

KID THOMAS

AMCD-10

I-3	Panama
I-2	Bucket's Got a Hole in It
I-4	Sister Kate
II-2	Come on Down to New Orleans
III-2	St. Louis Blues
III-4	Sweet Georgia Brown
III-5	Bucket's Got a Hole in It #2
IV-2	Sister Kate #2
IV-4	Kid Thomas's Boogie Woogie
V-1	Careless Love
VI-1	Marie
VI-4	Panama #2
II-3	Come on Down to New Orleans #2
V-2	Some of These Days
V-3	Sunny Side of the Street

DINK JOHNSON–CHARLIE THOMPSON

AMCD-11

Dink Johnson:

925	Stomp de Lowdown
926	So Dif'rent Blues
927	Grace & Beauty
928	Take Your Time
959	Indian Rag
960	The Stella Blues
961	Frisco Dreams
962	Las Vegas Stomp
963	Jelly Roll Blues
964	Yeah Man
967	Dink's Blues
965	Rag Bag Rag

Charlie Thompson:

968	Lily Rag
969	Derby Stomp
970	Delmar Rag
971	Slow Blues
2-1	I Had to Lose You
3-4	Weary Blues

BUNK JOHNSON 1944–45

AMCD-12

870	Milneberg Joys
833	Snag It
888	Old Grey Bonnet
604½	You Are my Sunshine

853	Shine
865	Noon's Blues
871	Cat's Got Kittens
603	Ole Miss
887	Lady Be Good
208	Precious Lord
823	Sister Kate
614	Blues in C
516	Alabama Bound
841	The Sheik of Araby
611	Ballin' the Jack
846	Willie the Weeper
615	Blues
610	Darktown Strutters' Ball

EMILE BARNES

AMCD-13

V-2	Tout de Moi
III-3	Billie and DeDe's Blues
II-3	Eh, La-Bas
II-2	Lonesome Road
IV-2	Careless Love
IV-3	St. Louis Blues
I-2	Shake It & Break It
II-2	Panama
III-1	Hindustan
VI-2	Some of These Days
VI-3	Ciribiribin
VI-1	St. Louis Blues
V-1	Careless Love

THE STRING BANDS

AMCD-14

Mobile Strugglers:

XIII-1	Cornfed Indiana Gal
984	Memphis Blues
XIII-9	Indiana Rag
985	Fattenin' Frogs for Snakes
XIV-1	Don't Bring Lulu
XIV-9	Original Blues
XIV-4	Billboard March

Louis James String Band:

—	Sweet Adeline (Schottische)
—	Next to your Mother, Who Do You Love?
—	Goofus
—	Rose Room
—	Down in Honky Tonk Town

—	After the Ball is Over (Waltz)
—	Exactly Like You
—	Memphis Blues
—	Please Don't Talk About Me When I'm Gone
—	Untitled Quadrille
—	Just a Little While to Stay Here
—	King Bolden's Song

BUNK PLAYS POPULAR SONGS

AMCD-15

930	In the Gloaming
931	I'll Take You Home Again, Kathleen
932	You've Got to See Mamma Ev'ry Night
933	Beautiful Doll
934	When the Moon Comes Over the Mountains
936	Where the River Shannon Flows
937	Ja-Da
939	Poor Butterfly
838	I'm Making Believe
106	I Don't Want to Walk Without You
105	Yes, Yes in your Eyes
842	Carry Me Back to Old Virginny
891	The Waltz You Saved for Me
892	Maggie
850	Sweet Georgia Brown
839	Amour
837	You Always Hurt the One You Love
860	Maria Elana
515	After You've Gone
890	Indiana

BUNK JOHNSON IN SAN FRANCISCO

AMCD-16

Bunk Johnson with Kid Ory's Band –
Geary Theatre broadcast:
—	Way Down Yonder in New Orleans
—	Basin Street Blues
—	Muskrat Ramble
—	High Society
—	The Wolverines
—	The Pearls
—	Dippermouth Blues
Bunk Johnson & Bertha Gonsoulin:
9	Sister Kate
16	Franklin Street Blues
14	Bolden Melody

5b	Temptation Rag
17	Sweet Georgia Brown
18	Darktown Strutters' Ball
Bunk Johnson with various groups:
26	Pacific Street Blues
—	Ain't Gonna Give Nobody None of My Jelly Roll #1
—	Ain't Gonna Give Nobody None of My Jelly Roll #2

BABY DODDS

AMCD-17

| — | Drum demonstrations |
Talking: Playing for the benefit of the band
827	Swanee River
826	Swanee River
901	Nearer my God to Thee
893	When the Saints Go Marching In
906	My Maryland
511	My Maryland
849	Listen to Me
852	High Society
212	Tiger Rag
880	New Iberia Blues
899	Just a Little While to Stay Here

NATTY DOMINIQUE

AMCD-18

—	Natty Dominique talking *(see page 140)*
—	Rehearsal Blues
—	Sweet Georgia Brown
—	I'll Never Be the Same
—	Shade of the Old Apple Tree
—	Careless Love
—	You Are my Silver Star #3
—	Chicago Slow Drag

AM BOOK CD

(enclosed on the inside back cover)
Full details of this CD can be found on pages 182-184

Notes

(1) **Bill Russell:** I remember one day, in 1944, when I was out in New Iberia with Bunk, we were sitting outside on his steps, and I was reading a newspaper, looking for old records. Seeing what I was reading, he said, "Some people say it pays to advertise, but the greatest thing is, it pays to think. You always got to think before you act." That was very much his motto in most situations.

(2) Bill Russell was employed in the test department of Electro-Dryer in Pittsburgh. The plant was engaged in producing transformers for use in heavy armorments. Bill visited San Francisco and New Orleans during his annual fourteen-day vacation. On May 16, he was waiting for the 8 pm train from New Orleans to return home when George Lewis rode up on his bicycle with a telegram from Bill's brother, Homer. It advised him that production at the factory had been temporally discontinued. Bill therefore remained in New Orleans for an extra month before returning to Pittsburgh.

(3) Bertha Gonsoulin had replaced Lil Hardin in King Oliver's band in Oakland during the band's California tour in early 1922. She was still with the band when they returned to Chicago and opened at the Lincoln Gardens in June of that year. Not liking the Chicago winter, she returned home to San Francisco in early December and was replaced by Lil Hardin.

(4) In the September of 1938, Louis Armstrong and his Orchestra were booked for a series of "one-nighters" for a tour of the South. When they appeared at the New Iberia Training School, Bunk met Louis Armstrong and invited him back to his home after the date for dinner. Louis gave Bunk a photograph of himself with the inscription: *Best Wishes To my Boy "Bunk" He's my Musical insparation* (sic) *all my life – yea man. From Louis Satchmo Armstrong.* Later, Bunk added his own inscription to the photograph: *A treat from my boy Louie,* and the photograph, as well as the endorsement, remained one of Bunk's proudest possessions.

(5) **Bill Russell:** The first time I met Ory was just after his brother had died in 1938. He was sitting in his kitchen wearing a bathrobe and playing *Muskrat Ramble* on a saxophone. He was friendly but had a naturally suspicious nature. He was always very secretive about money, and when he signed up with MCA he wouldn't show the band any contracts and paid them scale – about $25. That was the reason Mutt quit. When I was collecting interviews for the Tulane Archive I knew Ory wouldn't be too keen on being interviewed, so I took Manetta with me when I went to see him in Los Angeles. I knew he wouldn't refuse to see Manetta. Just before he died, I went out to Hawaii to see him. Trummy Young was also living out there and he used to go out to see Ory most Saturday nights, so I got Trummy to take me out to see him. Ory was hard to get to know, but when he felt you weren't trying to exploit him he was very friendly and helpful. His wife was more of a problem than he was.

(6) Eugene "Gene" Williams was born May 18, 1918. In the 1930s he attended Columbia College, where he met fellow enthusiast Ralph de Toledano, and in 1940 they founded the *Jazz Information* magazine, which Gene edited. Although the magazine lasted only a couple of years, it was influential in bringing many early New Orleans musicians (many of whom were still active) to the attention of a growing jazz public.

The magazine began reissuing Paramount records and sponsored Bunk's second recording session (October 2, 1942) in New Orleans, although Gene was unable to attend the session through ill health. Being employed by Decca Records in New York, he managed to persaude the company to record Bunk in Los Angeles for their subsidiary, World Transcriptions.

Ralph de Toledano recalled him as "a thin, pale guy who was always being argumentative about jazz." Others remember him as a highly strung young man with a single-minded passion for jazz and veteran musicians, that knew no bounds. His highly charged writing in *The Record Changer* would seem to confirm this. A legacy enabled him to promote Bunk and the band for the first of their Stuyvesant Casino engagements (Gene lost around $3000), and his Greenwich Village apartment (68 Washington Square) provided a home to Bunk and, for most of the time, the band during their time in New York. Acting as Bunk's manager, his failure to promote Bunk as a major attraction in 1946 was followed by his losing even more money trying to promote Kid Ory's band in San Francisco in 1947. Disillusioned, he returned to New York and committed suicide by jumping from a skyscraper, on May 5, 1948.

(7) Bunk's account of this incident differs slightly from Bill Colburn's report. Wade Whaley had told Bunk that, on his way home from the session, he had met Bud Scott, and Bud had told him: "Don't make any records with Bunk." Bill's 1944 diary reports: "He [Bunk] was especially bitter about Bud Scott, and said he'd never have anything to do with him again. . . . Bunk had looked forward to playing with Bud, as he hadn't seen him since Bud was playing with Robichaux, and he said he didn't care if he never saw him again." Although Bud Scott was probably acting under instructions from Ory, Bunk accused them both of trying to sabotage the session. Ory, on the other hand, was planning to fire Bud Scott and replace him with Frank Pasley.

(8) On being given the flute, Bunk took it into George's kitchen and began to play. Although Bill knew it was Bunk playing, he remained in the other room listening for a few minutes. When Bill entered the kitchen, Bunk (being proud of his musical prowess) winked and said: "I bet you thought that was George Lewis playing."

(9) Hugh Davis was a Chicago recording engineer whom Bill admired. He worked for Cebour Seeberg, who sold juke boxes and juke box records. The company also broadcast (via cable) recorded light music to factories. Davis advised Bill on recording techniques and mastered many of the American Music records. He was a partner with John Steiner in "S & D" (Steiner Davis) Records.

The problem of speed correction of many AM 78s comes from the incompatibility of Bill's and Hugh Davis's turntables. Bill's machine recorded at 80.681 rpm, whilst Hugh Davis mastered on a turntable that was locked to spin exactly at 78 rpm! Bill always delighted in telling how Hugh Davis would leave his turntable spinning all day to keep it in "top-class condition."

(10) Many specialist jazz labels in the 1940s exempted themselves from this clause by printing "Not licensed for radio" on the label.

(11) Although all of Bill's American Music recordings were non-Union, Bunk, and most of the band members, had joined the black local Musicians Union in 1944. However, they would have been unable to record under Union supervision, as the AFM had imposed a nation-wide ban on all instrumental recordings between August 1, 1942 until November 11, 1944. As noted in the text, Bill was often paying similar or sometimes above Union rates during the 1940s.

(12) Gene Williams stayed with Bunk in New Iberia in 1942 and heard him play a whole dance on tuba. As a teacher on the WPA Program, Bunk could play just about all wind instruments. In the 1920s he doubled on alto sax when playing in the orchestra at the Houston American Theater. He is quoted as saying: "I played the hell out of the alto sax." Bill also recalled when, in 1942, he played the *High Society* chorus on a clarinet that Hal McIntyre was buying for George. He also once borrowed Jim Robinson's trombone to teach Jim the *Royal Garden Blues* breaks.

(13) Ann Cook was born in Franzenville (St. Francisville) in 1903 and worked in Storyville as a prostitute.
Bill Russell: Louis Armstrong remembered her in his book, and when he found out that I had recorded her, he asked me to send him the record straight away. Manuel Manetta also recalled Ann Cook (or as he called her "Nann" Cook) when she worked in the "district" over in Algiers. The Algiers "red-light district" was situated near the levee. The main whorehouse was the Ping Pong, with its tin roof, but there were also a few cribs and cheap hotels nearby. Some of the girls, like Ann Cook, used to take their customers up onto the levee itself, so they wouldn't have to pay the 26-cent rent. George Lewis and St. Cyr were afraid of her, as she had killed a number of people in her younger days. George said, "Sometimes she'd shoot 'em, sometimes she'd cut 'em to death." When she recorded with Wooden Joe's band, after she left, one of the guys told a joke about her (which I didn't catch) and they all had a real good laugh about her. The next day Wooden Joe said with a smile, "She hasn't changed any." Ann Cook died in 1962.

(14) While there was a great deal of racial tension between the white Cajuns and black people in New Iberia, it is unlikely that many Cajuns could afford the services of a black maid, as they themselves were amongst the poorest paid workers in the South.

(15) In 1942 Bill met Louis Armstrong's sister Beatrice, in New Orleans.
Bill Russell: She strongly objected to Louis's "dance hall" version of *When the Saints Go Marching In*. When Louis heard his sister's

criticism, he dismissed her objections and said that she was in no position to criticize, as she would often go to church and then spend the rest of the day gambling.

(16) Manuel Perez (1873–1946) was one of the most respected cornet players and teachers in New Orleans. He retired from music in the early 1930s, and by the early 1940s was suffering from Alzheimers (senile dementia). When Bunk visited Manuel Perez (Thursday, August 3, 1944), Bunk reported that Manuel's son was home, having just been discharged from the army, suffering from mental instability. George later told a story which suggested that Manuel's son may not have been "all that crazy." "At his camps, he spent all his time going around the grounds picking up every scrap of paper, looking at it intently and then discarding it, shaking his head and saying, 'That's not it.' At last, when he got his final discharge paper, he picked it up and said, 'That's it!' " (George Lewis as told to Bill Russell). George took Bill to visit Manuel Perez on Monday, May 24, 1943.

(17) This was George's oldest daughter, Mildred (born 1919), from his first marriage to Emma Zeno.

(18) The San Jacinto Hall, the Artisan Hall and the Astoria Hotel (and maybe other dance halls and saloons) were owned by "Beansy" Fauria. He was a light-skinned mulatto, who also owned numerous bar-room slot machines and ran the "numbers game" in New Orleans. George Guesnon worked for Beansy for a while and was always proud of the fact that Beansy trusted him with the money he collected. In the late 1950s, Larry Borenstein rented a studio from Beansy, where he hired musicians, before Preservation Hall opened.

(19) **Bill Russell:** Some people would call the Perdido and Gravier Street areas the "Battlefield." There were a lot of low-class honky-tonks around there at one time. The Red Onion was in that area. But from people I talked to, the "Battlefield" district probably finished a block or two beyond those two streets. George and I went up in the daytime to see Shots. If it had been at night, George said, even he wouldn't have felt safe walking around there. Ann Cook lived up in that section.

(20) Many veteran musicians stated that "Red Happy" Bolton (1885–1925) was one of the best of all New Orleans drummers. He worked with King Oliver

between 1912 and 1916, with John Robichaux at the Lyric Theater (1918-c1920) and then with Peter Lacaze in the early 1920s. In 1925 Red Happy visited Chicago and Joe Oliver recommended him for a band that was due to tour Canada. Red didn't have any drums, so Joe persuaded Andrew Hilaire to lend him his spare set. When Red Happy died in Canada from an overdose of marijuana, the drums disappeared and Joe, who had underwritten the loan, had to pay Andrew Hilaire $80 for the set.

Christopher "Black Happy" Goldston (1894–1968) began playing with Amos Riley around 1916, then with Jack Carey (1917–20) and Jessie Jackson's Golden Leaf Orchestra (1920–21) with Punch Miller. But he was known mainly for his drum work in brass bands. From 1916 he marched with the Tulane Brass Band, the Tuxedo Brass Band, the Excelsior Brass Band and the Onward Brass Band. He worked with the WPA Brass Band during the 1930s, with Henry Allen's Brass Band in the 1940s and the Eureka Brass Band in the 1960s. He recorded with Papa Celestin (1947–51), and Alphonse Picou (1953).
(1953) and the Eureka Brass Band (1960).

There was a third New Orleans drummer also called "Happy." This was Remus "Brown Happy" Matthews, the brother of drummers Bill and Bebe Matthews. Bill Matthews later switched to trombone and recorded numerous sessions with "Black Happy" Goldston.

(21) Tom Benton (1897–1945) was a popular banjoist, guitarist and singer, who worked with Jack Carey (1914), the Jimmie Noone–Buddy Petit band (1915) and Papa Celestin (1915–16). Benton then played irregularly for many years, before joining Amos White for a tour of Texas (1926). Many musicians remember him mainly for his inventive, risqué songs.

(22) *I Can't Escape from You* (actually *You Can't Escape from Me*) does seem to be a favorite opening number on American Music recordings, e.g., Jim Robinson (1944), Kid Shots (1944), both issued as *San Jacinto Stomp*, and Herb Morand (1949).

(23) This was probably Leon Vajean, a former pupil of Bunk's.

(24) Skippy Adelman was a young photographer who worked for *Life* magazine. As Gene Williams had been contracted to write an article, "New Orleans Today," for *Jazzways* – Vol.1, No.1 (published 1946), Skippy was also hired to take photographs to illustrate the article.

(25) That week all clubs, bars and other places of entertainment were subjected to a midnight curfew. After VE Day (May 8) this appears to have been lifted.

(26) Memorial Day (May 30) was not a national holiday, but as Bill explained: "The colored people all celebrated it, as it commemorated the victory of the Union Army over the Confederate Army, whom they probably saw as their oppressors."

(27) Gene Williams's fascinating (if at times over romantic) article in *Jazzways* confirms all of Bill Russell's own recollections, with the exception of his meeting with Joe Petit. According to Williams, he did not meet Petit until the trombonist Albert Warner pointed him out sitting on a bench in the Artisan's Hall during Wooden Joe's session.

(28) Pointe a la Hache was a small country community, a few miles past Davant on the Delta Road, forty miles south of New Orleans. Bunk Johnson, Lawrence Marrero, George Lewis, Slow Drag Pavageau, Andrew Morgan and Abby Williams had been booked to play a white dance at the local school. By all accounts, this was one of the best-ever Bunk Johnson performances.

(29) 12" glass-based masters were used to record virtually all the American Music recordings in 1945, later issued on 10" 78s. In 1944, when the 12" 78s were being recorded, many of these were cut on 12", 13" and 16" glass-based (or occasionally steel-based) masters. All masters cut in 1943, 1944 and 1945 were center start, finishing at the outer edge.

(30) The *Esquire* concert (January 17, 1945) was the second all-American poll-winners concert organized by *Esquire* magazine. It was performed, simultaneously, in three different locations (New Orleans, Los Angeles and New York), each linked by radio. Part of each concert was broadcast coast-to-coast by the Blue Network. From the Municipal Auditorium in New Orleans, Louis Armstrong performed with Duke Ellington (in Los Angeles) and Benny Goodman (in New York) for one number. In New Orleans, Leon Prima's band, Mary Osborn, James P. Johnson and Louis Armstrong's Jazz Foundation Six played several numbers over the air. Louis Armstrong's band featured J. C. Higginbotham, Sidney Bechet, James P. Johnson, Ricard Alexis and Paul Barbarin. As Bill Russell and Gene Williams had been part of the voting panel, they, along with others, had engineered enough votes for Bunk to be part of the concert.

Bill Russell: During the broadcast, Bunk played one number with Louis's band, *Basin Street Blues*, when the Mayor of New Orleans changed the name of Saratoga Street back to Basin Street. I had to laugh when I read Leonard Feather's review of the broadcast. Louis sang a vocal and Bunk played the trumpet solo over the radio, which Feather wrote up as Louis's solo. Feather really had no time for Bunk, but on this occasion he couldn't tell the difference between Bunk and Louis! (Bill Russell in a letter to Johnson McCree, March 19, 1982).

Bunk also led a band of New Orleans musicians at the concert, which included George Lewis. This part was not broadcast.

(31) Vic Gaspard (1875–1957) marched with the Onward Brass Band and the Excelsior Brass Band before World War 1. He was much respected as a fine musician, performing with John Robichaux (1913–17, 1926–30) and as co-leader with his brother, "Oak" Gaspard, in their Maple Leaf Orchestra (1917–26). Had he not retired from music in the early 1930s, he would have been Bunk Johnson's first-choice trombonist in the 1940s.

(32) Bunk also told a story of how he once put some soap on someone's bass strings and how they couldn't get any tone.

(33) The Pig Pen was situated on Burgundy Street (between St. Louis and Bienville). This French Quarter nightclub catered mainly for white tourists and servicemen. The week before, Alphonse Picou had left Kid Rena's band at the Cadillac (a white cabaret dance hall near the Industrial Canal) to take the job at the Pig Pen. The band consisted of Picou, Kid Shots Madison, pianist and leader Sadie Crosby, and Charlie Sylvester on drums. Besides playing for dancing, the band also accompanied cabaret and "fake" striptease acts.

This was not the same Pig Pen in which DeDe and Billie Pierce later worked, at 1135 Decatur Street.

(34) Hoyte D. Kline was a record collector and one of the few people to receive a message from Bunk via Mary Karoly in 1942. In the early 1940s Hoyte made a pact with Bill: whoever died first, the other would inherit their record collection. (Bill admitted that Hoyte had the better collection.) While serving in the US Army in Italy, Hoyte was killed when his jeep ran over a land-mine – although the war had been over for several weeks! When Hoyte's wife insisted that the

pact should be honored, Bill sold most of the collection and, after dividing the proceeds with Hoyte's wife, used the rest to sponsor Bunk's Brass Band date.

(35) Dominique "T-Boy" Remy (c1886–?) was the leader of the Eureka Brass Band during the 1940s. Percy Humphrey took over the leadership when Remy moved to Los Angeles in 1946.

(36) The Ship Island Canal dance:

THE FIRST GRAND

MILLIONAIRE

Wedding of the Season

GIVEN BY

BORGNEMOUTH COL. SCHOOL

Sat., May 19, 1945, 7:00 p. m.

At the Y. S. and D. Hall   Violet, La.

MUSIC BY KID WILLIAMS

Dancing- 8 until late!

Admission   -   -   -   50 Cents

(37) Jelly Roll Morton lived with Dink's elder sister, Anita Gonzales ("the only woman I ever loved"), first in Las Vegas and then in Los Angeles (1917-22). Although he married Mabel Bertrand in 1928, it was Anita who was named as his "wife" on his death certificate and inherited his estate. His 1924 recording *Mamamita* (later copyrighted as *Mama Nita*) was dedicated to her.

After Jelly's death, Anita remained in California and died in the fall of 1956.

(38) Many New Orleans pianists, such as Sweet Emma Barrett, also preferred a high keyboard.

(39) Although Ed "Tudi" Garland had confirmed to Barry Martyn that he and Bud Scott had participated in this session under assumed names, for many years Bill would never admit to the true identities of the string bass player and guitarist. All he would ever say was that Dink got some Mexican musicians from a list of names scribbled on the wall, next to the phone. When I put "Tudi" Garland's statement to Bill, he confirmed their presence, but protested that he had given his word that their identities would be protected in case of Union problems. It is interesting to note, however, that they were paid slightly above the Union scale. Dink received $80, plus a $40 composers royalty, based on the number of records pressed. Tudi got $60 and Bud $40.

(40) Art Hodes and his Blue Note Jazz Men occupied the Stuyvesant Casino bandstand from January 13 to April 9, 1946, between Bunk's two engagements. The personnel was Henry Goodwin (tpt), Albert Nicholas (clt), George Lugg (tbn), Art Hodes (pno), Pops Foster (sbs) and Kaiser Marshall (dms). During the engagement, Albert Nicholas left to join Kid Ory at the Jade Palace in Los Angeles, and was replaced by Cecil Scott.

(41) "Sister Kate" was the nickname used by Bunk for Kathryn Richards, who was Bill Riddle's sister-in-law and a friend of Don Ewell. It was drummer Bill Riddle (also from Don's home town of Baltimore) who first got Don Ewell interested in jazz in the mid-1930s. A few years later, he introduced Don to the music of Jelly Roll Morton and, in December 1945, arranged for Don to sit in with Bunk's band at the Stuyvesant Casino.

(42) **Bill Russell:** Dink had very definite ideas on how New Orleans drummers should play. Shortly before I went out to see him in 1946, Buster Wilson had invited him down to hear the Ory Band. Ory was very suspicious and wanted to know why Dink was there. Dink thought it was a fine band, but he said they didn't play in the right style anymore and they were set up wrong on the stand. All he could hear was the trombone, trumpet and clarinet, and he couldn't hear any piano, guitar or drums. He said, "Ram just sat up there doing nothing. In New Orleans music you've got to hear the bass drum beat going *BOOM BOOM* all the time." He then gave an exhibition of how the snare sticks should be used to hit various things, including the bass drum, in order to make interesting rhythms.

(43) Although Bill was not able to record Ash Hardy with Buster Wilson, it is possible that Adrian Tucker recorded them later, and a copy of the record may be be in Bill's collection.

(44) This story is unlikely to be true. Although Paramount Records first began releasing records in 1918 (exclusively for the white market), it was not until the summer of 1922, when its first "race" records were recorded and released. It is therefore, safe to assume that the shop was not opened until after 1922. The five Artie Matthews *Pastime Rags* were published between 1913 and 1918 by the Stark Music Co. of St. Louis. *Blues Who's Who* (by Sheldon Harris) confirms that Edith's husband, Jessie Johnson, operated a record store in St. Louis during the 1920s and 1930s, and names the store as, "Jessie Johnson's DeLuxe Music Shop." The restaurant that Bill visited in 1942 was the DeLuxe Restaurant. Edith Johnson (1905–88) recorded for QRS, Okeh, Vocalion and Paramount between 1928-9.

(45) Robert "Bob" Hampton (b.1890) died in Los Angeles September 25, 1945.

(46) Bob Matthews recorded Wooden Joe with Ray Burke's Speakeasy Boys on May 11 and 12, 1949, in the back room of Orin and Harvey Blackstone's record shop. The session was recorded for Paradox and partially released in 1950 on two 78s.

(47) **Alden Ashforth:** Bob Thomas was obviously unaware of the LP and thought we were just recording a couple of 78s. After the LP was issued I gave a copy to each of the musicians, although probably none of them had a record player that could play LPs. Later George Henderson saw George Guesnon and said, "Did we really play that fast?" "No," said Guesnon, "it's called a Long Playing record. What you have to do is keep your thumb against the edge of the record to slow it down and it will play alright!"

(48) After Bill had declined to issue the Eureka session for cost reasons, Dante Bolletino of Paradox records agreed to purchase the session. However, before it could be issued, Paradox ceased operations in 1952. The material was then transferred to its associated label Pax, and was issued as Pax 9001. Bolletino later leased the recording to several associated labels around the world. Dante Bolletino never paid Alden for the session.

Index of Musicians

(italic type denotes photograph)

Index of recorded titles

(Readers will have noted that there was often variations and/or abbreviations to certain tune titles on American Music labels. Therefore these tunes are listed below under a common title)

AM BOOK CD
included on the inside back cover

Track 1:
WOODEN JOE'S NEW ORLEANS BAND
Artisian's Hall, 1460 North Derbigny Street, New Orleans.
Thursday, May 10, 1945
"Wooden" Joe Nicholas (tpt); Jim Robinson (tbn); Albert Burbank (clt); Lawrence Marrero (bjo); Austin Young (sbs); Cié Frazier (dms)

804   Tiger Rag   (Previously unissued – This is the first number in which Cié participated and contains some of Wooden Joe's most powerful playing – see page 53)

Track 2:
WOODEN JOE'S BAND
Dr George Nelson's Home, 1421 Touro Street, New Orleans.
Thursday, July 21, 1949
"Wooden" Joe Nicholas (tpt); Louis Nelson (tbn); Albert Burbank (clt); Johnny St. Cyr (gtr); Austin Young (sbs); Albert Jiles (dms)

XII-7   Sugar Blues   (Previously unissued – see page 131)

Track 3:
DINK JOHNSON
Associated Studios, 1032 North Sycamore Avenue, Hollywood.
Monday, October 6 and Tuesday, October 17, 1947
Dink Johnson (pno, clt and dms)

C2-1   Rag Bag Rag   (Previously unissued – see pages 102)

Track 4:
TALKING RECORD – following the Kid Shots session
San Jacinto Hall, 1422 Dumaine Street, New Orleans.
Saturday, August 5, 1944

715   Baby Dodds, George Lewis, Jim Robinson, Lawrence Marrero, Slow Drag Pavageau, Bill Russell, William Wagner and Alfred Lion
                            (An incomplete version was issued by Dan Records – see page 44)

Track 5:
BUNK JOHNSON'S BAND
George Lewis's home, 827 St. Philip Street, New Orleans.
Tuesday, May 15, 1945
Bunk Johnson (tpt); Jim Robinson (tbn); George Lewis (clt); Lawrence Marrero (bjo); Alcide "Slow Drag" Pavageau (sbs); Baby Dodds (dms)

858   Make Me a Pallet on the Floor   (Previously unissued – This take is very different from the other versions, as it is performed at the faster tempo that the Bolden band were said to have played it – see page 63)

Track 6:
BUNK JOHNSON & BERTHA GONSOULIN
Betha Gonsoulin's home, 1782 Sutter Street, San Francisco.
Monday, May 10, 1943
Bunk Johnson (tpt); Bertha Gonsoulin (pno)

24   Careless Love   (previously unissued – see page 9)

Track 7:
BUNK JOHNSON'S BAND
San Jacinto Hall, 1422 Dumaine Street, New Orleans.
Monday, July 31, 1944
Bunk Johnson (tpt); Jim Robinson (tbn); George Lewis (clt); Lawrence Marrero (bjo); Alcide "Slow Drag" Pavageau, Sidney Brown (sbs); Baby Dodds (dms); Myrtle Jones (vcl)

209   My Life Will Be Sweeter Someday (Previously unissued – see page 20)

Track 8:
BUNK'S 3-PIECE BAND
Cieferskor's Studio, 29 West 57th Street, New York. Monday, June 3, 1947
Bunk Johnson (tpt); Don Ewell (pno); Alphonse Steele (dms)

929   In the Gloaming   (Issued on Dan Records, but not included on AMCD-15
                               – see page 96)

Track 9:
ORIGINAL CREOLE STOMPERS
Albert Burbank's home, 2129 Lapeyrouse Street, New Orleans. Wednesday, July 13, 1949
Herb Morand (tpt); Louis Nelson (tbn); Albert Burbank(clt); Johnny St. Cyr (gtr); Austin Young (sbs); Albert Jiles (dms)

IV-6   I Can't Escape from You   (Previously unissued – see page 120)

Track 10:
Personnel, location and date as above

VI-3   B-Flat Blues   (Issued on AM 532, but not included on AMCD-9 – see page 120)

Track 11:
NATTY DOMINIQUE'S CREOLE DANCE BAND
Saber Room, Darbell Springs Hotel, 8900 West 95th Street, Chicago.
Monday, September 28, 1953
Natty Dominique (tpt); Preston Jackson (tbn); Darnell Howard (clt); Ralph Tervalon (pno); Sam Casimir (gtr); Bill Settles (sbs); Baby Dodds (dms)

        You Are my Silver Star #2   (Previously unissued –see page 138)

Track 12:
BUNK JOHNSON'S BAND
San Jacinto Hall, 1422 Dumaine Street, New Orleans.
Tuesday, August 1, 1944
Bunk Johnson (tpt); Jim Robinson (tbn); George Lewis (clt); Lawrence Marrero (bjo); Alcide "Slow Drag" Pavageau (sbs); Baby Dodds (dms)

386   Honey Gal   (Previously unissued –see page 23)

Track 13:
BUNK JOHNSON'S BAND
George Lewis's home, 827 St. Philip Street, New Orleans.
Monday, May 14, 1945
Bunk Johnson (tpt); Jim Robinson (tbn); George Lewis (clt); Lawrence Marrero (bjo); Alcide "Slow Drag" Pavageau (sbs); Baby Dodds (dms)

835   Margie   (Issued on AM 511 and Wolf, but unissued in AMCD series –see page 59)

Track 14:
Personnel and location as above, but recorded on Thursday, May 17, 1945

866   Do Right Baby (Noon Johnson, vcl) (Issued on AM 511 and Wolf, but unissued in AMCD series –see page 67)

Track 15:
Personnel and location as above, but recorded on Tuesday, May 15, 1945

855   Slow Drag's Boogie Woogie   (Issued on Dan and Jazz Connoissseur, but unissued in AMCD series –see page 63)

Track 16:
GEORGE LEWIS TRIO
George Lewis's backyard, 827 St. Philip Street, New Orleans.
George Lewis (clt); Lawrence Marrero (bjo); Alcide "Slow Drag" Pavageau (sbs)

97   San Jacinto Stomp   (Issued on Dan, but unissued in AMCD series –see page 12)

Track 17:
LOUIS DELISLE'S BAND
Rehearsal at Dr. George Nelson's home, 1421 Touro Street, New Orleans.
Monday, July 18, 1949
Charles Love (tpt); "Big Eye" Louis Nelson Delisle (clt); Louis Nelson (tbn); Johnny St. Cyr (gtr); Austin Young (sbs); Ernest Rogers (dms)

VII-4   Pork Chop   (Previously unissued – see page123)

Track 18:
EMILE BARNES NEW ORLEANS BAND
The Karl Kilinski Violin Studio, 315 St. Charles Avenue, New Orleans.
Thursday, August 30, 1951
Emile Barnes (clt); DeDe Pierce (tpt); Harrison Brazley (tbn); Billie Pierce (pno, vcl); Albert Glenny (sbs); Josiah Frazier (dms)

IV-1   DeDe and Billie's Blues No 2   (Issued on Storyville, but unissued in AMCD series – see page 146)

Track 19:
KID THOMAS ALGIERS STOMPERS
Hope Hall, Algiers.
Monday, September 3, 1951
"Kid Thomas" Valentine (tpt), Emile Barnes (clt); Bob Thomas (tbn); George Guesnon (bjo); Babe Philip (sbs); George Henderson (dms)

I-1   Bucket's Got a Hole in It   (Previously unissued – see page 150)